Good-bye and Good Riddance

Good-bye and Good Riddance

Valerie Hagenbush

iUniverse, Inc.
New York Lincoln Shanghai

Good-bye and Good Riddance

Copyright © 2005 by Valerie Hagenbush

All rights reserved. No part of this book may be used or reproduced by any means, graphic, electronic, or mechanical, including photocopying, recording, taping or by any information storage retrieval system without the written permission of the publisher except in the case of brief quotations embodied in critical articles and reviews.

iUniverse books may be ordered through booksellers or by contacting:

iUniverse
2021 Pine Lake Road, Suite 100
Lincoln, NE 68512
www.iuniverse.com
1-800-Authors (1-800-288-4677)

ISBN-13: 978-0-595-35099-5 (pbk)
ISBN-13: 978-0-595-79801-8 (ebk)
ISBN-10: 0-595-35099-2 (pbk)
ISBN-10: 0-595-79801-2 (ebk)

Printed in the United States of America

—Frankie—
who is sorely missed

Acknowledgments

A portion of this novel, in somewhat different form, has been presented on the Internet as *Dust Yourself Off* under "Your Short Stories" on the Rutger Hauer official site (www.rutgerhauer.org/stories). One day, as luck would have it, I chanced upon this special place, which was offering a unique opportunity for everyone to have their stories considered for the Starfish Tango anthology. The proceeds from its sale support the actor's charity, the Rutger Hauer Starfish Association. It is dedicated to providing help specifically for children and pregnant women with HIV/AIDS, as well as educating communities about this disease.

Grateful acknowledgment is made to Rowman & Littlefield Publishing Group for permission to reprint lines from the book *Tales of Fishes*, copyright 2001 by Zane Grey, the Derrydale Press, part of the Taylor Trade Publishing group.

I appreciate my husband, David Bauman, and my daughters, Emily and Taylor, for bolstering my spirit during this arduous, drawn-out process. It pleases me that my mother has been able to witness the completion of this endeavor. I am indebted to my friends, whose encouragement spurred me on, particularly Margaret Steinmann—everyone should have such a caring person in his or her corner for just such scary undertakings in life. I hope I can reciprocate. A heartfelt thank-you is offered to my sister-in-law, Jeanie Showalter, for giving me her highly valued opinion.

The professionals at iUniverse are to be commended for their insightful and expeditious review of *Good-bye and Good Riddance*.

CHAPTER 1

The phone smacked the table. Trigger-happy fingers stroked the safety latch of the garden shears, wielded, at the moment, like a gun. The showdown involving the adversarial caller was set for high noon. A screen door got the boot. Woe to the unwarned innocent who crossed paths with this typically dignified lady and her abrupt shoot-'em-up humor.

"Good morning," sang Sarah, cheerily hailing her passing neighbor, who barreled by without answering. She kicked up the volume. "Yoo-hoo. Mis-siz Gul-liv-ver…mor-nin.'"

Nothing. Feeling slighted, the fussy homemaker resumed sweeping the crevices of her orderly garage while muttering several choice words under her breath. A few minutes later, the woman with fixed purpose was darting past again, this time carrying a handful of pussy willows. The figure veered left, distracted by the hidden voice that had again called out her name (somewhat crossly this time). The branches, brutally severed at their stalks, repeatedly whipped her thigh as she stormed across the driveway. Sarah was taken aback by the unprecedented outburst:

"Janet just called…said she was swinging by to discuss Harry's college tuition. I asked what on earth she was talking about, and she wondered why I sounded upset!" The flat of her hand struck her chest, emphasizing what could only be interpreted as the brazenness of this demand from her own daughter. Evidently, Mrs. Gulliver wasn't thrilled at the prospect of helping to further fund her grandson Harry's education.

And hello to you, too, thought Sarah, as the tirade continued. She didn't see why the request seemed unusual; after all, didn't Mrs. Gulliver freely discuss how often she and her husband, Ed, helped their kids financially? Sarah once wished she could have been one of their brood for that reason, then reconsidered.

Mrs. Gulliver had a forceful way of delivering her opinions that intimidated the relative newcomer to the block. Even after three years of living next to her, and though Sarah's two little ones happily designated her as their "Aunt Maddie," the young mother couldn't bring herself to use the woman's first name.

Sarah asked dryly, "Is Harry the one you put through the Freedman Academy?" Freedman was the city's most prestigious private high school.

The implication wasn't lost on the seething grandmother. Following a curt "goes without saying" pronouncement of her love for the boy, Mrs. Gulliver clarified that the irksome part was the manner in which her daughter simply assumed she would get the money. "She and Dan never even asked whether her dad and I would help them. They expect all three boys to be Ivy Leaguers, yet they've barely saved a dime! The nerve…to think that we'd foot the entire bill!"

Sarah could have pursued Janet's rationale, but by then Mrs. Gulliver's ire had caused a vein to really bulge on her forehead. The jagged lightning bolt looked drawn on in blue ink. That was all Sarah needed—for Mrs. Gulliver to collapse on the asphalt from a stroke.

It was futile going on about the topic. Mrs. Gulliver apologized for the explosion, and started across the yard to her house. Halfway there, she turned and hollered, "Sarah!"

Stretched on tiptoes, Sarah pulled the broom down from over her head and peered out from the shadows. The dazzling backlight from the morning sun produced a halo around Mrs. Gulliver's stately physique. And framing her were soft-pink taffeta May blooms, newly erupted from the magnificent azalea island directly behind her.

"Sarah," she repeated loudly, "just tell me if it's none of my business, but…may I ask whether you and Mark have received much help from your parents?"

Sarah's perpetually serious, dark eyes took on an extra note of sadness, surely undetectable at that range. The question brought to mind a collection of hurtful name-calling incidents that had accumulated since as long ago as her preschool days and finally ended with her college years. Growing up, she would have greatly appreciated the smallest handout.

Sarah walked slowly, dragging the long handle until she could prop the broom against the basketball pole and continue. The diminutive woman straightened her posture with every step, so her countenance would better resemble that of Mrs. Gulliver's confident bearing. The revived embarrassments persisted, playing out from a heretofore consciously closed-off portion of her memory. She could hear her mother's unconvincing rhetoric about secondhand clothes serving their purpose. *You should be thankful for the roof over your head, Sarah.* This level of need was foreign to most of the locals, Sarah perceived, including the Gullivers.

Her elderly neighbors had by no means started out rich, but they belonged to families that were at least exempt from poverty. Their merchant culture profited greatly after World War II. By the time their rather backward Ohio River town transformed itself into a full-fledged center for commerce, the Gullivers, like scores of other city dwellers, needed relief from the choking congestion. They discovered unadulterated air only thirty minutes away, in a pearl of a place called Mount Sterling...and guarded it as such.

Initially, around 150 years ago, the farmers of this region had coexisted beside a few of the governing bigwigs' estates. But during the 1950s and early 60s, the trend was to divide this extensive agricultural land, which was unfortunately no longer viable, and turn it into residential property. Quite unlike the inhabitants of similar areas being developed on the outskirts of town—areas developed too quickly and without foresight—the newly established gentry of Mount Sterling took early action to protect its privacy. By inflating the price of land and enacting restrictive zoning laws, the citizens ensured against any disruption to their sought-after repose.

The continuity was maintained by returning offspring, networked into the social hierarchy by pervasive nepotism. This enclave recognized its favorable and enviable standing. Sarah could not understand what twist of fate allowed some such unfair advantages simply for being born here.

The inner club atmosphere grew even more exclusive during a real-estate boom in the 1980s. Curiously, new blood seeped in at that time. Professional two-career couples (an emerging phenomenon) learned the housing game of "buying up" and set their sights on the elite suburb, celebrating it as *the* place to be.

Sarah and Mark were among those divesting the cliques. The resident generations guessed that these young arrivals must have come into hefty inheritances; after all, the recently increasing cost of living there jolted their own sensibilities. But that wasn't the case. For Sarah, a tenacious girl with Appalachian roots who put herself through college with a humbling cafeteria job (and superior grades), the earned reward of finally gaining entrance to this island of civility was painfully treasured.

Sarah wanted to look Mrs. Gulliver straight in the eyes. Closing in, the supernatural vision gained detail and realness. With about five feet between them, Sarah raised a hand over her brows for shade and answered boldly, "None. Not a penny from anyone."

They stood contemplating each other. Maybe seven seconds passed. Embedded frustrations filtered through the mesh-like haze and rode out on the passing breezes. The taut lips relaxed into a generous smile, and Mrs. Gulliver proclaimed, "How wonderfully gratifying! You must feel extremely proud."

The words rang true—supremely true. In this briefest moment, the esteemed woman's praise imbued Sarah with a sense of accomplishment never conjured by her own mother, now deceased. Sarah felt she had successfully delivered her point.

They parted. Mrs. Gulliver, her anger vaporized, strode home, pausing on the flagstone path to sit on a weathered concrete bench surrounded by dense blue-green hostas and ferns. She pitched the pussy-willow branches into the wild garden, suddenly indifferent about the hallway corner they were intended to fill. Holding tightly to the edge of her seat, she arched her back until it ached, took a deep breath, then turned from side to side to untangle her muscles. An alarming thud—like a baseball whacking the ground—made her jump in her skin.

A seemingly lifeless squirrel lay at the base of the catalpa tree. Hopefully its little chest would stop rising, and the death not be prolonged. As unexpectedly as he had fallen, he righted himself, twitched a couple of times, then scurried into the adjoining woods. "Damn!" exclaimed Mrs. Gulliver. She continued to look after him even as she walked away, reiterating another "damn."

Once in the house, she moved from counter to counter in the kitchen, then started over in an ongoing loop. She caught herself and stopped, realizing she'd been doing that a lot lately—wandering without purpose. Also she noticed her emotions going haywire. She relived the yelling match with Janet; vile words and cheap shots collided in her skull. A migraine was developing. She opened a cabinet and reached halfway in for a vase for the now-discarded pussy willows, then felt stupid over her forgetfulness. Exasperated by her inexplicable behavior, she followed the sound of snoring, which provided her with a momentary distraction.

Her aimless body slumped onto a cloud of powder-blue chenille. There was seldom an opportunity anymore to enjoy the cushy loveseat. She had been spending inordinate hours with her philanthropic fund-raisers since she and Ed sold their parking-garage business two years ago.

Here, looking out of the floor-to-ceiling bay window, she used to find solace in watching each season rotate into the next, as if the scenes were all integrated on a giant platform, the kind one sees at a Disneyland exhibit. Birds were the constant: dousing their feathers in the birdbath during summer or establishing a feeding hierarchy at the suet in winter.

Her husband never witnessed the transitions these days either, forever languishing as he did in his fireside recliner. He spent his few waking hours outside, weeding the garden, or in the basement, constructing bluebird houses, which he presented to neighbors and local parks. He had planned on devoting his retirement to fishing with his best friend next door, and also with their son, the one who loved the pastime as much as he. Both were dead.

She turned and scrutinized the breadth of his ample, elderly girth. His protruding belly was attached like a useless mechanized prosthesis on his otherwise normal frame, rising and falling with metronomic regularity.

When Ed's hoarse breathing trailed off, Big Red's took over. The name Roly-Poly would better suit the slumbering, overfed fourteen-year-old golden retriever. He'd been given the only name everyone in the family could agree on—their favorite chewing gum. Nowhere from head to tail did his coat resemble the luxuriant cognac-colored sheen of his youth. She didn't want to dwell on Big Red's patchy, thin hair; it only served as a reminder of her own transformation over sixty-five years. Although she had good reason to gloat over her still-vital spark and arresting features, Madelaine Gulliver didn't kid herself when it came to facing that number; it wasn't twenty-five.

Her sigh joined the chorus.

A desperate Janet would be coming over soon. Maddie knew she couldn't discuss this latest development with Ed. For years, she had turned a deaf ear to his complaints. He blamed her for allowing most of their children to live far beyond their means. Why should they ever rein in their spending when blessed with a lifelong benefactor like her? But Ed backed off long ago in what was a gradual process, eventually permitting his wife to usurp complete parental control in the house. Then, as if it had always been that way, one might hear a relative or neighbor's description of them: "Oh, Maddie definitely decides everything...but Ed is real nice, always goes along. At least it keeps peace." How many times had she heard that from her friends? She was envied because she and her husband were beyond confrontation. Maybe that was what was gnawing at her now: she was witnessing the result of her liberal, unscrupulous giving.

Maddie succumbed to the rhythm of synchronous snoring and the blanketing warmth of the spreading sunlight. While floating in this dream state, she thought about her daughter's selfish tendencies. Janet was the third of her six children, the one butting horns with her incessantly. Maddie recalled the morning when the girl, only days out of high school, informed her parents that she was going to hitchhike across Europe. It was during the heyday of such endeavors, when many students were caught up in making the requisite trek. Ed and Maddie insisted that Janet wait another year or two, when she'd be more mature…and when she had some college credits under her belt.

But Janet announced she had already bought the ticket with her allowance through an older friend and was going to celebrate her graduation from high school in Paris…or Athens. To top it off, because it was a last-minute deal, she was going alone. Ed declared they should punish her by withholding her upcoming tuition fee; that would whip her into shape fast. To Maddie, that wasn't an option; no way was their daughter not starting college in the fall. Ed had thrown his hands in the air, the extent of his usual show of defeat. It was apparent to him that Janet had planned this deceit well in advance; she had gotten herself a passport.

Exhausted and impotent—that's how the parents were left feeling that summer. They still hadn't come to terms with the accident that stole the life of their eleven-year-old son Tim, even after six years. The pain was deeply buried.

Immediately following that tragedy, Maddie wanted to get pregnant, and they ended up having one more daughter. When Janet went on her carefree (and irresponsible) way that summer, Maddie was facing thirty-six—still relatively young, if the age were merely stated as a number. That period wasn't nostalgically revisited in Maddie's dozing dream, or ever. The mother clearly remembered Janet's insolence, still her most offensive and characteristic trait.

Suddenly, as if pinched, Maddie sprang up—so much for enjoying the view. She noticed the obvious length of their lawn compared to the neighbors'. Amy, her youngest, better be home to do the job. How typical for Maddie to get sidetracked by a task at hand…it kept her in constant motion, which offered relief from sorrowful thoughts. She used to pause and reflect a lot, before deeming it pointless—what could you change?

She stopped short of calling Amy's name from the bottom of the staircase when she heard the shower running. Annoyed by everything, Maddie eased herself down on a step and inspected the paint chipping off the baseboards.

With elbows propped on her knees, she pressed her fingers into her temples and slowly massaged, pushing forward until the brows on her scrunched face almost met her cheeks. She continued to roll the skin in tight circles, ending behind her ears. That felt great.

As if instructed, she stood and marched up to the second floor. The water rushing through the pipes had ceased. She didn't bother to interrupt the singer belting out *Memories*; the grass-mowing chore no longer mattered. At the end of the hallway, she pulled on a dangling chain, which caused the overhead attic stairs to drop in two successive hinged movements. She climbed with care, trying to distribute her weight evenly across the creaking and shifting wooden rungs, intent on finding a box that had been absentmindedly tucked away decades ago. It was imperative.

The sun illuminated the vaulted space. Having no rail for support, the final step was the trickiest. Waist level with the attic floor, Maddie grimaced as she placed her hands beside her on the gritty surface. Then she hoisted herself up over the ledge, crawling forward quickly to avoid plunging backward in the hole. After a heartfelt "Thank you, Jesus," she began the search, rubbing sore kneecaps along the way.

She swelled with gleeful expectation. Like a child who chances upon a sled during the first snowfall and makes a beeline for the nearest hill, she intuitively knew that this discovery was going to instigate some course of action. Her excitement forced uncharacteristically maniacal behavior: she heaved cartons and kicked aside giant trash bags filled with neglected keepsakes, all the while grunting from the sheer physical workout. She coughed her way through thick airborne puffs of dust. This hunt was completely dependent upon the faith she placed in her subconscious to guide her. And it did.

"JANET—COLLEGE." Maddie cursed the large cardboard box's four-flapped closure. She finally pried it open, dug into its contents, and found the tattered manila envelope...then dropped onto an old beanbag chair. Tired, she closed her eyes and inhaled deeply, huskily clearing her throat to expel any dirt particles left over in her lungs. Her lids felt puffy, and her eyes smarted when she opened them. She chuckled over the mess she had made.

The bold black marker letters endured: "EUROPE TRIP '73."

"1973," she mumbled, shaking her head in amazement. A broken bent-metal clasp secured the coveted contents. As she tilted the envelope, the thick stack of Janet's correspondence spilled across her thighs. Sitting knock-kneed and pigeon-toed, with strands of her trademark French twist coiled wildly in the air, she took care to methodically peel apart the fragile letters, studying when and where each had been mailed. By chance, the first postcard she plucked out of the pile was from Mondorf-les-Bains, Luxembourg, dated June 8, 1973—Janet's starting point. She continued to read letters sent from Interlaken, Switzerland, and Corfu in Greece…more cards from Rome, Belgrade, Salzburg, and several from Germany. Except for a few creases, the picture postcards maintained their enhanced brilliant blue skies and color-saturated flowers. Maddie's eager hands unfolded several small maps. She traced her finger along blurred pencil routes and connected the trail of destinations…Rome to Brindisi to Corfu to Olympia to Athens.

Leafing through a little address book, she recognized some of Janet's old friends. Other names were impossible to sound out; one contained eighteen letters, another had apostrophes interspersed. There were train and boat schedules, faded paper money in a variety of colors and sizes, pamphlets describing hostels, brochures for all kinds of museums, a bunch of beautifully decorated restaurant coasters, directories of university dorms, and the plane ticket: Icelandic/Loftleidir. Did that airline still exist?

"One hundred twenty-nine dollars round trip from New York. Wow!" exclaimed Maddie, under her breath, remembering how inexpensive that was, even for back then. Including the necessary connecting flight in Pittsburgh, the total amounted to one hundred ninety-nine.

She awkwardly repositioned herself in the beanbag chair amid the give of newly shaped dents formed by her pointy elbows and rear end. The once neon-lime vinyl was grayed, cracked, and tacky like a stale marshmallow. She stared up at the rafters, piecing together shreds of a life thirty years distant.

"Let's see," she whispered. "If Janet turned eighteen…then Amy was going to start kindergarten. Hmm, Carol would have been in the fifth grade, and Matt was getting ready for his second year of college…that's when Gary moved to Texas." Gary, Matt's twin, had elected to leave the university permanently.

Her mind's eye fleetingly revealed Tim in his casket.

Her arms reached high above her in a stretch. She placed her interlocked fingers behind her neck, satisfied over correctly placing the whereabouts of her kids. She recalled the sense of relief that came with Janet's letters in the mailbox…knowing Janet was safe. Ten-year-old Carol would read the updates during dinner, then save the mail in her nightstand. Maddie imagined the younger, impressionable little girl tucked in her bed, rereading the letters and picturing her older sister's exploits.

She and Ed had had their hands full at the time with adult stuff: managing their home, the family, and their evolving business, all of which had been occupying them for just over twenty years. It was mind-numbing to realize how much responsibility had already gotten packed into their marriage.

Her thoughts returned to the plane ticket. She honed in on an inner voice, a barely audible one, stirring up her newly mounting restlessness. She neatly reassembled the mess on her lap. Now for the fun part—escaping from the beanbag's ensnaring grasp, and then having to face the steep descent. Coaxing herself along and grumbling, she managed to grope her way to a standing position, then stumble over the clutter until she reached the open pit. She cautiously inched down the ladder. Both hands were needed. Stretching an arm between the slats, she let go and watched as the heavy packet dropped flat.

Crazy with impatience, she didn't attempt to fold the ladder back into the ceiling, but headed quickly to the den with her stash, logged onto the Internet, hurriedly typed "Icelandic Airlines," and waited in suspense.

"How 'bout that…still around." Icelandair was likely the same company.

For hours Maddie sat enticed by the hodgepodge of items sorted out from the slew of memorabilia. Her cheeks flushed. Fidgety fingertips, poised on the keys, itched to begin a new search if a site took "forever" to pop up, longer than the allotted five-second toe-tapping count. Her left thumb's cuticle was becoming raw from the nervous flicking of the next finger. Finally, she ended where she began, staring at the open spaces and the ticking cursor prompting her to fill in a destination and date of departure. How easy! She didn't question her impulsive decision—it was as certain as finding Ed engaged in midday snoozes.

"Enter. Ta-daa!"

A done deal.

CHAPTER 2

It was early in the afternoon when Maddie emerged from her bedroom, freshly showered and exuberant. She was relieved that Janet had failed to appear. She tucked the printout of valuable information in her purse and moved through the house with vigor. Grabbing her keys off the hook by the kitchen door, she skipped past Ed, who was on his way in after mowing the yard. It crossed her mind that Amy had lucked out as usual. Before Amy she got around to beginning a chore, her dad complained, it could have been done ten times…so he did it himself rather than listen to Maddie defend their daughter, which caused him to simmer longer. According to his wife, he should lay off Amy and be thankful she was a "good kid." To him, if Amy were truly endowed with that trait, she would willingly, and voluntarily, lift a finger occasionally to help out.

"Running some errands…back in a while," said Maddie, giddy over her intentions.

Ed acknowledged with a nod while downing a big glass of water over the sink.

The heady smell of freshly cut grass trailed her to the car and permeated the Eldorado's interior. *So this is what acting with reckless abandon feels like—pretty neat,* she thought. A second later, she was screaming out of fear at the top of her lungs.

The unrelenting horn blasts momentarily paralyzed her. Another driver barely missed slamming into her when she went flying through the intersection, oblivious to her stop sign. Unnerved, Maddie's hands and knees trembled uncontrollably. "Hallelujah!" she exhaled, grateful to have arrived at The Peripatetic's parking lot in one piece.

Her mad dash inside the store was thwarted when she nearly stepped into the ribs of a parked black Lab; she luckily caught her balance just in time. His surprise would have certainly catapulted her into the pitched tent and assorted camping accoutrements that overwhelmed the entrance. She remained teetering over the undisturbed dog, poised on the balls of her feet, with arms spread winglike in the air. In a flash, powerful hands grabbed her waist, steadying her until she could recover her equilibrium.

"Good Lord," she muttered, having squeezed her eyes shut to avoid watching the impending catastrophe.

"Mrs. Gulliver…I am so sorry. I put up the display last night, thinking it might be too close to the door. And Storm…I'm so, so sorry. Are you OK?" pleaded the young man.

She turned toward the distressed voice and opened her eyes, wondering who was showing this amount of concern for her. She hadn't come here in fifteen years. Her good friend Sam Browning had owned the place then—when it was sensibly called "Sam's Luggage."

"Considering what might have happened, I'm fine." Maddie looked down at the comatose hulk. "Please don't tell me he's stuffed."

There was no hint of a smile. The man gently led her by the arm away from the hazard.

"How do you know me?" she inquired.

The fellow's eyes lit up, reckoning how amused his almost future mother-in-law would be when he told her. "I'm Sam Junior…I go by Joel now, my middle name." That didn't register. "Amy…high school?" his voice went up, suggesting that should be the crucial clue.

Dumbstruck, Maddie enjoyed the best laugh. "Can't be." She held him by the shoulders. "Just look at you!" Mentioning his great weight loss might sound rude, so she immediately focused on another obvious change. "And your hair!" He'd always been hidden under an unruly dark mop. Given Amy's popularity-driven nature, no one could figure out her attraction to him at the time, especially since he didn't play sports.

Maddie didn't have to say it. Joel grimaced slightly when he remembered his former size. They exchanged a few memories, including some about his dad, who had single-handedly transformed this corner cow pasture by the freeway into a prospering business district. Most people visiting today would never guess how the area used to look twenty years ago. Joel told her that his parents recently retired to Palm Springs.

"Where's Amy these days?" he asked.

"She's still with us. Hard to believe, huh?"

"Jeez!" he exclaimed, shaking his head. "My prediction came true."

"What do you mean?"

God, how do I tactfully say this? he wondered. "You know how nuts I was about her?" He hesitated. "Well…when we split up, I told her I didn't think any guy could compete with how good she had it at home." Nervously he added, "There were just a lot of times when she refused to deal with things…she'd go back home, and that would be the end of it. End of discussion." He didn't like the direction of this conversation. "Anyway, how can I help you?"

Minus Joel's extra pounds, and because his features had matured, Maddie found herself looking at his mother; the resemblance was that dramatic. "This is turning into some kind of eye-opening day," she remarked.

Joel, believing she based her statement solely on his comments, apologized. "It was ages ago. I shouldn't have brought it up." He felt responsible for her solemn expression.

She looked beyond him, contemplative. No, indeed—there was nothing praiseworthy about a thirty-three-year-old still under a parent's roof. It was selfish to keep Amy around as a buffer, but Maddie feared that if her daughter were out of the picture, there'd be nothing left for her and Ed to talk about. Then what? It stood to reason that Maddie wouldn't contribute to anything that would send the girl packing.

If only their housekeeper, Ivee, hadn't retired when Amy finished college. Regarded as family instead of hired help, the woman's continuing presence would have offered Maddie the same security, thereby allowing Amy to take wing. All these years—ones in which Ed tried repeatedly to force the issue—Amy's mother dodged giving the arrangement a second thought, because if she did, she'd have to confess, as she was finally beginning to do, that having it as easy as Amy did was a veritable negative in life.

"It's true," she said, "not much has been asked of her."

Eyes widening, Joel exclaimed, "Much!" Uh-oh. "I didn't mean for that to come out like it did," he added hastily.

"You're right, Sammy…sorry, Joel. *Nothing* has been asked of her." Maddie sounded regretful. Walking past him, she said, "I need whatever lightweight stuff they make these days. Things I can easily carry."

He took the brusque change in tone personally. "Where are you headed?" he asked, glad to be on a different subject.

She gazed at the walls and admired the gloriously vivid travel posters. The images were a collection of blown-up vintage luggage labels from a bygone era, which depicted exotic island destinations, ocean ship voyages, and propeller airplane circumnavigation. For the first time, she was actually going to say the words. "I'm going to Europe," she declared, matter-of-fact.

"That's terrific," he said, adding, "The Gullivers stroll the Seine, sail the Rhine…"

She interrupted, "*A* Gulliver, Joel. One."

"Oh? Part of a group charter, or with a friend?"

"No."

"Well, then. Will you be renting a car or traveling with a Eurail pass?"

All right, here's the test to see how harebrained this idea really is. "Hitchhiking," she replied, followed a second later by, "mostly." Darn. Why couldn't she commit to that one hundred percent?

He cocked his head, and his teeth pulled on the edge of his lower lip. Maybe he was trying to guess whether she was pulling his leg. He didn't laugh. Stepping back, he examined her from head to toe: from the perfectly spiraled hairdo, to the distinctively crisp white shirt and tailored blue skirt, to the bright rose pedicure exposed by a pair of stylish (no doubt) designer sandals.

"And how long do you intend to stay?"

"I have an open return."

After a period of deliberation, an uncomfortable one for Maddie, Joel asked, "Mrs. Gulliver, have you really thought this through? Especially during these perilous times when there's so much…ill will in the world for some or another reason?" The words held such gravity. "Well?"

She ran her fingers across a mannequin's silky pants. "I honestly can't explain it. I have this undeniable…" she paused, unclear about what specifically was motivating her, "*need* to do this."

Joel mouthed the last few words along with her. "And this urge…or pursuit…has it come over you recently?"

"Today," she said, without reservation, studying his every nuance. She gauged the tone of his voice, the narrowing of his eyes, his negative body language (with arms crossed in self-hugging fashion), and the turned-up corners of his half smile (or smirk?).

Holding out his arm toward a wall stacked with hiking boots, he responded politely, "Why don't you sit over here? We should make a list…prioritize. Cut it down to basics."

Good plan, she thought. While Joel went to get a notepad, Maddie realized that, so far, she hadn't the slightest desire to back out of this trip. She caught sight of herself in one of those shoe mirrors propped up on the floor. The angle of it missed her lower legs and instead revealed a most unflattering perspective of her from the waist up. She felt quite disconnected from the figure looking back at her. There was so much drive coursing through her veins. This energy couldn't possibly belong to that aged-looking soul.

Joel sat down next to her, pen in hand and ready for business.

"I've had considerable experience planning the globetrotting for older travelers." He stated the word "older" unabashedly. She liked that. The comment made her curious.

"What kinds of trips? Please don't tell me cruises."

"You won't hear me knocking anything that earns me my bread and butter." He sounded sincere, then punctuated the remark with the quickest wink.

Grinning, she got up and tested hats and shoes with "memory." They sprang open after being compressed into small wads and amazingly retained their shape. While she continued to be awed by this magic, Joel thought he would relate some inspirational tales that involved area residents with whom Maddie was probably familiar.

The first took place during Joel's high-school years, when he worked there part-time. Five women, whose ages ranged from late forties to middle sixties, used the store for discussions about their dealings with cancer. They appreciated the privacy of the reading corner, which he had convinced his dad to make. The ladies were ahead of their time when they asked Sam Sr. to locate an outdoor retreat with rugged terrain where they could participate in activities designed to give them back a sense of themselves. Joel and his father believed the women were being unrealistic, but they kept their opinion to themselves.

Joel admitted to eavesdropping on their conversations. They despised that the idea of death would catch them off-guard in the middle of routine errands. They hated the added burden of comforting their worried families; it was enough for each of them to concentrate on making it to the end of her day, and they really resented putting on a false face so others could feel better. Listening to them, the thing that impressed the naive teen the most was their unwavering resolve to carry out this particular mission in order to reclaim even a small fraction of their former strength. Their purpose began to make sense to him: testing one's limits does ward off lapsing into self-pity and depression. It was a way to live entirely in the moment, with others who understood. The letter the women later mailed from the remote Wisconsin town which had been found for them, described their personal joy and gratitude to his dad.

Although the store meetings Joel recounted happened a long time ago, Maddie remembered having read two of the names in the obituary section of the newspaper.

While Joel carted a few things over to the register, he started in on the high-school chemistry teacher's story. A loved and respected man who had also coached decades of basketball, he considered himself fortunate because he was allowed to work past retirement age. Sadly, that following year he was diagnosed with prostate cancer. Elated over surviving the treatment, he dragged his sorry thin bones into the store and announced that he was going to the top of Mt. Everest—needed to. Both Joel and his dad didn't take their frail customer seriously.

His wife called and begged them to find her husband the warmest clothes made, because he was insistent about doing this. It took a year for the teacher to fatten up, and he exercised to increase his stamina. Joel had recommended a highly experienced guide; at least he would be in good hands.

Maddie followed Joel to the reading nook, where he poured her a cup of chamomile tea. She was aware of this story's outcome, having sat in the library audience a couple of years ago to see the climber's slide show. She recalled his advocacy of not deferring goals. His ardor was supported by breathtakingly pristine images from the top of the world. Those congregated were able to share that spectacular view. Upon emerging from the effervescent sea of clouds into a dizzying blue vastness, anchored on rock as old as the earth, the speaker prayerfully voiced the sentiment from the familiar twenty-third Psalm, "He restoreth my soul," to which his audience offered amen.

Back to the job at hand. Maddie liked the Velcro fasteners incorporated on just about everything—very practical. While she inspected a vest, she did a double take when Joel next mentioned the subject of yet another story: Irene Valentine.

This was a former bridge club partner who had lived on Maddie's cul-de-sac. When her husband chose to leave Irene for her best friend, she disjoined the regular world. Looking through the big front window of her house, anyone passing by could observe her bare feet rooted to the hardwood floor. She likely lived in a robe. This lonely form, partially hidden by her chair, sat hypnotized at all hours with nothing more than the dimensionless companionship of television life...and her Scotch. You didn't have to look hard to see the collection of bottles crowding a small table.

In the middle of every night, when Maddie got up for a bathroom run, she'd notice Irene's TV flickering in the blackness, a reminder that the place was still inhabited. After a couple of years, a For Sale sign appeared briefly in the yard. And then Irene disappeared.

Maddie took a break from her shopping and listened with fascination as Joel informed her about her friend's whereabouts. One day not too long ago, he had noticed Mrs. Valentine strolling through an aisle. (As an aside, he said she appeared sober. Mount Sterling was, after all, a fairly close community, so it wasn't unusual for Joel to be up on its gossip.) Following a perfunctory greeting, Mrs. Valentine confided to him that she wasn't sure if she felt more humiliated by her ex-husband's behavior or by her wimpy response, having submitted to the role of the pathetic cast-off wife.

Irene confessed that she was sixty-four and had this impulse prodding her to start over anew—far from Mount Sterling's watchful eyes. She wasn't inclined to move closer to any of her three children, all of whom lived in other states, because she feared she'd become overly involved with the ups and downs of their families. A dramatic change was in order. If she could survive something as frightening as having been left stranded in midstream, in late life, she knew she was ready to tackle anything.

While finalizing her selections, Maddie remembered that she still required some books and current maps—ones that didn't show a divided Germany. Janet had also traversed the length of Yugoslavia, but with its ongoing border disputes and violence, Maddie wouldn't even try to enter the country. As she weighed one tour guide title against another, Joel remarked that Mrs. Valentine had decided on a destination by looking at a book jacket on display about the Old Patagonian Express train. Maddie noticed the Patagonia labels on some of the merchandise and professed her ignorance, asking if such a place truly existed. She'd heard of it before, but thought it made up, like Shangri-la or Eriador.

Joel stepped aside so she could view a mural of a historical map, the focal point of the small reading area. His finger pointed to the "land of the end of the world."

She laughed in disbelief. "Irene is in Patagonia?"

"At its most southern tip...in Tierra del Fuego."

She assessed the distance from their midwestern city, taking in the scope of possibilities that lay as open to her as they had for Irene. Her eyes settled on Joel's. They sparkled like onyx gems. Placing a hand on her back with comfortable ease, Joel led Maddie to a well-worn brownish-greenish leather chair, the surface of which looked much like an old mottled tortoise shell. He placed an open atlas in her hands. His excited voice receded into the background as she studied the map. *God, Irene...what were you thinking?*

"Sammy"—she didn't correct the slip—"Irene couldn't possibly have taken a train."

"She did."

"Hogwash!"

Joel laughed, grabbed the book, planted himself on the floor next to her, and began leafing through the pages.

"True, she didn't start in Boston, like this author did. It made more sense to fly up to Chicago and begin there." He pointed in the air toward North America on the wall map. His arm dropped southward as he mentioned where Irene had found it necessary to take a plane a couple of times. They were short hops, bypassing some political hotspots. "She sent us updates. It was a blast following her."

"Unbelievable. If she would have mentioned anything like this when I knew her…" Maddie shook her head. "It is so preposterous."

"I can tell you that she wouldn't have cared what you thought, the same way you can't be dissuaded from doing what you feel you must. I've learned to believe those singular individuals who, when this flight of fancy plainly overtakes them, are definitely gonna do it." He slapped his thigh on that note for effect.

She would have much to mull over this evening. Before she returned home, she needed to choose that last essential piece: a backpack. There were so many different designs. She decided on one with a Patagonia label. It was lightweight with small wheels—in case she grew tired of carrying it. Most important, it would symbolize her divorced former neighbor's determination.

Although moved by the cancer combatants' tenacity and the teacher's grit in attacking not just any old mountain, Maddie wasn't able to put herself in these adventurers' shoes. She could, however, relate to Irene's want for escape. The nagging self-reproach that had plagued her friend was beginning to seep into Maddie's own life, leaving her confused. The underlying source of it was different, but the sense that remaining in Mount Sterling would only compound the feeling was the same. She needed to flee the tunnel vision. She wanted to explore who she was apart from the domain of her family and this town.

Waiting for the grand total, Maddie became transfixed by the melodic, undulating notes floating out of Peruvian pipes. They hovered in the air, ascending then plunging like the changeful flight of butterflies.

Joel followed her out, carrying the bundle. They sidestepped the old, fetal-curled Lab; he hadn't budged the entire hour. A twinge of sadness arose in her chest when she thought of Big Red, and certain people. What was it about being old and sleeping? You'd think everything would become more wakeful with age, not wanting to miss a blink of the precious time remaining.

When Joel opened the car door for her, Maddie couldn't resist asking what on earth the store's name meant. She admitted it sounded nonsensical. That didn't bother him. Simply put, a peripatetic moves from place to place. He felt that travelers, lured by the journey, were akin to Aristotle's followers, so named for addressing life's questions while wandering the philosopher's school in Athens. She eyed him warily. It seemed like a stretch, but she kept that sentiment to herself. Joel understood.

They both felt inclined to give each other a hug. It was a sincere gesture and encouraging to Maddie. As she slid behind the wheel, Joel pulled out a business card.

"If you ever need anything, give me a call. My e-mail is on there, too. Are you familiar with cybercafes?" She looked confused.

He explained how she could access the Internet in one of these places, which were scattered all over the world. He would be waiting for news from her. When she turned the key in the ignition, he poked his face inside the open window.

"Mrs. Gulliver," he addressed her, then paused. She could distinguish each of his black curly lashes. His gaze was direct and fervent. "Trust me on this: Leave yourself open. Shelve all of your preconceived notions and beliefs." He glanced down, trying to formulate his thoughts. She couldn't help thinking what a delightful son-in-law she might have had. "You're going to find yourself in unimaginable circumstances, making decisions without the scrutiny of anyone you know around you. It's going to be wildly exhilarating."

That was it exactly! What she was hoping for. Joel sounded so upbeat; it made her feel exceptionally optimistic—so much so, one would have guessed she was going with the pope's blessing.

She didn't enter the main street right away. Looking in the rearview mirror, she was relieved there was no car pressuring her from behind to hurry up. A few deep breaths were necessary to calm her. Mindful of her almost-fatal mishap during the drive over, she heeded her own advice and gave the road her full attention, momentarily forgetting that her upcoming life lay in her trunk.

CHAPTER 3

A week later, Maddie's enthusiasm hadn't waned. Ed was still in the dark about her plans. She wasn't certain what she'd say if he, or anyone else, questioned her impetuousness…or her mode of travel. Joel's understanding was undoubtedly rare.

The evening before Memorial Day, she busied herself fixing the customary tubs of potato salad, baked beans, and assorted dips. She looked forward to having the twins at home together; Gary seldom visited. Would Janet bother coming? she wondered. The two hadn't spoken since that eventful phone call.

It wasn't unusual for the spring to be this cool. Growing up, the kids had often spent the official opening day of the swim club shivering in the water. Besides the community poolside picnic, which marked the annual event, the families on this lane had appeared to share almost everything back then. The parents had taken turns rounding up the herd for tennis, horseback riding, soccer, and various other activities—then dutifully cheered from the sidelines. Ed and Maddie themselves had convened weekly with their neighbors for golf and card games, which, back in that era, included a cocktail hour, always laced with mingling cigarette swirls. But when the few youngest children entered high school, the support team had dwindled to only two couples (the Gullivers being one of them). This routine had run its course, and they could barely muster another hurrah.

The open and overlapping kid-friendly yards gradually dissolved into contained plots, seamed together by privacy hedges. Those hedges grew to represent a mature orderliness stemming from the chaos of adolescence—a change of pace readily welcomed by the currently toilworn older folks. Unwittingly, these green fences would irrevocably distance this blended family of friends from one another, more than was ever intended.

This holiday would follow the same pattern as the last fifteen or so years—that of every neighbor inspecting the lineage piling out of the parade of visiting vans. Oddly, all of the backyard grills would fire up at the same time, likely a residual effect from the old swim-club days. Because the smoke snaked its way over the hedgerow, invading the next perimeter, then the next, and so on, the parties couldn't ignore each other. Cursory greetings in the form of obligatory waving were sent across the acres, equally intended for the few newcomers as well as those once considered close as kin. The communal atmosphere had been supplanted by a detached politeness, not unlike the measured space sought by those who rethink the extent of self-revelations made to a new acquaintance.

The train of vehicles began pulling in at noon. By one o'clock, most of the Gulliver clan had begun to feast at the backyard setup. Janet arrived. She and her husband never formally greeted her mom, heading instead to the safety of a crowded table. The snub did not go unnoticed. The college-bound Harry and his two brothers did manage a hello before running to play baseball.

Small talk made up the afternoon. It had been a while since they last sat together as a unit. There were always spouses' families to take into account when deciding whom to visit during such holidays.

Maddie listened to the multilayered conversations, fascinated by the outcomes of individuals growing up under the same roof. It was disheartening to her, though, that her relationships with most of them lacked depth. She occasionally commiserated with several friends who claimed they felt the same disconnect with their children. Ignorant of a fix, they didn't belabor the topic. Only one person's company always gave Maddie unmatched enjoyment: that of Rima, her seventeen-year-old granddaughter.

Maddie figured she would sense an opening, then make the announcement. She wondered if there might be relief over having her gone, out of everyone's business for a change. During the last incident, she had vowed to limit her interference, but it was hard when she could see a mistake in the making. And didn't it turn out just as she had warned—with Matt's wife in the hospital after the two had decided on a whim to buy motorcycles?

It was almost dark. The adults, pacified by their full stomachs, caught-up gossip, and the lingering daze generated by a combination of beer and gin and tonics, watched as the children's' energized bodies targeted all the houses, running inside them and out, and over and over like ricocheting spring-driven balls. The lawns, strewn with every imaginable toy from roller blades to rideable electric cars, looked like the after-effect of a cyclone. The evening air was alive with quarreling, shouting, and laughing…and pervading the atmosphere was the unspoken truth that this scenario should play itself out more often than it did.

Gary's taxi arrived promptly at ten to take him to the airport for the red-eye flight to Vegas, his current base. It wasn't clear to his parents how anything could be so urgent that their son needed to fly back the same day he had arrived. Probably a new girlfriend took precedence over them…again. At any rate, one child departed without Mom disclosing her plans to him.

Janet and her husband, Dan, were prepared to leave next. They had taken advantage of Gary's departure to say their good-byes to everyone else. Their thanks got muffled behind the closing car windows. Maddie shook her head in disappointment as they raced off in their tank-sized SUV. She wondered if Grandma had been slated the "bad guy" to the boys. Would Harry mostly blame Maddie if his parents couldn't figure out how to get him into this particular school? When their fancy truck headed down the hill, Maddie remarked under her breath, "Yeah…you go. Riding in high style. That could be all four years at UC (the local college)." They were out of sight now and, as far as she was concerned, out of mind, too.

Matt, whose wife was home still recovering from the accident, finally caught his two girls, a blur of spinning cartwheels. They drove away also uninformed about Maddie's intentions. Maddie smiled after them. Where would that boy be without her? Born with virtually no focus or drive, Matt was irresponsible in a harmless way (until the motorcycle purchase). Nothing ever threatened his happy-go-lucky nature. After he drifted for too long after college, Maddie had convinced him to sell Mount Sterling real estate, which basically sold itself. Matt's lack of passion for anything really disturbed his dad. This son merely coasted through life—a sin in his old man's bible.

Carol helped Amy and their dad with the cleanup. Maddie was reluctant to mention her concern, but something was troubling about Carol and her husband's manner today. A solemn mood was evident soon after they arrived. Even Rima, their only child, was unusually nontalkative, preferring to ride a bike by herself throughout the neighboring streets. Her grandmother thought that she and her cousin Harry would have had a lot to talk about, since they both were starting college this year.

Carol and Tom gave her parents the customary peck on the cheek before sinking inside their 1969 Volvo station wagon. Rima, on the other hand, wrapped herself around her favorite person in the whole world, her grandma. She praised Maddie endlessly about the food and the pretty bouquets, then ended as she always did, telling Maddie how much she loved her.

All the while as she listened, Maddie rocked Rima where they stood, lovingly pushing her thick, honey-colored hair out of her face. This kid never held back. Right then, everything seemed all right. Maddie resolved to curb her overactive imagination.

They continued chatting through the open windows as the car rolled slowly down the driveway. Grandma Maddie walked alongside the (by now) vintage automobile. Its original, distinctive red paint was weathered like the strata of a geological specimen. The thinning topcoat bled into the bluish steel base, causing it to resemble a faded sixties madras plaid. The old car was used (and loved) like a threadbare heirloom quilt that couldn't be parted with. It summed up the family perfectly: practical. They held no pretense.

The words came out easily: "Rima, dear, I'm going to miss you so much when I'm away."

Tom hit the brakes, and she got bombarded with questions:

"What do you mean?"

"What are you talking about?"

"Where? Dad didn't say anything. Why didn't you say anything?"

"When?"

Three pairs of probing eyes zeroed in on her.

Maddie shooed them on with the wave of her hand. "It's late. I'm ready to drop. I'll call you tomorrow."

They did as ordered. Grandma had to laugh, though: Rima, smiling, had shoved her head and shoulder out of her back window in order to shake a punishing index finger at her. The same gesture had been done to Rima and the other grandkids—in jest—when they were little and had done something they shouldn't have.

Maddie observed Ed giving leftovers to Big Red. She thanked him for doing an outstanding job of grilling, as usual, and then suggested that they finish putting things away in the morning.

That morning came and went—along with the next one—without Carol getting a call from her mom. Maddie cringed when she read Carol's number on the ID display, and again when she deleted it—several times. She simply didn't feel like explaining herself.

She told Ed that several committee members were going to leave information for her, so she let the answering machine pick up. She did that frequently, so he thought nothing of it. He seldom picked up the receiver anyway, because the calls were mostly for her.

The countdown was nerve-racking. Maddie went where she always did to find relief. The pool continued to serve as her mainstay, where she would therapeutically stroke the distance with fortitude whenever events proved unbearable.

CHAPTER 4

It was 11 AM, and Ed was in his zone, snoring to his heart's content, splayed across his recliner—the seat and back of which stayed hollowed and configured to the ponderous load even in its absence. Big Red's unshapely form lay upside down in his corner, blocking the air vent on the floor. His paws twitched and cycled in place, chasing his dream's prey. Maddie sat on the footstool facing her husband, unamused by this too-familiar habit. She shoved his knees. A droopy eye opened halfway, then closed.

"Ed, wake up." She spoke calmly. "It's important. C'mon."

He followed his yawn with a limp push to right himself. He seemed sufficiently alert. The basic points were delivered in a straightforward tone. She could just as well have been reading instructions on how to assemble a bike, so unchanging was the attitude in the expression reflected back at her.

He cleared his throat. "I figured something was up."

He wasn't as inattentive as she thought.

Each continued to look at the other. He shrugged his shoulders, suggesting that if there was nothing more she was going to say…

She got up and strode out of the room with a knot of guilt in her chest. He deserved to know sooner than the day before. While she proceeded to the car, her emotions did an about-face: why should she feel bad when he had subjected her to years of sudden and irrational shifts in his behavior? Those moods came out of thin air, catching everyone off-guard.

Maddie diagnosed it twenty years ago, after watching a doctor on a talk show. His description of depression fit Ed to a T. Her husband's mood swings manifested themselves during the last half of their marriage. The cloud always formed in the middle of a fun event. There were fortunate periods marked by fewer episodes, but the sullenness had increased again that past year. Forget dragging him to a doctor, though—Ed's solution was to sleep more. Lord, how she longed to jump ahead to tomorrow and be seated on the plane. She again skedaddled to the swim club, where she could count on the sensation of sailing through water to quell her impatience and frustration.

The night passed without further discussion. Ed was in bed by the time she arrived home. There was no concern about disturbing him while she undressed and got in pajamas, because his snoring forced her to sleep in another room; at least that was the original reason. Before turning in, she set her gear in the garage for an easy getaway.

Very early the next morning, she opened and closed doors quietly. Tiptoeing through the kitchen on her way out, she heard the unmistakable sound of Red's nails scraping the wall. She swiftly backtracked. The full moon's diffused light showed off a bald belly. "Dear, dear, Red." Maddie got down on her knees and kissed the top of his old lumpy nose, the quirky pointed bump on his noggin, and his closed eyes, overlooking that they were gooey and caked. He curled his legs around her arms, enjoying the attention. She dabbed the tears on her cheeks with a paw.

It was 4:30 AM. Maddie stood in darkness on the driveway. The faraway bloodcurdling screeches from fighting raccoons intruded on the normally tranquil hour, which was usually filled only with chirping. Her heart raced. It struck her that she might never see this view again, or the faces of her friends and family. Panic didn't set in. In her heightened state, she became acutely aware of the content of her life. She marveled over the energy she had expended in her pursuance of solving others' problems, especially when no one bothered to follow her advice: not Ed, nor her children and their families, and not her friends. No doubt, others faced similar epiphanies at solitary moments like this in the predawn stillness. Should anything happen to her on this trip, she felt assured that she had completed the job meant for her here—everyone was able to take care of themselves, a fact worthy of admitting a long time ago. Entering this twilight stage, she could now afford to satisfy some curiosities about other parts of the world. When she was little, she had hoped to visit all its corners.

Although the Gullivers had seen many of the states, Ed wasn't interested in putting up with the hassle of foreign travel. He preferred the freedom of driving his own car, and bringing the children along when possible. Once, when Maddie actually persuaded him to fly to Puerto Rico, they got called back home after only two days at the beach; Gary had appendicitis, which required surgery. Another time, because most of the neighbors talked up Hawaii, Ed finally conceded to go. Their bad luck was unheard of: After tolerating seventeen hours en route, a message awaited them upon their arrival. Ed's mom, who had been at their house babysitting, had had a heart attack. That put the kibosh on future ocean crossings.

A glint fired through the evergreen branches as the shiny black limousine turned around the bend. It was on time to take her to the airport. Maddie hauled her pack to the street. She had no desire to make conversation with the driver. He was an elfish, shabby man who appeared hungover—fortunately, there shouldn't be much traffic. She got her desired silence.

Normally she would hate having the windows open on the interstate, but the sweet, doughy scent from the nearby bread factory clung to the humidity and reminded her of the grandkids' vanilla bath gels. The fragrant aroma permeated the rooms throughout her house when they spent the night. The moment felt wonderfully genuine, not surreal as she had envisioned. She already missed Rima and counted on her busy itinerary to keep her from dwelling on it.

Once inside the terminal, Maddie moved systematically from a departure screen showing that her flight wasn't delayed to the check-in counter.

Forward moving, forward thinking. With her Patagonia strapped on her back, and sporting an air of confidence derived from her ambitious undertaking, this unproven hitchhiker strode past all of the indifferent strangers' faces, fearless. Mrs. Madelaine Gulliver, former prominent socialite, focused on the course ahead of her, invigorated by the refreshing uncertainty of it. She had a commanding presence: five feet, nine inches of indubitable spirit, manifested by a disciplined, straight posture and easy, graceful gait. The curve of her angular jaw met the sweeping line of her auburn hair, which was pulled back and around in its usual style and secured with a black oval piece of tooled leather fastened with a wooden chopstick. It was among Janet's keepsakes and still, remarkably, carried the faint smell of the pungent patchouli incense reminiscent of the times' proliferating headshops.

Relieved to have successfully cleared the security gate, Maddie looked at the overhead sign directing her to Gate B19. Right when she launched herself on the people-mover, she whispered a parting sentiment, "Time to see what we're made of."

She glimpsed the nose of the plane outside the waiting area's windows. Home free.

While Maddie waited to board, she grew contemplative about this ride of life everyone was on, and about the times it was necessary to park off to one side and catch a breather. She'd had plenty of those recouping spells, but now she was zooming along again in high gear.

Who can say when this uncanny thought process began—the process that culminated in the mental picture of a particular forgotten box with the prize envelope? Maybe Maddie's psyche had been begging for a change for quite a while, giving signals that she kept ignoring. Eventually, as a matter of self-preservation, it devised a means for giving its subject the proverbial kick in the pants.

Maddie took her window seat in the comfort of first class. She relished this long-awaited event, hoping soon to conquer the idiot grin she was wearing.

CHAPTER 5

Madelaine Morrisey married Edwin Gulliver in 1953, days after Christmas and his return from the Korean War, events that also coincided with her sixteenth birthday; and only after he agreed to let her raise their future children as Catholics. They met at summer camp where Ed was a counselor and she was a tall, gangly twelve-year old. When he laid eyes on her the next summer, Maddie had been stunningly transformed. It was no exaggeration when admirers declared that her pinup looks rivaled Rita Hayworth's.

Sparks ignited, and they corresponded with letters throughout the year. Their words, poetic in nature, not bawdy, were filled with the idealized passion one would expect at their ages.

That spring Ed graduated from high school. Believing that service to one's country was a man's honorable duty, he volunteered for the army. The love-struck teen-age girl promised to be there for him when he returned from the war, even though they'd never been on an official date. Their intention to wed was not discouraged by her mom and his parents. Expectations were different then. Many girls were wives before reaching twenty, and there were children who didn't go beyond the eighth or ninth grade because they were needed on family farms or in their parents' stores. Ed himself could look forward to managing his ailing father's single parking-lot business. Before his tour of duty began, Ed had already scouted prime locations around town that he wanted to buy. He wisely anticipated a future filled with so many automobiles, that multiple level structures might be necessary in order to accommodate all of them. Maddie had a good head for numbers and asked to take on the small company's bookkeeping job, after completing her high school's secretarial courses. She never even started her senior year.

The newlyweds leaped into life together that December. It was an exciting period, especially when Maddie and Ed learned they were soon to become parents. Each had been an only child and agreed that they wanted many babies. Gary and Matthew were born on a torturous hot and humid night, a little premature, during the beginning of September.

The Gullivers were establishing the family life they had envisioned. Janet was born late the following spring, followed by Tim's arrival the next year. After Maddie suffered three miscarriages, Carol came along in 1963. By then, the topsy-turvy household was becoming too challenging; the parents decided they'd had their fill of interrupted sleep.

In the meantime, the company continued to prosper, acquiring more properties to hold all of those cars being used instead of buses. The couple was amazed as they watched their financial picture grow steadily rosier. It was during this boom-time that they made their move to Mount Sterling. The rural open spaces were opposite the tightly packed downtown row houses.

Their charmed existence lasted four years, until Tim was killed in a car accident. He was only eleven. The neighbor boy was driving him home from a swim practice, and didn't gauge the speed of the oncoming car when he turned into their street.

Shortly thereafter, Maddie's newfound obsession with having another baby finally swayed Ed, who at first had misgivings about the idea. He had already sensed something off-kilter in himself before his son's death, a feeling he shared with no one. His grief brought it to the forefront. Maddie's conviction on the matter made him rethink his stand; after all, a new baby might indeed help them endure this dark episode. Amy didn't quite greet the New Year; she expelled her first cry a couple of minutes before midnight on the last day of 1968.

Amy was a wanted "mistake," at least to Maddie. Wanted, because Tim's death had to have been a grievous error; one that God would no doubt correct by presenting her with another son, one as easy-going and loving as Tim had been. The mistake became evident when the doctor announced a daughter. The new mother was greatly disappointed. Ed responded better than he thought he would. The baby's unique, feisty personality directed his attention away from his sadness. Maddie, on the other hand, feigned interest in her. Comparisons were constantly, silently made as to how Amy was nothing like Tim, which kept him present in the mother's thoughts, and the pain of his absence alive in her soul.

By the time Maddie approached her forties, she was physically and emotionally spent. Her mournful condition resembled the state of the country. Toward the end of the sixties, a sense of despondency infiltrated America, continuing well into the next decade. Arguing and yelling matches ensued whenever the older boys came home. Matt was then in college. Gary, in particular, railed against his father during any discussion about the relevance of patriotism in the Vietnam-Nixon debacle.

Also, the ongoing race riots created an uncomfortable situation in Mount Sterling. Interactions with the household help were strained and self-conscious, because *all* were "colored," as they were called at that time. There were no safe topics. While in high school, Janet threw herself wholeheartedly behind the plight of the migrant farm workers, admonishing her parents for buying lettuce and for being unconcerned about the effects of treated, toxic produce. Janet organized sit-in demonstrations during Mass when she discovered that the wine served for communion came from California grapes, which were on the boycott list.

Maddie and Ed gave up when their eldest three children backed the legalization of marijuana. Like so many parents during that tumultuous period, they wondered how it was possible to have gone through the supposed steps for raising morally sound individuals, only to witness their efforts drastically backfiring. That upcoming generation was, for the most part, a cynical, angry, and disrespectful lot whose jeering hostility could not be excused. The kids tried their damnedest to make fun of their parents' values. One could never have imagined a day when calm would be restored to the divided nation.

Now, here she sat, thirty years later, having survived that episode. She was fully engaged in watching the passengers filing by, far removed from the particularly sordid history of the previous century.

Once airborne, the enveloping drone of the engines was like a steady rain enticing one to remain under the covers for the day. For a couple of hours, Maddie remained asleep, until the smell of roast chicken alerted her senses. Outside, the floor of clouds, lit by an evening sun, glowed with ripe peach hues. She checked her watch, disappointed it wasn't later.

Stiff, she took a moment to stand, before the advancing food cart blocked the aisle. The men seated on the other side of the cabin were traveling together. A rock band, she assumed. The four youthful faces, displaying shaved heads and rows of earrings, bandied ideas back and forth while the fifth member, slumped in the back-row seat, slept. His silky black hair ran in rivulets to his thighs, where the ends curled on the seat. It was beautiful. A girl, maybe ten, and probably his daughter, leaned against him. Her bare feet were hiked up on the seat. Maddie smiled; she saw only blue jeans and bright pink toenails and fingernails. *Harry Potter* was propped on the girl's knees, in front of her face.

Maddie sat, readjusted her clothes, and didn't neglect the importance of some ankle rotations. Viewing the heavens, she thought of the last book Tim had been reading—about fishing. It had belonged to Ed when he was a boy. Her son was thrilled to be going with his dad and their neighbor on the men's annual Alaskan salmon outing at the end of summer. Ed had the book buried with Tim.

The mom remembered her other children's favorite topics. Gary, always self-absorbed, was fanatical about *The Fountainhead*. He got hooked on it at the young age of fourteen and carried the tattered paperback throughout high school...and probably beyond. He was forever referencing lines—to the point of scaring her.

Matt, the consummate tinkerer, was enthralled with gadgets and contraptions he built using how-to books. His fascination required raiding the cupboards routinely. She thought of the mound of neatly folded toilet paper Matt left next to the sink when he needed the cardboard tubes. Rockets and kites called for a lot of those.

Miss Know-it-all Janet couldn't make her way through the Nancy Drew mysteries quickly enough.

Indicative of her patience, Carol loved intricate descriptions. She reread Hudson's *Green Mansions* for years. Maddie was upset when she learned her granddaughter was to be named after that book's main character, Rima. Whoever heard of that?

As for Amy—whose constant goal was being the most popular girl—she stuck with the teen romance themes and a series dealing with gymnasts.

These thoughts were interrupted when Maddie eagerly accepted her tray of food. Her lower back was beginning to hurt from so much sitting. She was grateful that Joel talked her out of flying Icelandair (which no longer went to Luxembourg, anyway). All of the airlines required at least one connecting service, which meant that the trip might last up to eighteen hours! Air France was the only one to get her to Luxembourg in less than eleven hours, with the briefest transfer in Paris. Life would be easier if she started in Paris, but it was more meaningful to begin where Janet had. She liked the idea of having a sense of history associated with the start of this adventure.

After eating, the passengers' background clamor subsided as they settled to watch the movie or sleep. Staring out the window into the gradations of night,

Maddie beheld an image from her childhood: ink-drawn swirls of hair streaming forth in all directions, a lovely face looking out of the midst of it like a moon out of a cloud. How could she have forgotten? As a girl, before leaving her home in England for America, she had adored her father's nightly readings of George Macdonald's *At the Back of the North Wind*. She recollected its cover vividly.

The story was about a servant boy who slept in a loft above a horse. The North Wind, in the form of a graceful and kind-voiced woman, visited him there, having blown in through the cracks of the poorly built walls. She then carried him away with her, over the earth. The details were fuzzy, but the remembrance gave her extraordinary peace. She'd hardly begun her journey, yet the worth of that memory alone was full payback for the effort of the trip so far.

Maddie started to question whether she was ready to face the inevitable revelations that were bound to surface during these next months of traveling. This particular jog to the mind had been like a gift; she guessed subsequent ones might ruffle her. The element of surprise was intriguing though, because there was little wonderment left in her daily existence. She loved that her hibernating imagination was being rattled out of its dormant state.

The plane flew quietly into the next morning.

Looking down over the expanse of runways made Maddie feel unexpectedly overwhelmed. After landing, she managed to step out of the crowd as it surged forward toward the exit. Her escape landed her in front of a uniformed information agent. When he checked her next flight number, she was immediately swept onto a motorized cart and transported to a plane parked on a runway far from the terminal. As soon as she was escorted to the last available seat, the engines and propellers started up. It was unbearably loud. That turned out to be fairly easy, she thought, then vowed to control her nerves, or she'd never last a single day on the road.

No sooner had the plane ascended, when it seemed to already start coming down. The morning sun shone softly above the crisscrossing green and brown quiltlike patterns of farm fields.

The Luxembourg International Airport was relatively small—although, according to Janet's account, it had been even smaller once. Going through customs was surprisingly brief. Maddie simply strolled out the door and sat on a bench, amazed. She was trembling a little. Slowly, calm returned to her.

She was dying to stick out her thumb, but the place was too busy to try hitchhiking. She stood in line at the curb for a taxi. With map in hand, she showed the driver the town of Mondorf-les-Baines. He politely explained (in English) that it would be easier to take a bus. She looked dismayed, believing that he simply didn't want to go beyond the city limits. Out she climbed, and she proceeded to the other side of the building. "Maddie, you've got the whole day," she reminded herself quietly.

Twenty minutes until the next bus. She watched as more people left the terminal, some looking as confused as she must appear. A couple of American women, in their mid to late thirties, approached her spot, looking back and forth from the bus sign to their map.

Maddie spoke up, "I overheard you mention the town where I'm headed. Do you happen to know of a place to stay there?"

"Sure," replied the one. "You can check the pension where we're going. It's only the start of the season—I'm certain there'll be a room available."

"You won't mind if I tag along?"

"Of course not," said the other.

Maddie learned they were also from Ohio, from Cleveland. Bev and Rhonda were nurses and both had recently divorced. They had purchased a one-month Eurail pass in commemoration of their freedom.

The bus was punctual. As it rumbled along, Maddie wondered: would she ever get over the novelty of being here? Every conversation she engaged in played along with an unspoken one recurring in her head. *I'm talking to someone in Europe,* she would say as they spoke. *I'm riding a bus in Europe…I'm looking at European flowers and cows and streets…*It was terribly annoying, but she couldn't shake this pesky habit.

The border town of Mondorf-les-Baines was known for its spas and casino, neither of which interested her. She wanted only a clean room and privacy—just at first, to take it all in. This was generally considered the quiet week before the onslaught of summer tourists. However, even years after the September 11 attacks, the number of visitors was still expected to be fewer than in the years preceding the horrific act. She would probably be lucky in regard to lodging. Hostels intrigued her. She liked the idea of random encounters.

The three women bought bread, cheese, and canned sardines minutes before a store along the way closed. They were the first and only guests in the pension so far. Maddie realized how lonely her first night would have been if these two hadn't arrived today. It was comforting to speak of familiar settings.

Alone on her bed, too drained to climb under the covers, Maddie grabbed the edge of the thin top blanket, pulled it halfway across her body, and didn't stir for the next ten hours.

CHAPTER 6

Clanging church bells produced a loud buzz in the loose window panes. The irritating rattle served as an alarm, waking the overextended guest. Maddie sprang straight up and immediately looked at her watch.

"Noon!" Her clearheadedness surprised her. One mighty push against the bed had her almost standing, but then she promptly fell back onto the mattress.

"Oh…my…God," she moaned. Each muscle group throughout her entire body felt as if it had undergone its own unique punishment. Accustomed to being in constant motion, her joints had suffered more damage from sitting so long. Right then, she despised her age—she wished she could have done this when she were closer to twenty, as Janet had. But considering she'd made it this far, she resolved not to allow another negative thought to sneak in and ruin her fun. She simply would find swimming pools along the way to relax her limbs.

She cautiously stepped over to the window. The leather barrette dangled at the end of some twisted hairs. Unraveling it tested her patience, so she ripped off the matted clump. It was too late to consider leaving; better to get an early start tomorrow. The weather was wonderful—perfect for a leisurely stroll. Maybe she would mosey over to the border of France just to see how long it would take.

As it turned out, she didn't get far before spotting an open space on a playground bench. She was content to watch these *European* moms and dads with their…yes, *European* kids. Her musing stalled when she tried to figure out whether they were referred to as Luxembourgians or Luxembourgites…bourgish? Bourgans?

The parents sounded like any others. The higher-pitched words of praise alternated with the sterner, deeper tones and clipped commands meant to keep a child in line—along with the family dog. The yapping dachshund continued to nip at the flying feet zipping past him at the bottom of the slide, in spite of his owner's tongue-lashing and animated attempt to catch him.

A day of recuperation was a good thing. Maddie tolerated some initial hunger pangs, but after an hour, she headed to the little market, where she encountered the two nurses she had met the day before. Unlike yesterday, the three ladies had plenty of time to gather an assortment of groceries. They fixed quite a feast back at the kitchen. As a welcoming gesture, the owner offered them a Riesling—a white wine. It was easy to understand her broken English. Between chopping and peeling, the women learned that their host had outlived three husbands and was currently living with a gentleman whom she had gone to school with as a child. The wickedly charming octogenarian shared a toast, then excused herself to go back to her designated portion of the house

In the meantime, these merry cooks were well into a third bottle of wine—drops of which actually made it into the coq au vin, the chicken dish they were preparing. Bev, the older, boisterous blonde, had them drowning in tears of laughter. Her depiction of the goings-on in her hospital (stories that included her former spouse) made it impossible to eat. It was much easier to grab another sip between breaths than to chew.

The woman's great breasts jiggled under her T-shirt as her arms flew in the air, trying to keep in sync with the related story points. Maddie admired her gusto. She could see how much Bev's poised and reticent traveling partner, Rhonda, opened up in the presence of her expressive friend. Maddie was curious whether either divorcee had misgivings about her breakup, but wasn't going to risk changing the mood by asking.

An hour of daylight remained in this fine summer day. The season wouldn't officially begin until after next week. The new friends said an early good night and headed toward their rooms, sputtering leftover giggles. Maddie's head dipped and rose like a buoy—secured, but nevertheless bouncing around its mooring. Her feet shuffled down the hallway. Leaning with her entire body against the door for support, she opened with it, then fell into the space. The heel of her outstretched leg caught the bottom corner of the door and pushed it shut, a move that propelled her across the bed, where she collapsed and lay prostrate for the second night in a row. Twice she woke, dazed. She never did undress.

A rooster belted out the kickoff of this noteworthy date. Maddie rolled over on her back. Anticipating pain, she breathed a huge sigh of relief when she discovered that she could freely stretch without wincing.

She hated running the shower so early. It had good pressure, but only lukewarm water. She tried to be quick, having heard the widespread opinion about wasteful Americans and their excessive water consumption, among other things. Her skin was still damp when she got back to her room. She shuddered while getting dressed. Everything was sticking. "C'mon, sun!"

After giving her tiny area the once-over, she headed downstairs to the kitchen, where she ate a roll and stashed a few for later. She poured a tiny cup of strong coffee made from a press, which the owner thoughtfully had waiting for her, then off she trotted in the direction of France.

The building that she was told was the checkpoint didn't look like the one on Janet's postcard. True, the exterior mural could have been painted on it later, but the orientation didn't appear to be the same either. And indeed Maddie was right. The former border guardhouse stood in the middle of a street and was now an office of tourism, albeit a small one. The current customs and immigration office was inconspicuous, blending in with the neighboring homes and businesses. It was situated near a picturesque pedestrian bridge that crossed a stream.

Maddie was ready to empty out everything on the table, but the guard simply opened her bag, felt around, and asked the usual questions. Another man gave the customary rundown of warnings, omitting any hitchhiking rules—which she purposely neglected to inquire about. If there were restrictions on thumbing for rides, Maddie could claim ignorance if caught by the authorities. The guards acted surprised over a foreigner traveling alone. She guessed it was because of her age. Her name was entered in their books. It reassured her. If anything were to happen, there would be a record of her whereabouts.

In ten minutes, she was on her way. She couldn't resist turning around to see if the guards' eyes were following her. She waved to them in a sweeping arc. They returned in kind, calling out, *"Bonne chance,* Madam Gulliver!"

VOUS ETES EN FRANCE, read the sign. *You are in France.* She would have gone on staring at it, if a woman driving by hadn't stopped to see whether she wanted a lift to the train station. A welcome offer, thought Maddie, but instead of the station, she asked how long it would take to get to the outskirts of town. "Hop in," came the reply. Maddie asked how the young woman knew to speak English to her. The driver smiled; she just knew. A few turns later, they were in the countryside. The baker, who smelled fantastic (having just finished an all-night shift), wished her a summer to remember, and winked.

Well, there she was! Heading south toward Paris, pulling the Patagonia pack behind her—alone—and not feeling the least bit lonely. Half the sun was in view; soon traffic would begin. Maddie had expected to see some cars by now. Not to worry.

Twenty minutes later, there still was no one. The tip of the town's steeple had disappeared; perhaps she should turn back. She sat on the top of her bag, smiling. The scenery was no different than if she were in the middle of a field back home.

"I'm in France." She repeated the words. The third time, she believed it. She resumed her slow march and wondered where she'd end up this evening; Janet had succeeded in getting to Paris in a day. She looked around. She could sleep in one of these beautiful fields tonight, if it came to that.

For the most part, her mind was blank. She didn't miss home. She was somewhere else on the planet; the recurring thought tickled her. She continued walking with the measured pace of the rising sun.

Maddie turned her attention to a charged-up tractor beginning to flex its morning muscle. The noise prevented her from noticing the dazzling, highly polished, turquoise Cadillac Coupe DeVille that had crept up slowly beside her, partnering her ambling gait. Startled, she stopped. The car stopped. She searched for the driver's eyes through the myriad of patterns reflected off the windshield. The door swung open, and a portly gentleman maneuvered his way out of the seat and pushed himself around the extreme perimeter of the hood.

Without taking into consideration that he might not speak English, Maddie remarked, "If I didn't know better, I'd have sworn I crossed the border into another decade."

His pudgy cheeks pushed into his eyes; it was the only way she could tell he was smiling. A full beard hid his mouth. He had probably wondered, too, which language was going to come out of her.

"Henri de Musset," he stated, shaking her hand rather finely.

"Madelaine Gulliver," she answered, casually giving him her full first name, even though she'd gone by her nickname her entire life.

"This *can* be a busy stretch." He straightened his tie while looking at the empty road from north to south. "Are you Canadian?"

Canadian? "American…I'm trying to hitch a ride to Paris."

"Did you lose all your money at the casino?" he asked teasingly.

"Yes. Exactly."

"Madelaine—if I may?" She gave the informal form of address an approving nod. "I would enjoy the pleasure of your company. I can go through Paris on my way to Vernouillet."

Henri spoke American English, not Oxford, and with no trace of an accent.

She couldn't believe his generosity. "I don't want you to inconvenience yourself by driving to the city if you don't need to. I'll be happy if you just drop me in the general vicinity."

He opened his trunk and firmly took the handle of her bag from her, heaving the bulky thing up and in. Maddie had sworn she would never allow her belongings to get separated from her. She wanted to grab her precious Patagonia back, but he closed the trunk lid too quickly. He motioned to the passenger door, and she graciously accepted his offer.

Please, please, please, don't be perverted, she prayed as she fastened the seat belt.

Henri de Musset did not embody any of the qualities Maddie had assumed about Frenchmen. Tucked behind fleshy lids, the small slits of his light blue eyes revealed an impish disposition, and up close, the plump, brushed beard looked as smooth as corn silk. She had to fight the urge to touch it.

His formidable size did not prevent him from wearing an elegant, custom-made beige suit. She admired the tailoring of the lapels and shoulder seams. It seemed that wearing a jacket while driving would be uncomfortable, especially when covering such a distance (and for anyone that size). Any second she expected him to announce, "We will sell no wine…" That was it! She wanted to mention his striking resemblance to the actor, then held back, supposing that being compared to Orson Welles (especially in his later years) might not be regarded as complimentary.

As soon as the wheels began to roll, the traveling pair were met by a barrage of blasting horns from a line of cars whistling around them. She eyed her rearview mirror, puzzled by their sudden appearance.

It was easy to begin a conversation about Cadillacs. In the midseventies, the Gullivers had owned a more refined Fleetwood Talisman. Gone were the huge fins that defined this model. One would see a lot of old BMWs and Porsches—or an occasional Jaguar or Bentley—in Mount Sterling, but never an old Cadillac. She could understand the appeal of a sporty Corvette or Thunderbird to a European collector, but not one of these showy gas-guzzlers.

The conversation turned to his other interests—planes and racehorses—which she knew nothing about. She continued to nod. He didn't grow tired of hearing his own voice.

Henri was not unlike some of the self-aggrandizing executives she was all too familiar with. Mount Sterling brimmed with them. Their pomposity served them well in business, but they were aloof when it came to understanding the hearts of their children and wives. Merely tolerated at home, this type lived for winning the deal, along with its inherent congratulatory camaraderie.

Henri was more or less retired from John Deere. He was returning home after a meeting in Belgium. He never took this route but for some reason had decided to today. Maddie said yes when he asked whether he could show her the cemetery at Verdun.

She remembered her grandfather in England talking about the World War I bloodshed. When the British declared war against the Nazis in World War II, he fretted that his own son (her father) might meet the same end as all those young British, French, and German boys had in the earlier war. It gave Maddie goose bumps to be standing where so many vital, expectant souls once had. The opposing sides must have watched with the same convoluted horror and curiosity as each other's lights extinguished. A staggering seven hundred thousand were slaughtered, give or take a couple hundred thousand…incomprehensible.

The two walked in respectful silence among the crosses, symbolic of the countless surviving families' thwarted hopes. Not only did the breadth of this extraordinary scene remind Maddie of her own terrible fears when Ed fought in Korea, but also of Ed's parents' sleepless nights. Her heart recaptured the indescribable joy she felt when she saw him step out of the car, alive and uninjured. She had stood frozen at the window—the emotion was more than a person could take. When Ed came to the door, he had to let himself in and walk over to her for his welcome-home kiss. God, how she had loved him! They had barely regained their wits about them when the boys were born.

The drive resumed. Monsieur Henri put in a CD of Handel's *Messiah*. This man defied pigeonholing.

The road into Paris was disappointing. Traffic was heavy and fast. The evening sky got lost behind a medley of crowded forms. The City of Light was as junky-looking as most large metropolitan areas.

Maddie noticed that she was fidgeting. It was a long shot to expect that the two places where Janet had stayed might still exist. They weren't on the Internet. Suppose there was no alternative accommodation close by? Henri could hardly be asked to find another place for her. What would she do? That would teach her to fly by the seat of her pants.

Henri followed her map to Rue de la Victoire. Incredibly, the copied address was still a dormitory. He caught the look of relief on her face and smiled.

She was glad to hold her possessions again.

"You picked a good spot, Madelaine. It will be easy getting around from here." He clasped both hands around her one and gently shook it. "I wish you a grand adventure."

"You've been unbelievably helpful, Henri. It's getting late…you must be so tired."

"Yes, I am looking forward to home."

She pictured it a lavish residence; after all, Monsieur de Musset's approach to life held no hint of moderation.

A few passersby gawked as the tank-sized icon of Americana rolled out of view into the night, swallowed by the looming linden trees that cloaked the long, narrow street.

It was ten o'clock. Inside the building, a small group of men stood waiting ahead of her. The student at the desk quickly checked them in. Italy was mentioned. Her turn. Did he have a bed for later in the week?

"No problem."

The overused catchphrase had always irritated Maddie, but right then, it was *the* best answer. She asked if he was familiar with the other place in question. He directed her right around the corner. Janet had arrived before the dorm was open for summer backpackers, but luckily had found a small hotel nearby. Maddie retraced Janet's footsteps, and there it was; it even still had the same name. She was astounded.

La Maison de Doumic was inscribed on a brass placard hanging on the weathered stone wall next to the door. A chiming jingle announced the guest. It was a plain, undecorated lobby.

"*Bonjour, Madam.*" The cheerful greeting came from a woman who stepped out from behind a dark, velvet-draped doorway.

"*Bonjour,*" answered Maddie. "Do you speak English?"

"Yes, of course." The reply was matter-of-fact, not rude.

Mrs. Gulliver pulled out one of Janet's old postcards. "This may sound a little crazy…but I would like to know if it's possible to check into the room where my daughter once stayed in 1973. It was one usually reserved for a pilot during his layovers."

"Seventy-three," the woman repeated, as if she hadn't heard correctly.

Maddie was hoping that if this lady didn't remember, she would ask someone else there who might.

"And how old was your daughter?"

"Eighteen."

The woman's pale gray eyes opened wide. "I was twelve then. You are asking about Captain Renard. You may have his room."

This streak of luck was unheard-of!

The woman's name was Catherine, and she offered a brief background as she led Maddie up to the second floor. Edouard Renard had become part of their family. They hadn't seen him since he retired, although he called them every Christmas from his home in Chicago.

The door opened to a small, stark corner bedroom.

Catherine's accent was thick, but her grammar was correct. She said she used to hate it when her parents would invite some of the guests to eat dinner with them, especially when she was a teenager. She'd just stare at her plate. Then, one night—Catherine remembered it like yesterday—she was lured into looking at this man with a deep, quiet voice. He told the story of a Jewish boy who was sent to live with an aunt in America. It was when the Germans entered France. His parents promised to join him there as soon as his mother gave birth. His aunt had received only one letter from her sister, telling her and Edouard that they were still safe and would be arriving with a baby brother.

Catherine pulled back a curtain, revealing a sink (no toilet, though). She sat on the edge of the double bed. Maddie stood by the window, listening.

The Frenchwoman described Captain Renard. Maddie could well picture his thick, wavy hair, the strong jaw and neck...soft, straight black hair showing from his opened collar, and also on his arms—not curly, Catherine pointed out. *What people notice,* thought Maddie.

"So he grew up to fly planes."

"Yes. He worked for TWA and always came to Paris. I guess the letter had been sent from somewhere on this street. But no one knew of his parents. Friends probably hid them until the Germans found them. I think he was wishing that maybe his brother had been placed with a family, and he would find him. He could have stayed at a fancier hotel, but he came here...for over fifteen years."

"Does he have a family?"

"Oh, yes, with three girls. Tomorrow I will show you a picture of him."

Maddie smiled, then went over to unzip her bag. Catherine took her cue to leave. "*Bonsoir.*"

"Good night, Catherine. Thank you for your help." The bit of history added a personal touch to the spartan room. The sink was a plus. Maddie took her time washing her face and moisturizing her skin from head to toe. There was barely space to turn around in.

It was almost midnight. Tomorrow was somewhere in the middle of the week; she didn't know or care. She lay on the fat pillow, watching the occasional bursts from headlights flash across the walls...just as Janet had, and the pilot. Being here didn't make her feel any closer to her daughter. That was never a goal for either of them.

She did imagine the loneliness of the accomplished pilot, who had felt compelled to return to this street over and over again. He had lain on this bed, knowing his mother's and father's love for him. His poor parents—how they must have suffered, wondering when they would all be reunited...then realizing they never would be. Captain Renard surely wept when he dreamed about his wife and children back home, and the long-lost uncle he wished to present to them. How long had it taken before he gave up his search? Or did he? Maddie slept with a heavy heart.

She woke up feeling relaxed and meditative. A comfortable teal jumper and short-sleeved white shirt had already been laid out last night. She would be testing her new black ankle-strap sandals with the supercushioned soles. Taking only an envelope-size purse that hung from a leather wristband, she set out on this new day—a hot, rainless one.

The preoccupied gentleman at the front desk said that Catherine would be working at her other job until the late afternoon. Sometimes she helped out at the hotel, but mostly she worked as a professional travel agent for Air France. Maddie wrote a quick note for him to give to her, about seeing the photo of Captain Renard. The musical door signaled her exit.

Maddie was anxious to compare her preconceived picture of Paris (mostly derived from Hollywood images) with the real thing. A bus ride landed her in the midst of streaming pedestrian commuters. The additional few inches to her height that her platform heels gave her, caused Maddie to stick out head and shoulders above the terrain of the French people's uniformly petite stature.

Ducking into a cubbyhole café, she ordered an espresso, just to sound like everyone else. She stood at the window counter, feeling lost and intimidated. A boy, maybe five, suddenly shrieked outside on the sidewalk in front of her. He was terrified to walk next to a dog, although it was behaving. The owner had the collie on a leash. Maddie watched the father hold his son by both hands and pull the boy close to his legs as they made their way around the animal. All at once, like on the plane, another childhood memory surfaced: her father's powerful hands gripping her tightly around her small waist, then hoisting her up onto the train where her mother stood. Both cried as they headed away from the man's comforting presence. The little girl couldn't know that he would never come back into her life. Odd, these flashbacks.

Experience had proven that if one simply placed one foot in front of the other, one would be in the game again. It worked. Maddie found herself on the street, looking for the subway. When she asked for directions, people were kind. What fun this would be if only Rima were by her side. For the first time since leaving home, Maddie wanted someone to share things with. Ed did not enter her mind.

She succeeded in landing at the base of the Eiffel Tower, only to find there was a good hour's wait to get on an elevator. Fine. Going to the top was a must. When, at long last, she got to see the skyline from that majestic symbol, she was amazed by the scope of the city. It truly was magnificent. She most enjoyed the communal atmosphere up there: complete strangers from different lands came together, smiling and nodding at one another, beaming with childlike wonder.

She followed that milestone experience with a walk around the surrounding gardens, taking note of the many other sole observers like herself, finding delight in this passive activity.

That was enough for one day. She made it back to her quaint hotel without a problem, and felt like patting herself on the back for a job well-done. As she paused by the door, she felt her bravery strengthen and considered going somewhere else; it was only the middle of the afternoon. She remembered that the dormitory where she would be staying after tonight had a television in a common room. Certainly no one would care if she sat there awhile. It would be helpful listening to some French. She jumped off the step and headed around the corner, pleased with this idea.

Having a flock of children afforded Maddie the opportunity of being exposed to a variety of interests, like French…three kids' worth of it. Their conversational homework ran as part of the nightly background track for close to a decade. She knew a lot of words. Forming sentences was a bear, though.

What a drastic contrast, going from the peaceful street to a lobby abuzz with different languages. She was glad she went in last night to secure a bed for herself later; there were so many people there today. She cut a path through the crowd and reached the openness of the adjoining room. Everyone made such a racket. She turned up the volume on the TV.

A drama (perhaps a soap opera) was long on emotive close-ups and short on the instructional dialogue she was hoping for.

"Oh, no!" she sighed—her turf was getting invaded. After all the chairs were filled, bodies squeezed into every inch of available floor space. Several laptops popped open in succession. Was it a class? As she listened to the nearby klatches, a very familiar vocabulary drew Maddie into their world.

"Play low on the heart lead, and hope East puts up the ace," explained a young Asian man as he pointed to the cards on the carpet in the middle of his huddle. They stared intensely at the configurations.

To her right, a German woman's no-nonsense lecture engrossed the members of her group. "One threat is protected solely by one opponent; a second solely by the other opponent; and a third threat, the 'common threat,' is protected by both opponents." Maddie recognized the description of a play known as "double squeezes."

Next to them, conversing with some Mideastern-looking men, sat a couple of ink-black gentlemen with French accents. Their eyes focused on the small screen they shared in the center of their table. One spoke in a precise manner: "To make this contract, you need two heart tricks. Playing the jack or king could never help…just play low." Another added, "You might still have a chance by running the nine later."

The room took on a sports-bar atmosphere; cigarettes lit up and hung from the sides of fast-talking mouths. Hands, busy dealing cards, failed to keep up with the dropping ashes. Beers abounded.

Maddie tried hard to refrain from laughing over the dead seriousness of everyone, especially those carrying on the weighty dialogue behind her. A man proclaimed, "There are many paradoxical cases related to Bayes's theorem. Consider the following two card combinations." She had to catch a peek; she quickly turned and pretended to look around. They didn't pay any attention to her. The man continued, "Proper play is to finesse the jack, then finesse the ten." Both fellows wore Stanford sweatshirts.

She could hardly believe what she'd walked into. During the height of her obsession with the game (beginning in the early sixties), she wasn't aware of any bridge-playing college students. At first Maddie and her neighbors approached this leisurely afternoon diversion as an escape from tedium. Then Greta Johannsen entered their lives. Her tiny, almost dwarf size, figure embodied an excitable personality. Greta had introduced them to a new realm of competitive playing. Unfortunately, interventions didn't exist yet to break them of that all-consuming addiction, which gripped their lives for over five years.

The relentless and charismatic woman's single-mindedness infiltrated their group, turning the once-relaxing biweekly bridge parties into a high-stakes contest. The new member had written books on the subject, started a column in the local newsletter, and coached professional players. The suburban ladies couldn't help but feel important when Greta asked to associate with them. They were only too eager and ready to accept the challenge of aspiring to a more disciplined level.

It was the defense aspect of bridge Maddie found most satisfying...and truly excelled at. She was good at containing her emotions and remaining flexible throughout a game. She perfectly understood the kinship currently enjoyed by those in the room.

It was too early to return to the hotel and too late to visit some other area in the city. Maddie resigned herself to being an invisible fixture. She stretched her long legs, crossed her ankles, and folded her arms on top of the colorful Turkish woven purse resting on her lap—a souvenir purchased today from a vendor by the Eiffel Tower. While staring at the drowned-out television, Maddie heard a friendly male voice call out, "Ma'am." After a pause, she heard it again, but the tone was more questioning. "Ma'am?" He had to mean her...who else here would be addressed like that? Certainly not the other females, who had to be under the age of twenty-five. She turned and met the eyes of the Stanford "boys."

"Are you with a particular school?" asked the student on the right.

Maddie shook her head no, loving the question. "I'm guessing that I've accidentally wandered into some kind of an international Bridge tournament for students, if such a thing exists."

"You bet they do," he replied.

"You've probably played, right?" the other fellow assumed.

"Yes, I used to love playing...but it *has* been a very long time." Maddie twisted around in her seat to face them better. "I don't understand how you can play on the computer." She had to speak loudly.

One of them stood and walked the few steps over to her. He grabbed the corner of her chair. "Sit with us, and we'll show you."

"Fine," she said, taken aback by the sudden gesture. He led her to a spot between him and his friend. "So, does Stanford pay for your expenses?"

They laughed outright.

"Robert Wellington, University of Michigan," confessed the young man who had been on the right and was now to her left. She looked at the other.

"Karl Oldenberg, University of Oslo."

"We masquerade as winners," said Robert. He admitted there wasn't much interest at school, and he mostly played online. This competition happened to coincide with a trip he'd been planning in order to study European architecture. However, Karl, an American exchange student in Norway, was given a small allowance.

"I am Madelaine Gulliver, representing Ohio…pleased to meet you both."

They sat close together. Maddie couldn't help but think how heavenly this situation would be if she were a young student.

Because of Gary's interest in computers, the Gullivers were not unfamiliar with them. Their son forced his parents to use them early on in their business. He had set up their accounting records and encouraged them to take courses periodically to keep up with the technology. For that, his mom would be forever indebted to him.

But Maddie had resisted giving computer games a chance, insisting nothing could compare to scrutinizing the opposition or handling the cards while figuring things out. How could you substitute the tactile element of fingering Scrabble, Clue, or Monopoly pieces? Even the boxes' distinctive cardboard smell lingered throughout a lifetime, reminding one of childhood. Her grandkids made the same nostalgia argument for calliopelike digital sound effects and joysticks…and perhaps the smell of factory-fresh plastic.

Karl did most of the explaining. Nothing he said was new. On the other hand, watching the computer, an inanimate object, analyze a player's tactics was disturbing. Enough with these exercises—she wanted to view a complicated board. Rediscovering the lure of competition felt good. Maddie found that her skills applied just as well in cyberspace as they had in reality.

Robert and Karl cast glances at one another: *Are you thinking what I am?*

"Madelaine," said Robert, "if you're going to be staying around here, why don't you meet us at noon tomorrow? We'll form some teams. You be on ours." He rested his right arm on the back of her chair and folded his hand around her shoulder.

"Or we can be on yours," said Karl, thereby letting her know they were impressed.

When it registered that she would have the chance to play with people, she was beside herself. She closed the laptop. "Yes, yes…people! Enough of this mind reader!" She rubbed her sore eyes, which had been glued to the monitor for three hours.

Both men stood and walked her to the door. She felt safe nestled between two figures considerably taller than she.

Maddie had just enough time to wash her face and put her feet up for a second before Catherine knocked and invited her to dinner. The dining room was elaborately decorated in sharp contrast to the entrance and guests' rooms. The orange glow cast by the unusual painted lampshades enhanced the cozy feeling, as did the dark wood furniture, richly embroidered tablecloth, and dark green velvet chairs. A whimsical wall-sized tapestry showed a young milkmaid seated beside a cow, entertaining some barnyard goats and chickens by directing a stream of milk into a cat's mouth.

A customary light supper was served: sausage, boiled potatoes, and the freshest crisp green beans. Catherine apologized for her family (six members were at the table), who couldn't stop talking about the pilot. They missed him terribly. Their guest's interest rekindled memories they hadn't thought about in ages. Maddie assured her hosts that she wasn't the least bored. Looking at a photo, Maddie saw that Catherine had not exaggerated the Captain's handsome features.

Later, while Maddie sipped her nightcap, an aunt positioned a zither on a specially designed table and began strumming waltzes. Maddie delighted in watching her; this was her first encounter with a zitherist. Catherine's uncle and her mother unrolled a flannel board and set it on the cleared dining table. They hummed the melodies as they searched through puzzle pieces of a fog-enveloped Golden Gate Bridge. Underneath them, on the thick Oriental, an orange cat lay curled in a ball next to Catherine's uncle's feet. A few times, the front-door jingle interrupted, and the family took turns checking in a guest.

So much had been packed into that day that it seemed like two days. When her eyes closed that night, Maddie had a lot more faith in her ability to continue with the trip. Tomorrow was going to be fun. She was living a life in France, not merely moving from point A to point B.

The weather hadn't changed the next morning. She figured she'd better take a stroll before it got hot, considering she'd be sitting all afternoon. Twelve o'clock couldn't arrive fast enough.

When it was finally time to play bridge, Karl met Maddie before she had her second foot through the door. He whisked the backpack from her and set it behind the front desk, assuring her of its safekeeping. The place was alive, just as it was the previous night. Karl directed her to a window table. Sonja, a small-framed blonde from a university in Germany, filled the fourth seat on the other side of Robert. Sonja offered a friendly hello and a vigorous handshake.

"Sonja has won the Junior division twice in the European championships," said Robert. "Now she's too old…has to play with the likes of us." He spoke without thinking and missed the expression on Sonja's face, but Karl left his mark on Robert's shin under the table. He reacted with an "Ow!" and a look of confusion.

Maddie didn't care. They were being overly sensitive about the remark. *Get on with a game, already!*

Some onlookers hung around, hoping to pick up last-minute pointers before their respective matches, which would start tomorrow.

Her memory was sharp, considering she hadn't played in over a decade. After a couple of hours, she and Sonja realized (with smug satisfaction) that they were on the same wavelength. They won easily—and repeatedly. Time for a welcomed break.

Maddie rode with Karl on his motor scooter while the others asked around to borrow some bikes. They all met at a café ten minutes away. This time she ordered café au lait, adding several sugar cubes. It definitely made up for the espresso yesterday. *Was that only yesterday?*

The students wanted to know why Maddie preferred traveling alone, what her husband and kids thought of her actions, and so on. She stated that she simply wanted to try being totally independent once. Then she asked about them.

Sonja, twenty-one, had dropped out of school a few times for undisclosed reasons. She hadn't yet decided on a major. The guys, both graduate students, were twenty-eight, several years older than what Maddie would expect of students who were getting their master's. Considering the cost nowadays, she presumed that they probably needed to work and save money before continuing with their studies.

Maddie had such a good time watching them and observing their characteristics, notably their youth, which was flagrantly emblazoned across them. And their eyes—those eyes shone with boundless enthusiasm as the three of them planned the upcoming decade. She licked the milk from her upper lip. It dawned on her that she was facing a future equally as exciting, one filled with untold possibilities…just not as many. After all, she might still be home with Ed and Amy, maintaining her status quo existence.

Maddie was at a disadvantage that she knew she couldn't hide from. Old Age, wearing a crafty grin, now engaged her in a game of tag, reminding her of its winning clutches. As yet, the minimal arthritis didn't interfere with her activities, and she could take a pill to boost her thyroid, but there was no denying that she was closing in on a period marked by greater problems. One couldn't forever stave off the increasing need for medications and surgeries.

Listening to the students' passionate discourse, Maddie thought about how time dissipates the highs and lows. In a way, she was grateful for that. Otherwise, the loss felt from the worst event of her life, which had been replayed daily in the ensuing five years since its occurrence, could never have suddenly vanished, which was what happened one June afternoon while she folded the laundry. She had paused in the middle of her chore, realizing with quiet astonishment that she'd gone through the entire previous day neither grieving for Tim nor thinking about him, not even for a second. So extraordinary was the absence of sorrow from her repertoire—a godsend, really—it had made her lightheaded.

After that, Tim's image only occasionally surfaced, and without the hurt that had been almost incapacitating. The flipside, Maddie thought sadly, was that the euphoria tied to the best moments was never truly recaptured, either. Alas, the emotions—the most cherished part of our mental snapshots—ultimately faded. Certainly, the greatest fear of the impending process was dotage—sitting by a window empty-headed.

A perceptive Sonja took note of Maddie's silence and distant look. "Madelaine." After pausing a second, she then asked, "What is it like hearing us go on about things?"

A poignant question, thought Maddie. She could see they were intrigued.

"It's like the years between us are miles...and I'm on Pluto...no, make that another galaxy."

Without hesitating, the girl leaned over and hugged her. "It's hard to imagine."

"Dear Mrs. Gulliver." Karl used too official of a tone, which matched the seriousness of his furrowed brow. She didn't like the sobering effect of her reply and wanted everyone to be laughing again. "Please tell us the most important lesson you've learned?"

She was tempted to offer a goofy answer, but she could tell that he sincerely wanted to know. Mirroring his expression, she said, "As long as there is another day, there's another chance...for anything. And that lesson had better be taken to heart before one's final day, so you're not faced with a mountain of regrets. How's that? Not as profound as you had expected?"

"I agree," Karl said. "It's all about taking action."

When they got back to the dormitory, separate rooms had been set up for duplicate bridge. The four played together and proved victorious.

Maddie declined an invitation to go celebrating at a bistro. She wanted to check out her new place.

The backpack! Worried, she wished her new friends good luck in their tournaments, then hurried to the entrance. Her bag stood in the same corner.

Maddie had just finished signing in when Robert appeared. He slung her pack on his shoulder as though it were empty and held out his arm to the stairs. They marched to the third floor. It was worth the climb. A student who lived there year-round had gone home to Spain for a couple of weeks; she had this all to herself.

The room overlooked a courtyard that was situated between the main house and a barracks-style dormitory. When she poked her head out the window, a pigeon sitting on the ledge looked back at her with interest, then hopped closer. She motioned for Robert to come over and see.

"I could stay here for months. This is perfect," she said.

While Maddie enjoyed the view, she was oblivious to the young man watching her...and admiringly so.

Maddie hit many of the tourist locales over the next few days. At first, she went with only a couple of others from the dorm. Then the group grew in number as more students lost their matches.

On the fourth day, she opted out and returned to *La Maison de Doumic* early in the morning to catch Catherine before she left for work. Maddie offered to fix dinner that evening. After a splendid morning of shopping at the colorful outdoor market, she spent the rest of the day in the kitchen, working at a much-needed leisurely pace. She concocted her own barbecue sauce for the ribs and mixed together a huge bowl of potato salad. The family was happily surprised and ate heartily. No guest, let alone an ex-guest, had ever done that for them before.

Back in her room, she was putting a chunk of bread on the ledge when a second bird landed and snapped it up. He then offered it to his partner in the corner. Smiling, Maddie grabbed her towel to go to the bathroom down the hall. As she opened her door, she gasped from surprise. Robert stood with his hand raised, ready to knock. Another second and his fist might have bonked her on the head. They laughed picturing it.

"Sonja's still in the running."

"That's fantastic. Who's next?" she asked.

He told her, then mentioned, "No one saw you today." He formed it as a question. It never occurred to her that anyone would care. He walked beside her. "We're meeting by the Sorbonne tomorrow. You'll come, won't you?"

"I don't know, Robert."

It wasn't that she minded hanging out with the young people. The problem was his constant proximity to her; she found it inappropriate.

"I want to go to Montmartre again," she stated flatly.

"We're going there Friday. You can come with us then. It'll be the weekend, and there's more going on."

"You're right. I wouldn't want to miss kicking up my heels when the nightlife's in full swing."

"Ma-de-laine." He wasn't put off by her sarcasm.

"You know what I'd really like? To find a swimming pool."

"There's got to be one around the university. Then we could meet the others for lunch."

We? She hadn't invited him along. But…if he could locate one…Reluctantly, Maddie nodded her assent.

"Great," he said. "I'll meet you downstairs at…what? Nine?"

Maddie was anxious to clean up and sleep. She agreed to the time. He gave her arms a quick squeeze, then left.

The next morning, the two met promptly on the hour and headed for the Left Bank. She didn't know what to expect, never having had any conversations alone with Robert. He showed an unusual degree of interest in her many pregnancies: Did she really want that many babies? Did each pregnancy feel different? Did she experience certain concerns with any of them? Was having her last child as exciting as the first? The line of questioning seemed bizarre—not the kind of stuff college boys pondered, unless maybe they were going into obstetrics. He asked if she ever wanted out of her marriage, and in the same breath, which authors she enjoyed reading, the type of music she liked best…and the list went on.

Maddie didn't feel talkative. She was on a mission, and she certainly wasn't going to get philosophical about her life. Women get pregnant, plus she was Catholic—end of story. She skipped over her relationship with Ed; it wasn't any of his business. She concluded by telling him that she went through reading spurts, and this was a dry period.

"What's the last book you read that wasn't for school?" she asked.

He had to give it some thought. Thank goodness it kept him silent for a moment.

The train moved swiftly along. They sat next to each other on one of the longer benches facing the opposite side of the car. She examined his profile. Robert stared at his crossed feet while trying to remember. He was going to mature into a handsome man; at this early stage in his life, though, he was almost pretty.

Directly across from them, two shy, giggling girls and a guy, all comically pretending to look out the window, had their eyes fixated on Robert. He seemed unfazed. He had to be aware of the glances wherever he went. His bright blue eyes turned toward her, and he named the book. He summarized the historical biography, which then led to a meaningful discussion about the founding fathers, which lasted until they parted ways at the aquatic center to go into the locker rooms.

Maddie had worn her bathing suit under her knit dress. In no time, she shot out into the lane. Her mind emptied on impact, as it was conditioned to do.

Robert walked to a bench to wait for her. Then it hit him—she was already in the water. He went and crouched at the pool's edge. Maddie's long limbs gave her strokes power and grace. Her kick was steady. He dove in next to her.

Eventually she glided to the wall. She offered Robert a weak smile, then studied the big glass-domed interior. Break was over; she inhaled deeply, pushed away from the side, and went streaming across the surface for another half-hour.

After dressing, the two still had a couple of hours to kill before it would be time to meet the others. Maddie tried to stay a step ahead of Robert, but the streets were jammed now. When they stopped to look at a window display, the right half of his body pressed against hers, and he rested his hand on her shoulder. She no longer had any misgivings about the type of interest he was showing in her, which went beyond friendly—*this is weird*—and she grew more incensed by the second. She couldn't think of what to say. Then they were walking again. Suddenly Robert took her by the arm and pulled her into a shop.

"I love this place. I could spend the entire day here."

Maddie surveyed the walls. The place was stocked with posters galore. She was relieved when Robert took off to go through bins of prints. It occurred to her that she might find an appropriate thank-you gift for Joel to hang in his store. She spotted a bold, red, vintage poster. Yikes, the price was steep. What the heck! He deserved it…and would appreciate it. Who knows, maybe one day it would grab the attention of another would-be traveler, and Joel would start in on the Gulliver tale. It was a heartwarming daydream.

Robert approached her and asked what she found.

"A souvenir for a friend. Thanks for taking me in here. Are you ready to go?"

On their way to the restaurant to meet the others, Maddie decided she would maneuver a way to keep from sitting next to Robert.

The sidewalk seating was filled. Karl stood on a chair and waved to them from the opposite corner, pointing to an open spot between him and another person. Robert took a chair from the next table and had to resign himself to sitting across from Maddie. The combination of heat and traffic exhaust was daunting. This time Maddie ordered a cold Coke with lots of ice.

When the perpetually cheerful Sonja arrived, she was greeted with resounding applause from her bridge cohorts at the surrounding tables. Third place was quite honorable. She slipped into a sliver of space next to Maddie.

Sonja mentioned that she almost got stuck in a huge crowd of protesters, specifically anti-Bush. An undercurrent of resentment pervaded the air here. So far, Karl, Robert, and Maddie hadn't encountered any harassment. They sympathized with the Europeans, who were being asked to send more support to Iraq, more troops, more boys and girls to play roulette with their young, unlived lives.

A Swedish student at the table brought up the subject of his travel plans. He was going to wander America and asked for their recommendations. Robert suggested they meet up, because he hadn't been many places himself, and the timing worked out well for him.

Sonja had visited Boston and Miami, and insisted that neither be missed.

Karl and Maddie talked over some ideas, then announced they had devised the perfect road trip. They had the Swedish student starting in Boston, continuing down the Eastern seaboard until he reached the Carolinas. There he'd have to decide whether to go on to Florida or head west. Either way, they assured him, he'd end up on Route 66 (a must for him). From there on out, it was pretty much a straight shot to the Pacific.

The fellow wrote quickly, admitting, "That's a lot for two months."

"Two!" Karl and Maddie said it together. They thought he had around a month.

"You *are* joking, right?" the student asked.

Maddie looked over the list and counted on her fingers the minimum number of days required for each destination. Then she assured him, "It's doable."

He shook his blonde head and raised his invisible eyebrows. "Then where?"

"Drive up the coast," said Karl, "at least to San Francisco. You can stop along the way in Carmel and Santa Barbara."

Sonja broke in, "Now I'm jealous. That's where I've always wanted to go. I'm going to fly to LA and meet you."

Karl remembered something he had read in a newsletter. "July…Long Beach. It's the North American Championship. The university should be pleased you did so well here. We should go online and find out next year's schedules. Maybe you could get your trip paid for."

As if Sonja could get any more excited today.

"Don't I ever go through Colorado?" asked the Swede. "I really want to see the Rocky Mountains…and Yellowstone."

"Yosemite is gorgeous. Go there instead," said Maddie. "Colorado could be the final destination. Fly home from Denver." She asked for a piece of paper and started roughing out a map. She was trying to think of alternate routes for the young man when she casually mentioned, "You are certainly welcome to come visit me if you ever get stranded."

"I'll take you up on that," said Robert.

Sonja and Karl exchanged glances. It was obvious to them that their friend had no qualms about showing their new acquaintance Madelaine an excessive amount of attention; he was getting nervy.

Maddie sat at attention, then unzipped her purse. Next, she tossed some photos in the middle of the table.

"There! I have a beautiful daughter, who is still at home. Maybe you'd be interested in dating her if you come."

Sonja picked up the picture. "She's very pretty. What's her name?"

"Amy." Maddie showed them a group shot of the rest of her family.

Robert stated unabashedly, "Your girls get their looks from their lovely mother." Maddie didn't bat an eye. After closing her purse, she pushed away from the table.

"I need to walk for a while. I'll go on back to the dorm and meet you later this evening. OK?" The young Swedish man stood up halfway to thank her and shake her hand.

As soon as she was out of earshot, Karl lit into Robert. "Why must you make her so damn uncomfortable!" The deep lines came together at the center of his forehead in the shape of the letter V.

Robert shrugged his shoulders and answered nonchalantly, "What? That was a harmless comment."

Sonja jumped in, "You do! You embarrass her to death!"

Robert was irritated by the sudden attack. "What's the big deal? I like her. You both like her. It's just a little teasing."

"Of course we do. But obviously not in the same way," said Karl. "I mean...Jesus...she could be your..." He stopped himself. "What are you thinking? Teasing? That isn't very kind!"

Robert glared back at him. The muscles jutted out on his jaws each time he clenched his teeth together. He shifted his steely stare to Sonja.

"Robert." Sonja tried to sound more sympathetic. "Don't you get it?"

He clenched his biceps as if to restrain himself. They waited to hear his rationale. He looked around. He didn't have to give them an explanation. Finally he asked them, "Why is it more acceptable for older men to hook up with younger women?"

"Are you serious?" asked Karl.

Sonja chimed in, "Acceptable to whom? Idiot business tycoons on their party yachts? In Hollywood, where renovated old coots are allowed to push their juvenile fantasies on the rest of us?"

If Maddie had been around to hear this, she would have agreed—to an extent. However, she would have taken into account Sonja's age. Speaking from her own experience, too often a sad truth emerges the longer people are together: It's not fun being with someone who's got your number, so the search for newness begins. It's often in the guise of youth, but not always; anything fresh and novel will do.

Karl spoke earnestly. "I can't believe you buy into the idea that if enough people do something, it somehow justifies it."

"Karl," said Robert sternly, "you can't deny that Madelaine is beautiful."

"I'm not saying she isn't. I bet she was drop-dead gorgeous at our age. That's not what we're discussing here. Even if I thought she could pass for fifty...just listen to what that sounds like!" He didn't understand why he had to make a case, which was exactly what Robert expected him to do.

"You know," said Robert, "if she were a painter or a singer, and liked a younger man, I bet her circle of friends wouldn't criticize the relationship."

Oh, boy...more comments to incite Sonja. It killed her to say nothing. She could write a thesis on the subject. No doubt her hard line resulted from her parents' split-up.

Robert rested his hands flat in front of him. "I enjoy watching how she moves. And she doesn't have a trash mouth like most girls today, present company excluded." He picked at the edge of the cardboard coaster. "It's like she's stepped out of another era."

Karl sighed and clasped his mooning friend on the shoulder. "It's not my business. I'm only saying you should put yourself in the lady's shoes. Your behavior makes her self-conscious. Madelaine isn't some artist…and what's insinuated is not a relationship, but a fling. She's got a husband, for Pete's sake." Karl stood. "I'm going to the poster shop." He sounded fed up. "I'll meet you after dinner."

"Fine," said Sonja.

The empty chair was immediately snatched up for another table. Sonja carried her seat over to Robert. A shoulder's width separated their faces. After a cooling-down period, she said, "There goes you."

He looked up to see what she meant. A teen with platinum, spiked hair was walking past them—Robert's very hairstyle (and color) years ago. He forced a slight smile. Switching the subject was working. She added, "He does need that black goatee to complete the picture." She had him.

He chuckled. "I wasn't as sensible as you at your age," he said, then glibly noted, "apparently I'm still not." He rubbed his eyes.

Sonja took in his features, starting with his dark brown hair, damp and matted at the temples from the heat, then moving on to his eyes. She admired the straight bridge of his nose, the slightly flared nostrils, and his sensuous lips. The backside of her hand slowly followed the line of his jaw. She had never been intimate like this with him before, and knew he had to be wondering about it. The smile she offered was that of a friend's. She understood how important their inviolate relationship was to him.

"I have a theory about your feelings." Her thumb slid around the curve leading to his ear. "Madelaine's like an Earth Mother. I can see why you'd be taken with the idea of her." His perfect, soft earlobe got inspected. "Don't make anything of this, OK?" Her focus was again on his eyes. "Why are you grinning?" she asked him.

"I have to get used to the fact that you've grown up," he answered. It was a tender moment. "I'll buy that," he added, referring to her Earth-Mother theory.

Sonja kissed his cheek. "Just a thought. Let's walk by the river before we catch the Metro."

Robert surprised Sonja along its bank when he suddenly raised her in the air, then acted as if he were going to pitch her into the murky water. She clutched his shirt and yelled to be put down, but he held on fast while trying to keep a straight face.

"The next time you stroke my ears, in you go!"

As soon as she hit safe ground, she swatted at him as if he were a pesky fly. Adjusting her clothes, she spied the back side of Maddie crouched over something. A tiny, recognizable red cap popped above her shoulder. As they headed toward her, Sonja asked, "May I make a rather tired Freudian observation?"

Robert assumed what it was and asserted, "Madelaine is a complete one-eighty from my mother." No sooner had he finished the sentence when the insight caught up to him.

When they reached her, he kept his distance. Truth be told, deep down, Robert had imagined that the older woman must be flattered by having elicited the attention of a younger guy. He would heed his friends' well-intentioned advice and back off. He couldn't put up with anyone regarding the degree of Madelaine's appeal to him as folly.

Maddie was delighted by their appearance, even if it included Robert. The antics of the comical capuchin monkey had to be shared with someone. *It's lonely laughing alone,* she decided. "When I relate my memories of Paris, I shall tell of a well-mannered gentleman, who stole my heart…and money. Of course, I won't go into any details." The little charmer graciously accepted another coin held out to him, then tipped his cap and kissed the top of her hand.

Laughing, the three started up the steps to the main street. Maddie accepted their invitation to return with them.

The dorm wasn't air-conditioned. Fans were useless. Everyone, limp from heat, dropped off to sleep for a nap. They were looking forward to partying all night.

The next stop was Montmartre. A group numbering about thirty squeezed out of the train, then quickly broke off into smaller bands of five or six. They drank and danced their way from one club to another, including a few in other districts. Different ages and nationalities mingled. It was heartening for Maddie to see a lot more of her contemporaries, several of whom she spun around the floor with. She partnered with Sonja on some rock 'n' roll oldies, then enjoyed a turn with Karl, slow dancing to a lazy sax rendition of *Moon River*. It was sublime—and unforgettable.

Ed had always managed to avoid the dance floor like a cat skirts a bath. He instinctively sensed when the situation might present itself, and would suddenly feign illness or a pulled muscle. Early in their marriage, his wife found an outlet for her favorite-but-missing pastime by tuning into the *Lawrence Welk Show* every week. She jitterbugged, polkaed, and waltzed with her kids before they learned to roll their eyes over having been subjected to anything so uncool. Later, of course, they looked back fondly at the fun they had had.

Around midnight, Maddie realized that Robert was nowhere in sight. In fact, she hadn't seen him since they had all parted ways earlier.

By 1:00 AM, her waning reflexes sounded her body's alarm for a needed break. She was dying of thirst. Her violet silk dress clung to her. The buildings' cooled interiors couldn't squelch the blasts of heat let inside with the frequent opening of doors. It was definitely time to go. Sonja begged her to hold out another hour, so they could leave together. Not a chance; another five minutes, and she'd be flat on the floor. *Wait until you're my age*, Maddie wanted to say, but vanity prevented her. She fell into the back of the cab. Although bone weary, she couldn't remember when she had last been this absolutely bursting-at-the-seams happy.

Maddie hesitated before entering the house. Paris lay in an eerie bubble of industrial, manufactured clouds. Their pale neon luminescence fluctuated between grayish green and lavender. Vibrations, caused by the distant low rumblings of thunder, traveled through her feet. The sky lit up intermittently, but no lightning was visible yet. There was a doomsday quality about it all.

The TV in the common room played to no one. Maddie hung on the banister a few moments, readying herself for the long climb to the top. Doorways stood wide open. There was the unmistakable sound of someone who had partied himself sick. Whooping calls and exaggerated moans filled another room. Internet porn, probably—now that bridge no longer consumed the players' thoughts. *When will this heat end?*

God, did she ever reek from cigarettes. She unlocked the door and grabbed a towel, programmed to wash her face at night, no matter what. Oh, to lie in a tub of ice water. The next best thing was to fill the sink and stick her face into it. She didn't bother to dry herself; it felt too good letting the cold drops strike her chest and belly. Her dress was beyond salvaging, anyway. She went back to her room and was hooking the latch when out of the darkness she heard: "Madelaine, don't yell. It's me."

Maddie rested her forehead against the door. *Sleep. Please God.* She only wanted to sleep. Acting as though she hadn't heard Robert, she went to the desk, leaned over, and brushed her hair. A quick twirl of the finger, and she pinned it back up.

The big windows permitted that exceptional glow from outside to infiltrate the room, lighting up everything with considerable detail. She was in awe of the moon. It was suspended high in the sky. And it was huge. Lemon-colored patches stood out between the gaps in the clouds.

"Your room was unlocked. I figured you were in the bathroom." His tone was subdued. "I got back to my room…next thing, someone started throwing up…other guys were already passed out snoring." He waited to see if she was going to say anything. "I was hoping you might let me sleep up here? The bed's big…I'd stay close to the edge." There was a doubting edge to his words. He watched as she unbuckled her shoe straps. "Even the floor…I don't mind."

She couldn't think. She nearly fell out of her sandals. Stepping around his seated form, she climbed onto the bed and placed her back against the wall, expecting some cool relief. It felt like a stove burner left on medium-high. She tossed a pillow out from under the one, punched hers, folded it over, and sank into it, closing her stinging eyes. At last, she was away from the smoke. Things couldn't be any better…even in a damp dress. The mattress tugged here and there as Robert lay down.

Outside, the thunder's ceaseless drumming caused the fixtures to rattle.

"Madelaine?" whispered Robert. He still couldn't get a word out of her.

Although Maddie bordered on unconscious, a part of her remained vigilant. She had her suspicions about this arrangement.

The approaching rain carried that distinctive odor she loved. She thought of Red, of his nose busily sniffing the air above his head. If he were there, he'd have already been pacing for hours in anticipation of the frightening bolts and the noise. The breeze picked up, and the gusts played with the chain on a lamp.

Robert cautiously inched toward her and cradled his head in the nook by her collarbone. She didn't like that his hair smelled from the nightclubs—but the soft feel of it touching her throat was tantalizing. He lay motionless; she thought she might finally drift to sleep…until he slid his left hand under hers and held it in a semigrasp. She listened to his breathing, and to his swallowing. There'd be no nodding off.

Giant raindrops began pelting the ledge. The birds cooed in their hopefully safe corner. She should get up and close the window.

Warm breaths marked her skin. When she repositioned her legs to get more comfortable, she touched bare skin. He had to know he was walking a fine line, half expecting that at any second he'd get kicked out. His heart must be thumping wildly, Maddie thought—like hers.

Bright flashes appeared through her closed lids. The rain came down harder. Her conscience served up a sister's long-forgotten warning, along with the perpetual scowl inscribed on the old nun's face. "Woe comes to any girl who gives in to momentary weakness." That this should surface now almost caused her to giggle.

Robert's thumb passed over her knuckles. She raised her chin to keep his hair off her mouth. The implication suggested by this scene was getting to her. It was well over a decade—maybe close to two—since she had last reckoned with any erotic feelings. Her hand slid from her thigh over to him. Maddie couldn't believe herself. To her astonishment, she acted on an impulse that was completely foreign to her. The sensation coaxed Robert's hips forward. She wasn't going to pursue this if he didn't want to. The keenness of her intention excited him.

Staying so long in this position caused her neck and shoulder to start hurting. As she was scooting to turn a different way, Robert awkwardly tried to catch hold of her and kiss her, but she had a knee-jerk reaction, not wanting any part of it. Before she knew it, he had her pinned, and was struggling madly to get her dress out of his way.

Madelaine Gulliver was not one to be undermined. She easily matched his will with her own. Using her foot and summoning all of her strength, she pushed away from the wall. Then she gained excellent leverage when she grabbed a huge handful of his hair. Robert tried in vain to lift his head, which made her pull it all the harder and caused him to start crying out her name—this time angrily. Her chest and face were flushed from guilt. She couldn't take on emotions of this magnitude. If only she had immediately thrown him out.

He stopped fighting her too readily. She opened her hand. Hopefully it wasn't a mistake. Nose to nose, in this peculiar bruising shade of light, they studied each other's faces, each other's eyes, listened to the rain, made their peace. Maddie liked the sensation of their bodies pressed together. A minor shift toward the foot of the bed was all Robert required. Because of the poetic bent of his imagination, he fancied he had plunged into the mysterious wellspring of life. It drove him senseless. Without inhibition, he shot into its midst, entering an unworldly place whereupon he fainted to sleep.

Maddie could barely drag her leg across Robert's anesthetized body. "You're an idiot, Maddie! A damned idiot!" she reproached herself out loud. Now she really felt like a total mess, and in need of a shower. And during a storm, no less—that always scared her. Her current distressed state jolted her out of her former inebriated one. As she inched toward the end of the bed, her insides felt stretched like taut rubber bands primed to pop. She curled up and hugged her knees. Something let go, and the rippling effect reached her groin and thighs. It was both pleasurable and painful.

This was an unforeseen development. Maddie had long ago come to terms with the loss of her libido, conveniently blaming it on the hysterectomy. After a lengthy bout with depression (having tried many ineffective remedies), she reconciled herself to a celibate life. Only occasionally had she accommodated Ed, whose decreasing desire eventually became nonexistent.

She sat there stunned, rocking in time with the surging climax that was nothing short of miraculous, and afraid for this event to end—in case it was just a fluke, never to be indulged in again. After it subsided, she attempted to stand, only to find her legs wobbling so badly she couldn't keep her balance. She tried, but couldn't talk herself out of cleaning up.

Somehow she reached the bathroom. The dress, plastered to her figure, had to be rolled off her body like a wet bathing suit. She carelessly pitched it in the trash can. Bracing herself in the middle of the narrow stall, Maddie simply stood and let the water pour down over her head. The steady pitter-patter was hypnotizing.

Every time she thought it impossible to get more tired than a previous night, she did it, becoming numb to the point of being brain-dead.

Thunder crashed outside. She lathered herself with closed eyes. For all she knew, the lights could have been out. The tile floor was a tempting bed.

Later, upon awakening, she would have no recollection of having turned off the faucet, of having walked back to her room—naked and wet—after which she detangled her hair with her fingers, then pinned it up out of habit, swallowed a couple of ibuprofen tablets, closed the window, and slipped under the sheet—at 5:00 AM.

The digital clock was flashing. She turned her head. Robert was gone. It was still raining hard, so much that the view out the window looked like a solid sheet of smoked glass.

Dare she move? She pushed up onto her elbows, let her head fall back, and twisted it from side to side. Not too bad. Getting her legs on the floor was another matter. "Oooh," she wailed, feeling battered from the waist down. Her wrist was extremely sore. A shiver ran up her spine. She was thankful to be clean. The temperature had dropped considerably, and already she was dreading a cold toilet seat. After taking a couple more pills, she quickly dressed in several layers. She grabbed her watch and reset the clock. It was two in the afternoon.

The mood downstairs was somber. The Nigerians had expected to leave early this morning, yet there they were on the floor, sound asleep, heaped over their duffel bags. The airport must be closed. Maddie was amused at the transformation from a week ago. Everyone had started out eager, aggressive, and confident. Now look at the bleary-eyed, hungover bunch...which also included her.

People managed only a raised eyebrow, a little nod, or a twitch for a smile as a greeting. There was a lot of head, eye, and stomach rubbing, along with mumbling directed at no one in particular. Coffee was the sole draw in getting them moving.

Maddie sat down slowly on a tattered leather couch, pulling her legs up for warmth. She set her cup on the window ledge, then held her sleeve over her nose, which had turned into an ice cube.

A kiss grazed the side of her head. Robert plunked down beside her, forcing her body up a few inches. She nervously eyed her hot coffee directly behind him. He slumped into the cushions and got comfortable, propping his long legs on the old trunk in front of him. He smelled good, like a pine forest. She was interested in what he'd have to say after last night. Hopefully he wasn't expecting her to go first.

When he leaned his head back, she reached over to move the coffee.

"Can I have a sip?"

She carefully carried it around the side of him. After he drank, he placed it on the trunk. He looked up at her from his lower position, and smiled. Then he watched as someone flipped through the television channels.

How casually the two of them sat there. Maddie thought about her appearance. She had never permitted herself to look so unkempt in her life. Sonja had insisted that she wear her hair looser, wilder. It couldn't get any more unmanageable than today. She quit fussing over her makeup and nails too.

The rain pummeled the earth outside. She didn't even notice when her eyes closed. Secretly, inside, recurring fantasies toyed with the sensible image she had of herself. Robert folded his hands over hers, which were now tucked between her thighs.

"Madelaine?" He thought she had perhaps fallen asleep. Her eyes cracked open, then closed again. "You know how some people just make you feel on cloud nine whenever you see them...or even think about them?"

"Sure," she replied dreamily.

"That's how it is when I'm around you. I can't help it." His warm hands felt wonderful. She looked at his sweet face, with its lovely mouth, and she could hear Amy dispensing her favorite line: *Time for a reality check, people.* Joel's pointed advice cropped up as well: *Shelve all preconceived ideas.* Amen, Joel.

Robert's stillness drove her to distraction, just as it had in bed. The way he managed to moderate his urges for the longest period completely engaged her. She thought of his hands lying relaxed to his sides, of his serene expression...and how he ultimately acquiesced to her touch. If last night had never happened, she would have remained clueless with regard to the extent that this appealed to her. She didn't understand how he could be so open with someone he barely knew.

Sonja and Karl's voices carried through the room as they came lumbering down the steps. Robert immediately let go of Maddie and removed his feet from the table. He rested his elbows on his knees and ran his hands through his hair. He was agitated. She felt relieved that her aroused state went unnoticed.

Sonja had Karl by both wrists and grunted as she tried to pull him over to them. His body defied any forward motion, and he tripped along clumsily. Little Sonja, only around five-feet-two, kept slipping between his legs. She then rolled behind him and pushed her backside against his. He would have flown across the table if Robert hadn't jumped up to catch him by his shoulders on his way down. Karl then got squished into the corner of the couch so he wouldn't topple. Robert leaned over his face and pulled an eyelid open.

"Hey!" he shouted. "Karl!" He turned to Sonja and stated the obvious: "Man, is he wasted."

Sonja went and sat on the opposite arm of the couch, next to Maddie.

"May I tuck my feet under you to warm them? They're frozen."

Maddie obliged her.

"Someone stole all my socks," Sonja continued. "I took a pair from Karl." They laughed; the heels of Karl's socks almost reached the tops of her calves.

Robert sat back down, gently this time. He didn't want to have to reposition his bulky friend.

"I bet it was the girl from Australia." She noticed the cup on the trunk. "I wonder if they have cocoa. Doesn't that sound good? Save my place." And she bounced off, the only person with any spunk today.

Karl's own snort woke him. He raised his head and looked straight at Robert, then Maddie. "Let's play a standard American...strong, no trumps, five-card majors, and weak two bids."

Robert went along, "Sounds good."

"All right then," he said. The two laughed when Karl's head fell back, and his mouth dropped wide open.

"Why don't you fill me in with a little background?" said Maddie. "Do you return home often to visit your family?"

Robert's knee supported his other leg, and he played with his shoestrings. "My mother never wanted me. I don't know who my father is." He suspected she would say that such a thing wasn't possible—that a mother loves her children, even if they might not think so. Realizing there was no opinion forthcoming, he resumed.

"My mother had me when she was sixteen…a year after she'd had an abortion. I was told the guy took off. She didn't get money in time to get rid of me…a mistake she never made again."

Maddie guessed that he had to have been an absolutely gorgeous child. How could his mother not have been proud…and not have wanted to show him off? She was struck with a pang of guilt for not showering Amy with a mother's love when she was born.

Robert told her he was sent to Iowa to be raised by an uncle and aunt. They had no children and were pleased to have him. His eyes were alive when he spoke about them. Then they turned sad. He crossed his feet on the table and slid his hands into the front pockets of his sweatshirt.

"I take it…they're no longer living?"

"My uncle is," said Robert. He told her how happy they had all been when his aunt learned she was pregnant. By then he was twelve. Unfortunately, she also discovered during that period that she had breast cancer—a fast-growing kind made worse by the changes in her hormones. Neither she nor the baby survived. "It's been a long time since I've thought about them." He liked how Maddie had a way of looking inside him when he spoke.

"Your uncle had to have been devastated."

He nodded.

"Did he start drinking?" She could tell from Robert's expression that he had. "He asked that you return to live with your mother?"

"Yeah. I ended up in Milwaukee."

A frantic student burst in the room; the cellar was flooding! His urgency produced a remarkable adrenaline rush in those still barely recovered from the night. Everyone glanced at each other, took some deep breaths, and scrambled madly after him to prevent disaster. Working at a frenzied pace, they passed boxes and old furniture to higher ground. There was already a foot of standing water caused by a powerful deluge that continued to pour through gaps around a window well. A bucket brigade rushed pails of water to the outside. Sonja waved to Robert and Maddie from the bottom of the dimly lit stairs.

After an exhausting hour, the rain subsided, but the lightning intensified, becoming as frequent and terrifying as during the early morning. This had to be a record-breaking storm. Ambulance sirens sounded in every direction. The group, successful in their efforts, was starving. Everyone volunteered for certain duties, and within a half-hour, a couple of pots of steaming pasta, marinara sauce, and baked breads were ready for devouring.

The bathroom showers ran until all the feet got rinsed. People were laughing and speaking excitedly over the incident, openly changing their clothes and running through the hallways, wide awake now. They convened on the main floor, recounting events of the past week, sharing chapters of their school lives, and making promises to each other for future rendezvous.

Sonja, Maddie, and Robert sat reunited around the trunk, eating their spaghetti. They were joined by six of the many Italians who were trying to leave Paris by bus. That was hardly going to happen today; the city had been brought to a standstill.

By now Karl was conscious, although very hungover…and extremely sentimental. With tears freely flowing, he went on and on about how much he was going to miss everyone. He welcomed the attention it brought, especially from the demonstrative and sympathetic Roman contingent. He returned their hugs and kisses. Robert and Sonja rolled their eyes at each other—typical Karl. When he drank, he spoke drivel and could cry over something as trifling as a dead fly on a sill.

Maddie was surprised to find Catherine standing in the dormitory entrance, motioning for her to come over. After sitting on the floor far too long, and taking into account what she had put herself through these last twenty-four hours, standing would prove difficult. Just as Robert was about to help her, two Italians, seated opposite them, immediately donned their chivalrous manners and, in a flash, grabbed her by the arms and waist, then lifted her in the air as if she were feather light. It was so fast, she momentarily saw stars.

Halfway to Catherine, she called out, "Is everything OK?"

"Yes, yes, Madelaine. We are fine." Catherine figured no one would be leaving, so she had baked a bunch of pastries for them to enjoy. She held out four large, full plastic bags. Although impressed by her thoughtfulness, Maddie disapproved of her walking over in the storm.

Maddie was out of hearing range when one of the young men who had helped her up admitted to his dinner companions that he'd had a dream about the *signora* after his group (with her in it) had visited the Louvre earlier in the week. Over the objection of his teammate, he started in on the details. At first, the mildly erotic account could be dismissed—until its content turned lurid.

That did it. Robert's dander was up. Madelaine was undeserving of such disrespect. He already had his hands in tight fists when, luckily, the Italian's friend jumped in again and convinced him to shut up.

Maddie raised one of the pastry bags in the air and announced loudly, "Dessert, compliments of Mademoiselle Doumic."

The place turned topsy-turvy as everyone made a beeline to the door. An inspection of the goodies produced a continuous stream of universally understood yummy sounds. Catherine became the center of attention and was wholeheartedly invited to join the spaghetti feast. The aroma of coffee (which Catherine also donated) canceled out the pungent garlic.

Maddie took her share of apricot-and nut-filled cookies, then tossed a pillow on the floor by the wall. Robert sat down cross-legged next to her while licking some glaze off his thumb. "People can be so nice," he said. She agreed.

"You were in Milwaukee, Robert…"

"I don't know, Madelaine. How 'bout another day?" He sounded tired.

"Were you around fourteen when you moved?"

He looked a bit annoyed at her refusal to drop the subject. She won.

"I had my thirteenth birthday with her." Maddie knew he was referring to his mother from the sad tone in his voice.

"Weren't you the least bit excited to be with her?"

"No. She never visited me at my uncle's. I never received birthday cards…or Christmas presents. People never mentioned her…at least not in front of me."

Maddie had trouble coming to grips with this. "She didn't act at all like she was happy to see you?"

"Jesus, Madelaine! No!" He instantly felt bad for being short with her, then quietly asked, "What don't you get? I was in her way. She had told her friends and the people at work that I was her baby brother, and she asked me to go along with it. She wasn't even thirty and could easily pass for being younger. I didn't care…as far as I was concerned, my aunt had been my mom."

Sonja delivered a cup of coffee for them to share, then went to sit among the few Greek students who, earlier this week, had been her rivals. Maddie could see how enthralled they were with her. Her fairness was part of the reason, but Sonja also possessed a celebratory attitude that put others in the mood.

Robert next described a life lived at school, recounting his activities. He only saw his mother in passing, along with the ever-changing faces of men she took up with.

"Weren't there other relatives you could have stayed with?"

"Not really. My grandparents offered, but my grandfather was a diabetic and required a lot of care. Besides, I hardly knew them. It would have been depressing." He crumpled his napkin. "I can't remember when I last ate poppy-seed cake. I love it...but I never order it." He pushed himself to the wall. After straightening his legs, he massaged his thighs. "I can't sit like this anymore."

Wait 'til you're sixty, thought Maddie.

"Didn't the school wonder who your parents were?"

"She must have claimed that her brother and sister-in-law were our parents. No one checked. Even if they had, my aunt was dead, and my uncle was a mental case. Come to think of it...she probably slept with whoever kept it under wraps."

"Did you have a good friend or teacher you could confide in?"

"I wouldn't risk that kind of gossip. I stayed busy. Things worked out."

They took a moment to look at all the bodies lounging in a satiated state. Karl had finally become more self-possessed and was strumming a guitar. The range of pitches and accents from the singers accompanying his playing was humorous. The setting was dreamlike.

The room had become stuffy. She and Robert followed suit when others began to remove their outer layers of sweaters. Maddie's head was against the wall, and she was taking a deep breath when she noticed the one Italian student who had helped her before staring at her. He lay sprawled sideways next to the trunk with his hand supporting his head. She watched him watch her, as did Robert. It didn't really upset her—mostly, it seemed very odd.

"So, Robert," she continued, "you said you never go home. What finally happened that made you sever the tie permanently?"

He looked at her solemnly. "There was a lot that led up to it."

"I'll consider that...go on. Please."

Robert told her that he had returned home from college in order to collect the remainder of his things. He was moving into an apartment that was going to be his permanent address. Before he set out to leave the next morning, he was fixing toast when, as usual, another stranger wandered in to make himself breakfast. Robert said he remained civil, even greeted the hungover sleepyhead with a friendly hello. He was so glad to be getting out of that house; there was nothing that could bother him—so he thought. Then his mother entered the kitchen.

"She had a look in her eyes, Madelaine, like 'you didn't tell him, did you?' Then...it was as if she needed to confirm it. She asked the guy if her brother had properly introduced himself." Robert's breathing picked up. Shaking his head, he said, "If only I hadn't looked at her right then." He clung to Maddie's gaze; it reassured him. "She winked at me, and gave me that shit-ass smile of hers...and I just blurted out to him that she was my fucking mother, and I won't say what else. It wasn't pretty."

Maddie had to ask him, "Why should she have changed her story for him?"

He chortled. "It was like all those other times when she'd said I was her kid brother; she'd give me that wink along with the lame smile...the 'our special secret' look. That fucking winking drove it all home. Sorry, Madelaine." He couldn't help swearing. "I mean, she'd done that ever since I was three or four. I certainly couldn't have understood the charade I had agreed to take part in at that age. I felt like a stooge for allowing her to play me all those years. I guess being older put an entirely different spin on the situation. At that moment, the humiliation...it all came back to me."

Maddie felt sympathy for the young man. Something came back to her as well while they sat in silence. She had forgotten that she had been talking to Ed about Janet when he ended the discussion as he always did—"damned ungrateful kid"—just as the phone rang, and the first words out of her daughter's mouth were about her grandson's tuition. If Janet had just called her fifteen minutes later, affording a period for some other distractions, Maddie might not have reacted like she did to her. The degree to which the timing of things shaped events was sobering. Maddie commented quietly, "It's remarkable how anything so small can set a person off." She asked, "What did you do?"

"I went berserk...I exploded. My mother tried to grab hold of me, and I almost punched her. I didn't want her touching me...I hated her touching me. Her boyfriend flew out of the house." Robert smiled and returned Sonja's wave. She was having a ball, dancing on the couch, and singing. "I tore out of there too. I don't even know what I was thinking driving back. I can't believe I didn't have a wreck. I was shaking so hard. God."

"How old were you?"

"Twenty-one."

Maddie noticed him absentmindedly twisting his watchband. "Then what?"

He brought his knee up and rested his elbow on it, while his hand hung over the top of his head. He closed his tired eyes. "It was late when I got back to the university. Sonja had been waiting for me on the main floor. I forgot I was supposed to meet her that evening."

"I thought Sonja was a lot younger than you?"

"She is. I hadn't met her before then. She came to the States to live with a cousin's family while her parents were going through a divorce in Germany. She was enrolled on campus because she happens to really be a genius. I was supposed to go over some schedules and strategies with freshmen who were interested in joining the chess team. Sonja was one of them. I guess she was with someone who knew me when they saw me go flying past them. I just wanted to get to my room. I don't remember anything after that.

"Sonja told me later that she had followed me because that was the only time in her schedule she could get the information. She had no idea something was wrong until she got to my door and could hear me through it." He turned toward Maddie. "Man...Sonja was only fourteen." He sounded amazed, as if he had just learned that fact. "I really freaked her out. She thought I was on drugs and called the police. I have no memory of being taken away...just of waking up in the hospital, calm...really, really calm."

Maddie was briefly distracted by the snoring Italian in front of them. Robert felt uneasy about knowing what the student was probably dreaming.

"Sonja came to visit me. I stayed locked up in a psychiatric ward for several weeks. After that, I had some therapy on and off for years." He looked fondly at the petite figure swaying her boyish hips to the beat. "A mere slip of a girl became my confidant...and still is. I don't know what I'd have done in her place. She was worried sick afterward, wondering if she had done the right thing."

Maddie wasn't going to be able to hold out much longer on the floor. She couldn't resist caressing Robert's chin before changing her position. His lashes cast a shadow on his cheeks.

"God, I was spacey for a couple of years," he said. "I'm grateful we weren't rich...I'd have had major surgery to change every feature resembling my mother's."

On that note, his face went blinding white. A violent clap of thunder caused more than a few shrill screams. The oil lamps had already been brought out earlier and were being lit. There were plenty of flashlights to go around. Calamitous popping surrounded them. Maddie wondered whether this region ever had tornadoes.

The next sensational bolt killed the power.

"I'm going to wait this out in my room," she announced, pushing herself up along the wall. She made her exit before Robert had time to react. He thought it abrupt, considering he had just poured his heart out to her. He jumped up and rushed to the staircase, covering three steps in one bound, then stood obstructing her way. Maddie raised her pen-size flashlight to his chin, creating the macabre effect that kids find so entertaining. Her behavior baffled him.

She advanced, forcing him to go up backward to the next landing. His heels had difficulty locating the steps. With her lips almost touching his, she said quite innocently, "I need to check on the birds." He moved aside to let her pass. She aimed her light at the third floor and continued up. He watched her from his dark corner, mystified.

Maddie went to the nightstand and lit the candle she had discovered in the closet earlier. Recurring power outages were the norm in the city this morning. At least the thunder didn't evoke the same threat as before. The lightning only crackled and hissed like a downed hot wire. The supernatural purplish green sky had become the usual steely blue-gray. She briefly stuck her nose out the window. The birds were huddled together and puffed up; they looked like one big fat pigeon.

Robert appeared in the hallway. He managed to slide inside at the last second, just as Maddie shut the door. He couldn't read her, and responded to their face-to-face confrontation with a short, nervous laugh. The mischievous glint in his eyes revealed that he wasn't about to take her seriously.

"You're a calculating one," he claimed, "luring me up here to have your way with me."

A mighty presumptuous assertion, she suggested—then reached down and gripped the vulnerable sides of his kneecaps, crippling him. He fell to the floor, kicking, while choking on his laughter. The second her strength gave out, he freed himself and scrambled to the bed, where he hugged his legs tightly against his body.

Maddie got up and plopped down beside him. His beauty distressed her. At that moment, she so envied his youth—anyone's. She felt foolish behaving as she was…but it was fun, and there were no witnesses.

His limbs relaxed, and he looked at her with adoration. "I'm going to remember this week forever, Madelaine. To think you've already experienced the world as a woman my age. I wish it weren't impossible for me to see things from your perspective."

What Robert couldn't know was—from her perspective—she couldn't stop imagining being younger. If she were, she would find him mesmerizing. She'd be speculating about marrying him…having his children…or meeting him again in some exotic place—anything that inherently included a future. She no longer tried to make sense out of their relationship, but simply accepted it as nothing more than a short dance between flirting molecules.

In the soft candlelight, Robert's eyes shone with marblelike transparency. The ongoing rain and intermittent thunder had become routine. It felt safe in the room, cozy. Stretching out catlike and displaying a captivatingly adolescent charm, he declared, "Anytime."

This playful spirit was new to them. Maddie hesitated, sensing she should exercise caution. She lacked the wherewithal to deal with another disturbing wrestling match—if for some reason it came to that. Night, that incorrigible voyeur, waited patiently for its thrills. Then, as if he could read her mind, Robert convinced her that he wouldn't be so intense this go-round.

CHAPTER 7

The following morning found students still lying where they had toppled, likely during a final fit of laughter. The rain persisted, exacerbating the widespread melancholia. The place was eerily silent. Even the chronic snorers teetered on the edge of deathlike slumber, which stifled their normally disruptive noises.

Late in the afternoon—at long last—the sky split wondrously apart. And as in a fairy tale, the dormant inhabitants of the great city slowly awakened; the sorcerer's spell had been broken. They weren't prepared for the unparalleled magic act nature was about to unveil before them. People were drawn to their windows and balconies; some came together in the streets. Fiery brass light passed through an ever-widening aperture, eating up the dark clouds. Here and there, the colorful segments of a grand arcing rainbow faded in and out along its leading edges. When the tired occupants of *Rue de la Victoire* staggered back inside their quarters, they could only stare at one another in amazement and shake their heads.

The four friends agreed to meet briefly for the last time in the courtyard. They grabbed some food from the kitchen and headed out the back door. It was a neglected area and looked worse flooded. As they carefully stepped upon the raised flagstones, the spongy earth could be heard soaking up the giant puddles. An ungodly number of croaking frogs leaped through the mud.

Maddie had taken a towel to wipe off the bench. It was useless. They were going to have to settle for wet butts. She checked out the location of her room, high up, and heard the pigeons on the ledge. She tore off a piece of bread for them and pocketed it, then handed off the loaf to Sonja, who passed it to Karl, who gave it to Robert. They shared a mineral water.

It was night now. The lights from inside kept the yard lit enough to see. Karl spoke up and suggested that Maddie join their online games.

"Yes, Madelaine! Absolutely! You must stay in touch with us," exclaimed Sonja, as she wiped a smidgen of soft Gruyere cheese stuck to her fingers on her jeans.

"How often do you play?" asked Maddie. It was heartwarming to feel included like this.

"Sundays, generally," she said. "It's only for a few hours once a month."

"We should form a club," said Karl, brushing off crumbs.

Robert agreed and offered to make some T-shirts. They had to come up with a name.

The words rolled right out. "The Peripatetic Bridge Group…or something to that effect," said Maddie, half seriously.

Karl leaned forward to see past Sonja. "Bingo, Madelaine! I love it."

The others also considered it appropriate. Maddie could have been a bit self-congratulatory, if she weren't ticked off that these three knew that darn word.

The members brainstormed. Which name sounded best: The Peripatetic Bridge Consortium or Association? Alliance? How about Aficionados? Players? Or the Guild? Maybe "bridge" should be dropped altogether. And what about a logo? They concluded that "Partnership" summed them up the best, but the initials weren't the greatest.

Tomorrow was on their minds. Each would be heading a separate way. Karl was returning to Oslo; Robert was traveling to Bonn, eventually ending his summer in Berlin; and Sonja asked to accompany Maddie on the train to Basel, where a friend was meeting her with his car to drive back to Freiburg, Germany. Maddie planned on transferring there to get to Interlaken, Switzerland—Janet's next destination.

They admired the constellations while feeling a little forlorn, hoping to sight the shooting star that would allow their mutual wish to come true: if only they could spend one more week together.

It was Sonja's fault; she started it, yawning so wide it hurt. Soon the others couldn't stop. It was decidedly time for bed. The ladies went ahead with their arms wrapped around each other. Sonja had become quite dear to Maddie. The fellows sauntered a few feet behind, also hanging on to one another's shoulders. The creaking stairs intruded on the stillness. Sonja and Karl drifted into their rooms, mindful of giving Robert a moment alone with Maddie.

Maddie mustered a slight smile. "We'll say our good-byes in the morning." He had to understand she was exhausted. She gently touched his hand, which rested on the banister, then started up to her floor. He came from behind and bound her arms inside a tight embrace. His heart beat against her spine, and his breath tunneled through her ear. She pried his fingers off her. "Good night, Robert," she whispered sternly. He kissed her neck and retreated to his room.

The morning arrived far too fast. It didn't take much effort to pack for the next leg of her journey. Maddie was just leaving the bathroom with her shampoo and toothpaste when Robert hopped over the last step. He greeted her with a huge grin and a clean-shaven face. She wondered if the conversation she planned on initiating would produce any regrets.

He closed the bedroom door behind them, then walked over to the open window. Taking the croissant from a napkin in his hand, he reached across the sill and watched the pigeon take it from his fingers. He inhaled deeply. "It seems like forever since the air has smelled this clean."

Maddie observed him out of the corner of her eye while she gathered some final items. Robert looked handsome in his clean white shirt with rolled-up sleeves. It was tucked into his jeans, and his hair was combed for the first time. They had all gotten rather shabby these last days. Some students shouted farewell to him from the other building. As he waved back, Maddie asked him to get tested for HIV—as if it were nothing. He was totally disarmed; her request came out of the blue. He turned and rested his weight against the skinny ledge, and hoped to God she was joking. His eyes searched hers. A couple of times, he failed to come up with something to say. He dropped onto the wooden chair beside the desk and kept watching her for any sign that this could be attributed to a wry, albeit cruel, sense of humor. Maddie sat calmly on the bed.

"I plan on it, too...as soon as I can." Her crossed leg didn't jiggle. She didn't nervously play with the bag's zipper, even though her fingers hung next to it. Her face conveyed maternal concern, of which he was principally ignorant.

The room closed in on him, caged him. "Why?" he finally asked.

"Why?" she repeated. "Because you had unprotected sex."

"You did, too," he fired back.

More silence.

"That's why I'm going to get tested." She spoke candidly. "When you went through your identity crisis, you said you took drugs...and probably slept around too, right?"

"That was over five years ago." He then admitted that he hadn't been with anyone in a long time, a really long time. "I've given blood several times since...I figure I'd have been notified if they found anything."

"You must have been holding your breath every time the phone rang." How irresponsible to potentially contaminate the blood supply, Maddie thought...what about the possibility of human error in the lab?

He folded his arms across his chest and looked up at the ceiling, acutely aware of his pulse quickening.

"Did you think because of my age, you could rule out the possibility of my having AIDS, or hepatitis...or any number of other things?"

Robert clearly wasn't in the mood for this. "Do you?" he asked. He couldn't determine anything from her expression. "Is that why you're traveling around...before you bite the dust?"

That was an interesting angle. She almost laughed, but it was Robert's life they were discussing here. She had no desire to lecture, mentioning only that her involvement in community health centers came about as a direct result from having lost friends to the disease; no one would have ever guessed these people could have contracted it. One had been their family doctor, a hemophiliac who had received a transfusion in the early eighties. Another, one of Carol's friends, had also received a transfusion during that period when she hemorrhaged after delivery.

Robert looked back at the ceiling. Maddie realized there was a slim chance of that happening now—then she thought of other women she had known.

"A couple of years ago, when I started volunteering at hospices, I came across three of my friends. I thought they had moved out of town. They felt so ashamed to have gotten the disease from their husbands that they didn't tell anyone."

Maddie almost got ready to say "in my day" but reconsidered in the nick of time (the platitude made her feel ridiculously ancient). Instead she plainly acknowledged that it wasn't uncommon for gay men to marry and lead a double life, or for straight men to experiment, and sometimes be in denial. That deceit would likely remain prevalent forever. She stood and pushed the rolling chair out from under the desk, then sat closer to him. "Can't you see? Any of us could be tragically affected...including me, right?" Her voice softened. "And then you would be, too."

Robert leaned over his knees and sank his face onto his arms. He bemoaned the reality of having to bring this up whenever one longed to get lost in the moment. Maddie remembered the dread of unwanted pregnancies…now there was this.

"I was so dumb for letting this happen," Maddie said. *Me, of all people*, she thought. If she hadn't known better, armed with the facts as she was—but she had no excuse. This could have been that one instance, and one instance was all it took. "You've barely begun your life, Robert. You can't imagine what's in store for you." She pictured his face staring blankly at the floor between his feet. "Is sex ever worth a chronic condition…or a terminal one?" She waited. "I'm not asking a rhetorical question."

With that, he stood and kicked the chair upside down. She didn't flinch. He pounded the floor from one side of the room to the other. It seemed he riled the pigeon, whose gentle cooing turned into a louder yodel. He stopped by the window. Placing his hands along its sides, he took in the fine summer day. "We're all drawn to a good mystery. There's nothing more compelling than when we are it, as volumes of literature bear out."

He flipped his chair back on its legs then straddled it. Maddie looked disturbed. Robert explained, "We have these secret areas that we're given a peek into every once in awhile. Then it's too late; it's only natural to want to peer in deeper. What we find is this ongoing, covert sensorial life as true as the one we can see and are physically living…and it produces special revelations."

She wasn't sure he was sticking to the subject.

He continued, "Its strangeness is so seductive. There's no way to predict if exploring it will turn out to be dangerous and maybe self-destructive, or enlightening…somehow moving us forward with new purpose." He deliberated a moment, then decided, "It does both, actually."

How was she to satisfactorily ascertain his answer from that? "Is that a yes or a no? Is sex ever worth that risk or not?" She didn't mean to be funny after his long-winded response, but he chuckled—at himself.

His leg cleared the back of the chair, whereupon he swept her up in his arms. He loved her for caring about him, and admired a quality he couldn't readily define. It was her resilience (an attribute that required yet more years of living for him to fully grasp).

"Yes! My answer is a resounding yes." With anyone else but Madelaine, he knew he'd be lying; a fit of passion was definitely not worth sacrificing one's life over…at least not usually.

"Reckless youth," said Maddie ruefully, generalizing. She held him around the waist and rested her chin on his shoulder, realizing she'd been equally reckless. Who was there to tell her off? "Please explain to me, then, what it is you've learned about yourself that warrants such stupidity."

Without a moment's thought, he replied, "I've never been able to completely let my guard down with anyone. Just with you. It's freeing." He took a step back, then asked in a somewhat injured tone, "Have you gained anything?"

Oh, boy—she hated being put on the spot. She was reminded of the first invitation to play cards. He couldn't fully appreciate its significance to her. Without knowing anything about her, other than she had an interest that the students shared, they had made her feel important. That was a thrilling feeling. At home, too many people assumed things about her because of where she lived and her connections. Maddie was the one who ordinarily elected the players into her world. When a group who hardly knew a thing about her decided that she merited their company, it felt pretty damn nice.

She tried to think of something more personal in nature. Glancing at her watch, she realized she had to get downstairs soon to meet Sonja. They were going to take a taxi to the train station. She stepped away to check her purse. "I'll be honest: I've never been above making snide comments about old men getting it on with girls half their age. Your persistence paid off, though, Robert; otherwise, I would never have permitted such a temptation to cross my mind. And in ways I can't describe—or rather, won't—you should know how tremendously rewarding being with you has been. I'm astonished…really." She could tell he wanted that last part clarified. The sigh that punctuated her words indicated he had heard all she was willing to share.

Everything was in order. Robert stood with his hands in his back pockets. "Aren't you anxious to get under way and study some more buildings?"

"Yes. Yes I am." For once, his face was deadpan. "Promise me you'll join our bridge games."

"Of course," she said. "I'm looking forward to it." She walked over and rested her hands on his shoulders. He remained steadfast. In the daylight, it really struck home: their involvement was ridiculous. She pinched her lips together over the image of the two of them.

His eyes began to glaze over. "I can't do this," he whispered. "My stomach feels like it has rocks in it."

Maddie couldn't say the same. In the kindest way possible, she told him, "You know, I've tried to make sense of this role I'm fulfilling for you right now…but it's beyond me, Robert. I sincerely hope you stay on course with your life and meet someone who appreciates your forthrightness."

He closed his eyes and cradled her hands on his chest. Giving them a quick squeeze, he let go and went to throw her Patagonia over his shoulder. He headed out without turning back, leaving her standing alone. She felt responsible for his unhappiness, then rationalized that he had brought it on himself. Impatient for a new adventure, she said a final farewell to the pigeon, then nabbed her purse and raced downstairs. It had been one and a half weeks since she set foot in Europe, and just look at what she had already experienced.

Perfect timing—the taxi had arrived. Maddie glimpsed her pack in the trunk as it was being closed. Karl awaited his hug. She had to wipe his wet cheeks. Robert smothered Sonja inside the front door. Maddie knew that he purposely had his back to her in order to avoid eye contact. Meeting Robert had been bittersweet.

"I'll be e-mailing, Madelaine. Please don't be a stranger," said Karl. He helped her get in the cab. Sonja took a giant leap over the front steps and jumped into his open arms. They didn't need any words. She scooted in beside Maddie and pecked her on the cheek. Wearing a joyful face minus any sign of tears, she announced with her customary enthusiasm, "I'm ready." The two waved to Karl.

It was a gorgeous, cool morning—perfect for hitchhiking. Maddie had to convince herself to forgo it when leaving a city this size. Even Janet had opted to leave Paris by train.

As soon as the ladies were out of sight, Karl proceeded over to Robert, who was sitting on the stoop in an inconsolable state. He had watched the departure and continued to stare after them. Karl tucked him under his wing, aware that he could offer no adequate words of comfort. A passerby would surely have interpreted this tête-à-tête as a tryst between the men. Throughout the years, they had resolved to be each other's keeper. They were guarded about mentioning to anyone that their close friendship had begun during their psychiatric hospitalization. Karl was alone like Robert.

"Are you going to do something foolish?" asked Karl solemnly.

The pressure in Robert's chest prevented him from answering.

"Hey!" Karl shook his shoulder so he would look at him. They were nose to nose. "Tell me you won't do anything," he insisted.

Robert blinked slowly. He cleared his throat. "I can't stop replaying everything that's happened." He wished he could elaborate, but it was too private. "I don't know how to deal with it."

Karl speculated about the nature of his friend's confession. "Before Paris...in your wildest dreams, could you have conceived of meeting someone like Madelaine and having the feelings that you do for her?"

Robert shook his head no.

"Then why can't you believe there's another woman out there who will move you as deeply?"

Robert's entire demeanor, including his voice, exhibited his crestfallen spirit. He lamented, "I never felt this content with anyone before in my life. I don't see getting that lucky again."

"Gee, thanks. Do Sonja and I make the grade?"

Robert poked him with his elbow. "That goes without saying." He spared Karl from hearing his thought. *I don't make love to either of you.*

It was time for Karl to leave. He hated worrying about his friend. He kissed him on the head as he stood. "I'm keeping my cell phone on. You call me whenever...even if it's three in the morning. On second thought, I'm calling you tonight. You'd better answer."

Miles away, Maddie and Sonja made themselves comfortable in the compartment on the train. Both delighted in the flurry of activity at the station and couldn't wait to view the countryside. Their eyes grew big when the whistle blew and the cars began to slowly chug down the track. In their excitement, they spoke passionately about a multitude of topics during the first hour. Then Sonja made an observation that struck a nerve.

"You are so easy to talk to, Madelaine. Please don't take this the wrong way, but...it's not often the case with an older person. I hope I become the kind of woman you are. It's great you don't lecture us all the time. You really listen."

Maddie's children would either have been incensed over Sonja's comment or rolling on the floor in sidesplitting hysterics. This wasn't the person they knew. So here she sat, presented with the secret for a successful relationship between the generations. It was a hard truth to swallow; it wasn't easy to let go of the presumption that what an individual learns over time holds any relevance for anybody else. Regardless of all the best-intentioned guidance in the world, lessons will always be custom-fitted to each of them.

Maddie had to wonder if her words back in the dormitory room would really convince Robert to alter his future behavior. Maybe advice only had an impact if the listener had a propensity for the teacher's way of thinking to begin with. That was probably why she got along so famously with Rima. Why, oh why, had she always been so hell-bent on sticking her two cents into everything going on, including the most mundane things? Habit? She continued in deep thought. The passing scenery didn't register.

Sonja chanced asking her a personal question: "Do you feel like you've cheated on your husband?"

Cows and flowers suddenly materialized. Maddie turned to the inquisitive face. She couldn't imagine Robert relating the details of what went on between them. But she couldn't help wondering exactly what was pictured.

"Honestly, Sonja, I wish I did." Because if she did, it would indicate that she had some residual feelings left for her husband, something in her heart to show for all their years of marriage.

Not one for unhappy endings, Sonja boldly made a straight-out prediction. "This trip is going to make a difference for the better. You must entrust to fate that your journey will lead to a gratifying conclusion. You will see."

Maddie had to believe her; she spoke too convincingly. *She should write fortune cookies*, Maddie thought. The girl housed a wise soul—something Robert must sense, too. Sonja's smile gave the old wife much-needed comfort.

CHAPTER 8

Back in Mount Sterling, Ed's days rolled along, as consistently alike as Maddie's were exceptionally varied. He resented being interrogated by his children regarding their mother's reasons for leaving and her precise whereabouts. They refused to believe their dad was in the dark about when she was returning home. What were their parents hiding?

They couldn't get over that Maddie hadn't confided a thing to them, especially Rima, who had hurt feelings. Rima understood her grandmother enough, though, to suspect there must have been a good reason for what she did. She trusted she'd hear from her soon.

Ed dealt with them in the way he did with most problems: he said nothing. Amy lost patience after a week and decided to stay with a friend temporarily. She clued in the neighbors as best she could with what little she had to go on, so they wouldn't come over to console him; he would likely snub them. Ed would gladly have maintained his humdrum schedule of snacking and sleeping if he weren't close to running out of food—and if the dog hadn't slipped on the tile floor. Red lay there splayed and helpless, waiting for the human to make things OK again. After all, Maddie always had.

Trying to arrange the dangling legs in a way that would make Red transportable was not unlike figuring out a Rubik's Cube. Ed contemplated getting Lorraine from next door. The idea of asking for help spurred his resolve to find his own solution to this predicament.

Although Ed had passed the local vet's hospital every day when he still worked, he had never ventured inside. It went without saying that the animals were his wife's responsibility. Over the years, they had included (besides the usual cats and dogs) rabbits, frogs, turtles, snakes, rats, hamsters, a ferret, an iguana, and the not-to-be-forgotten baby fox. Oh, yes, also a Canada goose, nursed back to health after he had struck it with the car.

An assistant greeted him in the parking lot with a stretcher. Ed undid the twine and fully opened the partially closed trunk. They heartily pulled on the tarp. He had been successful in dragging the dog to the car on it. Next he had scooped the ol' boy up in his wheelbarrow and heaved the handles way high up in order to slide him into the trunk. It had gone surprisingly easily.

Ed sat on the exam room floor beside the stretcher and waited for the doctor. He had difficulty finding a painless position, but wanted to stay in Big Red's line of sight, despite the fact that the poor animal was almost blind.

Then the whining started. Each breath began with a quivering, shrill pitch that diminished as the dog exhaled. A flood of emotion surged through Ed, who looked at his pal with the overwhelming realization that he would probably be going home without him.

The vet knocked and entered, telling Ed he could remain seated. She got down on her knees and placed her stethoscope here and there on the shaking dog. Ed didn't even notice the tears he was brushing off his face. He was concentrating on easing the nerves of his dear buddy. He gently stroked the solid rump and hoped with all his might, *Don't let this be the day...please, please...don't let it.* He wished he could pray, but learned of its futility back when he was a soldier.

The doctor didn't give him the feared verdict. It was considered a good sign when the dog flinched after she pinched his paws, although she had to do it really hard with an instrument. Nevertheless, it gave Ed hope. Blood was drawn, and she'd be able to tell him more in twenty minutes. She showed him how to massage a few areas on the dog's back to calm him. He was certain Red could detect the sense of relief in his fingers. Apparently Red's medical record showed a recurring history of badly pulled muscles.

While they waited, the vet explained that if Red's obesity was not brought under control right away, his days were definitely numbered. Unaccustomed to dealing with the husband, she asked if Ed wanted her to speak with his wife. He said she was out of town.

It was news to him that Maddie had already agreed to put Red on a diet. The aging retriever needed to shed some pounds before undergoing anesthesia for cataract surgery. The doctor stated that dogs could become increasingly fearful of their environment due to blindness. This led to inactivity and atrophy. The surgery might not help, but it was worth a try.

Ed got to go home with his dog. He sat in the kitchen and read the armful of information he had received, comforted by the warm body that lay snuggled between his feet and the chair leg. He was hell-bent on improving Red's condition. It felt terrific to have a mission. He promised to be Red's partner in this endeavor; they were going to do this together. That meant eliminating treats and starting an exercise routine. Ed felt responsible for making Red as comfortable as he could at the end of the dog's life; after all, Red had been an enjoyable constant during the multitude of changes otherwise going on in the family.

The regimen began the following morning—at 7:00 AM sharp. Ed refused to feel disillusioned when Red could only waddle as far as the mailbox; it was a long driveway. The dog's front legs bowed around his fat, wide chest, and he panted profusely. He also preferred standing to sitting; getting up from the ground was nearly impossible. Ed patiently waited the ten minutes for Red to recover. They headed back to the house at a snail's pace—or more appropriately, at a morbidly obese, decrepit, ancient hound's pace. Ed remembered that Maddie sometimes held a towel underneath Red's belly in order to hoist his hindquarters over a step. In this instance, it was required for the front end as well.

Only a half cup of kibble was served for breakfast—no extras. Red circled his dish once the appetizer disappeared in a bite, then pawed Ed's leg. It was a pitiful sight. Ed held his ground while eating his own small bowl of cereal. He yearned for a morning cup of coffee, but the can was empty. Heck, he could forgo it from now on.

Ed got to work weeding the yard; the dandelions and crabgrass had taken over. Big Red was no longer allowed to languish inside with daylong naps; instead, he had to go out and keep his "personal trainer" company. Every so often, Ed whistled and encouraged the dog to walk to another spot in the grass. He would then praise and massage him. Red caught on quickly. As soon as he collapsed in a new area, he rolled on his back, inviting a belly rub.

Ed didn't want to hurry the process, but he was astounded by the results after only four days. The dog had noticeably more energy, as did he.

A week later, Ed decided to get an overdue haircut and do the laundry…finally. He tossed the accumulating pile of clothes in the washer. The knobs couldn't be less self-explanatory. One came off in his hand. Instructions were in the drawer. Aha…push. He grabbed a belt before leaving and found that he could pull it a notch tighter.

Ed even managed to do "serious" grocery shopping before coming back home. It was a surprise to see Carol when he pulled into the driveway. She walked over from the garden bench to greet him. She always got the biggest hug from her dad. He had to admit he was glad to see her, having been alone without conversation for almost two weeks. The one-sided dialogue with Red, where Ed made up the dog's answers to his questions, wasn't the same. And although communication between him and Maddie had become limited lately, he was used to the sound of her voice filling the void. He realized he missed watching his wife flit around the house too.

As they carted the seven bags through the garage to the kitchen, he said, "You know where the key is, Carol."

"It's a beautiful afternoon. I could use the time outdoors. You've been busy…everything's growing really well. The flowers are gorgeous."

Big Red's waving tail would keep smacking a cupboard until he got noticed. Carol petted his lumpy head. He squinted with pleasure.

Carol's father wasn't oblivious to the inspection going on. She caught him eyeing her and smiled. When she went to sit at the kitchen table, she looked back at him with such a hopeful face. There was a small vase with fresh flowers. That was always her mother's touch; she thought Maddie had returned.

"I missed them on the table," he confessed, aware of her disappointment.

"When Janet saw you last, she described a gruesome picture…of you, and the house."

Ed folded the grocery bags, then sat with her. "That was then."

Carol looked bad. He assumed his daughter was worried about her mother. "I still haven't heard from your mom. Has Rima?" Surely Maddie would have notified her by now.

"No," she answered. "Dad, why should Rima hear from her before you have? I don't get any of this. It isn't like Mom. Is she sick? You'd tell us, wouldn't you?"

"No, no, it's nothing like that," he assured her. "I'm trying to make sense of it too, Carol." Her hands were loosely folded, and she stared out the window. Her golden glow had grayed. She bit her lower lip as she struggled to hold back the tears. Ed placed his hands over hers. "I'm certain she's all right. Someone would have called us." He was trying his best to raise her spirits.

Carol pushed her bangs back and just held onto her forehead. "I don't doubt Mom can take care of herself." She took a tissue from the counter behind her and blew her nose. She had an emptiness he'd never witnessed before. "I tried talking to her at the picnic, but it wasn't the right timing or place...and then she was gone."

The possibility of Carol and Tom divorcing entered his mind, though he knew of no problems. God, she was so haggard. It hurt him. He'd never had lengthy chats with his kids. He didn't know what Carol expected from him.

"Dad, I've hit a brick wall." She pressed her fingertips into her temples. He was reminded of her brother's death. The news must be grim.

"We have until the end of the day to pay the mortgage, including six months of penalties, before the bank forecloses on us."

He waited to hear more.

"The university closed down Tom's department and let go of a lot of people. He's been out of a job for almost a year. He really thought he would find another position by now. I hate going into Rima's college fund...and my social work doesn't give us very much."

Ed wasn't sure if he was being asked a question. Did they need money? Or want to live with him if they lost their house?

Carol sobbed, then immediately forced herself to stop.

Her dad just wanted to make her feel better. A story might help. "I'll never forget when you were around twelve...and you were eating dinner, right here at the table. You calmly informed your mother that you weren't going to go to religion classes and be confirmed."

Carol sat bereft over her impending loss. Her dad's tale came out of left field. Had he heard a single word she'd said?

Ed chuckled, remembering the image. "Your Mom was furious. 'No way are you going to get out of it!' she screamed. 'Sometimes you just have to do things you don't like. Too bad.'"

Along with everything else going wrong, Carol now had to concern herself with her dad's usual disconnect from anything involving serious emotions. He laughed...while she faced the worst crisis in her marriage.

Ed continued. "This was blasphemy. It was bad enough we let you go to public school." He took immense delight in telling the story. "Do you remember, Carol? You looked me right in the eyes and said, 'I bet Dad doesn't believe Jesus was born from a virgin either, do you?' Then Mom yelled that it didn't matter what your father thought, you were going to get confirmed." Ed got serious. "You repeated it, but not as a question. 'It doesn't matter what Dad thinks.' I'll never forget it. 'It matters to me,' you said. And you asked me again if I believed in the Virgin Mary. I never took on your mom when it came to anything having to do with the house or religion. But the look in your eyes.

And the kids' faces as they waited to hear my answer. No, I said, I don't. Do you remember that? You made me proud that day…that it mattered to my kid what I had to say. You and Tim."

Carol nodded a little, reminding herself that her dad shouldn't be blamed for his inept way of dealing with her plight; that was just how he was. She accepted the inevitable: tonight she, Tom, and Rima would be officially homeless…and penniless. Having resigned herself to that, her breathing became shallow, and she felt oddly at peace.

Battle weary, she got up to leave. Trying to make ends meet this past year had been all-consuming. She leaned over to kiss her father. "Let me know if you need anything." She sounded drained but nevertheless meant it. On her way out, she heard her dad's chair scoot across the floor.

"Carol?"

She turned as he was walking toward her. He gave a shrug and a questioning look. "Aren't we going to go to the bank?"

Ed caught his girl in time, just as she slumped into his arms—rescued. She pressed into him with a neediness that wore away the man's generally disengaged front. "Does Tom have to meet us there?" he asked.

She was gulping air, unable to speak. Ed called and made arrangements with her husband.

CHAPTER 9

Rima was never certain what to expect on any given day when she arrived home in the evening from her summer job. The situation had become desperate this month. The minimal and strained conversations were intolerable. Her despondent parents never yelled, but their daughter was beginning to think it would be a welcome change. She knew in her heart that her grandparents wouldn't hesitate to offer their help. Her parents emphatically told her, though, not to mention a word about their financial problems to them, especially her grandfather. Why did her mom think they were undeserving when her cousins' families had benefited from her grandparents' generosity for as long as Rima could remember? Those contributions were no secret.

Eight o'clock, and the sky was still bright. Rima wandered around the rooms until she saw her mom on the back porch. When she walked over to say hi, her dad came into view. He was sitting hunched over in the wicker rocker on the opposite side. The suspense was killing her. "How long before we gotta be outta here?" she asked.

"We got a reprieve, Rima," said her dad. "Grandpa helped us today."

Her father said it as if it were a good thing. However, considering the degree to which they hadn't wanted to accept any aid, especially from Grandpa, did this news warrant celebration? The entire situation left her confused and tired, but relieved. She wished she were already away at college—or with her grandmother, wherever she was. Rima was heading back inside when her mom called out to her.

"Rima, will you come sit with us a moment? It won't take long."

She was conditioned to expect something bad. *What else?* she thought as she sat down close to her mother on the rocker's matching loveseat. Carol forced a weak smile. She took her daughter by the hand and ran her fingers across the many rings she loved to wear.

"Grandpa gave us the amount we needed for the house…and then some. I realize I haven't handled things well these last months. I should have gone to him sooner." Carol shook her head in a slow, conscious manner. "Foolish pride." She looked at her husband. It made Rima uncomfortable to see her dad sniffling, his eyes glassy.

Carol explained that ever since she refused to get confirmed as a girl, her parents, at her father's insistence, had started putting money in the bank for her. The first amount had been from that particular saved expense. He believed it was only fair that she get what the others did. When she graduated from high school, they set aside what it would have cost to send her to parochial school. They did the same when she went to the local state university, because her brothers and sisters had been enrolled in private colleges. They even threw in the outrageous total spent on Janet's wedding extravaganza, because she and Rima's dad had married in a small ceremony at the courthouse. She almost forgot mentioning the down payments given Janet and Matt for their homes.

Rima couldn't believe her ears. This seemed to be heading in a positive direction.

Her mom was too emotional, so her dad continued. "When we were at the bank…and saw the amount on the check." Her father could only shake his head. *Hurry up!* thought Rima, *tell me*. "Not only was it what we owed, but it included the rest of the mortgage. We were shocked." Rima could only imagine. "After signing all the papers, he told us to follow him in the car. We ended up at his bank. He told your mom to take out her money today…money that was due her. Even minus the mortgage, it was still a whopping figure."

Rima thought somebody should show a modicum of enthusiasm over this unexpected stroke of good fortune, but she sat speechless with them now too. She always felt her selfless parents were deserving of so much more than what they settled for. They went out of their way to instill in their daughter a sense of self-reliance, as if that trait alone were the be-all and end-all to a purposeful life. She grew up admiring their integrity. But sometimes, because of her combined youth and inexperience, Rima couldn't resist the twinge of envy when she saw how much her cousins and most of her friends received for doing nothing—not just next to nothing. She hadn't been able to wait until she could earn her own money. It so happened that when she finally did, and could afford an occasional, frivolous luxury…the guilt was unbearable. She'd stare at herself in the mirror while applying an overpriced mascara or lipstick, and dwell on what those few extra dollars might have bought someone waking up hungry.

Maddie respected Carol and Tom's views regarding no lavish birthday or Christmas presents. It bothered Maddie, though, so she came up with a substitute for the absence of material items: when Rima turned fourteen, Maddie convinced her parents to allow the girl to go places with her…meaning every play and musical that came to town, along with the many charity functions she organized. For Rima, the doors opened to an enchanting world she wouldn't have traded for anything. She loved sharing her grandmother's company; the two really hit it off. Although Rima's mother had an aloof streak, Rima couldn't fathom why she wasn't closer to her very own mother. Everyone else seemed to enjoy being around her grandmother. Carol simply chalked it up to divergent interests.

Rima went to her bedroom, where she lay staring vacantly at her bare feet. Reality took hold and roused her out of this nowhere state. She acted on an impulse and called her grandfather. It was almost ten. "Hi, Grandpa. Rima." He sounded alert. "No, I haven't heard from her." He said he was looking at slides. "Can I come over and watch with you?"

She left quietly and drove the twenty minutes to his neighborhood. Upon entering his house, she followed the clicking noise of the projector tray, which led her to the open basement door in the front hallway. "It's me," she called down. She gave the big guy a hug and seated herself on the floor, ready for the show.

"There's your Uncle Tim, a month before he died."

Tim appeared made of copper. The combination tan and sunburn matched the color of his buzz. He was well proportioned for a boy at that usually ungainly age. It was Memorial Day weekend at the swim club. Ed and Rima laughed over her mom, who was about four at the time. Carol sat topless on a corner step in the water, turning a page in a plastic book. Her father, the photographer, must have just called out for everyone to look up at him. Carol stared directly at the camera. Her indiscernible blond brows were tightly knitted together, displaying an adult's look of consternation—to think someone could be born that contemplative. She was a pretty little girl. Still pretty, thought Rima, but her chronic seriousness distracted one from her otherwise vivacious features.

"You have to see this, Rima…this is somethin'."

Ed got another tray, humming all the while. Then he rapidly blurred past several pictures until he hit the right one.

"Look at that! Now that's your mom!"

Carol was maybe twelve. She was a speck at the top of the tallest oak in the bordering woods (perched higher than one would think possible to climb).

Ed told his granddaughter, "You can't see it too well in this one, but she's got the book up there with her…the one she pulled your name out of." They both studied the frame. "She'd stay up there for hours." Rima loved watching her grandfather's eyes sparkle from the reflected screen.

Ed advanced the slides. A telephoto lens caught a rare close shot of Carol in her tree, smiling ear to ear. A targeted beam of sunlight poking through the branches crossed her face and gave her gray-green eyes stunning clarity. Her strawberry-blond hair, pulled back in a ponytail, had loose tendrils that softly framed her face. She waved to her dad. Her other hand held the opened *Green Mansions* against her chest.

Rima was deeply moved by her mother's realized fantasy of someday having a daughter she would name after the character in her favorite story. Carol, though not a demonstrative type, gave Rima a symbol of an inspired love she could carry with her forever. It was a link to that idealized realm of childhood that often became jaded over the years.

Rima asked for the slide in order to get an enlarged print made from it. As far as she was concerned, she was looking at the time of her conception. Her mother, daydreaming in that tree, had no doubt formulated a list of qualities her future husband should possess…and she found him.

She needed to get home. Grandpa was tired, too. He walked her to the car. Rima always felt like a small child around him. They never got beyond the simple generalized topics of conversation. That was about to change. She wanted to make a conscious effort to meet him head-on as an adult. The awkwardness upset her. Nevertheless, it had to be done.

"Grandpa, I hope someday I can do something as wonderful for a child of mine as you were able to do for Mom today."

She was afraid he would be embarrassed and brush aside her comment, telling her it was nothing and to hurry on home. But he didn't. He looked thoughtfully at her. His glasses magnified his faded brown eyes. The spotlight above the driveway created harsh shadows, delineating the creases of his forehead. His white hair shone. "It's rewarding when it's truly appreciated," he said.

"It certainly is that," she replied.

"You know as well as I do that your mom would never have taken the money before now. That's just how she is. Your grandma and I were going to hand it over anyway as a twenty-fifth wedding anniversary present."

Rima briefly thought about the things she and her parents could have bought, could have enjoyed—like her cousins and her friends had—if they had gotten possession of the money sooner. That yearning for unnecessary stuff was disconcerting. Rima realized that had they obtained the money earlier, without showing true need, it might have proven detrimental to the sound state of her family life, which was an aspect of her existence that she truly valued. This crazy past year had been the first of its kind. Rima wanted her reliable life back. As she stood there with her grandfather, having been given a fleeting glimpse into the insidious nature of greed, her principled mother and father suddenly grew nobler in the girl's eyes.

"C'mon. You get going."

"Grandpa…I've been thinking. You know what would be great?"

"What?" he asked, smiling in such a way that she again felt five years old.

"I've often heard Dad say how much he wished his father had been like you…especially when you go on about fishing. At the end of every summer, he and Mom remember the trips you used to make to Alaska…and how you had planned on taking Uncle Tim. Why don't the two of you go this August? He's been through the wringer this past year. And I think he and Mom could use a break from each other."

Ed liked her dad, but couldn't imagine fishing with him—and besides, Tom was a novice. Tim didn't have experience either, but that was different. However, in light of his granddaughter's heartfelt intentions, he promised to consider it.

Rima drove away satisfied.

The rest of the week, Ed vigilantly continued to motivate Red. By then it took less coaxing to keep the dog moving. Their walk progressed to the stop sign at the end of the street. Red didn't have to catch his breath anymore. He'd turn around on a dime, sort of, and make a comical attempt to run up the slight incline as he headed toward home, eager for that belly massage. Ed openly laughed at the dog's goofy, swaying style of running. They repeated this outing four times a day.

This impressed the neighbors, who cheered them on. They'd lower their car windows in passing, asking for brief updates. Maddie wasn't mentioned at first, per Amy's request. Because Ed was out and about more, and becoming quite the talker, one gentleman who knew him the longest got roped into asking—curiosity was killing them all. "Oh," Ed started telling him, making it up as he went, "she's having a fabulous time in Europe…so wonderful, she said she might stay." And left it at that. Eventually man and dog trooped over to the next street, where they got to know the folks there better.

One thing Ed hadn't counted on was Amy's return. In order to thwart it, he resumed his silent treatment. That sent her off in a huff—for good, she said. He gloated over his success…about time she learned to fend for herself.

He was steering the riding mower into the garage when Lorraine Simms from next door greeted him. Red could actually jump when he recognized her voice, and appeared to take supreme delight in this newfound mobility; he wouldn't stop.

"Ed, I've got to give you credit, ol' Red is looking mighty handsome and trim these days. I wish I had some time-lapse pictures of him over the last couple of weeks. I can see the changes every day."

Ed straightened his back and stretched after his dismount.

"Oh…my…Lord! Look at you!" Lorraine stepped up to him and pulled his baggy work shirt away from his belly, which not too long ago had resembled a barrel.

"Yeah, yeah," he remarked, annoyed by her tone. He flicked her hand off him. Age and her husband's death did not curtail Lorraine's ever present flirtatious manner. At sixty-two, she was the youngest of their age-group on the street. Friends had always referred to her as foxy, but Ed was unimpressed with what he considered her crass behavior. She exhibited an unconstrained sauciness with other wives' husbands that was inexcusable.

The women believed her overtures with their men was unbecoming, but nevertheless harmless…little did they know. Ed thought Lorraine was conceited too. Packing a few extra pounds lately made her no less spirited, or more matronly. She seemed to relish the added bounce when she walked. Her hair was colored a vibrant burgundy, and she wore distinctively bold eye shadows that matched her loud outfits. She still had a remarkable porcelain complexion that he did not want to admit he found glamorous.

"Ed, how 'bout you be my dinner companion if I fix a good home-cooked meal?"

He answered in exasperation, "Sure," then headed inside. He remembered what Rima had asked. "Lorraine," he yelled back.

Her garage door was closing, but she reversed it. Ed waltzed over, forgetting that for two years he hadn't set foot there—not since his best friend's death. This had been their hangout, where the talk centered on engines, fishing, football…and occasionally the kids, specifically Tim, until the accident. There were always too many children flying in and out of the Gullivers' garage for Ed to take advantage of the space.

Lorraine witnessed the momentary effect her husband's absence had on Ed.

"Could I look over Neil's rods and tackle box? I want to take my son-in-law up to Alaska...he doesn't own a thing." He sounded humbled, as though it were the day of the funeral and in bad taste to be bringing this up.

"Anytime, Ed. Do you want it now?"

"No...I was just wondering." Then he walked back home through his silent garage. He remembered being hungry, but the feeling had left him.

Later in the day, his doorbell rang. He turned down the TV and shushed Red. He didn't want to leave the comfort of his chair and was glad when he thought the person had left. The pestering musical gongs started up again. He would sit it out. The dog's tail flapped furiously; he was primed to bolt. His eyes did a ping-pong number: back and forth, between Ed and the door.

Lorraine called out from the entryway, "Ed...Ed...you there?"

He couldn't believe it; she had the nerve to enter his home. On second thought, yes he could.

"Where else!" She clapped her hands together at the sight of him in his lounger. She had a great excuse to sit a minute—Red knocked her onto the couch. He loved how she roughed up his ears. She kissed his watery eyes and bristly nose, the way she knew Maddie did—he must be missing her.

Ed couldn't deny that the visit was good for the dog. He couldn't continue to keep Red all to himself.

"I brought the poles and boxes. They're next to the front door."

Why hadn't he locked up! He found it difficult to say thanks.

"It's only seven o'clock. What are you doing in your robe?"

"Can I take a shower and be comfortable in my own home?"

She grinned; it was how she liked to play off the fact that she got on his nerves. She missed it. He didn't. A black-and-white World War II movie was on TV, with no sound. She realized what Ed had done and was about to make a wisecrack, then decided against it.

Lorraine wouldn't take her eyes off Ed. He looked good for a man of seventy, with his full head of fluffy snow-white hair, which matched his thin, always perfectly trimmed mustache and short beard. It gave him a much brighter appearance than when he was younger, and his hair had been dark. People had regarded him as sinister-looking then. Funny how his temperament contrasted his coloring—he used to be amiable, way back then. And by no stretch of the imagination was he currently a cheery soul…these recent weeks being the exception, or so she'd been told.

Lorraine couldn't remember when she was last in the Gullivers' home. Things changed so much after Tim was gone. She and her husband never had children, and both did an excellent job of playing aunt and uncle to all the Gullivers, but they were especially fond of Tim, who had truly adopted them as family. The boy enjoyed doing his homework at their kitchen table. He needed to escape the constant commotion in his own place. Tim used to take their lumbering old Saint Bernard on a daily walk and faithfully wash the line of drool that dog painted along the walls.

Lorraine broke the silence. "Can you believe how quiet the street is? At some point, every day, it really hits me. I still have a clear picture of all the activity that used to take place. It's spooky…like in the movies where ghosts are carrying on alongside the living."

Ed didn't answer. He didn't allow the past to cross his mind often.

"We sure made grass-cutting an event to look forward to. It's too bad everyone switched to the riding mowers." She giggled more the longer she thought about it.

He grinned, slightly to the side (which she adored). She recalled how the "girls," after meeting for a cocktail (or two), pushed off with their lawnmowers shortly before the men came home from work, promptly at 5:30…back when the world revolved around a set schedule. Following their ritual evening martinis, the men took over while dinner was readied. There was a commendable uniformity to their street's matching zigzagging rows.

Ed chuckled. It did feel good to share a memory with someone—even if it was with this nuisance.

"Is Maddie coming back?" She didn't beat around the bush.

He gave a dismissive gesture with his hands. "I'm sure, eventually."

Like his kids, she wondered what the real story was.

Ed wasn't prepared when Lorraine leaned across him, simultaneously pushing the footrest flat against the chair, causing his bare feet to hit the carpet. "What the hell are you doing!"

She kneeled between his legs and propped her arms on top of his. Part of him was put off by her brazenness, especially because he guessed she had plotted this; yet he remained transfixed by her evocative posture. She peeled open the robe and wove her fingers through the curly hairs on his chest, under which his heart was pounding out of control. Maddie, seen during happier times, was watching from the pictures on the table behind the sofa. He should stop this immediately.

Lorraine's teasing nibbling won out. He had fleeting thoughts of the few times Maddie came close to doing this, then didn't. He had never cheated on his wife to satisfy his lust…had never wanted to. His wedding vows—like any promise made—were taken seriously. Discipline, after all, was what separated the civilized from the beasts. *Now look at me.* He was compromising that belief. He closed his lids and placed Maddie in this scene.

Using Ed's thighs for support, Lorraine pushed herself onto his lap. He found himself confronting the softest, pinkest-looking nipples. They were like dollops of meringue topping a couple of pastry puffs—and he had to touch them. His composure went by the wayside; Maddie's face faded. He couldn't pretend anymore. "Lorraine, this is crazy."

She agreed. "Isn't it, though."

Although he loved what he remembered about his wife's athletic body, this one was rousingly different, plush. And that ivory skin…

Red, worried by these newfangled vocalizations, whimpered; he'd never heard Ed so worked up.

CHAPTER 10

Shortly Maddie's train would be pulling into the mountain town of Interlaken, hours later than expected. There had been a minor misunderstanding in Basel; Maddie learned that she needed to continue to Zurich before heading south. Fortunately, it didn't take long to get rerouted. She called the hostel to make sure their doors wouldn't be locked when she arrived. As she watched the glorious alpine scenery, she couldn't ignore how much she was already missing Sonja. They had clung together on the platform before parting, as if whoever held the tightest might convince the other to go her way.

Sitting alone, she ruminated over the subject that consumed her thoughts during this entire ride, which had nothing to do with figuring out transportation or lodging. The long-running theme was strictly salacious in its content. Now that she knew what it felt like again, Maddie wondered how she had gone without any romantic interaction for such an unthinkable amount of time. All during her animated conversations with Sonja, she privately acknowledged the revived sensations going on inside her, provoked by vividly recurring memories of Robert. Like an infatuated adolescent, she obsessed over the image of him lying on the bed.

When Tim died, the grief-stricken mother's despondency left no energy for rekindling a lost libido. Her foremost wish—to reproduce the lost son—became a high-minded pursuit; any sort of loving display was deemed frivolous and a distraction. Later, disheartened by the unwelcome baby girl and the draining postpartum recuperative period, she sank into oblivion. To this day, Maddie couldn't remember those first few ensuing years. Time did work its intrinsic magic, though, and eventually she moved back from the periphery to the mainstream of her family existence—devoid, however, of those life-affirming longings.

The extent of the psychological damage hit home one day while she was waiting in line at the local meat market. Ten years earlier, ignorant as to what the future held out to her, she had walked into that same store and found herself stammering and blushing when she ordered from a newly hired young apprentice. The attraction was not merely one-sided. The two eagerly looked forward to their biweekly repartee, filled with innuendo. Although confident she'd never act on it, when their eyes met they blatantly signaled, "You never know..." It was tremendous fun.

As it happened on this one particular afternoon, while Maddie stood there observing the butcher go about his usual work behind the counter, she became acutely aware of the present...as she never had since Tim's passing. It was as though a hypnotist snapped his fingers, and presto! She instantly tuned back in. Her line of sight converged with the butcher's, and it was evident that the shared memory of their amorous feelings crossed their minds. The result, on her end, was nothing, absolutely nothing.

Maddie walked out and returned home empty-handed...and empty-hearted. The rest of the afternoon was spent on the back patio, where she struggled with what seemed like a partial amputation of her psyche. She didn't dare discuss the loss with anyone, especially her priest. Her way of dealing with it was to reprimand herself for having placed so much importance on this superficial aspect of her life. Nevertheless, she couldn't deny feeling robbed of a fundamental part of her identity. She tried to appreciate how much she still had in lieu of what she had discovered to be missing.

From that day, she resumed an active role in helping Ed grow the business, and she began organizing her charities. On one level, she was enjoying everything again, but she went to bed most nights with an unsettling sadness. No matter what she accomplished, it always felt as if she had just missed the mark. It was no sacrifice when she later had to submit to a hysterectomy. It couldn't make things worse.

This summer, twenty years later, and out of thin air, Maddie was inclined to believe that she was experiencing something akin to the phenomenon of phantom limbs, or in her case, organs. As preposterous as it sounded to her—and granted, it was long after the fact—what other explanation could there be?

Five minutes after disembarking, Maddie remained standing by the train, absentmindedly holding a map. She was still contemplating such a medical condition when a teenage boy and girl approached her. They offered help, having mistakenly assumed that she was trying to decide which way to go. She remembered that she was indeed hoping to locate the Wanderer's Villa. The two were nice enough to walk her there, trudging with their bikes alongside them, which they had taken on the train. It wasn't far; two right turns, and they said good night.

Maddie was quietly ushered into a darkened room with four bunk beds. She had requested a bottom one and luckily got it. Pulling the provided sheet and thin blanket to the top of her ears, she hastened to join the other softly snoring mounds.

In the morning, a towel-wrapped form kept passing Maddie, going up, then down, and back up the ladder at the end by her feet. Giggling filled the hallway…and squealing as soon as someone entered a shower. She gathered there was no hot water. The room was chilly. Oh, to dive down deep under the covers and warm her head. But she was afraid she'd never want to get back out—better to face the day. She recalled a photo of Janet in Interlaken. She was on a bench with a couple of other girls, surrounded by patches of snow that had accumulated on the first day of summer back in 1973. At least there was no possibility of that today.

Wiggling her way to a sitting position, Maddie removed a sweatshirt and insulated socks from her bag and put them on as fast as possible, fearing she might wrench a muscle in the process. Friendly faces greeted her as she familiarized herself with the layout of the hostel. The stairs led down to a large eat-in kitchen area, already filled at eight this morning. While standing there caressing a mug of hot chocolate, she was invited to sit with a family who had an extra chair.

Frank and Louise Washington, a retired couple from Atlanta, introduced themselves and their two grandchildren. They were hoping to give the preteens a valuable lesson about others' customs. After three weeks on the road, they wondered whether they would survive the next three months. They asked Maddie to join them later for a drive. Their previous objective of viewing the Jungfrau had to be changed due to severe weather at the top of the mountain. *Why not?* she thought, and agreed to meet them in front at ten o'clock.

While she got ready, Maddie learned about her roommates. They were from Norway. Two were teachers, the third a dentist. They had worked in their respective fields for three years and saved most of their salaries for this global excursion. They chose cities as they went, based upon the recommendations of fellow travelers.

Before embarking on her European journey, Maddie had been curious about the ages of the people she would find staying in hostels. There was a wide range here.

Riding in the rented Mercedes beside the lean Washingtons proved comfortable. She didn't think cars were manufactured with front single bench seats anymore. Perhaps it had once served as a taxicab, to allow for more passengers.

Interlaken had incorporated many of the outlying bucolic villages since Janet's sojourn through the countryside. The carload of sightseers crossed lush green valleys with prettily situated towns. Roads climbed through wooded country affording superb views of Interlaken, the surrounding lakes, but unfortunately not the three famous peaks that made up the Jungfrau mountain ridge. It was exciting to exchange observations with the Georgia couple, first-time tourists themselves. Maddie wouldn't have guessed that she shared so much in common with African Americans from the south. Like the Gullivers, the Washingtons had done quite nicely for themselves by offering a needed service that grew over the years. Their business evolved from a small mom-'n'-pop car wash station to a tristate chain. Frank and Louise were active in local politics and also supported the arts and charities. After working tirelessly for forty years, they agreed they must see a world they never made time for. Only a few months ago, the husband stepped down and let a son oversee the company operations. They explained that the grandkids belonged to another daughter, who was a newspaper journalist.

The afternoon got warmer than expected, but was still overcast, hiding the upper portions of the mountains.

Maddie felt sorry for the bored kids who sat in the back, obsessed with their handheld computer games and deaf to the adults, thanks to the headphones. They were decent enough to oblige her with a quasi-smile when she glanced at them. She'd been down that road too many times with her own children. No one could fault them for missing their friends...or wishing to be with others their own age. At least they spoke respectfully to their elders—but their dialogues were mechanical. She understood the grandparents' occasional embarrassment regarding the youngsters' lackluster responses; after all, here they were, being given this terrific opportunity, and they acted as if it were no big deal.

Many disappointed faces greeted them at dinner when they returned at six. Despite the warnings, a number had chanced a break in conditions on the mountain peak...and would have memories only of fog. The forecast didn't suggest clear skies for two more days—not long according to Maddie's travel schedule.

She reveled in the usual bedtime chitchat of her three roommates: of boys and dreams and places to see. It was easy to forget her age. The talk conjured up distant schoolgirl crushes and her ever-so-brief interlude as an unmarried person. She marveled over how short it actually was…and so did the others. Maddie had never fantasized about a life different than the one she'd had. Looking back, she was glad for it. She slept contentedly.

It was 9:00 AM. Maddie stood at the foot of a wooded hill that bordered the town and decided she'd check out the local real estate. Here and there she spotted corners of rooftops poking out among the trees. The homes must have spectacular views. Taking a big, inspirational breath, she braved climbing up a narrow, really steep road. Fifty feet in, she realized she'd better keep her eyes open for a strong branch to use as a walking cane.

Thankfully, the ground leveled off. Compact, fairy-tale cottages, separated by beautiful trellises and gardens, dressed the short lane. The occupant of this last home shouldn't mind a weary hiker resting on his or her stout rock fence. Maddie could hardly be perceived as threatening. If anything, she looked quite fetching. Her hair, worn looser since Paris, was held together tidily with the leather clip. The pale blue jogging suit accented her hazel eyes, expertly smudged with a smoky-gray shadow. She had substituted her bright lipstick for a natural gloss. A few lines around her brow may have tired her look somewhat, but one feature that maintained its youthful form was Maddie's mouth. There were none of the distinctive crosshatches pinching it together, so common in others her age.

She wiped beads of perspiration from her forehead. Her skin felt incredibly soft after traipsing through this humidity. She weighed whether to follow the overgrown road in front of her. It ran more uphill than the one before.

A restaurant was built into the rock somewhere above her. She had planned on grabbing a bite to eat there, but the slope had better not get worse. She fancied herself to be in fairly good shape, but this climb was testing her reserve energy.

Catching her second wind, Maddie sauntered up the well-hidden dirt path backward, exercising a different set of muscles in her shins and calves. When the charming house diminished from sight, she faced forward again, meeting a black Saab head-on. It rolled past, barely missing her toes. The female driver grimaced and raised her hand above the steering wheel in a wave of apology. Maddie wished she had it in her to give her the finger.

A clearing to the right exposed a wide area taken over by mushrooms. She thought she could distinguish a couple different varieties. During Janet's vegetarian stage, Maddie became fascinated by a recipe book extolling the plants' exquisite flavors and creative uses. She wanted to inspect them at a closer range, but the angle of the hillside presented a problem. It looked silly, but if she bent her knees as if preparing to jump, she could brace herself with one arm while inching along.

Once she started across, the minimal distance of thirty or so feet grew increasingly longer. It was as if a prankish stagehand were constantly pulling on the scene, preventing her from ever reaching the end of it. On impulse, she stood erect to gain a more extensive view—big mistake! Her ankles gave way, sending her crashing onto a turreted, decomposing tree stump.

The surprise left her mute. As she clumsily tried raising her body off the pointy crown, she began sliding down the hill, picking up speed as she went. She tried in vain to grab the few long grasses, but they were damp and squeaked through her fingers, leaving her with nail marks imprinted in her palms. Her rump struck the stone ledge like a door banging against a doorstop.

Maddie blinked rapidly, desperate to erase the momentary blind spots. Afraid to move, she remained frozen in this ungainly position, with knees and feet pointing outward. Slowly, she rotated the major joints. She couldn't be sure if she laughed; the memory popped up of the squirrel that hit the ground in her garden not long before she had decided to take this trip.

It wasn't until she attempted to find a more comfortable way to lean that the burning in her ribs and hip forced an audible wail. She succeeded in getting upright. Her folded legs jacked up her sore bottom off the rock. She closed her eyes and focused on reconfiguring her badly jarred equilibrium. A heady fragrance, perhaps wild onions, boosted her recovering senses. She was acutely aware of being the lone human in these woods.

Maddie looked up toward the mushrooms and wondered if they had warranted this. She'd been trying since the start of this trip to overcome her aversion to risk. Conquering it was imperative if she wanted to hitchhike. Normally she considered the potential downside to everything, which drove her kids nuts when they were growing up. This calamity could easily have been avoided. One look at that hill should have been enough. She reminded herself of her children's reasoning: harping on the negative limited one's experience. Of course, this wisdom prevailed best in cases where one's neck wasn't broken.

The perch served as a terrific observation deck. Even on this colorless and damp morning, the panorama of Interlaken's cozy locale, snuggled amid the mountains, appeared as picturesque as on Janet's sunny-looking postcards.

Her spirits picked up at the sound of wheels traveling below. There was no way to see, but the vehicle must be on the same winding road she'd been using.

She glanced to her sides and considered the strength of some lower branches. Next she imagined what would become of her when those branches gave out and she dropped over the edge. There was nothing else around to hold on to. "Oh, God, Maddie," she murmured with exasperation. "What now?"

Upon turning, she was startled by the sight of feet in front of her nose. She scanned up and found the warmest brown eyes studying her.

A man started yelling not too far away. He sounded angry. It didn't distract the figure from his unremitting watch over her. She was tempted to reach out to him, then thought it smarter to let him make the first move.

The commanding voice grew nearer, as did the crunching sound as the shouting man made his way through the dense brush. She hollered, "Can you help me, sir? I'm over here." It occurred to her that he might not understand English. He suddenly appeared where the trees ended, and was forced to stop in his tracks. At least he knew a dangerous slope when he saw one. His features were indistinguishable at this distance.

"Max, damn it!" he yelled. That was followed with further cursing (judging by his tone) in Swiss—she guessed.

Maddie looked back at the eyes still fixed on her. The unruffled dog turned toward his owner, who was decidedly fed up with the animal's cool response. In a display of helplessness, the fellow threw his arms in the air. "I'll call the police." He pulled a cell phone out of his jacket pocket.

Now that she knew his name, she felt more confident petting the dog. She'd never seen a breed like this; maybe he was a mix. He looked like a German Shepherd impersonating a…well, she wasn't sure exactly. His superlong coat sprouted straight out from his body, as though charged with static electricity, and looked removable. She wondered how he had gained his footing on this challenging obstacle course.

The man sat on the ground and waited. They didn't talk, because they'd have to shout to be heard.

The police and fire department showed up quickly. Maddie felt extremely embarrassed about causing so much trouble. Fortunately it was a remote area, so crowds wouldn't gather. The team could reach her best from the road below.

They extended a ladder along the side of the cliff. When she stood firmly on a rung, she looked back at Max, worried about how he'd make it down…but he was already out of sight.

The second her foot touched the ground, a paramedic insisted she go to the hospital. She knew she should, but asked if it was really necessary. This was all terribly inconvenient.

The gentleman who discovered her came running down the road with the dog. The workers greeted him as a friend. Gone was his temper. Enough with all the handshaking, she thought. Next they started giving Max hearty pats and shoulder rubs. He ate it up.

The tall, husky man came over and sat beside her on the back bumper of the ambulance. He took her hands and held them securely. Beefy fingers, she noted—not the kind she ever liked shaking hands with. They did feel wonderfully warm. His cold blue eyes turned kind and regarded her with sympathy. A sunnier day might have picked up platinum-blond highlights in his messed-up hair. In this light, the color was as nondescript as clear water.

"You OK?"

Maddie nodded, though she wasn't sure. "I feel really stupid."

He offered half a smile and waved some hair out of her face. Through the rips in her sleeve, he could see the gashes on her arm. "Tell you what," he began in perfect English, "you get looked over by a doctor. I'll meet you at the hospital and take you where you need to go afterward. My name is Marcus."

She wanted to say "don't bother," then thought about the practicality of the gesture. As he was leaving, she had to ask, "Why didn't your dog bark?" Max sat poised, staring up at her.

"Well, I guess because you weren't dead, or dying." He sounded indifferent; like he had better things to do. Motioning for Max to follow him, he said curtly, "Catch you later." She wanted to tell him to forget it.

The doctor was almost done. He was suturing a severe cut running across her left elbow, having finished the short but deep one on her hip where an imbedded twig had broken off. Good news from the X-ray: nothing broken. A neurologist confirmed Maddie was lucky to have escaped a concussion.

Maddie was anxious to leave, but she took her time walking to the waiting room, firmly holding on to the attendant's arm. As promised, Marcus was by the reception desk, happily carrying on with the nurses, who appeared unusually delighted to be speaking with him…or maybe the painkillers just made everyone look overly peppy, because she was reduced to this dismal, dragging state.

As soon as Marcus saw them, he hurried to Maddie's side and relieved the aide. Wearing a look of concern, he wondered aloud where he shouldn't touch her.

"My whole left side," she said drowsily. "It's so shot up, though; it'll probably be numb for hours."

"Do you need to get a prescription?"

"They gave me several days' worth of Percodan…or something like it."

He helped her out to the parking lot.

"You've got to be kidding," whined Maddie when the car door opened for her. The sporty BMW was level with the ground. Stooping down was going to be difficult—and painful, regardless of all the analgesics pumped into her. The convertible top was lowered so she wouldn't have to bend. She sat sideways on the seat and lugged her left leg up with her good right hand. Marcus locked her seatbelt from his side. She felt totally relaxed from the medication—he'd better be a trustworthy character.

"I'm at Wanderer's Villa. Do you know it?"

"Yes," he said, "but first you'll have lunch at my place and rest. The doctor said you shouldn't be alone today."

"I can't interfere like this. There are three other ladies in my room…and lots of others coming and going." She folded her arms over her stomach and closed her eyes. To keep her head from hanging, her right fist held up her chin.

A CD of Willie Nelson's plaintive renderings added to the soporific effect of the drugs. She enjoyed not having a care in the world. A voice—sounding like hers—answered yes about being married, "…but my husband doesn't like to travel." How long? "Almost fifty years," she mumbled.

Marcus grinned and realized the futility in asking her to think while she was this groggy. She didn't make any sense. Fifty years? That was absurd; she didn't look old enough to have been married that long.

A slam popped her lids open. She watched Marcus go through the steps of getting her out of the car. He leaned inside her door and helped raise her legs in order to slide her out. His hair looked so silky smooth. And he smelled great.

Tottering in his doorway, she exclaimed, "You're at the wrong place!"

Her fuzzy state amused him. "No, Madelaine." He pronounced her name Medlaynuh. She could be someone different again. "This is my home, and you're going to get some food in you." He directed her toward the tiny eat-in kitchen and sat her down. She resigned herself to being cared for. Marcus spoke briefly on the hallway phone, then returned and cracked some eggs over a skillet, humming one of Willie's ditties while he went about his business.

Shortly thereafter a woman entered the kitchen, carrying a bundle. She took Maddie's good hand and gave it a little shake. "Hello, Mrs. Gulliver. I am Claudia, Marcus's neighbor. It was a terrible thing that happened…but you are still very lucky."

"Yes, I know." Only the dog had yet to tell her that. She managed to smile. "Please, my name is Madelaine."

Claudia had a genuinely pleasing face, along with a trusting tone to her voice. She should have told her to call her Maddie—it rang more true.

"I've brought you some clothes." Claudia told Marcus she'd watch the eggs while he stepped out in order for her to get his guest changed.

Maddie removed her necklace, which had a flat folder hanging on the end of it that contained her passport and money. She was handed a gray warm-up suit. It felt like cashmere. The torn clothes got pitched in the trash under the sink. "Pity," said Claudia.

Eating produced a welcome change in Maddie's behavior. No longer sluggish, she wanted to discover who her shining knight was.

Marcus Roman, spoken like Romahn, with the accent on the second syllable, was a seasoned German actor who had been asked by a publisher to write his memoirs. After three weeks at this retreat, where he proposed to accomplish this task, he hadn't produced a single sentence. He looked to be around sixtyish.

As the eggs were doled out on their plates, Maddie thought about how to phrase her next question without insulting him. "If someone wants your autobiography, you must be very well-known. Have you made films in the states?"

He and Claudia exchanged a meaningful look. "Some, Madelaine." He still pronounced her name as Medlaynuh, even though he had heard her say it to Claudia.

"Sorry…I seldom go to movies these days."

Her thoughts stayed with this subject while he and Claudia discussed something or other as they ate. When they were almost finished, she inquired, "Whom might you be comparable to in America?"

Marcus wiped his mouth and, without a second's thought, replied, "My dear, I am in-com-pa-ra-ble—in a league of my own." To which Maddie let forth an uncontrolled (and unattractive) laughing-through-the-nose kind of snort. He raised his eyebrows and opened his mouth in mock astonishment. "What? You don't believe me?"

Uh-oh. She searched Claudia's eyes for a sign that he might actually be telling the truth. The neighbor placed a hand on her shoulder. "I hate to admit it," she began solemnly, "but this clown is indeed much admired and loved." Claudia pinched Marcus's cheek. "There is probably only one character more famous, and that is Maximillian."

"The dog? He's in movies?" Maddie asked.

"No," said Marcus, chuckling as he sipped his coffee. "He's a highly decorated police dog. He's saved many lives. People everywhere are familiar with the stories."

"Now that you mention it," said Maddie, "I do recall hearing about a dog in the news a couple of years ago. He ran into the path of a plane so it couldn't take off...I think it was in Germany. They seized someone on board."

"Yes, that was Max." He puckered his lips together then said, "But *me*, you've never heard of."

"You're making me feel terrible." She genuinely meant it.

"How do you think I feel?"

"Your poor ego will survive, Marcus," Claudia teased. "Don't worry about it, Madelaine. We actors over here are used to it."

"Speak for yourself." He started cleaning up the dishes.

"Is Max a particular breed?" Maddie couldn't wait to find out. The dog lay asleep by the back door.

"A Belgian Tervuren," said Claudia. "Isn't he too handsome?"

"Why do you have him, Marcus?"

"I'd been doing this detective series for German TV, and Max's owner was one of our consultants. I rented a guesthouse from him when we were shooting. Unfortunately, he died in a freak accident a little over a year ago." Maddie liked watching him tidy up the stove and counter. "His wife didn't want the constant reminder of her husband, so I offered to take him. He was good company for me, and I knew I'd soon be spending more time here. Lots of time," he moaned. "I will probably die in this house before ever putting one word to paper."

Marcus had to leave for an appointment. He insisted that Maddie make herself comfortable on the sofa. It was late—already three o'clock in the afternoon. Claudia said she could use a break and wouldn't mind staying with Maddie. These two neighbors apparently breezed in and out of each other's homes routinely.

Maddie waited until the car pulled out before confiding to Claudia that she recognized her from her Hollywood films, movies from decades ago, when

Maddie had gone out more often to see them in the theater. The woman was still curvaceous and beautiful; she also appeared to be very content. Most of her shoulder-length light brown hair blended evenly with the gray, creating a frosted effect. The black eyeliner didn't look harsh, as it would on most faces, especially older ones. The famous pout had lessened with age. Claudia proclaimed she was in fact very pleased with the substance of her life; that must have kept her vibrant.

Maddie asked about her background. The former sultry sex kitten (so labeled by the movie rags of that time) held a diploma in biology from a university in Austria. As a child, she had been influenced by the reports of Albert Schweitzer's humanitarian work in Africa. When she grew up, she wanted to help people like he did. Along the way, she got discovered. Realizing the influence a film career could have on furthering her cause, she had no qualms about playing up the sexpot image—an act completely opposite the conservative and bright girl that she was.

As Maddie listened to Claudia excitedly relate how a charity event she was planning would help build a school for girls in Kenya, the top of her head suddenly started to feel cold...then it lost all feeling. Her entire left side, especially her butt, hurt beyond belief. "Claudia," she whispered, "I hate to interrupt...could you get me one of my pain pills?" She was glad someone was with her. Claudia's face continued to go in and out of focus while the woman checked her pupils. A hard thermometer clicked against her teeth before sliding under her tongue. No way did she want to find herself back in the hospital. Maddie stretched out her arm and grasped the dog's soft mane. Max had jumped to her side at the first hint of a problem. She found peace in his solid demeanor and wasn't as reluctant to fall asleep anymore.

She woke to the sound of a belly laugh, along with some recognizable voices. "Isn't there anywhere left in the world that has escaped *Seinfeld*?" she asked, not quite sure whether she was dreaming the episode.

"Madelaine!" shouted Marcus, giving the name his usual peculiar twist. "Finally!" He turned off the program and helped her sit up. It was dark outside.

"What time is it?"

"Ten thirty," he replied, closely observing her behavior. It made her self-conscious.

"I need to go to the bathroom."

"I don't want an argument. I'm walking you over."

She winced with every step. Ten minutes later, after another pain pill, she could move more freely. Marcus reminded her of the antibiotic she also needed to take.

"I wasn't thinking," said Marcus apologetically. "For the sake of your muscles, I should have made you go to bed instead of lying on the lumpy sofa."

The sky was clear. She peeked out the French doors and saw a small, enclosed patio. "Could we sit outside? If it isn't too late?" He grabbed an afghan on the way.

When he was convinced that she sat comfortably on the (padded) wrought-iron chair, he went inside to make her tea. Fragrant roses filled the night. Maddie looked forward to viewing Marcus's garden in the daylight—if, that is, she would ever see him again.

Max strolled out and headed toward her, wearing his predictable casual air. If he were human, he'd be chewing on a blade of grass and jingling the change in his pocket. He acknowledged her with a short, light rub of his muzzle against her shin, then meandered to a favorite patch of grass, where he twirled around before sitting. His nose caught the scents. She was totally infatuated with him.

Tea for her, wine for him. "That's so unfair!"

"Trust me," he said as he raised his glass, "yours is much tastier than mine."

Her pitiful look won out.

"All right…one tiny drop. Here." And he handed her the cabernet.

She inhaled the aroma, then took a huge swig. Marcus wrestled the glass from her hand, because she refused to give it up. Her cheeks puffed out. If she swallowed, she chanced choking; if she started laughing as he was, it would burst forth and be wasted. Holding her hand tightly over her mouth, she hobbled to the bordering hedges and downed it in a couple gulps. The coughing made her laughing difficult.

"Serves you right," he snickered, adding, "This is the first time I've seen you smile. It's beautiful."

He walked over, took her by the arms, and studied her mouth. She thought for sure she'd get kissed. Instead, he lovingly wrapped her in a hug and rested his cheek against hers. A hand cupped the back of her head. Her lips touched his skin. His back felt powerful. He led her in a relaxing swaying motion—an adagio measured by the faint breeze and their easy breathing.

His hand glided to her opposite shoulder, allowing her head to drop back onto his forearm. She caught the stars twinkling through the ragged, drifting clouds. A clear outline defined the dark edge of the three-quarter moon. Maddie clasped her arms around Marcus's waist and drew him nearer. He kissed her ear and throat ever so softly, sparking a resurgence of emotional longings in her—not just physical. Magic like this had eluded her. It was admittedly significant that Marcus was closer to her age than Robert had been. Sharing a period of history with someone offered more connectedness. Without requiring more details of his life, she sensed being with a man who knew himself. She leaned her head on his shoulder. Could she possibly stay here forever?

"Let's go in, Madelaine," he whispered.

Her trance was immediately interrupted when he stepped away.

"Marcus, if you don't mind…I'd really like to wake up at the hostel." She didn't want to take him up on his earlier offer of spending the night here, or at Claudia's. "I can take my time getting ready after everyone's gone. My belongings are there." She had to convince him more. "I'm much better than earlier. Truly." She could tell he was deliberating as they walked inside. It went against his better judgment, but he got his car keys.

Even though it was after midnight, a couple of lights were on in the hostel, unlike the evening she had arrived.

"I can't begin to thank you enough for your help today."

He said nothing and got out.

It was difficult holding back a moan as she pushed against the low seat while he pulled on her good arm. Marcus asked her to meet him for dinner in a couple of days. She nodded. He gave her hand a quick buss.

She smiled to herself as she closed the door. He had an endearing quality. Her foolish heart fluttered.

Each step was slow and deliberate. Maddie passed a chorus of vomiting in the bathroom that almost caused her to do the same. It was distressful. The overhead light was on in her room. The three roommates appeared to be fine. They couldn't sleep because of the noise—apparently a case of too much alcohol. Seeing her roommates' worried at the sight of her bandages and bruises, Maddie gave them an account of her day: "Fell down…landed at the hospital. Only needed stitches. Gotta sleep…'night." She collapsed on her bed, in Claudia's clothes, grateful to at least not be retching too.

There was no keeping track of the date. Each waking morning was simply regarded as the next day. It was a welcome departure from a life that had revolved around schedules. Ever since Maddie was a teen, there was the marking of fertile periods on the calendar, followed by the countdown to delivery dates. Lucky for her that the rhythm method of birth control worked as well as it did. Then she was committed to the endless chore of raising those babies (and pets), which entailed ongoing doctor and veterinary appointments. Add to that the kids' umpteen sports programs, and their company's finances, which she managed…her stomach turned inside out when she thought about it now. If Ivee, their industrious maid who had turned out to be more of a nanny, hadn't happened along in Mount Sterling when she did, it would have been an impossible life.

While lying on her bed this morning, Maddie decided to reconsider her travel plans. She desired more spontaneity. Janet's route had served its purpose in getting her under way; now she was ready to pursue her own course. She was disappointed that she hadn't stuck out her thumb yet for a ride. Nothing would prevent her from doing it when she left here.

During breakfast, she discovered that she wouldn't have the peaceful hostel all to herself, as she'd hoped. Five sick students from Japan lay in agony in their room, racked with the dry heaves. She took only half a pain pill with a bread roll, then watched TV in the sitting room, relieved that the closed door drowned out the boys' misery. She would play the perfect patient today and rest as instructed.

One of the owners stuck his head in the room. He had heard Maddie had been to the hospital. The lean, tobacco-colored man propped his arms across a high-back chair and asked, in a thick accent, why she was up in the mountains…alone.

She was reluctant to say, but she told him.

"…next thing, boom! I hit the rocks."

He shook his head and commiserated with his equivalent of a tsk: "Nay, nay, nay." Before walking out, he held up his index finger, suggesting he'd be back in a minute. It piqued her curiosity.

In he came again, and sat next to her. She lay stretched out on her right side. He showed her a copy of a magazine article, written in English. "You read. Yes," he said sternly.

"OK," Maddie replied in the same incisive way he had asked—or rather, demanded.

He patted her knee, then left.

The subject was the thousands of fungi species identified in the world, and the importance of amateurs learning to distinguish which were poisonous. It was an eye-opener—not that she didn't already know many were deadly, but because there were considerably more than she realized. At the bottom was a list, which named several organized "morel-gathering" outings in Europe. One was planned for Switzerland in late September. That was something to think about doing.

Her Scandinavian roommates joined her in the afternoon. It had begun to drizzle, so they scrapped plans of going to the Jungfraujoch mountain top region until tomorrow. They asked her if she wanted to go along, since there would be little walking involved. Trains and cable cars would take them to the peak. Maddie was convinced she could do it, if she took a pillow to sit on.

Two young men from Russia who were staying at another hostel came to visit. They had met the Wanderer's Villa women while hiking. It was entertaining to observe how the genders sized each other up. Maddie continued to feel lazy, but wasn't nearly as out of it as yesterday. She remained the spectator, listening to the accounts of each storyteller as he or she tried to outdo the other with tales of bad weather, transportation nightmares, or encounters with crazy people. She loved being here.

The topic eventually got around to movies. By and by, she felt prompted to ask if anyone knew of Marcus Roman. The name galvanized the group—they spoke it like an exclamation. It was hard to tell at first whether that was a good thing, but it became obvious that he was in fact highly regarded. They were completely enamored with him, referring to his films with cultlike reverence. It seemed unusual to her when she considered their ages.

The German actor was discussed with bright-eyed passion for the next hour. Maddie reminded herself that a lot might be untrustworthy gossip. Movie titles popped up so quickly among the roommates; it was as if they were contestants trying to beat the buzzer on a game show. It reminded her of Matt and Janet's trips home from college, when they used to have lively discussions about Truffaut and Fellini, their two favorite foreign film directors. Maddie smiled over her own recent discovery.

The dialogue came to a halt when one of the Russians asked, "And what of his last picture...with Birgit Haas?"

Together they sighed, "Birgit Haas." That said it all...apparently.

"I give in," said Maddie. "Who is Birgit Haas?"

Lisa, the dentist, and the chattiest of her group, declared, "Only *the* best actress in the world." All agreed:..."the best"..."no one comes close"..."no American can touch her." Wow! Maddie's eyebrows kept going higher in accordance with the superlatives.

One of the fellows complained he was getting hungry, then the others said they could also eat. Pizza sounded easy. Maddie offered to buy. She walked upstairs to get her money, passing a crew that was busily scrubbing the vacated infirmary. The disinfectant made her eyes sting and her nose run.

She took pleasure in sitting in her empty timber-framed room for a few minutes. It gave her a chance to organize the events of Marcus's life. The windows revealed the mountain tops poking out from a belt of fog. She sucked air into her nostrils and inhaled as deeply as possible, relieved to smell the exposed wood instead of the permeating ammonia odor that had briefly deprived her senses.

Marcus was born in 1944. He was rumored to be the son of an SS officer who fled with his family to Argentina after the end of the war. No interviewer had ever been successful in procuring the facts from the actor. His mother supposedly returned to northern Germany with him a few years later, having left her husband. Maddie wondered if Marcus had been too young to remember the great journey. To avoid being ostracized, they changed their family name before arriving. Being a lover of books, the mother chose Roman, a German word for a novel.

When the boy wasn't yet ten, his mother died in a ferry accident. She was on her way back from visiting a relative. Marcus continued to stay with her friends, a British soldier's family who had been caring for him while she was gone. The father was part of the occupation forces. Although he wasn't entitled to go to their schools, Marcus did master English because of the living arrangement.

By sixteen, he was capturing the ladies' hearts, as they say. He stood over six feet and had wavy blond hair and the bluest eyes. His haughty manner, inherent to that rebellious age, was magnified by his innate self-confidence. His exiled father (if the story is accurate) would have been proud of his son's symbolic, radiant Aryan features. Not a noteworthy student, the teen possessed a superb talent for mimicry and was forever impersonating teachers and friends. Without effort, he could sing like several popular rock 'n' roll stars.

One day in Marcus's young life, something remarkable occurred. His class had gone to another city for a field trip. While the students were waiting for the train to return home, and the cutup was acting out as usual, some American GIs who happened along took notice of him. Impressed with his uncanny performance of Elvis' "Jailhouse Rock," they asked the assuredly disbelieving teen if he wanted to take his show on the road—that being the officers' clubs at the various U.S. army bases established throughout Germany.

Little was known about the next ten years of his life. Maddie could only guess how exciting the atmosphere must have been. The art scene, in all its forms, which had been denied under Hitler's dictatorship, really began to flourish again during that period, as it did throughout most of postwar Europe. Marcus became an integral part of it all when the famous Italian filmmaker Scotti gave him his first big break.

In her account, Lisa had guessed that the actor was around twenty-seven or eight when he made that western. That movie wasn't like others in the traditional sense. Marcus acted in several of these dreamlike, surrealistic visions that sprang from the imagination of this particular avant-garde director. At least Maddie understood why she wasn't familiar with Marcus's work.

From that point, Marcus's biography was well-documented. He married a woman who was not an actress. They had a son and daughter, neither of whom any of the ladies from Norway or the Russians had ever seen in photos. With increasing fame came drugs, parties, and the expected women (and men, according to the reports). Marcus must have always been sober on the set, though, because he kept churning out one successful film after another. They were produced in various countries. Having a knack for languages and dialects paid off.

In the late seventies, Marcus arrived in New York City with hopes of getting into theater. The film industry, with all it could promise, enticed him instead. The scripts were unmemorable, and the titles produced groans in the group downstairs. Disillusioned, he returned to Germany. The cinema in Berlin was gaining ground. He went there to portray a citizen who had been deformed by a previous generation's nuclear disaster. The character possessed an evangelical zeal that incited his countrymen to retaliate against an elitist government that was consumed with continuing its secret research, no matter the cost to humankind. It won numerous European awards and was up for an Oscar in the best foreign film category. That coup promoted a string of hits wherein Marcus played similar inspirational men, able to turn the tide of hopelessness for some complacent or impotent group or another: a Dutch minister encouraging black rule in South Africa; a British officer fighting for India's independence; the list went on.

Hollywood came knocking again. In deference to his European fans, whom he considered more loyal and appreciative, Marcus chose not to leave. That decision only boosted his already phenomenal popularity.

Several years ago, an Austrian director targeted the actor and asked for his help in developing a national theater troupe. Maddie knew of him; Rainer Hessel was indeed renowned throughout the world—which to her, conceitedly, meant America.

A voice from downstairs called to her. The food was ready for pickup. She returned and gave them the money.

Maddie wasn't finished with her self-serving interrogation. Once they started in on the second pizza, she asked if someone would elaborate on the actress they had last mentioned.

Originally from Belgium, Birgit caught the attention of a traveling British writer who happened to see her in a television production the one day he was passing through the country. She was only twelve years old. He ended up writing a screenplay just for her. The roommates guessed she must be in her mid-forties now.

Listening to the scads of fascinating storylines made Maddie want to run out and rent all of the movies, then sit holed up for a month to watch them. She felt as if she'd been deprived in life of a marvelous confection, and there was no way of ever getting enough of it to make up for the loss.

"So…what was this last picture about…with Birgit and Marcus?" Maddie asked.

One of the fellows and Lisa started talking simultaneously. He held out his hand for her to continue. She was seated on the floor and pushed her way over to Maddie, who had resumed her reclining position on the couch. A sprig of blonde and orange spiky strands jutted out from her hair clip and bounced comically in the air while she described the plot. Maddie found it difficult to follow, catching only phrases here and there. Her imagination ran wild.

She pondered the inconceivable number of people Marcus had met over his lifetime, including the daunting total he'd presumably had sex with. Lisa was looking directly at her, believing she was listening. "Uh-huh," said Maddie, pretending to look interested and nodding sometimes to show she cared about Lisa's effort. No wonder the man sat stymied, unable to begin his writing—with a history like his. And what a roster of players to consider.

"Marcus pretends to be a brainy and unobservant college professor, but he's really a clever detective who takes a room in this boarding house…"

The other Russian chimed in, "Wolfgang Schick. They should have made a series with that character. Sorry, Lisa."

And what happened with his family? Maddie asked herself. She'd look around for pictures the next time she was in his place.

"There's the scariest bathtub scene…he knows she wants to kill him…" There was Lisa's voice again. Maddie felt bad for ignoring her. But her current objective was to obtain her own firsthand information regarding the actor's enigmatic background.

CHAPTER 11

There sat Maddie, sipping her hot chocolate on top of a mountain. Thanks to Lisa's well-padded bicycle shorts (which she wore hidden under her pants), she was able to make the trip with very little pain. It had hurt more climbing into the snug-fitting elastic thing.

What a view! She couldn't fight the envy when she waved to her ambulatory friends outside, jumping and laughing in the snow like little kids. A couple of hearty women joined her at the table. The retired professors were bicycle enthusiasts who were making their way across several valleys. One was from France; the other (her partner) was originally from Holland. They'd been up here often, and wouldn't have bothered visiting today if it weren't for the incredibly clear sky. They had never experienced the summit under these perfect conditions.

During the polite conversation, Maddie acted nonchalantly toward the women's open displays of affection. She tried not to picture what they did with each other...which led her to thinking about Robert. Their involvement had been immoral and sinful, which was exactly her first reaction to these women. Though she had developed many friendships with gay individuals because of her community affiliations, it didn't preclude her from privately denouncing their lifestyle. She remembered what Joel had prepared her for before she drove away from his store—she wanted to keep an open mind; at the moment, it was spinning in circles.

If God were to weigh the nature of the offenses, she asked herself, would the women's situation and hers be comparable? Say that these ladies had remained monogamous throughout their relationship, but a straight person had strayed in her marriage, was it worse being homosexual—no matter if they upheld their commitment to each other? Or was being a cheating heterosexual more reprehensible? Things weren't nearly so cut and dried now that she was personally caught up in the dilemma—up went the defenses, time to start rationalizing. Maddie surprised herself; she concluded that trustworthiness had to win out.

So why didn't she believe there was a spot reserved for her in hell? She had no compulsion to go to confession and unburden herself. All the years of playing by the rules—of spouting off to others with smug self-righteousness—this was where it landed her, acting with the same two-faced behavior she so loathed in others. The lack of remorse she felt was plain crazy.

Although she didn't regret going, Maddie pushed herself too hard on that day trip and paid for it on the weekend. She slept on and off, looked at the various foreign magazines left behind, and made new acquaintances.

The Norwegians had gone to Geneva and were replaced with two nineteen-year-olds from North Carolina and a tiny, wiry seventy-five-year-old Spanish woman. Even though she wasn't completely blind, the elderly Maria traveled with a Seeing Eye dog named Paco, a beautiful, muscular chocolate Labrador retriever.

New faces appeared at breakfast, too.

Maddie thought about home a lot, which bothered her—not too much about friends or family, but about the sense of comfort derived from walking through one's own kitchen and sleeping in one's own bed. This was only the beginning of her fourth week, yet it seemed as if she'd been gone the entire summer.

Claudia called Sunday afternoon to see if Maddie would like to go to Bern, the capital city of Switzerland, the next day. Half an hour later, Marcus phoned, wanting to spend tomorrow together, too. She declined both. She was going to treat herself to a day at the pool, alone. The owner of the hostel had offered to drive her to a spa in the morning, where she would attempt to swim, despite still suffering from limited movement. He was also going to find some waterproof bandages for her two wounds. The anticipation made her restless, and she hardly slept that night.

It was a new day. Maddie looked at the water, into her rippling features. Her feet dangled weightless below the surface, then down she slowly sank, past her fluid reflection. Nothing was more calming. She floated up on her back, keeping her eyes closed. This tranquil state inspired romantic fantasies. There was no particular man, no specific setting; she was simply in love with the sensation. Hollow lapping sounds got amplified in her ears. She pictured minuscule curious sea creatures skirting around her body, investigating.

She had some time before she was supposed to join her roommates in the kitchen downstairs. She curled up comfortably on her bed, then hit the automatic dial button for home on her cell phone. It would be around noon or one o'clock there. She had no idea what she was going to say to Ed.

"Hi, Mom," answered someone else's excited voice.

It threw her for a moment. "Carol?"

"Yes! I saw it was your number."

Maddie breathed a sigh of relief. A conversation with her daughter would be brief and to the point. She began, "I know I've been irresponsible for not checking in sooner…or for that matter, taking off like I did." Carol didn't interrupt. "Is Dad there?"

"Red's getting his cataracts removed today. I was going to help get him inside when they come back home."

Oh, boy, did she feel guilty. Everyone could take care of themselves except Red. And she had put his medical needs out of her mind completely. Amazingly, Ed had come through for him. "You mean…Red lost the weight he needed to?"

"Yeah, he looks great. So does Dad. They've been walking buddies."

Maddie sat in disbelief.

"You know, Mom…Dad gave Tom and me the money he said you two had put aside…in case I ever needed it. Is that true? Was that really mine?" Carol was never going to get over this windfall.

Maddie thought a split second. "Yes, of course, Carol." There was silence. The mother remembered her misgivings about Carol and her family's mood during the picnic. Look at how father and daughter worked things out. It was pointless to mention the concern she had felt for them that day. "How's Rima? She must be getting antsy about starting college."

"She is. She wanted to go away for a bit. I don't know if you remember the one tutor who helped me with calculus? Anyway, we've stayed in touch over the years. She's on the faculty in Berlin. Rima's always wanted to take her up on her offer of visiting. Maybe she'll go for a couple of weeks in the beginning of August. Are you having an interesting time?"

"Yes. Very."

"Dad and Tom are going salmon fishing at the end of summer. Can you believe it?"

No, she couldn't. "Really," said Maddie, giving her head a slight shake.

"Rima misses you terribly. I can't believe you haven't phoned or e-mailed her."

She could use Claudia's computer. "Tell her I'll send her a long message in the next few days, OK?"

Maddie knew Carol had what she needed: she learned her mother was fine; they had relayed the basic news...anything more was unnecessary. That was Carol's cut-to-the-chase mentality, resulting from years of bureaucratic dealings that her job in social services entailed. However, Mom wasn't willing to hang up yet. Maddie grew more sentimental as she listened to the sound of her daughter's voice.

"Carol...has Dad said anything about my leaving?"

"Hmm. Not at first. I'm sure, initially, he was hurt...maybe embarrassed. Wouldn't you be if he had done that?" There was no accusatory tone, and she didn't expect an answer. "I think he's only now beginning to try to figure out what's going on."

"Do you know?" asked her mom.

"I think so."

Maddie smiled. In all likelihood, Carol knew better than Maddie did herself. This kid had weeded out the true nature of things since she could talk—something the mother realized only in hindsight. Hindsight was also responsible for allowing Maddie to finally see that she had given far too much credence to trivial matters over the course of her life. The damaging influences from the era in which she grew up couldn't be overlooked. Everyone wanted to emulate the posed, smiling TV and magazine images of what a family should look like, be like. It seemed silly now—it should have then. Her religion couldn't be excused either—the way it put the fear of damnation into one as early as childhood. Not only could God observe her every move, he was also able to witness her every thought...every teensy-weensy fleeting one. Then there were Maddie's own mother's insecurities, which the fearful woman had projected onto her daughter. Maddie was made to think that danger lurked behind every corner, because that, sadly, was her mom's take on the world. It became more pronounced after Maddie's dad fell in love with someone else in England during the war—after she and her mother had traveled to the States to be safe. Feeling safe was a condition that would elude his ex-wife up until her death.

"Please tell your father...please tell him that I'm sorry." And Maddie truly was. Sorry for circumstances that summon one person to act, leaving another with no choice but to react.

Carol didn't recognize this apologetic tone. While she listened to her mother describe Paris, she contemplated telling her about the way in which her dad was opening up. She sometimes accompanied him on his walks with Red, and was learning about a whole other side to him—that part which was indelibly affected by his stint in Korea.

Ed and two other infantrymen should have died with their unit when they were attacked by the Chinese; they would have, were it not for the fact they'd been sent on foot to obtain help and deliver the message that their men were sitting ducks. The unit had outdated and nonworking munitions, and a faulty radio. After the atrocity, the army simply told him to put it out of his mind when he returned home, like others had…like you were supposed to do.

As often happens, the more children and life experiences Ed enjoyed, the more he thought about his fallen comrades and what they were missing. He gradually plunged into a depression that escaped his understanding. Vietnam deepened the gloom. Although he wanted to side with the antiwar movement, he felt as if he would have been betraying the honor of those lost buddies. Vietnam wasn't a garage topic he might bring up with his best friend. Neil had been gung ho about sending the troops overseas.

Matt and Gary were so antagonistic toward the military during that period; Ed could never carry on a meaningful dialogue with them. And the alienation firmly established between Carol's dad and mom obviously left everything undiscussed.

Carol wanted to tell her mother how happy she was that Tom could talk to her father about it. Although her husband had been a conscientious objector, his method of exercising his beliefs was to live quietly by example instead of spouting off with heated rhetoric. The heavily laden veteran found solace in his son-in-law's contemplative nature and thoughtful words.

Maddie had finished her summary. "Carol," she said, "I'm sorry to you, too, honey." She had never before used a term of endearment. The mother could see her little Carol now, in all her glory, perched high in her tree. She felt bad for having insisted that this noncompliant, enlightened child should have unquestioningly followed her rules. If it weren't for Carol's own formidable will, the girl's evolution would have been permanently stunted. Maddie's eyes were wet. "I'm proud that you've lived by your convictions. You're the most honest person I've ever known. I just want you to know that." It sounded ominous, as if she were expecting something terrible to happen. "Carol?"

"I'm here." After a pause, she said, "Thanks, Mom. That means a lot." Carol decided that the recent revelations about her dad should come from him to his wife.

Maddie didn't know how to end this. "I guess I'll go now." Her selfishness was beginning to intrude on her conscience. "I'm glad you were home."

"Me, too. Be safe." And she hung up.

The tears started down her cheeks. Soon Maddie was really weeping. It felt good to miss home. It hurt, but it meant she cared. She was not suited to playing the gypsy. Oddly, today's connection made it possible for her to continue her journey. She simply needed to hear a familiar voice. What might she have done if no one had answered?

Paco, the dog, sensed her sadness and hopped on the bed. She had offered to watch him, because Maria wanted the freedom to join some new friends, one of whom had a car. He sniffed her face and swiped her salty cheek with a big lick. She pretended to be put off, but the dog knew better. He lay on his side and snuggled under her comfy bosom.

At dinner, Maddie ate quickly and spoke little, anxiously looking forward to getting back to bed and resuming her daydreams with Paco beside her. When she did return, her thoughts stayed on the room; it was a sight to behold. The current occupants' belongings lay all over, including Maria's. At least Maria had the excuse of not being able to see where her stuff landed. Paco had his job cut out for him when the time came and he'd have to sort her items from the others'. Their lack of consideration really bugged her. She had to fight an impulse to leave and check into the nearest hotel.

It was a lovely, rare, cloudless evening. The windows were wide open. Her thoughts thankfully drifted to ones of Big Red. In her mind's eye, she watched Ed's caring hands (he had beautiful, long slender fingers) stroke their aged dog, who would be confused this night from the lingering effects of his anesthetic. A feeling of overwhelming tenderness flooded her heart for her husband. Her breathing slowed, matching that of Paco's…and Red's. And then she enjoyed a restful sleep.

Maddie had already been sitting at Claudia's computer for a couple of hours when Marcus's booming voice disrupted the peace. He rambled on about something in German…to Claudia, who wasn't home. He must have asked a question, because when there was no answer, he yelled again, "Claudia?"

Poking his head around the kitchen doorframe, he exclaimed, surprised, "Madelaine!" always still pronouncing it in his unique way. "Why didn't you answer?"

"I don't know what you were saying."

He shook his head in exasperation and walked over to peck her on the cheek. He gently held her chin up and lingered a moment to admire her. She was no longer disagreeable to the touch of his fleshy hand upon her as she had been during that first hand-holding handshake. He stroked her lower lip softly with his thumb. Just as in his garden that evening, the expected kiss was not forthcoming. Glancing at the screen, he asked if she was finally letting the folks back home know she was alive.

"I did that earlier. Now I'm helping Claudia raise money for the school in Kenya. I know some people back home who, I'm certain, would like to donate to this project."

He pulled up a chair beside her swiveling one and reviewed the list of names. "That's admirable of them."

"Well...yes. But they've been promised something in return," she said, hesitatingly.

He leaned over her armrest. The fragrance of her sidetracked him. He sucked in the scent and held his breath a few seconds before allowing it to trickle back into her ear. Immediately she got goose bumps. He stayed within his breath's distance from her, playing with the wisps of hair around her neckline. The heat from his body was unhinging her.

In a sobering tone, she told him that there were a few who wanted to attend the charity event being held at Lake Como in person. Their generosity would equal their gratitude, if they could have a more personal one-on-one with the celebrities—maybe have lunch with them.

"You can't mean me, right?"

She clucked her tongue over the remark. "Only if you're agreeable to the idea."

Marcus balanced his right foot on the chair and rested an elbow on his knee. "Hmm." He gave his head a little scratch. The other hand moved from her curls to the side of her shoulder. She was completely aware of his thumb rubbing against her skin as they spoke.

"Some really want to meet me, eh?"

"Well, there are four at the moment. I planned on checking with you first before finalizing anything. I wouldn't want to get their hopes up for nothing."

He took boyish delight in these well-meaning strangers' offers. "Who are they?"

"Let's see. There's Trudy, who is Austrian. She's involved with all of the theater events and has seen many of the Hessler productions." Maddie pointed to the screen, to the amount Trudy was willing to pay.

"Are you serious?" he asked. "That's a lot."

"The comma's got to be in the wrong place," said Maddie.

"You're mean, Madelaine."

"Look here." She read the e-mail. "This is what Dr. Morgan Hernandez is willing to donate!" They looked at each other in astonishment.

Marcus was excited. "So much! That must mean sex."

"Noooo." She gave him a quick, teasing bop to the forehead with her pencil. "Good grief."

He laughed. "If I paid that, I'd expect it. Hell, I'd expect it for fifty bucks." Then he stated emphatically, "A lot of people think I go both ways, but I won't meet a guy if he's going to put the moves on me."

"What!"

"This doctor. Why would he offer so much?"

She looked back at the name; it did sound masculine. "Dr. Hernandez is a single female cardiologist. She earns lots and is a workaholic. Obviously, she takes the time to see movies."

"Imagine that! Is she pretty?"

"Does it make a difference? It's for charity…not an official date, you know?"

"A dog, huh?"

"Name me one ugly dog."

"C'mon, Madelaine. Pretty or not?"

She thought back to when she last saw Morgan; it was recently, on a tennis court. "She's probably in her early forties…has noticeable dimples. Is a little chunky—only a little. I would consider her voluptuous if I were a man. Dignified. Dark-haired. Overall, a very handsome woman."

He stared straight at her. "That's no help."

"And if she were homely? Which she is not."

He groaned. "Will honesty win out here?"

"Marcus, Marcus," she sighed. "Here you go…this girl states that she's a twenty-year-old college student. Bet you don't care what she looks like."

"Now that's not true!" He squeezed her tight. "I prefer them more mature…at least twenty-six, or twenty-seven."

"I'm beginning to think this is a terrible idea," she muttered, in jest. "How on earth does such a young thing from the States know who you are, anyway?"

He gave a little shrug. "The wonder of cable, I guess."

Maddie was relieved when Claudia returned. A diversion was imperative. The sexual tension she felt was becoming intolerable. She wanted to jump out of her skin.

"You ready to go, Maddie?" she asked as she entered the study, having quickly acknowledged Marcus with a noisy kiss on the top of his unruly mop.

"Hours ago," she replied.

"Ah, yes," said Marcus, "Bern today. Can't I go, too?"

Claudia patted his cheek. "Sorry. Girls only."

He stood and shook the stiffness out of his leg. "Being like a brother is no different than a sister. Let me go along, Claudia. Please," he pleaded. Then he looked to Maddie for backup. "Maddie?" He took note of Claudia's more familiar reference to her earlier, and felt entitled to do the same.

Claudia positioned herself squarely in front of him and, with her hands on her hips, delivered a scolding. "Marcus Roman, you will go to your room immediately and begin writing. Today! This hour! Enough of your..." She got stuck.

"Dillydallying," proposed Maddie. The German word suddenly popped into Claudia's head, which probably meant the same here...maybe worse.

Maddie shut down the computer. Before rounding the corner as they headed out, Claudia shot another scornful look at the procrastinator. "*Du Bummler!*"

"Ow!" he yelped. His mouth broadened into that sly grin of his. He followed them to the front door. "Dillee-dalleeing. I like that...I am a dillee-dallee-er."

CHAPTER 12

The women talked nonstop and laughed so much they got headaches. Claudia zipped around the numerous tight curves, loving the control she exercised over her midnight-blue Porsche. They stopped for coffee at a pleasant roadside inn and vowed five minutes of silence to relax their jaws.

The regal pair possessed an ease of manner derived from the kind of self-acceptance that developed over time. Their decision to wear something a bit more elegant that day set them apart as well. Claudia's emerald formfitting dress suited her shapely figure. Maddie wore a flowing, low-cut, maroon tunic top over khaki pants. Her amethyst and diamond necklace (which Claudia lent her) rested between the soft mounds at the start of her cleavage—the first point of interest to anyone glancing at her.

At last they calmed down, and Maddie gave her curious friend some information about herself. As an aside, Claudia mentioned that Marcus couldn't get over her age, quickly regretting the comment when Maddie asked how he knew. Had he glanced at Maddie's chart at the hospital? Not that she kept her age a secret.

Claudia acted uneasy. She crossed her legs one way, then the other, constantly bumping their small outdoor table. "Please don't hold this against him." She studied the rural scene. The bright sun directly overhead eliminated shadows and played with the perspective. White, immovable blocks of cows appeared suspended against the flat, green field, like in a folk art rendering.

Picking her words carefully, Claudia told her that Marcus had guessed Maddie was silly from the pills when she told him how long she'd been married. That evening, he snooped inside her passport, which she had left on the kitchen table, to see her birth date. Maddie saw nothing wrong with that. She'd probably have done the same.

Claudia explained that while Maddie was asleep on the sofa, he had inspected her hairline and features in order to find seams from cosmetic surgery. Claudia emphasized how much she had wholeheartedly disapproved of his impropriety. Hopefully, the action wouldn't be interpreted as a personal violation. Claudia could just as easily not have revealed this, but it was on her conscience now.

Knowing Marcus to the extent that she did, Maddie could see him shushing Claudia while he tried to find one blemish that might be construed as a remnant suture. "What was the verdict?" she asked.

Claudia's eyes smiled, even if she felt reluctant to. "He was going to wait and find a good time to ask the name of the surgeon."

Maddie chuckled. "I guess that's flattering, right?"

Embarrassed, Claudia played with her fork and cake crumbs. She felt like an accomplice and wanted to kick herself for bringing it up. Then again, it would have gone on bugging her if she hadn't.

"No harm done, Claudia."

They reached Bern. In a rather twisted progression of linking thoughts, the conversation evolved from the town's historically famous citizen, William Tell, shooting the apple from his son's head, to a discussion about fathers in general. That in turn led to Claudia describing her marvelous relationship with her dad, and concluded with Maddie's account of her disassociation from hers at a young age.

The women walked arm in arm in the customary fashion, exploring the many shops while carrying on about the men in their lives. Claudia couldn't accept that this daughter hadn't seen her father in more than fifty years. How was such a thing possible? And he still lived! More improbable was the fact that they continued to send each other an annual Christmas card, signing only their names. Messages had long ceased to be included.

"That's insane, Maddie! Absolutely insane!" Claudia was oblivious to the people she startled around her.

It was funny what one got used to doing. Maddie never gave the ritual a second thought. The corner of her mouth involuntarily jerked to the side, implying that it didn't matter after such a long time. She didn't realize that her well-intentioned companion remained inanely preoccupied with this topic for a good half hour. When they found a little fountain tucked away in a cobblestone alley and were enjoying its cooling spray, Claudia faced Maddie and took her by both arms.

"Maddie. You must promise me that you'll go see your father before you return home."

She knew Claudia's heart was in the right place, but Maddie simply couldn't understand her persistence. "I don't get why it bothers you this much…he's a total stranger at this point. All right, I admit, it is dumb that we've continued to still send cards. I'm sure he doesn't even acknowledge them. Considering his age, a caretaker likely signs them out of courtesy to me. He's got to be…ninety-two or three."

That didn't produce the reaction Maddie had hoped for. Claudia didn't let up. "You're in no hurry to get back home…there's nothing to lose by going. He's your father. Your father! You are still someone's little girl. Think of it!"

"It's not possible. Really. It isn't."

Claudia released her and started pacing. One might deduce from her hopeless expression that she had just learned of a terminal illness. Maddie's indifference affected her as profoundly. It was irrational. "What harm is there in going?" Claudia implored.

"None. It's just pointless. He wouldn't recognize me. It isn't like we'll ever plan on visiting each other in the future. Don't worry yourself so much over it. God, Claudia."

The tortured pacing stopped, and the eyes widened. Then, as if gripped by an epiphany, Claudia announced, "This is why we have met." The melodrama was comical.

"Oh, please." Maddie's hand pounded her forehead to show her growing impatience over Claudia's single-mindedness. Maddie truly didn't want to hurt the woman's feelings, but Claudia was clearly going overboard. The day had been such a joy until now. The subject was dropped. It put a definite rift between them. They walked back to the town square in silence, maintaining their distance. Maddie couldn't stand it any longer, nor could Claudia—but neither could figure out how to get out of this.

They sat in the park and watched the people. While staring straight ahead, Claudia began to talk. "Marcus cares for you a great deal."

That was unexpected. "He told you that?"

Claudia crossed her ankles and pushed her skirt between her knees. Without turning toward Maddie, she said, "He doesn't have to." She paused to apply lipstick. "I've known him since I was in my early twenties. We've been friends for maybe twelve of those years." She stole a glance to the side. The underlying tension was still there, but they were mature enough to try and get beyond it.

Maddie couldn't refrain from asking, "Have you ever been involved with him?"

"No," Claudia answered, quickly adding, "and I've never wanted that."

Their wills melted, and they simultaneously took one another's hand. "I think I'm the only woman who can claim that," Claudia said, with a short laugh.

On that light note, it was comfortable again between them. "Marcus has grown over the last years…better late than never, right?"

Maddie wondered in what ways.

"When I first met him," said Claudia, "he was just starting to get bigheaded from the fame. On second thought, he was already bigheaded. Fame made it that much worse. I steered clear of him after our first and only picture together. He began to drink heavily…and use drugs. Although I've never talked about it with him, his family had to have gotten ignored. There was nothing to admire. I couldn't enjoy watching his films anymore…which was a shame, because he is definitely talented."

Claudia walked over to a vendor and bought a couple of ice-cream cones. When she sat back down, Maddie asked how the two had met.

In between licks, Claudia began with a brief description of events that led up to the film she and Marcus made. She was already well-known in Europe by the time she was twenty-two. Next stop, Hollywood, where she appeared in films with some of the biggest stars. She admitted that the casting couch was very much a reality, and she worried that her career was going to stall out, because she absolutely refused to go that route. Maddie could tell she had that way about her. Claudia said it didn't matter if men said things behind her back about how well-stacked she was (the standard term back then), or if they were devising ways of getting her in the sack, as long as they behaved like gentlemen in her presence. And, for the most part, they did.

After three years, she returned to Europe to star in an Italian cowboy picture with an actor who was beginning to get a lot of press—Marcus Roman. Even though the script was a strange allegory that made no sense to her, she looked forward to dressing up like a saloon-hall gal in a corset and petticoats. By then, Westerns were passé in America. Unfortunately, she regretted every day on the set. For some reason, the film crew delighted in making her the butt of their daily jokes. They behaved like stupid teenage boys, though most were almost thirty—and some older than that. It was the first time she called home and cried to her father. Claudia's hands waved through the air as she expressed her humiliation and despair. Her father was ready to leave Austria, along with her two brothers, and put these despicable "jerks" (she cleared her throat to insinuate a choicer word had been used) in their places. She resolved there and then to fight her own battles, but it was good to know she had backup waiting in the wings.

That very week, while shooting a scene, Marcus was fooling around and grabbed her breasts, then made some insulting remarks into the camera. Before anyone could see it coming (including herself), she slapped her hands together into one mighty fist and punched him across the face like a batter cracking the ball into the stands.

Claudia's intense, dark eyes narrowed as she recalled her outrage. "Maddie…I was so mad! Like a raving lunatic! Someone came running to help him, and there was screaming. Just my luck"—her eyes twinkled—"we were shooting in a telegraph office, and I spotted a sharp letter opener on the table. Marcus was backed into a corner, and I jumped on him. I threatened to cut him if anybody tried to come near, or even spoke." Maddie wasn't sure whom to sympathize with. "The director didn't take me seriously; he said my name…so sweetly, Maddie…like a grandparent bribing a naughty child with candy. I pushed the blade in Marcus's throat. He barely flinched." Claudia placed her hand on Maddie's forearm and leaned into her. "Then…Marcus tilted his head up and gave me such a look…I don't know…so cunning, as if he'd been waiting to see how much I could take before I'd break."

Maddie hung on her every word and could easily see Marcus's face, even though she didn't want to believe he was capable of such cruelty.

"A little blood trickled down his chest. I held the handle of the blade with both my hands and spoke quietly in his ear so the microphones couldn't pick it up." She demonstrated how close they were. Maddie felt her breath. "I asked him what his wife, or his little boy and girl, would think of his disrespectful behavior toward me. I hadn't met them yet, but I could only hope he was human enough that they mattered to him on some level. I said I hoped he thought highly of his mother. How would she feel if she learned she had raised a son who mistreated women?"

"That's a good one," said Maddie.

"Then I asked him what he would tell his daughter to do, if one day she met a boor like him. And would she fight the bastard he caught joking about his wife?"

"What did he say to that?" she asked, on the edge of her seat.

"The police came. They were trying to get me to come to my senses—as if I had started this. It hit me then, that I was going to be arrested. Strange...but I can really remember Marcus's lashes whenever he blinked. I leaned back in order to see him better. His expression had changed, and his body relaxed under mine." Maddie couldn't wait to hear whether Claudia ended up going to jail.

"I pulled out the blade...and the police grabbed me while a medical team took over. Marcus pleaded with them to let me go...he wasn't going to press any charges. I couldn't believe it."

Maddie stared, riveted.

Claudia sighed and sat up straight. "I went home, sat awake all night drinking one glass of wine after another. I didn't know what I felt. I wanted to phone the hospital to see if he was all right, but at the same time, I didn't care. Several days later, the director came to my apartment. He apologized for the lack of professionalism among the men, and then he asked if I'd show up on the set in a week."

"How fortunate for you," said Maddie.

"That's not how I viewed it." Claudia got up, signaling for them to start heading back to the car. "How were Marcus and I supposed to face each other when we resumed shooting? I had never backed out of a contract, but I sure wanted to then. When it was time for our first rehearsal, we took our positions on a staircase. We stood about a meter apart. My chest felt as if an elephant were on it. I thought I might faint dead away. Marcus spoke my name, then waited for me to look at him. God, Maddie...it infuriated me that this obnoxious brute could be so beautiful. I tried to find the scar, but it was hidden under his shirt collar. Next he said he was sorry, that everyone on the set was as well. They felt ashamed and wanted more than anything to put this incident behind us. His eyes searched mine. I imagined that perhaps he wanted vindication. I absolutely refused to give it. Somehow, we got through the next several weeks, although we never spoke outside of our film dialogue. The attitude during that period was strictly businesslike...which was fine with me. I was grateful to be taken seriously."

They squeezed their packages into the small trunk. The convertible top stayed up so they could use the air conditioner. This heat was new. As Claudia was pulling out of the space, Maddie asked about the film's success.

"It was really popular; after all, it had Marcus in it. Get this, Maddie: during the premier, I sat with my mouth wide open when I saw that the knife scene was left in."

"Oh, no..." Maddie laughed.

"Yes! It was distributed as an underground movie in the States...remember those?" *No, not really*, thought Maddie. "After that, I decided to work only on the stage. I found a wonderful family of actors and playwrights in Hamburg. They would tell me whenever Marcus was in the audience, but I never invited him backstage. We'd see each other from time to time at parties, but I ignored him there too. And neither of us ever discussed that scene in interviews. People could speculate all they wanted."

Now that she was tired, Claudia took into account her delayed reflexes and didn't wind around the maze of curves as quickly as before. A German singer with a pleasing, effortless voice played in the background while Claudia told of her marriage to a Swiss fashion photographer. He had won her heart when he made her causes his own. Together they documented the pitiful conditions of some of Africa's starving populations in order to raise awareness, often facing hostile government troops in the process. On one particularly daring attempt to leave a remote dirt airstrip, her husband was shot. He was a paraplegic for a decade, enduring numerous health problems. A couple of years ago, he died abruptly. Claudia spoke with no emotion. Maddie could relate to having exhausted them.

Ever since she and her husband first began raising money, Claudia told Maddie, she could always expect a check from Marcus twice a year, on her birthday in August and at Christmas. She responded to his generosity with a curt, obligatory thank-you note. Then, Claudia said, something totally unexpected happened when she was in a television studio one day. Marcus caught sight of her chatting with a group of people and came over to them. He excused himself for interrupting. Next he asked her point-blank if she would be his friend.

"Just like that, Maddie. He said, 'I could use a good friend.' He looked worn out...maybe sad. So much time had gone by. I found myself nodding yes. It seemed like a big leap of faith for him to ask this, and in front of all these people. I automatically put my arms around his neck, and he just hung on me. I don't know how else to describe it. It was so intimate...and made everyone uncomfortable. They left us alone." Maddie loved watching her face. "We stood there the longest time."

The CD switched to the reposeful guitar of Villa-Lobos. The music was a perfect accompaniment to the final rays of the setting sun. They watched without speaking. In less than ten minutes, it was dark.

Claudia resumed. "I gave Marcus my phone number. He'd call regularly to discuss work...things like character motivation, or ways he wanted to change his appearance for a role...nothing ever philosophical. He said he enjoyed hearing my voice and knowing I was there. He would always end the conversation by asking about Carlos." Carlos had been Claudia's husband's name. She glanced at Maddie. "I still have no idea what came over him. I figured if he wanted me to know, he'd have told me." She slowed down, having spotted a big shadow ahead on the road. It was a dead deer. She continued, still grimacing from the sight, "We ended up doing a comedy together at Hessler's new playhouse. God, we had fun! It was the turning point in our friendship."

Both took turns yawning and sighed when they started up again. Maddie asked if Claudia had ever met Marcus's wife or children.

"Not Marta, his wife...but his son and daughter, several times. They are clones of him. It's downright spooky. Marcus was legally married, but there was no marriage to speak of. That's a whole other story." Her remark caused her to think about some problems Maddie had touched upon when discussing her marriage to Ed.

They pulled up to the hostel. Maddie almost forgot, standing there with her packages—she wanted the necklace removed. Before walking inside, she looked at Claudia. "You're certain Marcus has a thing for me?"

"Without a doubt." Claudia flashed an encouraging smile before climbing back in her car.

This night when Maddie sank in her pillow, she was restless. What an informative day. There was no end to replaying it. She looked forward to spending the next day with Marcus, especially knowing what she did now. They were going sightseeing in town. She checked the glowing numbers on her wristwatch often: 11:00, 12:00, 1:00...when she next looked, it was 7:00.

The place cleared out early. It was going to be a gorgeous day, and everyone had hurried to take advantage of it. Maddie herself was anxious to leave. She grabbed her last clean shirt, a black one that would go well with the block-printed skirt. *Better make time to do laundry,* she thought—maybe that evening.

Marcus was already waiting for her outside at eight thirty. He didn't bother to restrain Max, who was rambunctious after their sprint down the path. The hostel owner had stepped out to greet him, and they discussed what she assumed was the weather.

Marcus waited his turn; Max got first dibs on kissing her cheek. Marcus dabbed it off with his hanky before planting his own less-sloppy one. Casually slipping his hand over hers, he directed her toward the river that ran through Interlaken.

"I could not wait for my day with you," he stated joyfully. It made her feel important. He swung her arm in a carefree, childlike manner. She loved the soapy-clean smell of him; he looked fresh in his mint-green, safari-style shirt. The sleeves were rolled and buttoned at the elbows. His forearms were strong. At some point, she'd have to touch his silky hair. Why put it off? She stopped, causing him to bob back a step. He looked at her with equal interest while she studied his face. A few deep creases ran across his broad forehead, and there were many lines at the corners of his clear blue eyes. She pictured those eyes looking at Claudia, needful for a friend.

"What is it?" Marcus asked.

She wasn't finished. His nose had a bit of a high bridge, and was a bit long. By the time her scrutinizing gaze reached his lips, they were spread wide. Individually, his features had quirks, but the sum of them, along with his impressive stature, drove home an image of daunting masculinity. If it weren't for one of the most engaging smiles she'd ever seen, she'd find him too imposing to approach.

"Marcus," she began, matter-of-fact, "I must run my fingers through your hair. It's always in the back of my mind when I see you."

Having expected something direr in nature, his eyes lit up over the simple request. He crossed his arms and waited. "Be my guest."

He wasn't sure what to make of the earnestness in her hazel eyes. Maddie laid her open hands gently on the sides of his head. Using her thumbs, she began to stroke the soft hair by his temples. Her fingers ran through the layered strands in a deliberative move. When she reached the ends, she began again, drawing out the waves.

"Mmmm...you're putting me in a trance." He exhaled another visceral moan. She massaged behind his ears. His head swayed with the same circular motion. He latched onto her waist. She couldn't resist kissing his throat.

They went and sat on a bench for a spell, leaving space between them. She needed to sober up as much as he did.

"Have you finally written anything?" she asked.

Marcus stretched back and ran his own fingers through his hair before clasping his hands together behind his neck. His eyes closed. He wanted to savor the sensations a while longer. "Ahhh...why did you have to bring that up?" Following a big sigh, he admitted, "Nope." Then added, "There's simply too much I want to say." He sat straight and folded his hands on his lap. "After all these years…I've finally got a relationship with my kids. I'm concerned about hurting them."

Maddie was moved by the disclosure. "They're adults now. Surely they'd understand."

He shrugged his shoulders. "I don't know, Maddie." He sounded resigned to putting off the venture.

Just then, Max got an earful from an angry swan he had annoyed one too many times. He shot up into the air, then darted over to the safety of the humans. Marcus held him to his chest. "There, there, my friend. He showed you who's boss, eh? I won't tell anyone."

Maddie asked innocently, "Why didn't you divorce Marta?" He regarded her with suspicion. She thought it OK to inquire since he had brought up the subject of his children. She didn't know that he was trying to ascertain exactly how much she had found out about him. "What?" she asked, perturbed.

"Didn't you and Claudia talk about me?"

What ego! she thought. "To some degree." She couldn't figure out what specifically was eating at him. "We spoke mostly about our own families. She did tell me about the circumstances of her first encounter with you…during the filming of a movie. Is that a problem?"

He grumbled no.

"She merely mentioned that she had met your son and daughter, but never your wife, and that your children resemble you." She was relieved to see a smile.

"Yes, I'm grateful for that," he said. "We all take after my mother's family."

"Why…is there something terribly wrong with your father's side?" It was intended as a harmless ribbing.

Again he looked at her with mistrust. She now presumed that the Nazi story wasn't fabricated. If Claudia hadn't gone off on that tangent about her dad and upset her so, Maddie might have remembered to ask the truth behind this tale. "Are certain things taboo to talk about?"

"I'm sorry." He took her hand. "It's just that I used to trust people too easily. Or maybe I talked too damned much when I was drunk. Stuff from what I believed were private conversations ended up in those stupid tabloids. I realized everybody could be bought…for the right price."

"No wonder Claudia is special to you."

His look softened.

She presented him with a scenario: "Do you think I purposely fell down the hill, because I knew you were in the area and expected you to come across me? That I've lied about not knowing your name? All to get the scoop?"

"No," he admitted, "...but now that you suggest it..."

Hallelujah! Back in his good graces.

"To answer your question: Marta and I didn't see the point of getting a divorce. We would deal with it if one of us ever wanted to marry someone else."

Maddie soaked up the scenery as they continued their walk. Max stayed close beside them, in case the menacing swan trailed him.

A Laundromat proved interesting. Maddie watched through the window as a long, cylindrical revolving drum pressed the duvet covers flat. How practical. Next their noses led them to the corner bakery with its freshly turned out breads and pastries. The strudel couldn't be passed up.

Senior townsfolk, considerably older than she, impressed her. Many still ran their errands on bicycles. Others walked hurriedly through the streets with sure-footedness. They were distinctly different from the large number of car-dependent septuagenarians in the States, who succumbed to a creeping vulnerability.

They came upon a flower shop. Expensive irises were abundant today. They were the theme of a nearby international convention. Whether in Brazil or Japan, incredible smells awaited the individuals in this line of work every day. *Bakers and florists have it made*, thought Maddie.

Often, when she awoke in her bed at home—her indelible spot on the earth—she visualized in what manner other inhabitants around the globe were preparing for their day. Barefoot moms in its poorest corners, balancing empty jugs on their heads, had already journeyed for hours while she slept in order to collect precious water from distant wells. She would watch as they stepped across her wide-screen ceiling, bored by the miles of same old scenery, and weary. Regardless of whether the restaurants were in Seattle or Paris, coffee was brewed by someone still sleepy and wishing for the later shift; at scads of resorts, lifeguards punched holes in the dawn's damp sand for the beach umbrellas; in many harbors, in many lands, boat captains readied fishing lines, already picturing their day's anticipated catch...This musing could keep her occupied for hours, if she let it. But, like all the rest, she'd get up and take her place among the multitude going about the unnoticed busyness of the everyday world.

As they strolled, Maddie loved having a head full of thoughts one moment and nothing but a primal, sensual response to the colors and smells the next. She enjoyed saying hello to everybody who passed, even when an occasional dour-looking sort acted as if she were intruding on his or her day. She observed that the citizens, by and large, were accustomed to seeing Marcus. One would not have guessed his celebrity from their reactions. It was amusing when the eyes bugged out of the sockets of five jabbering young backpackers who stopped mid-sentence at the sight of him.

"Are we anywhere near that restaurant on the cliff?" asked Maddie.

Marcus pointed to an elevation to their right. "It's probably a good forty-minute hike...uphill, mind you. We have to backtrack to reach a closer path."

"The one I took the other day?"

"No, there's a more direct one."

She thought it over. Off they went. The effort was worth it. Mountains met clouds, and the town in the valley was scaled to the size of a model railroad layout.

While Marcus went to the restroom, Maddie took a seat by the window and reflected on some of the subjects they had touched on as they plodded their way up the narrow road. She had mentioned the actress, Birgit Haas. He said that he respected her a great deal. That's all she could get out of him, which irked her. He had at least opened up about other aspects of his past...like when his daughter Renata (then in her early thirties) visited him a couple of years ago.

Marcus had only seen her a few times since she was around ten, which was when he and his wife separated. He never gave the matter much thought, assuming he had caused his family enough problems, and they must have been glad to be rid of him. During their awkward attempt at conversation, he had the distinct feeling that she was scoping out his apartment. He told her that he wouldn't mind giving her money, if she needed it. She railed into him like no one since Claudia. Fortunately, there was no knife—he smiled sheepishly, referring to that. His daughter claimed she was strictly doing her mom a favor; it was important to Marta that the child should at least have a civil relationship with her father. That didn't sound like Marta to him, but he wasn't about to voice his doubt, not with Renata in that state.

They parted on a bad note. The meeting continued to trouble him, and he decided to get to the bottom of it. Instead of calling Marta, Marcus went to visit her for once. He drove to the hamlet, rang the bell, and waited nervously on the porch. His wife never moved from the town where they had lived together—a place he had considered too provincial during his quest for worldliness and fame. She had switched to a bigger, newer house, but it was still small compared to what he had imagined his family would be living in. He did always send them a generous amount of money...always. He made certain to point this out to Maddie, as if it would absolve him from a degree of guilt for having abandoned them. He continued to wait, clueless as to what would tumble out of his mouth when he saw her. His heart raced when the door opened. The gaunt figure then rendered him speechless.

Marta immediately sought to allay his shock. She had to pull on his arm to move him inside. Her fragile body was close to losing its fight with leukemia, having successfully overcome it once before (unbeknownst to him). Little time remained. He explained his reason for coming. He could strangle the girl for not mentioning anything so important. Not only had Marta never encouraged their daughter to see him, she was also ignorant of her trip to him.

Maddie's thoughts returned to the present. She wondered why Marcus went over to the front desk to talk to the manager. Before sitting down, he helped himself to a kiss on her neck, then caressed her shoulders. Looking around the room, he said, "I had to slip them a hundred for this private lunch."

"You didn't!" she gasped, half believing him because the place was empty.

He laughed. "It's between meals. They're actually closed now, but we can stay."

They could already taste the schnitzels with potatoes being prepared. She then asked him if he stayed at Marta's house until she died, and he replied that he had.

The food arrived. It was difficult to keep from eating it too fast. Hopefully the chef wasn't witness to them skimming the forkfuls across their water glasses to prevent burning their tongues. Not a word was uttered until their plates were empty. Marcus leaned back and stroked his belly. "We can walk on a path built into the side of the cliff. Then we'll have coffee."

"Sounds good to me."

They exited through a side door, which led to a completely different kind of landscape. The colorless, cragged area was wedged between two smaller mountains. With its wide spectrum of shadows and irregular scrawl chiseled in the rock, the gorge resembled a scene from a Chinese hand scroll. The thin waterfalls looked like lead-filled tinsel; they fell so straight, and shimmered like silver.

Soon Maddie realized she had overdone it that day. When was she going to learn? Her legs felt as if they would give out any second. Marcus noticed her two-sided limp. She flinched with each step, but remained composed.

"Stop, Madelaine! Why won't you admit you're in pain? I bet you still have a lot of bruising."

He sat on a protruding stone shelf, then tucked her between his thighs and began to massage her gluteus. Embarrassed, she glanced around to make certain there were no onlookers, then rested her arms on his shoulders. His manipulation felt therapeutic, although it was accompanied by several loud "ows."

Interlaken was out of view. Maddie wished she could go around the next bend, and the next, to see if the scenery changed. Instead, they headed the short distance back. She slid a steadying hand along the wall. It was slow going, and it made her feel miserably old—something she was not at all accustomed to.

They resumed their place at the restaurant table and savored a mocha torte with some exceptionally strong coffee. When the cups were refilled, she asked if he would please reconsider telling her about the film with Birgit. He said that the events with Marta led up to it; he tried to remember where he left off.

"We had a fun couple of weeks before Marta became bedridden. Her friends were the same ones from when we first moved to the town. They still lived there." His tone reflected that this was an unthinkable concept to him. "We played cards and joked about the old days. It was especially meaningful for me to remember when my children were born." He folded his hands on the table. "I never talked about myself or my work. I knew they weren't impressed with me. I had been a rotten husband and a lousy father."

Maddie's disposition soothed him like a tonic. Instead of the condemning face he half expected to be glaring back at him, he met one filled with grace. He found her to be uncommonly genuine. It was safe to divulge more. He looked out the window, at the clouds drifting almost imperceptibly above the peaks.

"That first day in bed, I stayed beside her, and we talked about everything imaginable. She tired easily and would doze off for short periods. When she woke, we would start up again. I confessed to Marta that, even though I came to talk about our daughter, I also wanted to finally ask for a divorce. I had been going out with a singer for years, and suddenly she could only talk about marriage and children. At that point in my life, I got sentimental about taking another stab at fatherhood. Marta asked me to truly think the matter through. She said I shouldn't make more babies if I didn't intend to take full responsibility for them."

He turned back to Maddie. "Just when I thought I was making a smart move…she made me doubt myself." He slumped down a little in his chair. "She said that it was only fair that I first be a father to the children who already existed. My son supposedly adores me, even though I've been absent from his life. She said that he's proud to tell everyone I'm his father. He studied to be a film editor just to be in the same profession as me." Marcus lowered his head. "I couldn't believe the things she was telling me. Then I thought about my daughter, Renata...there was no way she could want a relationship with me. Marta acknowledged that Renata didn't care...at least not for herself. She had come to terms with those feelings early in her life. But now she was pregnant. She confided that she would like an *Opa* to tell the little one about his grandmother someday."

By now tears crept down both their faces. They quietly laughed over this picture and used the napkins to dab their eyes.

"Is this really leading up to the movie?"

"Yes, yes," he answered, then cleared his throat. He licked the chocolaty prongs of his fork and resumed. "Anyway..." He took a long pause. "After Marta's funeral, I went back to Munich. I was already under contract to begin a new film. I honestly thought the project would help me get over my grief. I put the marriage idea on hold, which my fiancée didn't appreciate. She left."

Before continuing, he suggested he call a taxi for them. He went ahead and paid the bill, then they walked outside to wait in the garden. The electric yellow and orange zinnias excited the butterflies.

Maddie sat on the bench, crossing her legs as well as her arms, as if somehow hugging herself might ease the pain. Her rump really ached. With care, Marcus gently placed an arm around her and got in on the hug. She couldn't hold a thought whenever he came this close to her. Because it happened to cross his mind right then, he asked, "Have you never had an affair during all your years of marriage?"

Maddie had begun to shake her head no. How easy to misconstrue what took place in Paris. That wasn't an affair with Robert, was it? *What* exactly was it?

"Aha!" He sounded as if he just caught her in the act. She immediately felt defensive.

"It doesn't count," she declared.

Her refusal to admit to her actions amused Marcus. "I'm sure he'd be happy to hear that." Then he asked, "Was he younger?"

"What difference does it make?" She hated herself for having answered so fast. The words sounded false.

"That much!" he exclaimed, exposing an ornery side.

Shrugging his arm off her shoulder, she could feel her face and neck heating up.

"It had to have been Paris," he said. "The young man was no doubt a finelooking student...and to think it happened so soon into your travels. Wow, Maddie! That's damned impressive."

She stood and stared with contempt into his smug face. He raised his arms in mock defense, not putting it past her to slap him. Why was he deriving such entertainment from riling her up like this? The taxi came; now she'd have to ride with him in this idiotic mood.

"Madelaine," he pleaded. "Come on. I wasn't accusing you of anything. Please...look at me." He truly didn't understand the fuss.

In minutes they reached his place. Max's head popped up in the window. Once he got out of the car, Marcus leaned over to give her a hand. Maddie pushed it aside and tried to pull the door shut, but he stepped in the way. Only then did his thoughtlessness occur to him. Without knowing the circumstances of her liaison, he realized she had given in to temptation for probably the very first time in...what? Fifty years! Good God. That was definitely nothing to make light of.

"I'm going home." She meant the hostel. He stood there, trying to think of something to say. She watched the driver in his rearview mirror. He appeared indifferent and was simply waiting for further instructions. Then she heard a quietly delivered, "Shit," followed with another, along with a thump on the roof. She presumed it was directed at her—her sullen behavior.

Marcus had actually cursed at himself, for ruining a perfectly great day. He hunched back inside the car, then handed the driver more money to take her into town. He wanted to kiss her...to right matters. Couldn't he simply rewind to fifteen minutes ago, and keep his trap shut? He gently closed the door and watched as they drove away. He went in and sat beside Max on the couch, then confided to him in German, "There comes a time when one isn't allowed to be this stupid anymore, you know? I'm surprised you pay me any mind." Max put his head down to sleep again, indifferent to his master's troubles.

Sitting there, Marcus pictured himself as the young man in Paris, catching Madelaine's eye in a café. She'd have hooked him with that direct, guileless expression, not to mention her refined manner. He rubbed Max's shoulders as he wondered which scenario ultimately led to that fellow winning her affections. One way, the easy way, involved alcohol...with lots of slow dancing, in perhaps a jazz bar. And who wouldn't enjoy a picnic in a meadow worthy of an impressionist's brush, or a stroll along the Seine after a concert? A stimulating argument couldn't be discounted, followed by the simultaneous merging of passions. He wanted to know how this boy had managed to break through her reserve. The longer he contemplated it, the more he couldn't fathom Madelaine being that naive. This had to have been mutual. He knew for a fact she hadn't instigated it.

Neither television nor music could distract Marcus from the unmitigated self-reproach he suffered that evening. He had undeniably acted like a dolt.

Maddie, on the other hand, escaped her conscience by getting to know her new roomies from Greece, a mother and her two teenage daughters. She liked their CD by a Greek pop star and tried to remember his name. The father, who was sleeping in the men's corridor, was meeting them later for dinner. They were excited to go to the restaurant where she had been.

Maddie ended up calling Rima. It was the middle of the afternoon there. She got the latest regarding Red's recovery: He no longer hesitated at the steps or when rounding corners. Rima's Uncle Gary was starting another job—which didn't require a move, for once. Aunt Janet told Rima's mom that she was taking out a second mortgage to send Harry to college. Uncle Matt and his family never came over anymore to visit Grandpa, whereas, Rima said, her mother was with him all the time, when she wasn't at work. Visiting Ed was usually something Carol didn't often do. Aunt Amy had collected her clothes and moved in with a girlfriend.

Maddie was glad when Rima moved on to her own life. She sounded good. She was still up in the air about visiting Berlin. Her grandmother tried talking her into going. Maddie almost told her that she had met a nice boy who was going to be there in August. It would be good for Rima to have contact with someone closer to her age. Had she lost her mind? How could she consider anything so foolhardy? Rima then asked her why she didn't call Grandpa. Maddie told her that she tried once, but he wasn't home. Rima asked why she didn't try again. Then her granddaughter wondered if Maddie was leaving Ed. No, said Maddie.

As soon as she hung up, Maddie took a couple of Advil, then curled up on her bottom bunk. Half dozing, she enjoyed listening to the foreign singing and chatter. The corners of her mouth turned up when she remembered the innocent delight of touching Marcus's hair this morning.

Marcus found no rest. He hated being on bad terms with this woman, who had managed to captivate his imagination entirely too quickly. He had her cell number programmed and almost hit the key several times. He finally left it in the bedroom and walked away.

Later, when it was dark, he poured himself a Scotch whisky, tasted it, decided he didn't want to numb his senses, and then watched the ice melt over the next hour. He sat in silence in the living room.

The house phone rang. It was on the table beside him. "Ja?"

"OK…so you start filming with Birgit. In a nutshell, what happened?"

The sickening lump in his stomach magically disappeared; her call was a godsend.

Maddie waited. "...a nutshell," she prompted.

"Yes," Marcus chuckled "I'll try." He was grateful he wasn't drunk. "A week into shooting, it was obvious that I was never going to be able to remember my lines. Everyone understood, but they were also at a loss over what to do about the situation. I asked to bow out of the production...it was so early into it. The director refused to find someone else. After a couple days, they came to me with a unique approach. I needed only to listen to the other actors and react to them with my expressions and manner. They worked my dialogue into their roles. It turned out to be interesting...Maddie? I've probably gone beyond my limit. Should I stop?"

"Very funny."

His heart smiled. He felt wondrously cozy, speaking softly in her ear. She might just as well be snuggled up beside him. He continued in a sleepy, slightly raspy voice. Maddie was surprised to hear an accent. "We shot in sequence the following two months. During that time, I lost a lot of weight and started looking...well, awful. But it worked with the story, because my character was being victimized throughout it...and worn down in the process." He cleared his throat and closed his eyes, wondering if he really wanted to continue. His breathing picked up.

"Please...you can't leave me dangling like this." She thought she heard a weak laugh.

He proceeded, speaking haltingly, "It's the last scene. I'm in the bathtub when Birgit's character walks in on me. She doesn't realize that I've set her up, just as she has done to me in order to kill me. She comes over and sits on the edge of the tub. I don't recall anything after that, Madelaine, except the steam rising from the water. Then it's all a blur." He paused. Maddie could barely hear him, but she wasn't going to break his train of thought by asking him to speak louder. "I take a deep breath...and feel the water as it enters. It's so very relaxing. I see Marta. She looks at me, then past me. I turn...I want to see what she does. And we float away together."

Maddie didn't say anything for a while. Finally, she commented, "I don't mean to sound funny, but please tell me they didn't keep that in the film," recalling the knife sequence in his movie with Claudia.

That produced a smile at his end. "No, not that. But I got the best reviews of my life. The critics were impressed that I let my body go to hell like that. Can you understand why I don't want to see it?"

"Were you suicidal?"

"No. I don't believe so." This was the first time he tried to put into words exactly what he had felt. At the time, he couldn't share it with Claudia; she had been dealing with the death of her own husband. "I wanted to understand what the transition felt like, you know?"

"Yes…I do," she said.

"I must have realized on some level that I was in a safe place; I'd be rescued. It was unfortunate what I put the others through, though. They were scared out of her minds." After a moment, he followed that with, "I did find peace." He was curious that Maddie had said she understood, and asked why.

"Death is an absolutely solitary experience," she said. "Who doesn't want to have an inkling of what it will be like?"

Marcus wondered aloud if she had ever done anything like he had.

Her story went back further than his. She told him about the accident that killed her son. A month after the tragedy, she began to hesitate when turning onto her street, at the spot where he was struck. She would watch as the oncoming cars appeared from over the hill, timing their approach. When one was almost on top of her, she would accelerate, causing the driver to veer and blast his horn, and—no doubt—give her the finger on his way down the road. It became a compulsion.

One late afternoon, she realized she was there at almost the exact minute Tim had been when the noise of the crash exploded throughout the neighborhood. The sun was low in the sky to her right, shining on her as it had on him. She waited in the middle of the road. The few cars that came up from behind were able to pass in the bicycle lane. As soon as that moving shimmer of a reflection appeared at the top of the hill, she heard the woman who lived on the corner start yelling her name.

For one amazing moment, Maddie said she had the sensation of actually being in Tim's young body, of sitting on the passenger side on his wet towel, of being famished after a day of swimming and looking forward to dinner, and of talking to the boy who was driving. By now, the panicked bystander looked ready to fly out in front of the unsuspecting driver, to make him stop. Maddie cut in front of his car. The man must have miraculously taken a visual cue from her neighbor, because he slammed on his brakes, tapped her back bumper, skidded sideways, then swung in a circle and traveled well beyond her. Next she pulled her car over to the grassy portion of the road and simply sat there in a serene state, satisfied that her son couldn't have anticipated the horror. She couldn't begin to describe how tremendously relieved and grateful she was that the poor soul in the spinning car had not died or been injured because of her imprudent deed.

Marcus mourned the loss of the boy.

Maddie contemplated how differently her relationship with Ed might have turned out if they could have shared their thoughts as Marcus and his wife had done before she died. She wished they could have made love right after Tim's death. Instead, in order to suppress the inconsolable grief, Ed began sleeping all of the time, and she threw herself into a swimming schedule that left her exhausted and mindless at night.

Marcus didn't want to hang up without asking for forgiveness. He was really out of line at the restaurant. Maddie agreed. Then she took this opportune moment to bring up the subject that she knew had to be addressed now—definitely not later. It concerned their sexual health.

He asked if they could get together tomorrow.

"I'm going to rest…do the laundry. How about after tomorrow?"

"Fine. I had wanted to go horseback riding, but that's not a good idea if you're hurting. Do you like to sail?"

"I'd love to ride. I'll be better. We just won't go for long, OK?"

They took comfort from having reconciled and said good night. He wished he could convince her to leave the hostel and stay with him.

Shaking walls woke Maddie. There was a shouting match going on downstairs. She checked her watch—only six thirty. It sounded as if chairs were being thrown. Repeatedly, President Bush's name came up—in conjunction with the f-word. So far, she had successfully avoided embroiling herself in any heated discussions about political issues, which invariably turned into explosive arguments—all of which, one way or another, were linked to the war in Iraq. The Greeks propped their chins on their pillows and looked questioningly at one another. The pulsating sirens grew louder, then the disruptive parties were carted away.

The day started out overcast and muggy, with a high expected in the middle nineties. The cold shower felt especially good. Maddie examined her injuries. They were healing well. Then she noticed her hip bones, which shouldn't have been as visible as they were. Skinny old people, with sharp-edged bodies, looked downright ugly to her. This serious condition called for more cake.

In the afternoon, the guests played international Scrabble, which meant players had to trust their opponents not to cheat. One of the Greek girls played in English and Italian. A German and a Spanish student were included. Maddie proudly came up with a few high-scoring French words. She didn't bother to correct the English misspellings; she assumed the others were giving her a break as well.

At five o'clock, when she was beginning to think about dinner, she received a call from Claudia asking her to come over. A friend was visiting tonight, and Claudia was preparing goulash. She wanted Maddie to join them.

The horn tooted at six on the nose. Claudia had never acted this bubbly.

Maddie asked if she could quickly check her messages on the computer. Karl and Sonja had checked in. Robert was signed on from Bonn. He wanted only her opinion of the logo design for their bridge club T-shirts. He did close with a "Love, Robert." It always put her in high spirits to see her friends' names. A feeling of embarrassment swept over her upon seeing Robert's. It was especially ridiculous because she was sitting alone in the room, free from Marcus's taunts. Whatever magic had charged her insides when she was with Robert in Paris, it prevailed and kept her slightly on edge. She hoped she was succeeding at maintaining a facade of decorum. It was work taming this voracious need; she had never faced that task in her entire life.

Her designated job was to twist the dough for the breadsticks. She caught sight of Marcus through the open door. He sat on the carpet and was busily reading wine labels. He blew her a kiss. Claudia just finished preparing the salads when the doorbell rang.

The dinner guest would leave the American starstruck the entire evening. He had only been referred to as Michael. Maddie nonchalantly shook his hand—great acting on her part. The dark, intense screen presence was the opposite of the expressive and approachable face she presently greeted. The gray in Michael O'Keeffe's shoulder length, thick and wavy dark hair was growing out at the roots. Black lashes accentuated his strained, glassy blue eyes, which were half shaded by his heavy lids. He was tanned and hadn't shaven for a while. Unlike the hair on his head, his beard was completely black. His crumpled, denim shirt showed the wear of the fourteen-hour drive up from Italy. He asked to grab a quick shower before eating and left with Marcus to use his bathroom.

"Now there's a man to die for, huh?" Claudia raised her eyebrows and kissed the air with a smacking sound.

No kidding. Maddie didn't say it, though.

They lit some candles for the table and arranged a bouquet of bright yellow and red roses from Marcus's garden, which Maddie still hadn't seen in the daytime.

The initial dinner conversation revolved around recipes. Michael loved to cook, and they all enjoyed recounting places where they'd had their most unusual meals. The war news was briefly mentioned. Solutions were beyond their grasp; it was so complicated. Then there was the matter of the weather. The heat throughout Europe was unheard-of, and there was no letup in sight—and it wasn't even July. Not *even* July, thought Maddie. Out of the corner of her eye, she could tell Marcus was observing her...her interest in this other man.

Having finished his meal, Michael needed to get up and move around. He made himself useful by clearing the table.

"Maddie." Marcus addressed her rather sharply. He then stated sarcastically, "I suppose you know *Michael's* work."

"Some."

He shook his head in consternation. She read his face: *Why his?*

"Name some that have impressed you." Michael detected that Marcus came off sounding confrontational and glanced at Claudia.

She could name a lot, going back as much as thirty years; however, she claimed to be bad with titles. The Irishman's stage work excited her these days. Maddie told him that the art council she belonged to recently spearheaded an effort to get his ensemble to come to Ohio after seeing a production of his in Chicago. The actor remembered. Other commitments prevented it, he said, but the troupe did look over their schedule to check whether they could accept the invitation at a later date.

To break the tension, Michael stated, "I like American expressions...'right off the bat.'" Amused by the phrase, he noted, "You said you couldn't name any titles right off the bat." He then added, "I also like, 'shooting from the hip'...and I love 'he bought the farm.'" His tired eyes showed delight.

Maddie appreciated his diplomatic gesture and hoped that Marcus would change his soured tune. "True," she said, "one uses them a lot...forgetting what they sound like...or how they even originated." She remembered several of her mother's peculiar Irish phrases.

At once a hurled breadstick clipped Michael on the chin. "I know where you're going with this, my good friend," said Marcus. And the two eyed each other like smirking teenage hooligans, having agreed to a major dare.

Claudia muttered something in German as her head dropped down into her hands.

Maddie looked confused.

"Just see if you can get this story out of them," she told her as she got glasses for after-dinner drinks.

"Well?" asked Maddie, exchanging looks between the men.

Marcus, in a mannered movement, gently lowered himself onto the big burgundy chair, taking care not to spill the schnapps in his right hand. With his other hand, he rubbed his face and pinched the corners of his eyes, and started laughing quietly to himself. He looked up at Michael. The fellow was punchy from no sleep and now eager for the chance to let loose; he baited Marcus with his devilish expression.

Maddie figured it an in-joke. She didn't care if she couldn't fully appreciate it. It tickled her to observe the glint in their eyes. They had already had too much wine, and Michael, being especially wasted by fatigue, stood no chance of fighting off the urge to vent some emotion.

Claudia giggled and excused herself to clean the dishes. "I guarantee, Maddie, they can't finish."

The anticipation was unbearable. "OK, OK…start!" Maddie demanded. "I want to hear." She kicked off her shoes and sat squarely in the middle of the sofa, waiting for the entertainment portion of the evening.

Admirably, the men pulled themselves together—a testament to their professionalism. As if the two of them were mimes changing their faces behind the screen of a hand, Maddie beheld an astonishing transformation. Michael, taking center stage, stood in darkness by the shuttered windows. He began his serious narrative.

The year is 1944. He described a scene in which the Nazis have captured an American outpost in Bavaria and have taken possession of top-secret maps that identify field positions and intended attacks against the German forces. He and Marcus play German agents who must trick another U.S. troop, on its way to this station, into believing they are the Americans. They are coming to pick up the important intelligence for safekeeping at another camp.

Michael stepped forward. His prominent features took on the warm glow cast by a stained-glass lamp. He moved a corner pillow, then sat on the couch, never yet having taken his eyes off Maddie's. The seductive mood of his slowly paced oration, coupled with the light, embraced the languor of a dying fire. With pupils grown big, he sucked her into their depths, eliciting the response hoped for by any performer—to make the audience's heart skip a beat.

Marcus sat stooped in a prayerful posture and studied the ground. He spoke in German to Michael, who turned to answer him. Although she couldn't understand, Maddie recognized that the words were delivered solemnly and precisely, every syllable being carefully enunciated. Marcus translated for her benefit.

He explained that the Germans have devised a scheme. Once the Americans arrive, an explosion will serve as a diversion and get blamed on someone who managed to infiltrate their group, and who then fled with the maps. It is assumed that the GIs will likely depart immediately to find the thief. Michael nodded in agreement with the facts.

How could Marcus look so sinister? The militaristic resolve he demonstrated was disconcerting. His eyes were narrow and cold, the jaw muscles tight and stern, and his lips ran a straight, mean line. The German agent stood up tall. The sound of running water in the kitchen and the clinking of dishes didn't distract anyone.

Marcus next related their surprise when the U.S. soldiers come ahead of schedule, undetected by the Nazi guards. The strategic positions are lying in full view on a table. They are told that it is feared the Germans have been tipped off, and the U.S. soldiers have come to seize the maps before the Germans can.

The two men stole a glance at each other, privately signaling a warning. You'd have thought the enemy was actually in the room. Maddie looked on, enthralled.

Michael picked up the storyline. The Americans quickly gather what they came for, and in a matter of minutes, are on their way out the door. The Germans must think fast.

In order to get the Yankees' attention, one German thumps the table. Marcus used the coffee table in front of him, making Maddie jump with surprise. He then yelled toward the patio doors (in the direction of the GIs).

Maddie watched as the imaginary soldiers turned back to face who they believed was an American officer. Marcus then commanded them to…

His chin quivered. Immediately, both Nazis rolled onto the carpet in a silent fit of laughter. And they continued to roll and hold their full stomachs.

"To what?" she pleaded, feeling gypped. She couldn't refrain from smiling.

Michael managed to stagger behind his superior officer in an effort to stand him up and restore his dignity. He almost succeeded, until Marcus tried to say the line again. They collapsed on each other, moaning.

By now Maddie was laughing. This was like Tim and Janet, except they used to make her angry. It made no difference if she ordered them not to speak; they intuitively made the same comical observations at the same time. It might be church, the grocery store, the dry cleaners…frequently it was at the dinner table. The spit seeped from between their clenched teeth. They tried so hard to hold it back, which one knows only makes the condition worse. Their shirts at times got drenched by the tears.

Thankfully, a winding-down phase allowed the clowns a moment to recuperate. Their faces and necks were a fiery red. Michael, sprawled across the carpet, supported his chin on Marcus's knee. Marcus, half sitting, leaned over Michael's back.

History had taught this mother they were good for another round.

"I've gotta piss so bad," wailed Michael in agony.

"First, tell Maddie what I had to say."

They reclaimed a semblance of calm. Michael charmingly cocked his head to one side and peered up at her. They were ten-year-olds masquerading as adults. He was going to try really hard to do this.

"The German said…" He swallowed and searched to find the focus he needed in her face. She thought she'd help by making herself as deadpan as possible, even though the merriment in her eyes shone through. "As they were leaving, the soldier was ordered to hold…hol…" His voice broke into a yodel. The snickering got the better of him. Marcus flew flat back, howling. With that, Michael clawed his way up the chair and ran to the bathroom.

Marcus curled into a ball, hugging himself tight to alleviate his stomachache. He was finally wearing out.

Maddie hopped over the back of the sofa and skipped to the kitchen. Standing in the doorway, she demanded Claudia tell her. "Hold what, for God's sakes?"

Claudia's dimples poked through her cheeks like the hollows at the ends of a plum. "Hold the phone there, Mac!"

"Oh, brother." Anticlimactic, indeed…but what an absurd thing for a Nazi to come up with. The audience must have agreed.

The women listened to the quiet. There was heavy sighing. Marcus headed to the bathroom next. Michael had thrown himself full-length and facedown onto the couch. Claudia dried her hands and Maddie joined her to sit on a loveseat facing the prostrate body.

When Marcus reappeared, his head and shirt were wet from a slap in the face with cold water. He then keeled sideways across the chair. His legs dangled off the arm, and his neck drooped backward over the other arm.

Annihilated, the soldiers couldn't summon up a peep.

Claudia elaborated upon the movie. "Marcus begged to have the line changed. He realized he could never say it with a straight face. He claimed that no German would understand that expression and actually use it. The director refused to listen, stating that's precisely why he was keeping it. If they were to be believed as Americans, they needed to use slang. Plus, the director had it in for Marcus. He had never wanted him for the role. That was the studio's choice. Later, during a critical scene…one where the Germans line up Jewish French villagers…and are getting ready to shoot them…those stupid words pop into his head and crack him up again."

"Oh, no." Maddie laughed, picturing it.

"Michael, along with the rest of the cast, couldn't deal with him anymore. Eventually someone else dubbed the scenes. It sadly became a contest of wills between the director and the producer. Everyone lost. The picture never made it to distribution. Michael had nothing to do with Marcus after that. He blamed Marcus for ruining his opportunity of making it in Hollywood. That wasn't true, though. Around ten years later, when they were both famous and had gained the confidence that comes with steady work, they crossed paths at O'Hare and were hauled out for being drunk. They had merely begun to reminisce about the unfortunate experience when the memory got the better of them. Can you imagine this behavior tonight at an airport?"

The ladies scrunched up close together in the small space and shared the drink Marcus never finished. They were like schoolgirls on an overnighter, disclosing their private thoughts at three in the morning—when antics are replaced by the whisperings of individual aspirations. They spoke about Africa and the upcoming charity event, American suburban life, husbands, loss, and children. Although Claudia never had any, they were dear to her.

As an afterthought, Claudia mentioned that Marcus considered the bungled episode a sign. The decision to never portray Nazis took him out of the running for many important future roles.

The women watched these wasted, but nevertheless brilliant, snoring fools, bestowing on the men the familial smiles of protective sisters. Nothing could wake the boys from their sound sleep.

They never did nod off, so Claudia returned Maddie to the hostel right before daybreak.

CHAPTER 13

The four hours of sleep felt like eight. One couldn't ask for a more beautiful, clear morning to go riding, but Maddie gave up on the invitation, figuring Marcus would want to spend time with his company. While tidying up, she wondered where her next roommates would hail from. She reeled from surprise when Marcus, giddy with good humor, bolted through the doorway and smothered her with a bear hug. In his exuberance, he began to rock her side to side in a mad morning dance. He was dazzling, absolutely *wearing* the sunny day. She clung to the back of his shirt to keep from losing her balance.

"Enough, already!" she called out, giggling.

His hands slid down her arms, and he reached for her hands. "To the ponies, right?"

"You bet!"

They made a pit stop at Claudia's for a pair of jeans. Maddie hadn't packed any, because she simply never wore them, not even for gardening. She was offered riding pants, but the fit wasn't good.

On their way out, they caught Michael enjoying a soft-boiled egg and coffee at the cramped kitchen table. The quaint homes were not spacious. He wasn't the least disturbed by the flimsy gauze curtain that repeatedly flitted across his cheek and shoulder.

The Irish actor's participation at the Lake Como fund-raiser was announced. Maddie tuned out while the three discussed it. She was struck by Michael's metamorphosis since the prior evening. Clean shaven today, his sculptured features looked smooth as polished marble. Gone were the curls. The damp, air-drying hair was fluffy and somewhat frizzed at the ends. The thick layers on his left side curled up slightly from the direction of the breeze.

A royal blue T-shirt flattered his eyes. He nodded a good morning to Maddie while he chewed. No matter the cheery morning light, this man had dangerous eyes—the kind that could extract confessions. Her knees would buckle if he were to stare at her indefinitely.

Marcus gave him a quick kiss on the temple and a cordial slap on the cheek. "Promise us you won't drive so long without stopping when you're tired. Our old eyes can't take it anymore, you know?"

That was her cue to shake hands good-bye. Michael began to stand. "Please, please…stay seated," Maddie said. "I've really enjoyed meeting you."

"Oh, dear," he said, "and that's based on last night?"

She grinned. "I'm sure no one will ever understand the humor I find in Nazis from here on out."

He looked at Marcus, who reminded him that he had been the one who started it. Michael told her as she walked out that he hoped to someday make it to Ohio.

On their drive to the stable, Maddie couldn't get over how real everything felt. Homesickness didn't trouble her—not since that last lapse, when she had to hear a family member's voice. Communicating with Rima over the Internet helped. It definitely gave her the needed oomph to continue her adventure alone. Their messages mostly centered on the direction her granddaughter was thinking about going with her impressionable, young life.

The drama that had revolved around raising children, keeping a marriage going, and operating a business amounted to nothing more than a mental file of snapshots to flip through sometimes if Maddie needed a context for a particular date. She loved being attuned to the here and now. Growing up, she knew only to anticipate and prepare for unseen eventualities, something her own mother wanted control over. What a huge amount of time had been wasted over second-guessing outcomes. And the underlying fret was always what happened to you if you didn't follow the rules…the Church's rules, the government's rules, the school's rules…everyone's rules but one's own. Maddie was still learning, and trying to take the lesson to heart, that until whatever was going to happen actually did happen, one could never be ready for it psychologically. So…why worry?

"You're especially quiet, Madelaine." Marcus sometimes preferred her full name, and she now preferred his pronunciation.

The top was down. It was noisy, but she heard him. Yes, indeed—abiding by all those rules was paramount…it secured one a superior spot in eternity. What an ambiguous destination in her current frame of mind.

"Maddie?"

Failing to gain her ear, he pulled over to the side of the road. She didn't question his action, nor did she look at him. There was a magnificent willow tree. Its tassels drifted in a southerly direction, as did the tails and manes of the three white horses grazing by the pond's edge. It was an incredibly lovely setting.

He used the German word denoting the same affection as "dear," then asked, "Where are you?"

She faced him. "I'm here, loving your sky blue eyes…the horses, the fields…"

His mouth met hers. He brushed some hair off her face, then quickly repositioned his lips, mindful of restraining his excited tongue. He sat back behind the wheel and waited for a response. Was she being coy? Her eyes conveyed a hint of pleasure—perhaps. He turned the key in the ignition, and within twenty minutes they were in stirrups, weaving down a trail.

Mounting Hilda, the tall, elegant horse, hadn't been easy for Maddie on account of her smarting rump. She would have chosen a smaller mare, but this one was guaranteed to have an easygoing disposition; no need to land in the hospital again. Marcus rode a handsome, stalwart buckskin, anxious to run. He had good control of the reins, but he couldn't let up for a second. He mentioned that a horse had fallen on him once, injuring his left leg. Daily exercises and an occasional cortisone shot prevented a stiff knee. Maybe Maddie should ask the doctor for one in her hip.

There was no one else on the path; this place wasn't intended for the general public. They reached an open field, where they cut loose with a hard gallop. For Maddie, the prospect of future discomfort was deemed insignificant when compared to this rush of adrenaline.

Resuming a trot, Marcus willingly talked about his children when she asked more about them. Marcus said he had often asked Kurt, his son, to go skiing or sailing with him when the boy was a teenager, but at the last minute, the kid always backed out. He therefore saw no point in continuing to invite him. During one of their last illuminating conversations, the reason Marta gave for their son's behavior was that Kurt felt he would be in his father's way. There were always so many fascinating people surrounding Marcus, vying for his attention; the man couldn't really have wanted to be bothered with the likes of him. His son realized he was a stranger to his father. Maddie understood Kurt's position. So could the father, even though it broke his heart to hear that.

They couldn't distinguish each other's features very well under the pine canopy. Momentary flecks of sunlight shot their faces through the blowing branches.

Maddie missed out on enjoying the relaxing aspect of the sashaying rhythm. She was getting used to the abrupt twinges of pain that accompanied every clippety-cloppety step along the uneven ground. It traveled the nerve that ran from a dime-size spot on each buttock to her tailbone.

Marcus's horse became rowdy when they reached a narrow bridge. She reminded him of what the worker back at the barn had said: if they got as far as the water, Marcus was to back his horse over the bridge.

He laughed. "Maddie…he wasn't serious. I've been around horses most of my life. He just needs some firm handling."

Right, she thought, then made the case, "Surely you've seen horses with quirks. They develop phobias, too. Maybe a tree limb fell across a bridge once and spooked him…or a loose plank pulled up and startled him. Try it! Or you might get thrown."

His horse continued to spin around with every effort made to cross.

"Come on, Marcus. We'll be here all day. I'll stay and follow. That way he can look at Hilda."

He couldn't dispute the fact that the horse held still when he had him facing away from the bridge. "I fucking don't believe this!"

She did. What she couldn't believe was Marcus's stubbornness. The horse likely had a legitimate reason for his.

The path on the other side was graded, which made a big difference to Maddie's bottom. Hilda didn't mind when Marcus brought his gelding alongside her. Some of Maddie's hair had bounced out of its tight knot, and she liked the feel of Marcus playing with the loose strands, just as he had done that time back at Claudia's place.

It was a perfect moment, and she almost said so; however, she wanted to qualify it by adding "if we were only younger"—and that would certainly have ruined the atmosphere. She thought of an old black-and-white film about an enchanted cottage. A romantic spirit allowed the guests to look beyond their physical limitations and find love, but only as long as they stayed within its boundary. Couldn't this forest hold such a mysterious power, returning to both their youth? She wanted to touch on the subject at some point—to know how he was dealing with it: getting old, not just older.

Although she wasn't one for staving off the inevitable with cosmetic surgery and antidepressants, Maddie couldn't deny how helpless it felt sometimes to stare in the mirror and count a new line, or observe those already etched growing deeper and longer. When people complimented her over her attractiveness (which was often) she would finish their thought in her head with, *for your age.*

Rima alone made Maddie feel ageless, because Rima took total delight in her grandmother's company. Maddie used to think that being around young people maintained one's vivacity. Now she saw it clearly had more to do with keeping one's own interests alive. What she had found pivotal in Paris, and expected to continue to find throughout her travels, was the importance of discovery—of everything. It was a never-ending quest.

Marcus took off in a canter, putting a halt to her daydreams. She chose to lag behind, keeping with the smooth gait. The boys ran far ahead, then raced back, kicking up the dust while doing circles around the ladies. Hilda, like Maddie, was unfazed.

"Learn that shooting spaghetti westerns?" she quipped.

His laugh was wicked. He was having the time of his life showing off. *How does he get away with being so full of himself?* she wondered. It carried him far in life, too.

He had to set her straight. "Those were not your everyday, run-of-the-mill cowboy movies. No siree, Bob. They were art."

"Ah, forgive me. I take it that line was in one or two of 'em."

He liked her teasing. His horse, in similar stud fashion (castration aside), began strutting tight figure eights in front of Hilda. Marcus boasted, "I'm quite proud of them. Some were, after all, based on Zane Grey's stories."

Something apparently struck a chord. "What is it?" he asked, when suddenly confronted by a most bewildering look on her face.

She hadn't heard that name in ages. The mare sensed the mood and was stilled; she didn't so much as shift her weight. "Zane Grey," Maddie repeated, flatly.

"Yes." He parked sideways, directly in front of them.

If ever there were a name to zap her out of this make-believe wonderland, that would be it. The scenery of a previous act was pulled in front of her face, hiding Marcus. Tim lay in his coffin. Ed had placed a book on his chest and positioned his dead son's hand on top of it. "*Tales of Fishes*…by Zane Grey." She unconsciously said it out loud.

Marcus wasn't sure what to say or do. Without prompting, her horse decided to slowly step forward, butting his out of the way. She trusted the animal's instincts, and only held the horn of her saddle as they ambled down the road. Marcus stayed so close that their stirrups scraped a couple times. Her horse paid no mind. Maddie finally turned to him; the sun struck him full in the face. His expression was amicable. She apologized for the baffling behavior and explained, "That's the book my husband buried our son with. I haven't heard the author's name in such a long time." Marcus stayed quiet. "I guess he used to be a popular writer, but I don't think kids read him anymore."

"That's probably true," he said, then questioned her about the subject. "You said 'fishes.' I thought I knew all of his westerns…I don't remember any fish in a title."

"I guess he wrote about that too."

That struck Marcus as peculiar. "What was the story about?"

"I don't know. I never read it. Ed was going to take Tim salmon fishing in Alaska that summer with our neighbor, and gave him that to read."

They headed back to the stable. They had been out longer than planned and now were hungry. While dismounting, Marcus asked her if she wasn't even a little curious about the book.

"No," she said, "I assumed it had to do with lures and lines…fish stuff. I never liked to fish." Speaking of Tim made her think of his son. "You were going to finish telling me about Kurt."

They walked the horses around the corral before taking them inside. Marcus told how he had kidnapped his son from work. "Last year, I planned a skiing trip for the two of us, but Kurt didn't know. I wasn't going to let him get out of it. I got a friend to take over his job for a week…he was editing a commercial. I showed up at his studio and told him that he had to come with me. Off we flew to Colorado. Just like that."

"Didn't it feel forced?" she asked.

"Mm…forced?" He wasn't sure of the word, but thought he knew what she meant. "Maybe, at first. But I couldn't take my eyes off him. It really hit me that I was with my son. And he was a grown-up man. Wow! Whenever he looked at me, there was so much love. Damn, if I didn't tear up the whole time. I felt so bad for him when I thought of all those missed trips."

"For him? Not you?"

"Not like you might think. I could never have been a different man, Maddie. It's just too bad that a baby can get stuck with an irresponsible galoot like me for a parent. It's a crapshoot."

"I'll grant you that," she said, thinking over her own family's disconnected status. She smiled over his choice of word. "Galoot" was perfect for cowboys.

When at last they got to the car and eased themselves onto the cushy leather seats, Marcus asked, "So how's your popo?"

"Could be worse. A pill and I'll be shipshape."

They made sandwiches back at his place and ate them in the backyard. She got to see the roses. Incredible—especially the ones with coral-colored petals, tinged with the faintest purple—especially, too, the crisp, unblemished, solid-white, perfectly shaped blooms. She couldn't claim a favorite.

Although it was by no means hot like in most of the major European cities, it was warmer in this mountainous region than its citizens were accustomed to. Bizarre weather loomed over the entire continent, and it wasn't budging. This summer would go down in the record books. Marcus and Claudia had only window air conditioners in their bedrooms, which was enough to make the rest of the small space comfortable. Max was glued to his cooling station, the kitchen floor.

While she changed back into her skirt and sandals, Marcus spoke through the bathroom door; he had an idea for what to do with the rest of the afternoon. She was up for anything.

"A retired pianist lives down the hill…you know, that little jog in the road with the three houses? He practices every day for an hour and invites me to come over whenever I want. Then we talk a bit, share a brandy. He adores Max. Would you enjoy that?" He put his ear up to the door.

"Very much," she replied, having always liked the company of artists, particularly musicians.

CHAPTER 14

Maddie stood transfixed. Scalloped doilies dripped from every ledge like icing piped along a multitiered cake. They decorated the chairs' headrests and arms, the mantel, and all the tables—even the metal covers that hid the steam radiators. The gentleman found comfort in his recently deceased wife's vast accumulation of collected lace. Every trip the couple had made (during the span of their sixty-year marriage) resulted in a purchase, all of which looked, for the most part, to be on display. Up close, the detailing was exquisite. They were hand sewn out of the finest cottons and silks, and elaborately embroidered with white stitching, creating an embossed design. A Youghal Needle Irish lace runner lay across the piano. Maddie recognized its particular intricacies from pieces handed down to her from her maternal grandmother. A solid square, with an Austrian snowflake trim, hung over a parakeet's cage.

The private nurse who greeted them said Herr Menzel was freshening up after a nap. This was second home to Max. He crept under the piano, spun around several times, then several more, then landed behind the foot pedals, which were scarred by years of habitual playing; Max had chosen the primo spot for capturing the distinctive traces of this long-lived human.

Maddie took advantage of their time alone to ask Marcus how he eventually reconciled with his daughter. He came up from behind and put his arms around her while she was reading the titles on the overstuffed bookshelves. "You already know far too much about me," he whispered.

"Seriously. I want to hear how you managed it. Maybe it will help me turn things around with a couple of my kids."

He sat down on the footstool next to her. She looked down on his head and was tempted to comb her fingers through his hair again, but instead went and rested her weary behind on a chair with an inviting, velvet-tufted seat. The craftsmanship of the boldly carved, wooden arms, with their imaginative griffin-inspired hand rests, was a sight to behold. She pushed herself for a spin, then stopped by dragging her tiptoes on the floor.

The two studied each other with uncommon intensity, as if this silent exchange should transfer thoughts. Right as he began to speak, a feeble voice sounded from around the corner. "Marcus, Marcus…where are you, my good man?"

She had expected Herr Menzel to speak German.

Marcus stood and stepped out from the hidden nook. His overzealous hug appeared to crush the frail fellow, but the little man took to it. Skin from his hanging lids almost completely curtained the eyes that peeked over a shoulder and noticed the stranger. Maddie immediately came forward for the introduction.

It made sense now. Besides the fact that English was widely spoken when he played with international orchestras over the course of his lifetime, Los Angeles had most recently been the German's base—for twenty years. There he discovered the lucrative business of recording film tracks and commercial jingles. Now the eighty-nine-year-old called this former Interlaken getaway home.

With no malice intended, Maddie regarded Herr Menzel's out-of-kilter form perfectly suited to the cubists' world. His wide (eerily so) forehead narrowed into a pointy chin. A sharp, protruding shoulder blade poked out under his brown satin smoking jacket. Like a coat hook, it pinched folds in the silky material. A hip bone punched out of the side. Through the opening of the jacket's loosely tied front, the other hip looked to run downhill, which offset the legs. The right knee bent much higher than the left. Somewhere was a torso. Skeletal fingers, with arthritic swollen knuckles, grasped Maddie's hand, then held it—delicately, to her amazement. His hunched posture permitted only the slightest of bows in which to kiss it. Marcus empathized with a consolatory smile. She courteously returned a greeting, counting the eight dark wisps of hair drawn across his liver-spotted crown. Maddie worried when he next looked up at her, if he would recognize her pitying thoughts. However, behind those slits were eyes that shone with gaiety, and she delivered a genuinely felt kiss on his cheek.

When Herr Menzel learned of Maddie's chosen method of travel, he shared his own hitchhiking history with them, relating stories that predated autobahns and interstates. He extolled the romantic, unencumbered life led by hobos who camped by the side of railroad tracks when he thumbed across America as a young man during the late thirties. Many times he ate and spent the night with them. His take on the Hungarian and Romanian gypsy families he encountered when he returned to Europe after World War II was entertaining. Of course, their mode of travel was carts, not cars. Every driver who picked him up had a special place in his memory. It was a joy listening to him.

They sipped a California brandy, which Maddie at first declined, disliking the eye-watering effect of such liquor. Marcus egged her on: she really should try it; it was so smooth. The flavor was remarkable, she admitted. It smelled of citrus and tasted spicy. And her vision wasn't impaired by its vapors.

As a first-time guest, she got to request the musical selection. It put her on the spot. Dare she say Chopin, Tim's favorite? The men waited expectantly. Of all of her children, he was the one who had truly loved the piano. The others did their time, as if it were punishment, then called it quits. Initially, at the age of six, he picked it up on his own by watching his siblings. At the time of his death, he was considered very accomplished for his age. He loved recitals and would have been a real showman.

Marcus could tell there was a problem that went beyond simply choosing something. At last she addressed the lopsided figure who sat balanced on his bench and ready. "I'll be honest with you, Herr Menzel…I had a son who believed that Chopin was the be-all and end-all…that the sun rose and set on him." The gentleman noted the past tense. So far, so good, she thought; her voice didn't even waver. "I would like nothing more in the world than, after all these years, to picture him playing. But I don't want to disturb your concentration if I start wiping my eyes…or blowing my nose."

An infinitesimal smile passed over the pianist's thin lips of which only he was aware. His twiglike fingers rested briefly on the keys. Then they floated across the passages that were second nature to him, more so these days than eating or walking. It was a wonder that his gift was spared from any afflictions. Compositions flowed forth that were the foundation of every student's repertoire, but notably interpreted here by a master. Maddie remembered them all. While observing the singular performance, Marcus realized that this illustrious musician, nearing his own end, was paying homage to a peer. That Tim was unknown to him—and, because of his age, unproven—was irrelevant; the boy was no stranger.

After an unforgettable, uninterrupted hour, the old man excused himself; he was overdue for another snooze. This had been draining. There wasn't the energy to look up at his guests when they shook hands to leave. Maddie wanted more time to convey how appreciative she was, but Marcus tapped her elbow and raised his eyebrows, signaling to go. The nurse instinctively knew to enter.

They watched as the musician shuffled down the hallway with her, his individual parts moving as clumsily as the wayward limbs of a marionette in the hands of a novice puppeteer.

When they reached the front stoop, Maddie's eyes were shiny. Marcus dabbed a corner with his thumb. He led her by the wrist down the stone walkway. Once they passed the gate, his pinky finger latched on to hers, and side by side they hiked slowly up the path. Hours of daylight remained, albeit hazy ones. The humidity had grown worse. Poor Max. His rapid panting created a wide-eyed look of desperation. He ran ahead, then turned and barked ferociously; *hurry up*, he demanded.

"Will you tell me about your daughter...Renata?"

Marcus nodded. There was an open area where he made the dog rest. Marcus lay down beside him and felt along the inside of Max's back leg. The pulse was racing. "A hundred and sixty," he said, counting the beats with his watch. "That can't be good. It's like he's just run for miles."

Maddie shared his concern. "How old is he?"

"I'm not sure. At least...eight or nine."

"That's getting up there for bigger dogs. If it doesn't slow down, I'll carry one end of him." She looked around. Tiny violets, with laser-bright yellow centers, dotted the shaded floor. Not far were some moss-flanked trees. Mushrooms, lots of them, ascended from the spreading roots and grew in stair-formations up the trunks.

"Don't even think about it!" warned Marcus, having followed her eyes. She grinned.

She sat beside Max's paws. The birds twittered loudly. They listened for a while, then Marcus began to tell about the night that gave him back his daughter. He needed to state first that his grandson was born about five months after Marta had died.

"It felt good to focus on something positive when we were still feeling so sad. The baby was a perfect little guy...hardly fussed, always smiled. Renata and her partner let me spend as much time as I wanted with him. When he learned to walk, my son would visit, and the three of us would go to the zoo or the playground. I told Kurt that we had the same fun when he was small. Too bad he couldn't remember. Kurt said his mother used to bring it up. They often looked through a box of pictures that showed us all together. He loved to hear her tell about how she and I met."

Max finally regained a regular pattern to his breathing. His eyes closed. Marcus sprawled out and rested on an elbow.

"As the baby grew, I'd be playing with him…in his little swimming pool or sandbox…and I could sense my daughter always keeping an eye on me. I hated the way in which she glanced at us when I was in a room with him. It filled me with guilt, like I hadn't earned the right to have this kind of fun. Although I was fulfilling the role of a grandparent, I was aware that I could never live up to being her father. I had tried to put Munich out of my mind, and the hate that kid had shown toward me that one time. But it wasn't possible. Those angry eyes of hers, Maddie…Jesus! She beats my meanest face any day. My skin crawls thinking about it."

He turned on his back. Maddie stared at the curve of his neck and had wonderful thoughts about it. He gazed upward. "I'd dream of her…waiting for me to make one wrong move so she would have an excuse to keep me out of the boy's life." He folded his hands together under his neck and crossed his ankles. A nearby woodpecker started hammering into a tree and didn't let up. It was annoying.

"Finally, I couldn't take it anymore. One night I drove the three hours to their house. When the baby's father opened the door, he asked if I was drunk…and said he wasn't going to wake Renata for any reason." Maddie guessed Renata hadn't ever married the baby's father.

"She heard us, and told him it was all right. He stepped directly in front of my face. I thought he was going to slam his head into my forehead, but he sniffed my breath, then left the room."

Max made an attempt to sit up, then flopped back down.

"I just came right out with my feelings. I told her that I needed to know for certain what was going on. If she really didn't want me around, I'd do her the favor and leave." He faced Maddie. "I got scared then…What a dumb thing to say. I couldn't imagine not seeing my grandson. I started walking in circles like a fool. She ordered me to sit…and she called me Daddy—*Vati*—which she had never done."

Maddie thought about the complicated nature of family relationships. No one was spared. She tried picturing his daughter.

"I sat down beside her, nervous as could be. She wished I had mentioned this sooner, saying I could have saved myself a lot of grief. I had it all wrong. Every time she looked at me, she saw the man her mother had fallen in love with…and remained in love with until she died—the one who gave her peace at the end. She said her mom helped her to see that I couldn't be any other way. When I was with the baby…and Kurt too, Renata said…there was a feeling of great affection toward me." Marcus had to clear his throat. "Next she said, 'I think it's tragic that you missed out on us growing up, not just the other way around. Who knows the man you might have become because of us?'" He paused. "I didn't bawl 'til I got back home." He watched Maddie absentmindedly pluck a flower apart.

She cast him a sympathetic look. "It's the old moral of not second-guessing anyone, right? Just think if you had never brought it up…and went on believing she hated you?"

"Trust me, that crosses my mind once in a while. Worse though was admitting that I could have been different…and I chose not to be."

Max sprang to his feet and licked him on the nose.

"Feh, Maaax," he whined, and wiped the wet smear off with his sleeve. "I see we're ready to head out."

They took it easy. Marcus barked orders to his mate, insisting that he slow down and heel. After a couple of freewheeling years as a retired police dog, Max had ceased to register the command. By the fifth time, he matched strides with them; the past conditioning from his working life had won out.

"You know, Marcus…about being stumped with your autobiography. Why don't you begin by explaining the importance of your children in your life now…then go back to your earliest memories? That might be effective."

He fell into deep thought and studied the ground in front of his feet as though he had to decide where to place each step. The cushion of pine needles felt good under their tired soles, but Max had to have the barbs tenderly pulled out of a paw once. When his home was in view, Marcus placed his arm around Maddie's shoulders, and she in turn held onto his waist. They were damp with perspiration. "We talk a lot," he stated.

"This is true."

"When we get back, could we just kiss for an hour or two?"

She caught the twinkle in his eye. "One or two?"

"OK…make it three."

She offered a little laugh, not realizing he meant it.

When the door opened, Max made a beeline for the kitchen floor.

Maddie felt sorry for him. "You should think about getting him shaven…just for the summer. That's a lot of hair."

Marcus placed some ice cubes by the dog's chin. "Maybe." He left while she got herself a glass of water.

"Madelaine, come here," he called. She entered his bedroom. He was standing in front of the air conditioner with his arms straight out to his sides. "This is heaven."

She pulled her blouse out of her skirt, then reached inside to hold the bra away from her sticky skin. They appeared meditative, standing so still, and with their eyes shut; it was as if they were before an altar.

"This is making my clothes cold." The hair stood on her arms. They chuckled at the sound of the dog's loud, jaw-breaking crunching.

Marcus bounced on the edge of the bed sideways and patted the spot beside him. Maddie didn't need convincing. Cozying up next to him, she then looked around with interest. It was obvious that a wall had been removed to make the room bigger. "How long have you had this place?" she asked.

"Oh…ten years or so. Claudia and her husband were already living here. He grew up close by. This house went up for sale after the owner died. I liked that it was out of the way. When I was still in school, my friends and I used to stay here at a *jugendherberge* (hostel) and go skiing. There are many good memories." He took a deep breath and arched his back. His one bent leg on the bed warmed her thigh.

The sumptuous atmosphere sharply contrasted with the minimalist-style living room. Richly colored tapestries, used for the upholstery, called to mind shades of reddish-gold cognacs and velvety-black wines. Metallic gold, lavender, and chartreuse threads shimmered in the weaves. The beige walls reflected the room's warm pigments, producing a rosy sunset glow across them. Two contemporary rugs with geometric patterns broke up the floor space. Overall, it looked busy, yet it felt comfortable. Lacking was a well-fed cat; a coppery-eyed, gray-blue wooly one would suit the scene nicely. Whimsical tarnished metal sculptures of monkey men and flying frogs and walking fish got lost in the patterns. There were no framed family photos. Her exploration stopped at three drawings—unmistakably by Van Gogh. That conclusion was derived from her strong personal interest in the post-impressionists, and particularly in him. Granted, the artist produced an inordinate number of sketches, but Maddie was familiar with a good many of them—and she didn't recognize these from gallery catalogues, or from any art books. Good copies? One was definitely of Arles from the late eighties.

"They're authentic," he said.

She gawked at the famous characteristic strokes, stupefied over being this close to originals. She had to ask, but didn't want to make him surly. "Was your father in some way connected?" It was common knowledge that the Nazis had confiscated many works of art.

"Yes. But I don't wish to discuss it now." His voice was soft, and not on the defensive. He removed the leather barrette, then shook her hair until her auburn tresses hung loosely on her shoulders. In a balletlike movement, Marcus gracefully wrapped his right arm under Maddie's knees and lifted her legs. She was pushing herself back a little when suddenly his other arm caught her from behind, and they went down together onto the puffiest feather pillow, sinking inches into its center. He propped himself above her face and ran a fingertip along her lips.

"It would feel good to get a shower," she said.

He seemed to ignore the comment and began to tenderly kiss her cheeks and neck, unbuttoning her blouse to reach her shoulders...for starters.

His chest lay across hers; the rest of his body was at an angle to her side.

"Can we listen to some music?"

He determinedly carried on with his objective. Maddie met resistance when she tried to push him off, and it drew an unwelcome response from her. It bugged her that he was probably accustomed to easily and always getting what he wanted from women. She knew she was being irrational about this; her own desire was the same as his. Nevertheless, the situation was reminiscent of her few dates before getting married. A boy invariably waited for the chance to feel up a girl, which put into question any previous gentlemanly behavior. Ed was the exception. She wriggled out from under him and walked to the CD player. It was on the table in front of the drawings.

"Should I keep the ones that are already in?"

"Sure."

He sounded fed up. She could tell from the one word.

There was a picture light mounted to the wall. She couldn't resist. Just then a silvery melody from a blues tenor sax sailed into the room and held onto notes that squeezed the senses out of her. The moment was indescribable. She was privy to a specific hour on a specific day, over a hundred years ago, when Van Gogh felt inspiration. If it were possible for a heart to weep from joy, hers would fill buckets. The two smaller pictures showed the backsides of farmers digging in a field. They were solitary figures with boneless-looking limbs. Gnarly, spiky trees stood isolated in the distance, and wavy wisps of clouds blew across the gloomy scenes. She studied the countless drawn lines.

Max strolled in; maybe he liked the tune. He jumped on the narrow chair alongside the window. The blast of cold air sent his long coat flowing straight back.

The break in action offered necessary time for reflection. With the events in Paris branded in her memory, Maddie asked herself if *this* was always going to happen to her on the road. Sex never factored into her reasons for making this trip. It was proving to be an undisputed central issue in the overall experience. She rested on the corner edge of the table, wondering whether she should allow the evening to continue in this direction.

Marcus realized she was having misgivings and wanted to kick himself for permitting such a perfect opportunity to slip by. He could pretty much give up on the luscious romp in the sheets he was expecting. She appeared resolute in maintaining her distance. He turned and faced the ceiling, searching its corners in the detached manner of a bored patient in a hospital bed.

He hadn't heard correctly—couldn't possibly have. He looked back. Maddie's pensive expression hadn't changed from before. He wanted to taste her mouth again. Dare he say *Pardon me, would you mind repeating what I thought you said* (which was to undress)? It must have been a subliminal auditory trick…wishful thinking on his part. He was painfully aware of his deep breathing and the pulse drumming in his ears. She continued to watch him…with no intimation of any interest. What if he did get out of his clothes…what was the worst that could happen? Her running out? That was likely being considered anyway.

He unfastened the button on his pants. Pausing a second, he quickly unzipped them and hastily pulled them over his feet. He didn't risk glancing at her. Off came his briefs. An elbow got stuck in a shirt sleeve. Maddie straddled him to help. His blood reached boiling. She planted a kiss—gratefully received. The pillowcase felt refreshingly cool. Patience, Marcus warned himself. After more than a year of no sex, the first of its kind, he had better not say or do anything wrong…which, minutes ago, he was convinced was already the case. He hadn't felt the inclination much since Marta's death, and was secretly relieved when his fiancée said good-bye to him during the emotional period.

Maddie looked at his hands draped casually over her thighs. Her skirt was hiked above her knees, and his fingers were lost in its folds. His pose was irresistible to her. Marcus reveled in her touch, which she appreciated watching. There was a time, when she was first married, that she got to enjoy this picture. But after only a few years, Ed stopped lingering in bed—stopped enjoying simply lying beside her. Once the act was executed, he immediately rolled over to sleep or got up to do something or other.

The sustained midrange hum of the air conditioner was hypnotic. The CD switched to a rainy-day voice that matched the brooding mood of the darkening interior. Nina Simone brought back memories. She served as one twin's inspiration when he used to write his papers in the middle of the night during high school.

Ms. Simone's songs blended into the next artist's, and the next…none of whom Maddie recognized. All were equally soulful. It really was possible to go on kissing this man for hours. She did need to straighten out while she still could. Positioning her elbows beside his head, she brought her knees together, then used her feet to push Marcus's ankles apart. She rested inside his legs. Holding him securely in place, her inner thighs turned as slick as their working tongues. Maddie found it all fascinating. Internally, things somersaulted. Until this summer, the idea of an illicit relationship (especially at this age) would have seemed as farfetched as taking up with the man in the moon, regardless of the fact that her marriage hadn't represented a meaningful union since ages ago. The strong hands held her with the kind of wanton brute force pervading hackney romance novels. Marcus then whispered, insistently, he didn't want to finish yet. She stopped moving. He was finding it difficult to do the same.

She climbed off. *Now what?* she wondered.

"Aren't you going to take your clothes off?" he asked.

"Uh-uh."

"That's not fair…"

Maddie gave a little shrug, and looked a bit teasing. Her arms hugged her bosom, increasing its fullness. He looked admiringly at the breasts and started to say something…but quickly became tightlipped—too chancy. "Out with it," she said, curious. Marcus regarded her with such intense longing that she felt the ache. She pulled him along with her when she tumbled onto her back. He carefully balanced above her on his knees and unhooked the front of her bra. After delighting in that fantasy for awhile, he began to kiss her mouth again. She firmly pushed him upright in order to inch her way down underneath him a bit more. He watched as he repeatedly vanished from view, only to re-emerge on those sweet lips. Maddie savored the notion of still being able to excite a man, especially one she cared for this much. The evening reached a satisfying conclusion.

Max's snout was tucked tightly under his legs when she rubbed his ears before crawling back in bed beside a sleeping Marcus. She shook open a coverlet by their feet and pulled it to their hips. The giant pillow had been knocked to the floor. Nose-to-nose, Maddie took drags off Marcus's deep breaths. The gap between his lips was inviting. The tip of his tongue passed over her front teeth. Aha…still awake…albeit with leaded lids. Maddie nudged him, and he grinned. His hands, in open prayer position, found a snug fit between her breasts. Her fingers glided lazily over his wrist and arm, then marched across his broad shoulder in a tapping manner until they reached the back of his neck, where they hit a ticklish spot. As she rubbed the muscles to relax them, he purred. "How do you do that?" she whispered.

"Hmmm..." mingled with the vibrations. She pressed an ear against him, next to the idling motor, skeptical of this ability.

Without opening his eyes, he found her mouth, cupped her breasts in a protective fashion, and slid inside.

It was dark...except for the illuminated corner with the Van Goghs. Hours were passing. This latest music suited her; the ethereal melodies plucked from a harp were like fairies moving with celerity among the field of stars where she was beginning to fall asleep.

CHAPTER 15

It was three in the morning when Maddie slipped noiselessly out of the house and began walking back to the hostel. She quietly laughed over this newfound gumption. No one who knew her would believe this middle-of-the-night stroll; she certainly didn't. The iridescent white clouds formed an umbrella around the earth, keeping the sky lit. The fragrant pines cleared her head. Her lone footsteps made her acutely aware of her existence. It felt splendid. But it didn't prevent her from stopping now and again to listen for another's. Would she really have the presence of mind to use the open Swiss army knife she carried, if need be? She had to admit, she felt perfectly safe winding down the wooded path, tangled with shadows.

She had written a note to Marcus, briefly explaining why she had taken off. It didn't seem the right thing to do, but she was accustomed to sleeping alone and wanted to wake up on her own time. Besides, he had to fly to Germany later this morning for a few days. She had hesitated when it came to signing her name. Just "Maddie" would have lacked warmth, but "love" was out of the question. She settled for "Enthusiastically Yours." That sounded so ridiculous now, but it was all her discombobulated brain could piece together at that hour.

It wasn't too late—nine o'clock—when she woke up. She snickered when she looked herself over—once again, a total mess. It had been another typical drop-into-bed-with-clothes-on night.

It was the first week in July, and Maddie didn't give any thought to the Fourth. The room was empty, made ready for new arrivals. She checked her phone messages. Rima sent one occasionally, if something noteworthy happened that couldn't wait…like when she received a scholarship. Maddie thought about a previous one, informing her that the last few times her granddaughter had gone to their house, Grandpa was at Mrs. Simm's (the neighbor, Lorraine's). Rima felt she should know. Maddie realized it must be unsettling to the girl, since Rima didn't want to report the news in an e-mail, in case a friend was sitting with her grandmother and might see it. Maddie dismissed it at the time. It was impossible for her to relate to whatever was happening in her husband's life. Today, however, she contemplated Ed also having such glorious nights. Although she wouldn't have put it past Lorraine to pursue her husband while she was gone, what she found most interesting was Ed's willing involvement.

Maddie knew without a doubt Ed had genuinely loathed their neighbor; he had disliked Lorraine for the trait he had now apparently fallen victim to. No one understood the Simms' marital arrangement. Before his death, Neil Simms, Ed's best friend, loved his wife despite her character flaw. And his wife appeared to love him very much too. Maddie recalled the word used to describe women like her back then: *nympho*. It had since fallen out of fashion when ladies began to speak openly about their sexual exploits in the same manner men traditionally had. Lorraine's lack of morality didn't stop Maddie from being friendly to her. She realized the important role the woman and her husband played in her son Tim's life. Maddie would return to thinking about this later; right now she saw a text message from Marcus.

Shame on you, she read. That was open for interpretation. *Will call tonight.*

She continued quasi-napping for another half hour. Yesterday's events captivated her imagination. Several times she sighed contentedly, freeze-framing choice moments. Then she thought about showering while she still had privacy.

Building up lather wasn't easy with this low pressure. At least the meager stream was lukewarm, not ice cold. There were jobs that could no longer be put off. Her hair needed coloring…maybe a trim. She should let the roots grow out; the auburn was no longer a prominent identifying feature like when she was younger, and it was also redder. She appreciated when people associated its color with her Irish ancestry. Nowadays, because girls and women alike altered their hair shades on a whim, that special connection was lost.

After much thought, Maddie determined more time was required before she could accept such a dramatic change in her appearance. It couldn't be that abrupt. She'd go a little lighter every month.

She needed to find more disposable contact lenses (what a godsend these were). It was also imperative to swim…spend time in an art gallery, swim some more, go to a movie…and swim, swim, swim. She simply wanted to hang out by herself.

Maddie dutifully stuck to that schedule for the next three days, caving in only twice when a few of the hostel's guests asked her to accompany them for a bite to eat. This new group comprised three doctors. Maddie was intrigued by the backgrounds of everyone she was meeting. These women were Janet's age and had hitchhiked back in 1972, when they were undergraduates. One was now an oncologist; another was a pediatrician; the third was a dermatologist. Although it had proved difficult, each finally managed to set aside a month for this reunion. They were revisiting all of their old haunts (except Morocco), bemoaning the fact that they had a ready supply of cash to help them out of an unforeseen jam, if the need arose.

That odd complaint required an explanation. They told Maddie that their first trip had been a true adventure, because they had to stay within a modest budget, which constantly necessitated improvisation. Their resourcefulness saw them through the summer. This go-round, though, they slept in private cars on the train; they had been eating in notable restaurants and attending plays and concerts. They were living the life they could only daydream about when they were poor students, sunning themselves on the beach in Greece. On a recent afternoon, while staring at each other in a Four Seasons lobby, they admitted to recurring feelings of emptiness. Bottom line: they missed connecting with people…time to go the hostel route again. They were pleasantly surprised to learn that some of the same ones were still in operation.

When they inquired about her, Maddie explained the circumstances. "What guts!" one of them said, and the others nodded in agreement. Maddie was surprised by the "you go, girl!" slap on the back she inspired from the baby doctor. It felt great.

Marcus called all three nights. He could hardly wait to return and begin writing. Her suggestion was a tremendous help and got him off to the start he needed. He missed her.

She felt torn. She didn't want to look forward to his calls as much as she did, to hearing the soft voice with the studied pronunciation. It was time to move on, before she became any more attached to him…and Claudia. The farewell was going to be difficult.

When Marcus returned, he headed over to his neighbor's, where he could count on finding something good to eat. On the kitchen table lay a big sign with *Italia* beautifully written in calligraphy (a hobby of Maddie's; she often addressed wedding invitations for friends). It was illustrated with grapevines.

She was leaving. The impending loss hit him hard, and his great body sank onto the chair. He outlined the letters. The cardboard was protected by a smooth, laminating sheet of plastic wrap that had been tightly pulled across it.

Claudia breezed in with a few groceries and began putting them away.

"So how is our overworked Wilhelm?" she asked, referring to their mutual friend in Munich. Silence. She turned around and saw the fattest tear rolling down his cheek. She could only think about the fun Maddie had yesterday designing her poster.

Marcus toyed with the salt shaker on the table, then the bottle of vitamins. He inspected its label. "You know, I steal one of these whenever I'm here." Claudia looked at him, puzzled. "I figure they're no different than men's…just a marketing angle." He set the bottle down and looked into her lovely, concerned eyes. "I thought they might have hormones. I've never been this weepy in my whole life."

"Oh, Marcus…" She pulled a chair in front of him. "You're simply a late bloomer when it comes to recognizing the essential stuff of this life." He rested his head on her lap. "She can't stay…she has places to see. You know that."

For once, Claudia offered him no solace. What goes around, comes around…he was feeling the kind of hurt he had inflicted on others for having done whatever he wanted, whenever he wanted; not maliciously, of course, but nevertheless thoughtlessly. The result was the same. So many had endured his general indifference to the important role he played in their lives. Madelaine was that important to him.

Early in the afternoon, Marcus stood waiting in the clearing. With her hair dancing loosely and a smile stretched wide, Maddie bounded up the path, trying to reach him faster. They jumped into each other's arms, laughing from sheer joy. Their hearts met. Her hold around his waist almost raised him an inch off the ground.

Surprisingly, they didn't end up in bed, but returned to Claudia's for lunch. The conversation revolved around their childhoods. Considering the grueling daily character-building tests imposed during that period, all agreed the present was preferable…well, almost all.

"I saw your artwork," said Marcus. "Very eye-catching. You're certain to get a ride…right off the bat." He winked, recalling the expression, then asked when she was thinking of leaving.

"At first, I thought I'd wait until it got cooler…but the heat's expected to continue. I'm glad I'm not in Paris now. Have you heard the reports about people dying?"

Her enthusiasm over getting back on the road didn't take into account his feelings at all. It pained him. Claudia couldn't watch and excused herself to go work on the computer.

"I guess I'll go after tomorrow." Maddie looked at his pretending face. "I can't wait to read about the many things that have happened in your life. You actually began the first paragraph?"

He got up to grind another espresso—and to hide his disappointment. "Thanks to you…and your suggestion." A shooting pain hit him smack-dab in the middle of his forehead.

She looked through the transparent curtain, which hung stationary, and remembered the way it had blown across the Irish actor Michael's face. "I miss Max. Why isn't he with you?"

Marcus informed her that Herr Menzel had fallen and sprained some muscles. His nurse asked if the dog could keep him company in the afternoons until he was better.

The remainder of the day was spent tending to the rose garden. There was a man who regularly looked after it, but he was ill. They worked quietly, pausing every now and then to sit and sip a chilled chardonnay. They ate a light dinner back at Claudia's kitchen. Every few weeks, Claudia got caught up in a cooking marathon; this was one of those times. They were presented with a wonderful skillet of scallops, noodles, and peppers. Gin and tonics replaced the wine. Claudia appeared happy about something. She couldn't hold back her excitement any longer: she had met someone she really liked, and the feeling was mutual. It was a celebratory night, new starts for all.

Maddie sidestepped the issue of spending the night with Marcus by declaring outright that she had made plans to meet her roommates later, which wasn't true. Her inner voice was helping her move forward with her trip. It was tempting to stay. She was afraid he would try to persuade her to make an excuse to get out of going. Instead, he briefly regarded her with dismay, then let it pass.

She accompanied him to pick up Max, and the three continued back to her place. The silence was unsettling. It was obvious she needed to distance herself from him. These intense emotions placed constraints on the grand trip she had proposed for herself.

Deep down, Marcus understood that her parting was for the best. There could be no distractions if he was to finish his book. It took more effort to accept this on his part, though.

When Maddie pulled the handle to get out of the car, she looked to Max to butt in and offer comic relief. The weary dog addressed her with a raised eyebrow. *Thanks for your help!* She aimed the sarcastic thought right at those big pupils. It apparently registered, and he whined. She proceeded to get out.

Marcus nabbed her left wrist before her getaway. She sat halfway in and halfway out. His grip was disturbingly tight. She slumped against the seat and waited to be let go. His eyes stared vacantly past her out the window. Was he thinking at all? This guessing game was taxing. How absurd…she was getting the heebie-jeebies from his making like a statue. She pushed the door wide open with her foot and tried working her hand free. "Marcus!"

He held it tighter—hard enough to crush her bones if he inadvertently squeezed a millimeter more. Now he looked at her. His disposition was frighteningly grim. She refused to be subjected to this bullish behavior. "Stop it!"

The growl from the backseat was low and ominous. The hand ejected hers.

Maddie massaged her sore wrist while she watched Marcus get out and go around the car to her side. With gentle hands, he helped her out of the seat, then walked her to the front door, just as he had on that first night…when she had been preoccupied with his hair. She looked at it under the dim overhead light, studying the strands that framed his face and the ones twisted over his collar. He stood with his arms to his sides. It went against her better judgment, but she couldn't resist smiling at him. He buried his face in her neck.

Maddie didn't wish for these cravings to be stirred up again. She was relieved to find her feet stepping away from him.

His eyes beseeched hers. "Tomorrow?"

She knew what he meant and nodded OK. Satisfied, he kissed her, then flew to his car and sped down the road.

Maddie went to bed at nine thirty. It didn't matter that the stark globe ceiling light was too bright or that her roommates were carrying on with visitors.

Mrs. Gulliver and Herr Roman awoke in their respective beds that Wednesday morning, refreshed and ready to tackle their day's agenda with businesslike urgency. Aided by quadruple shots of espresso in his cappuccino, the writer watched the sun come up in front of his computer. The constant, soft clatter of the keyboard was the only sound in the room as his fingers transferred outlined remembrances at a hurried pace. His adrenaline carried him through hunger and the usual midday sleepiness. The answering machine was on; no one had been deemed important enough to sidetrack his dedicated effort—that was, until Maddie called at six thirty in the evening, right when he had stepped out to the garden to stretch his legs for the first time.

She, likewise, was up at dawn, but she was at the gym, preparing herself physically for the next leg of her journey. The only noise came from the muffled sound of closed-off generators and pumps. Maddie was standing on the east-facing platform, set to dive, when the sun popped up between the mountains and smacked her in the eyes. She tore through the water. Miniature bubbles escaped her smile. Later, she ate heartily, packed, and reviewed some maps before calling Marcus at six thirty. When his voice completed the message, she began hers.

"Hello…just wanted to let you know I'll be in my room the rest of the evening, if you…"

"Maddie…I'm here." He breathed fast from running to the phone.

Neither was upset by the other not calling until then, so certain were they of inevitably meeting today. He needed to eat and would pick her up afterward, in thirty-five minutes. He always gave exact time frames—and adhered to them. It amused her.

The evening's program proceeded without a hitch, as if both had already mentally rehearsed it. No background music tonight; only the persistent air conditioner played along with the lovemaking. Holding hands, they fell asleep.

Thursday morning they showered, dressed, and ate with hardly a word spoken. Maddie had bid farewell to Claudia the day before. Too bad Claudia couldn't be the one taking Maddie to the entrance ramp in an hour.

After collecting her bags at the hostel, they returned to Marcus's car. She felt keyed up and ready. He wished he could discourage her from hitchhiking.

Patches of fog carried drizzling rain. One could literally walk in and out of it. The slab of sky was pewter gray. Maddie was too excited to care. The dog sat between them and worked at regaining his footing after every turn. He could smell her sense of thrill and hovered over her face, licking it now and then as show of support—at least, that was how she wanted to interpret it. She needed someone to share in her eagerness.

Yay—the highway! Both fellows were given a heartfelt caress and the breeziest kiss. Maddie moved quickly, insisting on getting the backpack out of the trunk herself. Within a minute, she stood several yards ahead of them by the side of the road, proudly displaying the oversized *Italia* sign in front of her. A triumphant smile appeared when she aimed her thumb high in the air and wiggled it nonstop. She motioned for the driver to continue on his way. Marcus complied, passing her as he left.

He hadn't gone more than a few kilometers when he decided that this silly idea of hers had to be squelched once and for all. It simply wasn't safe. He hit the brakes just as he was about to bypass the street that would lead him back to the ramp. The dog flew to the front. Marcus cussed out loud—at himself, at Maddie, at other people...evil-minded ones, those hell-bent on destroying lives. Fear over her welfare gripped him.

He couldn't believe it...simply could not believe it. The car remained idling at the side of the road while Marcus sat there, bereft. At first, pursuit came to mind. Maddie couldn't be that far ahead. He rolled up to the main road and looked south. A curtain of gray obliterated his view. His forehead sank onto his hands, which clutched the top of the steering wheel. Max felt helpless and pawed at his arm. Marcus wiped his face on his shirtsleeve and tried seeing out of the windshield. His vision was too blurred. Some honks were directed his way as others made sure the driver wouldn't pull out in front of them.

As a last resort, he did what he had done during Marta's last days. For the first time in his entire life, he had prayed to a God and begged that his wife die without pain. Since it worked, he now placed one hand over the other in a pious gesture and asked, with all of his heart, that this woman...this friend...be free from harm.

"Please protect her," Marcus whispered. Then he headed home in a most lonely and despairing condition.

CHAPTER 16

❦

A shift in the weather helped Maddie reclaim even more of her original zeal. The clouds were dramatic. Fighter planes, flying in formation, suddenly ripped through them and delighted the siblings. They craned their little necks. The sight placated them for a while. Tedium from the long hours on the road had begun to undo the family, an Italian father with his daughter and son. They had been traveling from Bavaria when they picked up Frau Gulliver (her newest form of address) in Interlaken.

The girl and boy were the same size; Tony was small for a nine-year-old, and Lucia, big for seven. They were admirably proficient in English, since it was part of their curriculum since kindergarten. Antonio, their father, could manage the simplest sentence.

Maddie had acted guarded when she first saw the oily, unkempt man through the lowered passenger-side window. Then she glimpsed the children in back and felt better about accepting the ride. It wasn't until she had herself strapped in the seatbelt that the possibility of him being a kidnapper sped up her heart rate. Within a split second, she sized up the children's expressions and decided she could relax.

She ascertained from the son that his dad was taking them to Italy to see the dentist (where it was cheaper) and to stay with their grandparents—who lived nowhere near Rome. She'd need to find another ride after they crossed the mountains.

Maddie's excitement and curiosity matched that of the kids when the old Mercedes rolled onto a platform leading to a railroad wagon. Antonio turned off the engine and immediately asked for the brown paper bags on the back seat. The family offered to share their sandwiches, but Maddie declined. She did accept the wedge of apple held out to her. She in kind reached deep into her rucksack to locate a couple of chocolate bars. Eyes grew big.

The train slowly made its ascent up the mountain. They exchanged glances before passing into the tunnel. It held the drama of an untried amusement park ride and produced similar squeals. In a flash, the stark interior lights hit them, creating harsh shadows. The father's face looked downright horrific. Residual pox from acute adolescent acne made his head look like some crude papier-mâché construction. Maddie focused on the children's precious faces.

It was in the tunnel, with no place for escape, that Maddie feared officials might in fact be searching for their car. A clue came from one child—the boy noted sadly that their mother would be sorry she didn't get to kiss them before their papa had picked them up from their summer Bible school. Antonio read the lines of concern evident on Frau Gulliver's face. He then attempted to relay, as best he could, how their mother had divorced him and wouldn't let his parents in Italy see their own grandchildren. He didn't understand why. He had always been a hard worker. His family never went hungry—they lived in a nice apartment. The boy's big green eyes studied Maddie as an adult's would. *Is there anything comparable to an Amber Alert in Europe?* she wondered. After reviewing the situation, she didn't doubt that the children were really going to end up at their grandparents' home…their mother would know this. That fact still didn't sit well with her, though.

A new scene abruptly materialized—one that revealed a sprinkling of snow across a desolate shelf of hard, brown earth. A thick haze obscured the peaks surrounding the alpine plain. It was bleak and otherworldly. Strong winds agitated the loose white powder, creating mini-twisters that swirled in a graceful, clockwise fashion, barely sidestepping one another. When Lucia huddled into a ball, scared, the brother said he had told her these were ghosts of all the railroad workers who had died up here. If the spinning specters could touch any of the bodies on the daily trains, they'd be given new life. The spirit of the person whose body they stole would take their former place outside, until the next train came, when the souls whose bodies had just been stolen would get a chance to reclaim their life by taking another body. Just as he finished, one of those phantoms skipped above their railcar and the girl shrieked, at which the dad lit into the boy in Italian. His arm was too short to deliver the smack across the face. Tony retreated to the corner, where he sat with his hand over his mouth, laughing. The father looked back at her in exasperation. Maddie agreed…"kids!"

After five minutes, the tunnel swallowed them again. The next time they emerged, the view couldn't have been more opposite the scene they had left behind, robbing Maddie instantly of her breath for a second. The satin-blue sky shone above a broad terrace that was even and green, like a billiard table. In it was stamped a single concrete road, which wound toward infinity. A distant, white church steeple stretched high above a promontory like a beacon for anyone found stranded in the middle of this beautiful, but lonely, patch of earth.

Maddie regretted how quickly the hours were going by. It was already noon, and they were at the Italian border. Antonio parked and motioned that he'd only be a moment; he went over to speak to someone inside the station.

His daughter lay sleeping. A page of her open book was caught under her chin. Some drool was ready to soak it. Tony followed Maddie's eyes and slid the book out from under his sister. Then he took Maddie by complete surprise. Dangling his small frame over the front seat, the boy wrapped his scanty arms around her neck and kissed her cheek. It was such an ingenuous display of affection; she reciprocated. His sweet voice proclaimed, "You are beautiful…like our mamma." He unlocked his arms and rested his hands on the seat. He spotted his dad. "Look how little Papa is."

What a noteworthy observation. Maddie didn't know how to console the child; after all, the comment expressed the son's own fear, whether he understood it yet or not. He must regard her as a giant. She brushed the boy's dark ringlets off his forehead and tried to make him understand that every generation was bigger than the one before. She wasn't completely lying; the rule applied over the long term. She added, "Don't worry about it, OK?"

"OK." He liked saying that. Then he squished her cheek with another unabashed, heartfelt hug. What a dear soul.

When the drive resumed, Antonio offered a history lesson. Tony enjoyed translating many of his words. Unfortunately, most of the information was going in one of Maddie's ears and out the other—but not because it was boring; it was really interesting. The problem was the sinking sensation, growing worse with every passing kilometer, the farther she traveled from Marcus and Claudia. She longed to be in the cottage on the road tucked away. It was indeed a magical place. She missed the fragrant backyard roses. She missed Claudia's kitchen, with its lingering aroma of ground espresso beans, and the simple gauze curtain. She wanted another opportunity to stand before the stashed Van Goghs, another chance to delight in Herr Menzel's playing…and to stroke Max's soft fur.

Lucia woke with a start and announced that she desperately needed to pee. There was no reason to look for a rest stop. Janet's letters had prepared Maddie for the lack of modesty she was certain to encounter. The ladies squatted behind a few slim trees that bordered the roadside. The little girl had obviously held it in for the better part of the day. Maddie forgot how tricky this position was. She pressed her hand against the trunk to keep from keeling over. Her skirt was tacked under her chin. Her knees shook like crazy. She felt vulnerable, like a giraffe off its center when stooping by a watering hole. This maneuver should have been practiced a few times beforehand.

An hour later, they stopped to eat at a modern restaurant chain. After much coaxing, the dad finally backed down and allowed Maddie to pay.

The driving was taking a toll on Lucia's well-being. She already had the car door open as her dad was slowing to a stop on the shoulder. The trajectory left a trail on the road. She sat sideways on the seat with her head between her legs. Her pitiful moans caused her brother to tenderly cradle her small backside. He sat on his folded legs, stroked the back of her hair—conveniently pulled together in braids (thank goodness, thought Maddie), and rubbed her shoulders.

Maddie grabbed a water bottle and wet a tissue. She got out on her side to go and wipe the girl's mouth.

Antonio's plan had been to drive nonstop to their destination. His daughter wouldn't last the remaining four or five hours. He expected the American would want to get on with her trip.

There was no way Maddie could leave while the child was in such wretched condition. She agreed to spend the night with them at a truck stop (in their car). She thought twice before suggesting that she would pay for a hotel room…since no one questioned the sleeping arrangement.

The worst over, the pale girl returned to a sitting position and clicked her seat belt. She feigned a weak smile, indicating they could continue. They hadn't gone far before securing their spot for the night.

Lucia perked up. She was understandably grateful for not having to spend another second in motion. The youngsters walked around in search of others of their kind.

Maddie cordially declined to take a stroll with Antonio. She towered over him and pictured how farcical their juxtaposition would appear. His son would certainly make a mental note if he witnessed them together. Later in his adulthood, he would recall when that giantess had lied to him. Hadn't she practically guaranteed that he would stand taller than his father? He'd better, she prayed.

The air was suffocating. The freeway traffic only made it nastier. This was going to be a long, long night. Maddie couldn't stop thinking about the children's distraught mother who, by now, would be dealing with their abduction. She pictured her hysterical with fear—or rage. Why hadn't she continued on her way when it was suggested?

The group squeezed themselves into their bedtime positions. Lucia cuddled beside Maddie on the backseat. Maddie could tell that her presence was reassuring and appreciated. It abated the earlier misgivings about staying. The boy rested on the front seat with his feet on his dad's lap. The man's slight body was hunched against the door. His head was pressed into a stained, well-used pillow, which he had propped on the window. His folded arms rested on his chest. He couldn't look any more uncomfortable, and yet he was first to fall asleep. At least he didn't snore.

The thing that was most distressing on the momentous occasion of Maddie's first night in Italy was how stiff she could expect to be tomorrow. She lay on her back with her right knee bent. The leg area was fully packed with things for the family's journey. The girl's head was situated below Maddie's breasts; the rest of Lucia had Maddie's skirt pinned down so she couldn't turn if she tried. Maddie had to chuckle over this picture and guessed that the discomfort was likely going to be worth it.

There was no need to wake up the following morning…because she hadn't truly slept. Maddie supposed that her face probably looked even puffier than it felt. She poked at her sticky eyes and cleared away flaky mascara grit. Her fingers tried in vain to untangle her matted hair. Making her way around the sleeping girl, Maddie climbed out of the car stealthily to go freshen up in the bathroom. Her flat passport holder contained a small comb and some disposable scrub cloths for such instances—maybe not quite like this one.

On her way back, she witnessed the father relieving himself directly behind his opened door. She stopped in her tracks, realizing that his penis was clearly visible. The sight repulsed her, to the point of stimulating her gag reflex. He stared down at the puddle of mud forming, still half asleep and oblivious. Shaking her head in disgust, Maddie continued in an arc to access the car from a different direction. She was prepared to go in search of a ride to Rome, but to her surprise, the place was vacant. It was only 6:40. She surmised that she had to have nodded off after all; otherwise she'd have noticed the commotion. That was a lot of people.

They woke the children, who ran lickety-split to the toilets. Everyone was anxious to get the show on the road. Once under way, the children started singing German songs. Their dad interrupted with an Italian selection. *When in Italy*...thought Maddie. Italy was their new home. Too bad she'd never know how this story would unfold.

Their tummies began to grumble. They hit the first restaurant; it was rundown, and occupied only by truckers. The place already packed a cloud of cigarette smoke. It looked like a sports bar back home. Maddie watched, amused. The men's fingers pinched toylike handles of *demitasse* cups. In between sips of espresso, their hands waved wildly in the air. The stirring topics could only be politics and soccer.

The conspicuous family sat by a wall next to an open window and ate some hard rolls and salami. Before finishing, Antonio stood and started making his way down the counter of men. Whatever he was saying, it couldn't be good. He'd jabber something to a driver, then they would look over at the table. It didn't deter him when the guy in question shook his head no; the little man would move on to the next fellow. It dawned on Maddie that he was trying to find her a ride. She wasn't sure whether to be incensed or humiliated—thankful never came to mind. She wanted the control of choosing her own company.

Maddie tried to cool her reddening cheeks with her hands, which felt like ice in comparison. A strip of skin above her breastbone began to burn, too. She considered fleeing. Just then, the jubilant man strode over with a trucker in tow. How could she get past the anger she felt over his presumptuous action?

"Frau Gulliver," he said. He held out his hand and presented her to the driver. "Jakov..." (J pronounced like Y).

"Strmski," finished the young man, helping the Italian father out with his last name. He shook Maddie's hand and told her that he was going close to Rome. She couldn't hide her uneasiness. Jakov leaned forward over the table, relaxing his weight on one leg. His arms were slender but strong. In a genial tone, he said that he could speak some American that he picked up from the movies...some German...and a bit of Italian.

She hated looking directly at him, knowing her face was still red. "Any French? *Francaise?*"

He shook his head. "Sorry. That's how you say?"

She couldn't pretend to smile.

The driver told Maddie not to hurry. When they were through eating, she could take her belongings over to his bright green truck. She'd find it parked ahead of a couple of others by the side of the road.

While exchanging hugs with the children, Maddie prayed she would be spared having to do the same with Antonio. Heaven forbid he should expect a kiss on the cheek. He must have read her thoughts in the cartoon bubble above her head. After carrying her bag to the rig, he only politely shook her hand.

"Good Lord!" exclaimed Maddie. This had to be the biggest truck she'd ever seen. Jakov came up from behind her, laughing. She admired his dark features and light skin; the exception was his left arm, tanned from hanging out the window. He was at least six-five or six-six and had a marvelously lean, muscular physique—a swimmer's body. She couldn't be sure if he was in his thirties.

Maddie balked at the imposing height of the passenger-side door, and didn't think she could possibly hike her leg up far enough to climb in. Holding a straplike handle, she raised a knee to her chest and set the ball of her foot against the edge of the step.

"Ally-oop!" grunted Jakov, as his boldly positioned hands pushed her up. She flew onto the seat, yelling as she went. He hoisted her pack and slid it inside the cab. He hopped in on his side. His eyes shone as black as his hair. His smile was infectious.

There was minimal vibration when he powered up, but the resonance from the engaging parts brought to mind an image of rocket boosters. He had to be a good driver, Maddie told herself, to be entrusted with an expensive machine like this. There was the sense of hauling too much weight…that somehow, they would begin to slide backward. They crossed that threshold, and within minutes were cruising through the countryside. This was magnificent. She commended Antonio under her breath; the Italian had come through for her.

Jakov Strmski was Croatian. He explained that both sides of his family were extremely tall; a girl cousin played basketball in Germany, and a professional team in the U.S. was trying to recruit a nephew. The only son of five children, he had to quit college temporarily when his father became ill two years ago. It was his duty to help out the family financially. His dad had since died. He had to fulfill a contract transporting these steel sheets before he could resume his studies in medicine. It took a half hour to get all this from his broken English.

Maddie then gave what had become her standard drivel. To make it easier, though, she raised fingers to represent her number of children, and the amount of years she'd been married.

He looked at her questioningly, and had to ask…how old was she? He did a double take—and watched her hands for her to repeat it.

Jakov's naturally pensive expression, marked by several deep creases on his forehead and the sides of his nose, added at least five years to his thirty-one.

Maddie was in awe of the responsibilities he'd taken on in his life compared to someone like Amy, who was slightly older.

The radio played. Listening to the Italian rock bands was fun. So far she'd heard too much American music, especially country and western. She noted the driver's well-worn buff-colored cowboy boots. His left pointy toe was enthusiastically tapping out the beat. The boots didn't seem comfortable for the road. The foot action stopped; he had to concentrate. There were lots of curves, and the traffic came barreling out from behind the rock walls. They climbed higher and higher. The truck felt like a living force.

Maddie was worn out from trying to communicate with him, and was happy for this break. At last the road straightened across a valley. She pictured Marcus, in western garb, riding at breakneck speed across it on a stallion, fleeing a hail of gunfire and aiming a six-shooter at the bad guys. Maybe his Italian flicks had no villains. The way they had been described to her, perhaps there was only a symbolism-filled prairie that needed conquering. It would still require guns, she decided. Jakov sang the lyrics between long drags on his cigarette. She wouldn't ask why a medical student, of all people, would risk his health.

Jakov wanted to know why Maddie was hitchhiking. To meet people like him, she replied. He reached over and gave her forearm a friendly squeeze. If he visited America, he asked, could he stay with her family?

Without reservation, she gave him her home and e-mail address on a slip of paper. It unnerved her that he read it while holding the wheel. When the truck slightly swerved, she feared it would continue to spin out of control. Jakov slipped the information in his shirt pocket, then reached for his wallet on the dash. Maddie expected to see pictures of his family. Instead, he handed her a photo and tapped it with his finger to emphasize the subject matter: twisted metal.

"Summer...last year...Jakov lucky, no?"

Maddie looked at his upside-down body. The legs dangled halfway out the window. Although bloodied, he was nevertheless smiling and waving to the observer who, unbelievably, had the gall to snap this scene. Emergency trucks surrounded the wreck. She didn't need to see this, especially now, with the drop-off on her side of the road.

When asked if it had been his fault, he assured Maddie that the other driver, the dead driver, had been drunk.

She couldn't even imagine what Jakov's poor mother must have experienced, having recently lost her husband...and then to almost lose her son. For a moment, the anguish from recalling such a penetrating grief was so severe, she thought she might throw up. She held her breath during each hairpin turn and continually gauged their proximity to the embankment.

They hadn't been driving more than a couple of hours when Jakov apologized for having to nap. He'd been up since three o'clock. Maddie admitted that her lids were growing heavy, too. Lying crooked in the back of the car last night was not restful. He pulled into a spot where a couple of others were taking an early siesta as well. They looked pretty lined up: the bold green truck next to the candy-apple red and royal blue ones.

Jakov was so quickly and severely hindered by sleepiness that his rudeness had to be overlooked. He rolled out of his seat, then staggered to unlatch the overhead cot. It dropped to an upper-bunk position. He immediately sprawled across the lower bed. Maddie understood too well. The air from the cracked side vents felt great. It was easy to stand and walk upright in the cab; the roominess amazed her. This mattress was a cloud. Her last image was of the burled walnut dashboard—like that of a luxury car. *What a swanky rig*, she thought.

Maddie dreamed of being back with Catherine's family in Paris. A harplike dulcimer—which really was playing in the background on the radio—reminded her of dinner with them. It gave her a warm feeling of well-being. In her half dream, the front seats took form, along with the driver who was again behind the wheel, and she remembered where she was.

During a bathroom break, Maddie found their location on the map. She wrongly assumed that after leaving Switzerland, the Italian family had been aiming for the country's western coast. They had actually been driving more down its center, which turned into a good thing. Jakov's next delivery wasn't until the next day in Florence. He suggested she stay the night in Bologna. He'd go to a truck stop and could easily pick her up at any number of locations in the early afternoon. She didn't want her energy to peter out and preferred to do most of her running around in Florence. Travelers in Interlaken had gone on and on about the place. He insisted on at least driving through the city.

The sun was taking its lazy time setting. The rose-colored light made the hectic urban life somehow mellower. Even the ever-stretching shadows contained a blush of color. The driver and his passenger observed in comfortable silence. Though the street was wide, Maddie admired the Croat's patience for guiding this monster vehicle down it. Drivers punched their horns nonstop at each other. They were like insults thrown out during a family squabble—nothing serious, everyone just getting in their two cents' worth.

It was almost dark when they finally escaped the bumper-to-bumper congestion. She didn't have to convince Jakov to let her treat him to a special dinner. Heading out of town, he mentioned a restaurant he had passed before on this route. He rubbed his thumb and a couple of fingertips rapidly together to show it was pricey. She would never have thought of that gesture if she were trying to convey that idea. How did these things become universally understood? Both were on the lookout for the isolated stone structure with an arbor growing out of its side wall. They were famished, and there'd be no backtracking if they accidentally missed it.

Impatient drivers flashed their lights and whizzed around them. They spotted the rustic building at the same moment. *Ristorante Montonari*. There was plenty of space to brake ahead of it and pull off to the side of the road. It would require a short hike to the entrance. Back-to-back, they dressed in fresh clothes. Maddie was salivating from the divine aromas blowing their direction—her eagerness caused her to twist an ankle. Following her nose, she had jumped to the ground too quickly. Not to worry, though. She held on to Jakov's arm and hobbled just fine, and at a fast pace.

Two dignified waiters placed before them the freshest porcini mushrooms, braised with an exact amount of garlic; antipasti with *aceto balsamico* (balsamic blended over decades of aging in a local time-honored tradition); and artistically molded ravioli and tortellini. The tiny surprise packages were filled with spinach, artichoke, and other unknown savory morsels. They enjoyed shrimp and monkfish soup and sampled cheeses that included greenish mozzarella balls made from buffalo milk and a nutty tasting variety that combined sheep's and cow's milk (the likes of which neither of the dinner guests had ever tasted), and ate scallops embedded with black truffles. And these were only the first creations. There was much more to follow.

The guests at the surrounding tables were entertained by their gasping responses whenever an additional tempting plate was set in front of their eyes. They'd been there once themselves…and by now had toned down a little.

Maddie and Jakov languished over the feast. Two hours later, the festive mood had become more serene. Several people were nice enough to have stopped by their table before they left. They recalled their first time eating there and discussed some of the chef's exquisite preparations.

It was eleven thirty, not late for Italians—and for once, not late for Maddie, who had benefited from the midday catnap. She and Jakov made a point of not drinking much wine in order to keep from getting sleepy; the food was too special. When they finished, they leaned back in their chairs and looked across the table at each other, content—weren't they the lucky dogs tonight! They had agreed before dinner that dessert was a must. First, a break. Maddie scanned the richly decorated dining room, never wanting to forget it. The colors were those of Marcus's bedroom. The memory of his winsome manner caused a transitory pining. Jakov tapped her foot under the table to bring her back around. Without knowing her thoughts, he gazed at her sympathetically.

They strolled the narrow, mosaic paths of the backyard herb garden, greeting some others making room for dessert as well. The spray from a raised fountain was refreshing. The water circulated around a statue of St. Francis of Assisi, flanked on both sides by the usual animals. They discussed the sights that Jakov wanted to visit in the States someday, and he gave Maddie an insight into his medical studies. Then it was time to enjoy the air-conditioning again.

They chose to share the ricotta cheesecake. An assortment of fresh berries was layered between slivers of pastry sheets and heaped with a Chantilly cream. After the last forkful, an exuberant figure suddenly appeared at their table. They stood and shook the elderly chef's hand, complimenting him all the while. The wiry and galvanizing gentleman went on about something with Jakov, although he'd been informed that the driver's Italian was limited. Maddie didn't believe Jakov was really making heads or tails out of it.

Time to square up the bill. While Maddie waited for the grand tally, the woman who had seated them asked that she follow her to a back table, where she poured her a cognac. She told Maddie, in her broken English, about a visit she had made to a sister in Minneapolis, in the middle of winter. No one could pay her enough to go back. They toasted to peace. Such a crazy world…filled with far too much sorrow for its mothers. The drink was potent.

Maddie didn't bat an eye over the bill—even after she added the 30-percent tip. Tomorrow she was bound to think she had lost her mind. Tonight it didn't matter.

Jakov polished off her drink and away they went, arm in arm, buddies…tipsy, fat ones. She was too tired to ask about his words with the chef. They each just wanted to get to the cab and sleep. The truck would have to remain alongside the road for the night.

In the early morning darkness, Maddie searched for toilet paper, then quietly sneaked outside to go in the field. Darn if she didn't turn her other ankle this time.

CHAPTER 17

They designated a fountain by the river for their rendezvous. After his delivery, Jakov was going to spend the night on the outskirts of town. Maddie was welcome to stay another night in his truck. He guaranteed it would be easy for her to get a ride back into Florence in the morning. She had all day to decide.

Maddie's itinerary was short: see the statue of David and some art galleries, and find a hostel. Shopping by herself didn't interest her. As she followed the route leading to Michelangelo's famous sculpture, copies of it jumped out at her from every direction. She hoped that the original wasn't going to be a letdown. There he stood, in all his naked glory, on beach towels and umbrellas. A statuette could be substituted for the hood ornament on your car. She couldn't resist giggling at the rather obscene version of "pin the tail on the donkey." Next to it on display was a shower curtain. She left the store, pleased with that purchase.

The midwesterner was surprised to feel this at ease in Florence. After a few hours, Maddie daydreamed about what life would be like if she rented an apartment down any of its quaint streets…preferably an upstairs one with a balcony. She could see herself working at a job here—in a little shop where she would sweep the front sidewalk early every morning. She wasn't at all uncomfortable eating alone in a restaurant, nor had she found shopping by herself to be disagreeable. Neither Paris nor Interlaken grounded her like this medieval city.

A similar experience had happened only once before. The family's car had broken down on their way to a New England lakeside resort, right during Boston's rush hour. It was towed and required a major fix. The Gullivers stayed at a hotel and made the best of the crisis by sightseeing over the next couple of days. During that period, Maddie noticed that Boston had a rare calming effect on her, despite its chaotic atmosphere. If told she had to make the city home, right there and then, she would have thought, *Great!* She couldn't put her finger on what had made her feel so comfortable then, and she couldn't now, either.

By early evening, she had found a wonderful escape from the crowds in the Semplici gardens. Getting back to the arranged meeting point on time was out of the question. Jakov would understand if she bowed out of continuing the drive with him. Unfortunately, he still had her backpack. Although Maddie vowed to keep the Patagonia always within her sight, Jakov appeared trustworthy. Besides, dare she stay another day? Who knew how long that day would turn into? It felt so right here. Maybe another town would yield a similar influence. After contacting Jakov on her cell phone, she was relieved to hear that he would have no problem locating her.

Off came her shoes. Her toes wiggled freely. She searched her purse for a small book. It contained observations about Tuscany by eminent visiting writers. Leafing through the pages, she saw that Janet had highlighted so many lines it had become pointless to pick out anything special. After reading a bit, she could see why: it was all special; each sentence was succinct. The quotations came from such diverse thinkers as Henry James, Charles Dickens, E. M. Forster, and Edith Wharton. One who didn't embrace the region was D. H. Lawrence. *Impossible*, she thought. She shook her head over his shortcoming, then immersed herself again. She read, with utmost fascination, about the periods of history in which they wrote.

Jakov smiled when he spotted her on the hill, lying stretched out on her stomach with her big toes twirling in the grass. The concentration she showed for the subject matter under her nose belonged to that of a college student during exams. She didn't notice him sitting down next to her. He cleared his throat.

She sat up on her knees and looked at the sky. The sun was ready to drop behind the horizon. Jakov's presence brought her back to reality, although there was no discernible difference from the fabricated one in her head that she had been steeped in for the last hour. Her soul swelled with emotion and demanded release.

The spontaneous display of tears didn't worry the young man. He slipped his arms around her and waited for the feeling to subside. Tired, and self-conscious, Maddie started laughing and began wiping her face with her skirt.

Jakov anticipated a similar reaction...when he saw the Grand Canyon someday. Yes, she could tell that from his nature.

Unfortunately, she did not find relief from the outburst. This city, the little book that painted big landscapes with mere words, this kindly medical student...it was an episode that demanded to be shared with a best friend; nothing else would do. One of Maddie's classmates from her junior-high days came to mind. She was going to be a painter and live in Italy someday. The girl with unconventional aspirations was from another planet to the young Maddie, who only thought about marriage and babies, like most of her friends during the fifties. Maddie hoped that friend got her dream. The stream of tears would have continued, except the source had emptied. She also thought about her granddaughter. Nothing would be lovelier than to hold Rima's hand at this moment, to kiss her brow.

The radio remained off. There was no conversation, no whistling...only a humming engine for the next couple of hours. They reached a spot to overnight. Maddie stared at the roof directly above her cot, hoping to feel more positive in the morning. Searching fingers crept over the edge of her bed in an amusing attempt to locate her hand. She smiled and placed her palm over them, then gave a gentle good-night squeeze. Jakov muttered something unintelligible; it was probably a sentiment spoken to his mother at bedtime. He must get incredibly homesick, too.

In the morning, after slapping cold water on their faces in the facilities, they embarked on another day of driving—an entire fifty minutes' worth. At first, Maddie didn't question it when they turned off the highway. After a while, she realized they had left all traffic behind them. The surface became increasingly bumpy, and there were huge dips in the road that had to be avoided. She was about to ask where in tarnation they were headed when Jakov stopped and climbed out. He went over and jumped on a ridge to inspect the countryside. The truck continued to idle. Should she get out too? A sense of dread filled her, sending a message of flight. She hated feeling cynical about his motives.

He opened her door. "The end of line, Maddie." A wide grin spread across his face. "I say right?" He hopped on the step and took her by the arm. She pulled away and bolted to his driver's side, bumping her ribs against the steering wheel before dropping in the seat. Jakov looked at her, dumbstruck. "Maddie?" His questioning tone hushed her fear—momentarily—then her foolish ideas got the better of her again.

She knew she was acting paranoid, but Jakov was giving her good reason. She stared out the wide windshield, seeing no people. Jakov remained posted by the door frame. The cause for her erratic behavior was becoming clear to him, and it made him uneasy. He never perceived himself to be a threatening type. It felt demoralizing to be a man in this situation—to be lumped in the same category as those capable of hurting women.

"Regalo, Maddie...it is present, from chef at Montonari, the restaurant." He hated giving the surprise away. She still wouldn't turn toward him. He leaned inside and rested on an inch of the passenger seat, insisting that she look at him.

His hand lay spread across his chest, above his heart—a sign of his good intentions. He held his other hand out to her, and she sheepishly took it.

"What do you mean...present?" Her voice was a whisper.

He didn't know how well he was going to be able to explain this. Maddie wished she hadn't forgotten to leave the electronic translator in the room in Paris. She had been getting by fine without it until now. Jakov remembered the words the chef told him...just not the order, or their exact meaning. She got a piece of paper. *Nascosta*, she wrote. Hide, he said, not too confidently. OK, next. *Persi*. Lost. *La valle*...valley, and *cuochi*...cooks. What a riddle. Jakov rubbed his strained eyes. She asked him again, "This is the surprise?"

He got his other pants. He had made a note to himself, and it was still in the pocket of those pants. It amounted to nothing more than a few lines drawn freehand, which showed where to exit the freeway. The same words were written that he'd already given her...except *cucina*...kitchen.

"All right," she said, "we've got a kitchen with cooks. That makes sense, but what does it have to do with being out here, in the middle of nowhere?" They played with the word order. "The hiding cooks in a valley's lost kitchen." No, definitely not. "The valley of the lost cooks' hidden kitchen. Hmmm...that has a certain ring to it."

Jakov agreed; it could very well be the name of the school, he mused.

Maddie looked at him, speechless.

He grabbed her bag from behind the seat and set it on the road...the empty road. Wearing the most incredulous expression, Maddie blurted out, "Are you nuts?"

"No," he said quietly, reaching up to her. "Please come."

He helped her down. Heat poured out from the underbelly of the rumbling truck, which loomed like a dragon in this peaceful setting. Jakov aimed a finger in the direction of a stony path leading toward a mesa-like formation. He would take her there if he could, but the semi could never be steered down the skinny road. They were able to make out the shell-torn-looking buildings perched atop the distant hill. Jakov pointed to his wristwatch, showing he needed to stay on schedule. Maddie pleaded with him, unconvinced that this wasn't a joke.

Her body simply hung there when he hugged her. When he let go, she turned and walked away to escape the hot engine. He hated leaving her like this.

"Is really school, Maddie. Of chef sister. You tell persons his name."

"Tell *persons* his name…sure, Jakov…who on earth is going to be living in that godforsaken place! And running a school?" Some seething life crept back into her.

She studied the distance. *Cool down*, she told herself. Hadn't she promised not to overreact to things? Here was a doozy of a test to see if she could regain her composure.

Jakov glanced at the time again. Maddie pulled up the handle on her Patagonia, collected the two over-the-shoulder bags, and started to walk to "town." *Why oh why*, she thought to herself, *didn't I stay in Florence?*

"Maddie," he entreated. Then he jogged ahead to stop her in her tracks. The iciest stare met him.

"You wanted me to hit the road." Maddie's tone was flat and made him feel like shit.

If only he could explain the situation better—that she was headed for something truly unique. There was no question in his mind that she would appreciate what the chef had asked him to do. He refused to leave without first kissing both her cheeks. She softened, to her surprise.

"You'd better be right about this. Or I'll find you." Jakov had no doubt. She held his face as if he were a dear son and kissed the corner of his mouth. He was grateful to carry the picture of Maddie's smile with him.

CHAPTER 18

For the first twenty minutes, Maddie walked in a mindless trance, facing the ground. Step after step, nothing changed; always gravel and weeds, and the clickety noise of the little wheels on her bag as they bumped along. Every so often they hit a rut, which jerked her backward and caused her ankles to bang against the bottom edge of the bag. The scrapes had begun to hurt, and her heels were probably getting bruises, but she didn't care.

All at once, a darling little inquiring black face entered her field of view, peered way high up at her…then spoke. "Mmwoarg?"

"And mmwoarg to you, too," she retorted and leaned over to scratch the ears. The cat welcomed the stranger by nuzzling its nose in her hand. The petite-framed feline stood on its hind legs and gently kneaded Maddie's shins with its front paws, which were carefully lifted off before they snagged her pants.

Maddie shoved the handle down and sat on her bag, gulped a swig of water, and opened the wrapper of a biscuit. How pleasant to have another dining companion—a much cheaper one, she admitted. The cat daintily licked the crumbs she dropped.

Her wide-brimmed hat offered considerable shade from the sun, but now that she was actually observing her surroundings (and not the ground), she pulled out her sunglasses. She was pleased to be making headway. There was still no one in sight, though.

The kitty jumped on her lap, startling her. It balanced comfortably on her thighs and continued to look her in the face, examining the dark sunglass frames to the point where Maddie felt compelled to remove them. The small, curious animal stayed put. "Maybe you've got hours for this, but I certainly don't." Maddie set her down, deciding that such a delicate creature must be female. "So, are you here to direct me, Miss?"

The feline replied in her throaty vibrato manner.

"Great! Let's go."

The cat ambled ahead a few paces and occasionally glanced back at the slowed but undaunted hiker, offering encouraging meows. As they pressed onward, Maddie entertained the idea of a cyclops rising out of the ancient ruins. She was really on a peril-filled odyssey of mythical scale, designed to test her mettle. Her wise little traveling companion would give her the necessary clues for outwitting the ogres and sorcerers. She must prove victorious, or face…

"*Ciao!* Signora Gulliver!" trumpeted a voice from out of thin air.

"Huh?"

Maddie found herself standing bosom to nose with an old woman whose makeup was applied disturbingly outside the lines. Maybe she looked like her brother, the chef from the restaurant; it was hard to tell. He had called his sister earlier and said she should be on the lookout for an American woman who might possibly show up. Her name was Liliana, and she welcomed the guest to her "home," which Maddie was yet to learn meant the entire village—all of its six inhabitable buildings. The loquacious feline was introduced too, as "our" *petit* Brioche.

Our Brioche? Maddie looked for evidence of other life.

The spent traveler followed the woman's hasty steps, listening all the while to her soliloquy. Brioche threaded herself around their legs, challenged by these moving obstacles. Traipsing on uneven ground had grown old, and trying to keep up with this scurrying character was no easy feat. There had to come a day when she didn't look so forward to bedtime.

At last, thank God. The host raised a thick iron latch from an equally huge iron slot, then pulled apart the massive wooden doors. Maddie strode into a salutatory kitchenful of company. Her mouth froze, gaping open. She was ushered in and invited to sit at a ceramic-tiled center island that was covered with all kinds of colorful and textured foods. Someone wrapped her fingers around a wine goblet. It was impossible not to feel comfortable in the hospitable atmosphere.

Introductions were made. The seven guests accompanied their handshakes with the clink of their glasses and the briefest bio. Last was Maddie's: current status, derailed hitchhiker.

It was a moonless, starless night. A mixed-up crowing rooster didn't realize that the new day was nowhere near ready to begin. Maddie fluffed her pillows and rested against the ornate headboard. Her eyes adjusted to the dim surroundings.

This was an agreeable spot: good size, no frills, and scrupulously clean. She had kicked off the crisp white sheets; they lay in a muscled heap at the foot of her bed as if she were hiding a lover. The curtains were merely yards and yards of fabric, falling twisted to the ground. In the daylight, they shone with a mother-of-pearl luminescence. The bathroom door was kept closed; it connected her room to another. It was elaborately tiled in royal blue and bright yellow circular designs, unlike the plain walls in the room where she slept. A bouquet of sunflowers stood like a cutout in front of the window, framed only seconds ago by a light that was now catty-corner to her decorative, unusable balcony. She guessed it was enough space for the maid to stand and shake out the bedding.

Curses were hurled across the fields over the premature revelry. It tickled her when, as if to spite the angry lot, a second cock-a-doodle-doo erupted, shriller and more directional than the first.

While lying comfortably in her bed, Maddie contemplated the age and history of the place; it boggled the mind. She'd been told that the castle had been under constant construction throughout most of the eleventh century. As was the case with other towns, the area was abandoned when the merciless plague infiltrated the region. The spared locals refused to return long after the disease had been brought under control, fearing another infestation of sorts—from ghosts. Maddie couldn't blame them.

She wrestled the sheet in order to pull it up to her chin, but not because she was cold; on the contrary, she wanted to raise it, then let it float down to help evaporate the sweat on her damp skin. It did the trick. The infernal racket outside continued.

By now all the lights were on, which helped her discern the dangerously uneven cobblestones. Maddie saw no reason she couldn't go sit in the front courtyard. Her flimsy gypsy skirt pleasantly fanned the air between her thighs when she moved. She circled the inactive fountain and ran a few fingers along the surface of the sitting tepid water. She thought of Marcus. Her casual movement elicited a remark.

"You look unfazed by the ruckus."

She didn't startle, but looked over her shoulder—enticingly so—then faced away, disappointed that she needed to abbreviate the ending to her stimulating reverie. She squeezed her arms tightly, as if chilled, then turned on her heels to greet one of the men enrolled in the course, Stanley Krupnick. His eyes drifted down to the lacy border of her camisole, then they lingered on her breasts. This stranger's insolence was deserving of a slap in the face. He realized the impropriety, then unapologetically and sincerely stated, "It's been a while." His smile was honest. She forgave him, and they went to investigate a winding passageway.

It was hard to believe that this mild-mannered guest was the angry man he professed to have been when he got off the plane right before coming here. While Stanley related his story, the hurt started to show through in his words. At forty-six, he had up and walked away from everything: his wife, family, business, and country. His sloe-eyed face looked to Maddie for consolation. She remained nonjudgmental, and curious to no end.

This Jewish, Brooklyn-born, second son had worked in his family's meat market since he was old enough to hold a broom. He assumed the position of the firstborn son after his brother took off to follow his own calling instead of taking over the business, as was expected. Now, when his father was ready to hand the shop over to him, the delinquent brother returned to lay claim to what was rightfully his, according to custom. The timing was unbelievable. More unbelievable was that the event was met with endless celebration, and marred what would have been a joyous and proud occasion in this diligent son's life.

The two found a small, lit alley by a backdoor delivery entrance to sit and talk. The noise from the roosters was buffered by the angle of the thick walls. They admired an abandoned wood-fueled oven directly opposite them. Stanley turned to her. He was good at looking directly into her eyes…from homing in on customers' faces, Maddie thought. Another butcher's eyes came to mind. She slunk into the thin shadow, hoping her flushed face would go unnoticed. What was going on with her these days?

Continuing his story, her new acquaintance explained that the prodigal son had returned, so to speak. His brother, who had no background in butchering or running a business, was given the store; it wasn't up for discussion. Maddie witnessed the devastation in his face. Stanley's response was to chuck it all. He had married a girl whom he never truly loved, only because the union was encouraged by the families. Thanks to the long hours he routinely put in, his grown daughters and son barely knew him, which didn't seem to upset them.

A month ago, while in the bank with the day's deposit, Stanley said he took out an amount he deemed rightfully his and went straight to JFK. He called a friend, told him where his passport was in his house, then asked him to bring it to the airport. He would try to get a seat on the first flight that coincided with the appearance of his ID, which turned out to be heading for Milan. The fellow's speech quickened as he recalled the excitement he felt. Maddie's heart raced, too. She understood precisely. Maybe this was not uncommon—adults running away.

They looked questioningly at each other over the sudden, piercing silence.

Stanley helped her up, and they returned to their rooms. His mustached lips grazed her hand, and he thanked her for listening. He was only now able to speak about the ordeal.

Not every second was going to be spent cooking. This morning at the breakfast table, Maddie was to vote with the others: morel gathering or touring the ancient roads today? That was easy, given the twinge of pain she still felt at times. She didn't need a reminder of the mishap.

She got the lowdown about the place from the dark and elegant gentleman to her left, in between bites of his herring and hard-boiled egg. Mr. de Palma, executive chef, ruled an exclusive kitchen in Miami. She'd been advised not to call him by his first name. He did come across as arrogant.

Maddie was floored to learn that Liliana's husband and two sons met their improbable fate on 9/11. They were in the World Trade Center's North Tower, at Windows on the World, in order to discuss a business proposal with a friend who worked there. They were seeking financing for converting a remote Tuscan village into a culinary establishment.

After taking the absolutely longest sip of tea, the man went on to explain that the three sisters and mother refused to give up the dream. With the help of many friends, and particularly Liliana's brother, the chef at Montonari, they forged ahead and developed the place…then the widow took a nosedive as the tremendous loss caught up to her. She became scatterbrained and often talked about the missing half of her family as if they were in the next room. A sickening, hopeless feeling took hold of Maddie…that "nowhere to run" one. She wasn't sure if she could eat the rest of the day. The hole that occupied the space of poor Liliana's annihilated heart defied description.

The afternoon yielded glorious sights of rolling hills and crumbling structures lost to time. The students had a couple of hours to themselves before preparing the dinner. Maddie was informed that the postman came mornings at ten. Relaxing on her bed, she filled out postcards. There were unfortunately none to be bought of this extraordinary place. Task done, Maddie closed her eyes and thought about the other guests.

Liliana's circumstances intruded on her thoughts. Who, on that particular September morning, and for weeks afterward, didn't contemplate its aftermath and wonder how such an event would transform their own lives, as it had the many others' that day? Maddie believed it when she swore to God that she would act with more understanding toward her family. It lasted awhile—for as long as all the others held to their own lofty promises made after that jolt to their sensibilities. Trying to maintain that state obviously wasn't normal, because normalcy returned.

That month was when Maddie became aware that she and Ed were merely locked into a habit of sharing space. If either of them got knocked out of the picture, it would be like a potted plant disappearing from its usual spot—a vacancy that sometimes took weeks for anyone to notice. Lying there with her postcards, Maddie wondered if Ed might be starting to miss her. She sat at the desk. There was stationery. *Dear Ed,* she began. *I saw kids swinging from tree vines today and remembered the fun I had at camp doing that, while I watched you play baseball with the boys in the open field.* It was nice to write a long letter. She described Tuscany. She wished him a big catch on his upcoming fishing trip. *Give Red a kiss from me.* She stared out the window, almost done. How to sign it? What did she feel? She studied the bouquet of sunflowers. Hmm. *Fondly.* She could live with that. Then she went to eat.

The next morning, the guests pondered the roosterless night. A cheesemaster proved an interesting subject for the next field trip. Tasty as the products were, the unpleasant odors of his profession left a lasting impression. A variety of samples were brought back and enjoyed with an afternoon wine tasting. Maddie had curled up beside a couple from Michigan to learn more about their bed and breakfast. Later they ate that evening's successful assignment: a foamy-textured Bolognese lasagna.

Maddie loved the school, and wanted to partake more in the actual hands-on cooking, but she felt guilty for not having paid. She doubted the others knew that, but still, she felt they should get their money's worth. She simply told them she preferred to watch. The instructor, a gregarious and portly—yet dignified—man, who wore the crisp white uniform of his trade with a regal air, demanded that she find one thing to make, so the experience would be truly memorable. She knew he was right.

Biscotti?

"No!" Too ordinary. He looked at her disapprovingly, tapping a wooden spoon with a teasing impatience. "Zuccotto!" he ordered—and that was that!

When the dome-shaped sponge cake made its grand entrance the following afternoon, wheeled in on the serving cart, Maddie held her breath. The luscious strawberry, chocolate, and orange layers agreed with everyone's palate. The chef smiled from across the table and kissed his fingertips.

On this eighth day of classes, Maddie's sixth, the sense of camaraderie made the place feel more dormlike. The students walked nonchalantly in and out of each other's open rooms to chat or find new reading material. Maddie would discover a page-turner by an author of westerns named Estleman...a favorite of the hoity-toity Miami chef (of all people). Janet's old postcards were a hit. Everyone tried recalling what they were up to in 1973. Poker was popular during the evenings. One night included a spontaneous jam session using the guitars and tambourines stored beside an old upright piano in the dining area. The chef had his beloved violin.

With only two days left, Maddie wished she had discovered the crafts room earlier. It was down the hall from the huge kitchen. The rafters, walls, and tables overflowed with dried flowers, herbs, nuts, and the skins of certain fruits. The combination of smells produced the Old-World nose of a brilliant wine.

She sat and watched the young woman painstakingly thread together a wreath. Maddie didn't have many opportunities to talk to this guest. Her name was Stella, and she spent most of her time where the cheeses were made. That process had apparently captivated her imagination.

The students were encouraged to create an aromatic sculpture in the craft room at some point during their stay. The school was famous for them, giving the proceeds from their sales to a local hospital.

With her ingredients gathered in a mound in front of her, Maddie inhaled deeply before laying out her pattern.

"The initial pungent earthiness, of a woody sort, mellows when it diffuses in the sinuses, and one can differentiate the citrus and floral notes," said Maddie.

Stella then added, "I detect a bit of oiliness in the aroma and a hint of spiciness in its finish, redolent of concentrated peach."

"Aha...I bow to the connoisseur," laughed Maddie.

"Will you please tell me what in heaven's name redolent means? I read it once," said Stella, "and it stuck in my head."

Maddie shrugged her shoulders. "Dunno." She kept trying to figure out a way to attach the pomegranates. It was hopeless. "All this time, and I never found out much about you." Maddie had told Stella a little about herself once over dinner. "How long ago did your husband die, Stella?"

Stella was searching the scraps for intact bay leaves. Her fingers were long and tapered. "Three years." Then she admitted, "There was no love lost." She had a grin that veered off to the right side of her face, giving a half-believable quality to everything she said. Maddie found its inherent cynicism appealing. She asked the woman if she had ever cared for the man, hoping the widow didn't mind talking about this subject.

Stella didn't answer right away, but tried to help Maddie control the wire she'd been fighting with. The widow blew her long, wispy bangs off her face. The rest of her shiny hair was pulled back into a sleek, expertly rolled chignon. Her bony frame gave her the appearance of being considerably smaller than she was. Sitting, the two women were at eye level with one another. The color of Stella's eyes perfectly complemented her reddish-brown hair...as did her galaxy of freckles. Maddie found herself wanting to count them. Once Maddie was well under way with her wreath, Stella began.

"I pretty much hated the man every day of our marriage. Since his death, I kinda reinvented myself. You should've heard me before an intensive year of speech therapy. I couldn't be happier with this new me. Sometimes I still wonder how that's possible...for it to feel so normal, that is." Done with her project, Stella sat back and relaxed. Every so often, she poked her nose into Maddie's handiwork to help out. While Maddie coaxed her fingers into reclaiming a lost dexterity, she listened, totally absorbed, to the woman's tale, that began in Tennessee. By the time Maddie's wreath was finished, she'd been given one more perspective on the self-preserving measures people will resort to when up against a wall.

The youngest of ten girls, the woman had been born to parents who were only too anxious to unload the extra mouth to feed. Girls served men's needs in the iron-producing region she hailed from. Stella said she was thankful she didn't have to care for all the younger siblings, like her older sisters; they went directly from one set of screaming faces to another as soon as their fertility was put to the test. Considering what lay in store for her, the skinny redhead was lucky to have had the number of carefree years that she did. When she wasn't yet ten, she was dragged out of bed late at night to meet someone in the living room. She fought having to sit on the baggy-faced geezer's knee. Her mother swiped her butt and told her to behave in front of her future husband. Scared out of her wits, she ran screaming to her room, where she jumped out the window.

Maddie didn't mean to laugh so heartily, knowing full well Stella must have paid for that action later. Stella laughed, too. How she liked that kid version of herself. A short time later, her cheerful spirit would sour and languish for decades.

The cat, Brioche, watched and listened with interest from a corner sill. Every so often, the dried silks from the corn cob crackled in her mouth. She tightly held her "catch" in her claws, in case the thing had a mind to scurry away if she let up her grip. Stella didn't dwell on the details of the next twenty years. The story of the kept wife who endured beatings from her drinking husband and miscarriages from the punishment was the tired topic of daytime TV.

Help arrived one day in the form of a clever Quaker nurse who hatched a secret plan that would free the tormented victim. Stella and the nurse met at the hair salon where Stella was permitted to work on Saturday mornings, only because her husband wanted to sleep off the consequences of the usual Friday-night drinking binges in peace.

Maddie asked her age. She was thirty-five. Stella's son, her joy, was twelve. He had been a lucky gift. During her pregnancy with him, the would-be mother worried that the baby would get beaten out of her, as the others had. She kept the news to herself. When she finally did show, a broken femur suffered on the job left her husband immobilized until she delivered. Maybe it was because of all the congratulatory handshakes and slaps on the back he received from his buddies (as if he had any control over choosing the gender), but the boy was left alone. For that, she braved the continued punches, growing wearier every year.

Maddie could picture the bilious and deteriorated man, whom the widow described as looking to have one foot in the grave by sixty-one—of course, Stella added, that could have described him at forty-five. Without investigating his health history, the nurse knew Stella's husband had to have the common ailments linked to alcoholics and smokers. This scheme the nurse concocted required a great deal of patience, possibly a few years of it. In the end, though, she promised the sad wife that, not only would she be physically free, she would also be financially free.

The women got the man to unwittingly sign the necessary insurance papers, with the help of the son, who told his dad through the man's usual fog that his signature was needed on some forms so he could go on a class field trip. The nurse made the quarterly payments, knowing she'd get repaid. From then on, this wife changed her tune and began killing her husband with kindness. The widow's grin was more beguiling than ever as she related this part. She made certain her husband always had a cigarette burning by his side. She fried up the greasiest bacon every morning and cooked him the thickest biscuit gravy. She said that he actually got mushy, asking her why his life couldn't always have been this good.

A year later, Stella's husband required oxygen support; coincidentally, it was the year his official early retirement was to begin. When he slept, which was often, she turned down his tank, never allowing her son to catch her in the act.

Maddie couldn't get over Stella's confession. Then Maddie wondered whether she was capable of doing the same under similar conditions.

Stella said that the neighbors thought her a saint. How could she continue to care for this old goat? It was no secret how she had been treated.

After two years of interminable waiting, her husband announced he was going for a drive. He sat up straight, then slumped back down. There was no second attempt. Stella recounted how she stood in the doorway, pitiless. The rehearsed sequential phone calls were placed according to plan. Then, with suitcases hastily packed, she and her son jumped in the old Pontiac Sunbird and headed lickety-split out of town. The nurse's cousin awaited them in Pennsylvania. Freedom made them absolutely giddy, as well as the sizable death benefit soon to be in their possession.

After all was said, there seemed nothing unusual to Maddie about sitting in the company of a self-proclaimed murderer of sorts. *Another runaway*, she thought.

Her wreath complete, Maddie went to her bedroom to lie down. She wasn't tired…not depressed exactly…just feeling kind of nowhere. Thinking back on that tricky smile of Stella's, she wondered if she had in fact been duped into believing the woman's fanciful tale. Maddie was beginning to wonder if perhaps she had reached the limit to the number of new faces and events she could handle. A time-out was in order to rethink things. It disturbed her that escape, in one form or another, was the option commonly chosen when people were presented with the short end of the stick. She herself could be taken to task for avoidance. And then, rather than figuring out a way in which to deal with this fault in character, Maddie napped.

The knock wakened her.

After the extraordinary lamb dinner, the bed-and-breakfast owner jokingly made the heretical comment that she could no longer go on eating these superb epicurean wonders. She craved a peanut butter and jelly sandwich. Lest the instructor misinterpret her tone, she muttered it under her breath. Her classmates snickered. Their snobbish dining companion quietly murmured, "Bologna, heaped in mayonnaise on the softest, spongiest white bread." And with a clucking noise, he added, "That sticks to the roof of the mouth."

"No!" cried the chorus of disbelievers.

"What is it?" implored the chef at the far end of the table. He was concerned that something wasn't to their liking.

Without missing a beat, the self-important Miami chef (in his customary droll manner) reassured their fastidious teacher, "I simply told them the pay of my waiters." Mr. de Palma savored his wine, pretending as if he had never confessed to the plebian indulgence.

Stanley Krupnick, the former butcher (formerly) from Brooklyn whispered, "You'd all get hooked on my potato knishes if you ever tasted them. Yum!"

"Herr Kr-r-rupnick's kar-r-rtoffel knishes," Mr. de Palma said, rolling the r's. "May I include those on my menu in Miami?" A case of silent giggles erupted. The erratic shoulder movement was a giveaway. They shared this one with their host. Everyone agreed, tomorrow's appetizers would be the butcher's specialty. Stanley was beside himself with excitement.

Before retiring, Maddie wrote a note to send to Liliana's brother at Montonari, which the instructor was kind enough to help her translate. It was the easiest thank-you she'd ever written. While she was at it, she also scribbled a few words to Jakov, letting him know about the rest of her stay. The suspense had been too much for him, and the chef had fortunately given Jakov Liliana's number along with the directions to the culinary school, so he was able to call Maddie that first night to find out about the ghost town. Cell phones didn't work at that remote location.

The next morning, at an ungodly early hour, the smell of cooking potatoes and onions filled the hallways before the guests' eyes opened. This last day flew by.

The Krupnick knishes were indeed a hit. As the students ate, Maddie acquired more names for her growing collection of addresses. The friends convened for a final stroll. They wound around the vegetable and herb gardens, the henhouse, and the dairy barn—all of which were out of view from the path that Maddie had taken into the village. (There was a bigger road on its opposite side, but no way for Jakov to have accessed it.) They all ended up sharing an emotional toast beneath the ligneous embrace of a venerable grape arbor. It shielded them from a soft rain that had been holding back all day.

Maddie was invited to head out on their shuttle bus the next day. She could hop off on the main road and continue to Rome. It would have been great fun if her compatriots' plans included an excursion there. Nevertheless, she was extremely grateful. The offer gave her peace of mind. She slept soundly that night and dreamed that no one believed her when she told of this special place. The Hidden Kitchen in the Valley of Lost Cooks was, after all, discovered only through word of mouth and by way of inside connections. The senses were the sole recorders of its inconspicuous existence.

Such a clever gimmick, thought Maddie while she continued to ponder the place on the new day's hazy morning as she stood thumbing a ride.

Hours away, back home, it was the middle of the night. Ed was sleeping in his recliner. The several times he woke, he reread his wife's letter, then nodded off again while holding it on his lap. When he had pulled the mail out of the box the previous afternoon and recognized Maddie's handwriting, he became apprehensive. He went in the house, locked the doors, then sat at the kitchen table, staring at the envelope. Finally, he flipped it over to open it…and saw the tiny drawn heart. Then he smiled. That had been his fiancée's way of letting her sweetheart know when he was in Korea that he was not receiving a Dear John.

CHAPTER 19

It took four rides to cover the short span to Rome. The last one scared the bejesus out of her. When the impudent driver reached over with lightning speed and tweaked Maddie's tit, she darn near lost it, and yanked the door handle equally fast. A hundred-mile-an-hour wind tore through the crack. The foulmouthed lecher swerved to the shoulder and barely missed wrapping up his nifty Porsche in a ribbon of barbed wire. Maddie wished she could forget his profile. He wore sleek sunglasses and had a thick-bearded jaw that matched the color of his black leather jacket. His face had remained steadfastly fixed on the road while he waited for his resourceful pickup to exit. She was glad her backpack had been crammed under her legs and not thrown in the rear seat or trunk.

The city appeared distant. Maddie caught sight of a moving bus at the end of the ramp. At least she hadn't been dropped in between towns. This little stretch was a piece of cake. While she walked, a feeling of helplessness still overwhelmed her. She had been lucky. God, was that stupid…stupid, stupid! Her number-one rule was to never get in a car with someone whose eyes she couldn't see. Damn, she was stupid!

There was no official bus stop, no posted schedule—only a broomstick-size pole with a small, round sign affixed to it. She guessed the word on it meant "temporary," and she was probably in for a long wait. She would flag a taxi if one happened to pass.

It was a gorgeous area, a moneyed one. It would be so easy to simply stay put and find a hotel. However, everyone she had met who had visited there said it was best to be centrally located in Rome.

Her bags proved burdensome. She was going to have to lug them on the bus, then off, then somewhere else. Why not throw a few necessities in the Turkish purse and the other smaller pack, and ditch the Patagonia on the spot? But then she wouldn't have a chair when she needed one…like right then.

Her thoughts were interrupted by abdominal cramps. Maddie tried to remember when she last had a bowel movement. Because she was never plagued by that problem, she had presumed nature would inevitably remedy the situation. When she counted back the number of days—perhaps as many as nine or ten—she grew scared. The pangs subsided. The more she thought about it, the more weighted she became.

Maddie's hilltop view reminded her of all the calendar covers she had incidentally glanced at over the years on bookstore shelves. And now she sat superimposed on one. Unlike the disassociation she had felt upon arriving in Luxembourg, her mind accepted that she was physically here—parked in Rome, Italy (the outskirts counted), imbibing a Mediterranean landscape.

The bus circled back toward her. The sign over its windshield switched from the previous destination to that of the train station, *Roma Termini*. The driver was forgiving when the foreigner couldn't produce the required pre-purchased ticket. He pointed to his watch to let her know it would still take close to an hour to get to the *stazione*, even though the word Express was visible in the corner window. Fine…she'd enjoy the sights along the way.

The cramps began again, accompanied by a new discomfort in her chest. Soon she'd have a room to wait out that inconvenience. She was told that *pensione* operators hustled the incoming tourists at the train station. Most of their places were nearby. Would she survive 'til then?

Bathroom dilemmas were likely to do her in before anything else on this trip. Although Janet had been very thorough in her letters about describing these predicaments, her mother mistakenly didn't appreciate the problems they presented.

The sporadic jabs made her shiver and sweat at the same time. For brief moments, they disappeared. Tight corners brought them on again. Maddie tried to hold herself straight in the seat as best she could. It was impossible to concentrate on the scenery or enjoy people-watching. When the bus finally arrived at the bustling inner-city streets, things inside her appeared to have quieted. She tried self-hypnosis to fend off any more debilitating bouts. Hordes of mostly sightseers stuffed themselves in the aisle in front of her. She barely noticed.

She wanted to move slowly when she stepped onto the curb, but knew it was smarter to skedaddle to the information center in order to avoid the pickpockets—notably the shameless, roguish children who hung around and stood ready to pounce.

"Hold off...hold off," Maddie begged her innards. So far, so good. She received a city map and had just unfolded it when a hand came from behind and X-ed a location in the middle. She turned to meet the warm brown eyes of Papa something-or-other. He bowed his head slightly as a formality and introduced himself as the owner of the establishment listed on his card. His accent was heavy. She couldn't understand, but nodded in agreement...of course she would stay at his place. He grabbed her bag and started motioning for a taxi when she immediately stopped him.

"No, no...please! Not yet, but soon." He had moved too quickly for her.

"You stay, no?" He waved his card under her nose again. "Clean...is very, very clean."

She pointed to her wristwatch. "In one hour...*uno* hour." She held up her fingers to let him know she'd be back at two o'clock. He waved his arms to signify she had wasted his time, then ran after a group of confused-looking backpackers.

Actually, she would gladly have left, but all of a sudden there was a pressing need for a restroom. To her dismay, the closest one was closed; she was forced to go downstairs. As she descended, she kept a sharp eye out for approaching thieves. She'd read that rolled-up newspapers were a giveaway. They were used to nab and hide the valuables as the culprits escaped. The only thing trailing Madelaine Gulliver, however, was the evocative smell of McDonald's fries that reminded her of home.

The stacked bags made moving inside the stall difficult. Maddie wanted to ask someone about taking turns guarding each other's belongings while each went, but she had no way of knowing how long she required. Her brow was knotted from the pain, which no longer let up. Her intestines rumbled and squeaked. She buried her face in her hands, pushed her elbows into her thighs, and bore down, convinced that the relief following this ordeal would produce a euphoria equivalent to childbirth. Her head rolled back. The base of her neck was wet. Cobwebs hanging above her got inspected. She couldn't stand up if she tried. It had been ages since she was completely at the mercy of her body's functions. It was a truly humbling experience.

At last. Now her fear was that her entire insides were leaving her. Out of breath, Maddie encountered yet another problem. Without a doubt, the bowl would overflow—but she couldn't leave it. Even though she was alone, she turned beet red from embarrassment. She felt sorry for the poor, underpaid attendant who would be coming across this. When she couldn't hear any more footsteps, she plunked her bags down safely by the sinks, dashed back in the stall, quickly flushed, and hightailed it out of there.

The nearby waiting room that adjoined the railroad tracks was a godsend. She would sit briefly with the train passengers before going back upstairs. Secretly humiliated, her knees shaking, the disabled traveler desperately needed to collect herself. Upon entering, Maddie immediately encountered cigarette smoke that assaulted her like a joker's pail of water, balanced above the doorway of its unsuspecting victim. Right away her eyes stung. A sneezing fit followed. Through the fog, she searched out a seat farthest from the gang of ogling soldiers who were mostly responsible for the toxic cloud. *Good grief*, she thought, listening to their silly come-ons as she wove between their strutting, juvenile bodies. Clearing the air with her one free hand as she went, Maddie wondered what would happen if she duly smacked a few of their wiseass faces in the process.

It took a minute before she grasped that a naked foot, not an armrest, was supporting the back of her left elbow. The sight of the dirt-encrusted, overgrown, and curling nails made her sick all over again, in a different way. Her string of bad luck today was becoming more than she could bear.

Suffering still from an occasional twinge of trapped gas, Maddie hugged her belly and prayed for an end to this torment. It occurred to her that the unsavory specimen splayed across the bench beside her had in fact died…and had been rotting for days. She watched the indifferent faces, none of which showed any concern about anything. Her focus returned to her bowels. Maybe there'd be relief from the pressure if she kept shifting her weight from side to side. God, how she hated that she'd be coated in nicotine after leaving here.

It was imperative to substitute the image of the derelict next to her with some other faces. Turning to her right, she noticed that none of the families were speaking Italian. Most of the women looked thick. Some wore babushkas. There was one teen, a girl in a seat diagonally across from Maddie, who captivated her with her beauty. She sat alone, absorbed in a paperback. Sensing something, the girl shyly looked up and faced the older woman's scrutiny. Maddie wasn't aware that her admiration might seem rude. If it weren't for another sharp pain, she'd have gone on staring. The girl's features were straight out of a painting—the artist escaped Maddie's memory. Although he had an Italian name, she was certain he wasn't; it would come to her probably in the middle of the night. The mass of rose-brown hair cascaded to her waist in perfect spirals. It was a strong face, enhanced by graceful brows and gorgeous pale-blue eyes. The butterfly-flared nostrils, along with the curved (almost curled) lines that branched out from the two pronounced center peaks of her upper lip, gave her a haughtiness that disappeared the moment she smiled. The vile, smoky air actually produced a lovely, soft aura around her.

Maddie leaned across her lap and hugged her knees. It felt good. Even though no one paid attention to her, she thought that crouching over like that must look foolish, so she pretended something was in her shoe.

A second later, she wondered what could possibly be pressing so hard against her cheek. Why was she remembering when a fork had pierced her heel...and the resulting pain that had shot up her legs to her neck? There was a similar sensation right now, only her temples felt perforated. The agony spread down her arms and spine in the same fashion. She tried to pull her thoughts together, to collect the words twirling in smoke swirls. Her body felt lightweight, suspended; yet her face still contended with a hard surface. And why this darkness? Were those her own fingers tugging at her eyelids? A few scrabbled letters fell systematically into place, giving form to a single simple sentence that filled her with terror: *It's a stroke.* Was anyone going to help? Maybe they were as indifferent to her plight as they were to the bum beside her. Under these circumstances, it seemed strange that she remembered him.

Her eyes opened. She definitely lay sprawled on the filthy floor, which, strangely, was heaped with debris. Without effort, she pushed herself up onto her elbows. The quiet was eerie. Those intolerable currents of pain no longer invaded her head—just like that, they disappeared. Maddie scanned the room in an exhaustively slow movement; similar to a forlorn wretch balanced on the cliff's edge, grappling with the wide sea. Gone were the annoying soldiers...and the girl, the Rossetti masterpiece. A name she would never forget now. A plume of smoke drifted gracefully upward and outward beyond the newly opened roof and past the sunshine, turning the sky a dusty pastel apricot and lavender. A glittering rain fell, from shards of glass propelled heavenward by the blast. It was beautiful until a rising gray-white curtain encroached on the colors, finally erasing them. Screams echoed far away.

Maddie's eyes met up with those of the vagrant. He'd been jolted out of his comatose state and was now lying on the floor too, and looking around. Together they took in the embattled scene. Large pieces of glass had blown inward across the room with razorlike precision, mortally wounding those standing or sitting...upright. It was a ghastly sight.

Before Maddie could begin to conjecture why she and this particular man had been spared, she heard a girl's pleas and a baby's cries that came from beyond the waiting room…close enough to reach. It took several attempts to roll atop her bag. Her legs had a will of their own. Every inch of her was shaking wildly. Her vibrating jaw caused bites along her tongue. There were no adult voices; she had to help those children. Half standing, and aided by part of a chair, she clumsily maneuvered her way toward them.

The smoke began to thin out. Maddie pieced together the figure of a dark-haired girl who was heading her way. Her hand was grabbed, and she was pulled so hard she tripped over her own feet. The child was frantic, but not crying. The thin arms pushed the large, unwieldy stranger along. Together, in a creeping motion, they came to rest beside a fallen body. An eight- or nine-month-old boy sat a few feet away, feeling lost and shrieking at the top of his lungs. The girl quickly picked him up and carried him over, making certain that he faced away from the gruesome sight. Hugging him close, she assured him that Mamma was here. Maddie was impressed with her presence of mind, considering her mother lay there bleeding profusely. Several other seriously hurt people were lying near the track. One massive train car had been thrown completely sideways. The other tracks looked fine, untouched; the ceiling was still intact above them.

The injured young mother looked searchingly into the foreigner's eyes. Tragically, she was beyond help. Maddie was surprised that she hadn't already slipped into shock. The infant's shrill pitch hammered their eardrums. He fought his sister's hold.

The anguished mother repeated her children's names over and over. "Angelina…Gianni…"

Maddie tenderly combed her black hair with her fingers and caught the tears heading for her ears. How could Maddie tell the woman she would make sure her babies would be safe—that she'd get them out of there and return them home? Something was said to the daughter, who began to unbutton her mother's blouse. Maddie helped, and they positioned her brother so he could nurse. The girl snuggled her lap underneath her mother's shoulders and head. The familiar and comforting breast instantly pacified him.

Approaching sirens blasted in all directions. Angelina, who was maybe ten, gently lifted the necklace from her mother's collarbone and held the gold crucifix in her hand. She spoke in her mother's ear. It occurred to Maddie that there might be other children back home. She felt helpless. Then, miraculously, words from long ago were revealed to her: the memorized Latin Mass from childhood. She continued to stroke the mother's forehead.

"*Deus, cujus Unigenitus per vitam mortem…*" (O God, whose only begotten Son, by his life…).

There wasn't enough energy to carry the weakening voice, but the woman's lips attempted the syllables. When they started a new prayer, "*Gloria Patri, et Filio, et Spiritui Sancto,*" a most serene expression glided across the dying face. Her daughter scooted to the side a little so her mother could see her better. The mother placed her fingers on the girl's dear, small mouth, and gazed upon her with the kind of love only a mother is capable of offering. Then the eyes found their new focus in the next life…and she was at peace. Even now, the girl remained calm. She studied her mother's disappearance. Her brother was falling asleep.

Maddie didn't think it proper to take on the role of a priest, but trusted she would be forgiven. Praying again in Latin, she asked, "May almighty God have mercy on thee and having forgiven thee thy sins, bring thee to life everlasting."

Angelina undid the necklace. They placed the wedding band on it for her father. Maddie hooked the clasp around the brave girl's neck. They sat, not moving, not speaking.

The station had become a madhouse.

With a rush, the limp boy was swooped up from their midst. Before Maddie or the boy's sister had time to react, they were themselves lifted to their feet. The man's eyes conveyed to them the urgency of getting out of there. While he held the sleeping child in his one arm, he ushered them to the stairs. Maddie quickly grabbed her blood-spattered bags along the way. This newfound burst of energy gave her a grip on things.

She and the girl followed as the man wedged a path through the hysterical crowds. He whistled and caught the attention of a taxi driver. Moments later, when Maddie and Angelina were seated in the back, he leaned inside to gently place the baby on their laps. The little guy stirred, but never woke. When the man lovingly placed his hand on Angelina's cheek, she didn't recoil from his filthy fingers, which matched the appearance of his feet. She placed her own hand on top and turned to kiss the inside of his palm. The gesture did not elicit a word from him. His face was a mere few inches from Maddie's. He looked directly at her. Contrary to the drug-induced veil Maddie had imagined, his brown eyes were intelligent—and clearly in the moment. Nor did his tattered clothes stink. The faint, medicinal odor of eucalyptus and menthol clung to him. He nodded to the driver, closed their door, and that was the last of him.

It seemed to take forever just to go a block. Then, in a flurry of activity, the threesome was escorted from a hotel's entrance to a grand suite—during which time Mrs. Gulliver was addressed by her name. They must have looked through her belongings; she hadn't recalled anyone asking who she was. It caused her to check for the passport around her neck. Dazed, she planted herself by the window. A nurse had taken charge of the baby in the lobby and presently had him on the sofa, where she was changing his soiled pants. The boy had fun playing with her dangling crucifix while she bent over him. His blubbering noises would have seemed comical, earlier this same day. Angelina went to Maddie's side, and together they stared across the crowd-filled square that was situated between the hotel and the train station. It was pandemonium.

A doctor entered. Thank goodness for the girl's sake; there was someone to listen as she described where her mother lay and how to contact relatives. Only then did the tears come. The girl began sobbing to the point of choking. She refused to go back out there when the doctor wanted to send her and her brother to a hospital. Maddie declined going too.

The hotel staff did a remarkable job of caring for them. After the physical exams, the beds were turned down, and clean nightgowns spread across the sheets. That was all well and good, but Maddie needed only to pee and fall onto the mattress.

Angelina curled up beside the American lady. They slept in their smoky clothes. Her mother's blood had long since dried on the girl's skirt. She refused to step out of it. Her small fist secured the ring and the cross; wrapped around her knuckles was Maddie's comforting hand. An opera played in the background. Someone was thoughtful enough to find music to drown out the calamitous street noise.

The urge to pee woke her—and no wonder. It was the next day. When Maddie came out of the bathroom, she noticed the empty bed. She recalled the girl having been beside her. The saddest eyes greeted her as soon as she opened the bedroom door. They belonged to Angelina's relatives. They grieved quietly; the initial news had barely sunk in. It sounded callous, but Maddie was extremely thankful to have missed their arrival. Angelina ran to her and squeezed her around the waist. That was all it took. One by one they came forward: the father first, followed by aunts and uncles and grandparents...thanking her over and over.

The hotel had supplied an interpreter. Plus, the nurse who was still keeping an eye on them could speak English. Bits of backgrounds were exchanged. The child had given them her version, but they also required the play-by-play account from the American. Being in the middle of this sorrow was intolerable, like being flogged. It must have manifested on her face. The nurse announced that Mrs. Gulliver needed to get in touch with her own family. The mournful lot nodded in agreement and filed past her on their way out, again offering their heartfelt hugs and blessings. Maddie promised the girl she would call soon to see how she was doing.

Her own family! "Oh my God," Maddie repeated, after being informed that the hotel had contacted her home yesterday.

"Ed!" The phone hadn't even made it through the first ring.

She got them in the nick of time. He, Carol, and Rima were prepared to go to the airport. Matt and Amy planned on it too, depending on the news. With suitcases packed, they waited anxiously, allowing her only one more hour in which to call. Although the hotel reported that Maddie was safe and resting, the family needed to hear it from her. She apologized and explained the craziness of the past day. The three were on the line at the same time, asking her questions. Through them, Maddie learned that the blast was blamed on a gas leak, and not terrorists. It didn't seem possible…not with that kind of damage. At any rate, Maddie said she was fine and wasn't ready to return yet; there was still much more that she wanted to see. It was quiet on their end. Even Rima had nothing to say—that hurt. They were likely pretty fed up with her escapade.

Ed told Carol and Rima that he wanted to speak to Maddie privately. Again there was silence. "Maddie…" She heard him breathing. "What's going on?" It was spoken like a scolding. She could understand why they were upset with her, but it didn't change her mind. The lack of dialogue continued. Maddie searched the hotel room in the same manner Ed was looking around where he sat.

"That's not acceptable, Maddie." More silence. "I want an explanation. This isn't like you."

Nothing was coming out of her. No one was hanging up. There was much sighing while she waited to hear her own answer.

"Ed…it's like having an addiction."

"What is?"

"Traveling on the fly. Hitchhiking. Something new every day. I'm only beginning to get the hang of it…and I would hate for it to end now."

"You would hate for it to end now? Jesus, Maddie…it almost did, for Pete's sake. I'd say you were goddamned lucky."

He was right. He was being an excellent voice of reason. She sensed her inappropriate response to this tragedy, but she had no control over it. "I've gotten used to just picking up and going…I love it. I can't imagine stopping suddenly."

"Are you saying that the only way we're going to get you home is with an intervention?"

She gave a little laugh. "No." She knew he was serious and really wanted to get to the bottom of her behavior. "Ed, I simply want to do it a little longer…that's all. The ordeal was absolutely terrifying. And home…seeing everyone's faces…would be wonderful now. But I can guarantee that after a couple of weeks, I would regret that my time doing this was cut short. I'm getting excellent attention here at the hotel. They have a nurse. Ed, I know how this is sounding to you." These gaps, with no one talking, were irksome.

"Will you call me once in a while," he asked, "or is that asking too much?"

"Ed…" She was put off by his tone. He was justified. More silence. "Of course I will."

"…'Kay. I'll let you rest. I'll tell the kids you love 'em. Bye. Oh, Maddie…I just want to tell you that I was happy when I read your letter. Bye-bye now."

"Bye."

She continued to stare into space, remembering that she really believed she had had a stroke.

Maddie finally convinced the nurse that she would be fine on her own. She relaxed in the great big tub, continually replenishing it while she watched a movie on the television in the corner. It was an older French film, subtitled in Italian. She was sure that the recognizable actors had since died. In it they played a couple whose tired marriage disintegrated into a bitter disunion. The wife, no longer the object of her husband's affections, nor he of hers, grew jealous of the attention he showed his cat. In the meantime, their home underwent demolition in the background. Maddie loved the actors' faces and being let in on their thought processes. When it ended, she felt comforted by the fact that she and Ed didn't actually despise each other as those two did. The characters' acceptance of their stalemate bothered her. They even derived a certain glee from harassing each other. Maddie wondered why countless people, regardless of status or intelligence or culture, resigned themselves to living under those conditions…and on an ongoing basis.

Time to climb out, before falling asleep and slipping below the suds.

The next morning, the manager personally delivered a message: Mrs. Gulliver was invited to stay until she felt fit to travel again. There was no charge. The staff was trying to do its part in helping the victims. He asked if there was anything she needed…anything. They would accommodate her.

Maddie was understandably skeptical. In her opinion, the offer went a tad overboard. The hotel had already replaced her damaged Patagonia with a new one, exactly like hers. She didn't buy the gas-leak story. Was something being covered up about the disaster, or did the Italians suspect she might be a typical lawsuit-toting American? She stared the ingenuous man in the eyes. He was a good actor.

"Thank you, but I hope to be on my way soon."

He bowed slightly at the waist, respectfully, and headed for the door.

Maddie's hopes for getting under way were dashed when the sniffles turned into a miserable head cold. After being laid up for three days, she'd had it with herself and decided she could just as well lay out by the pool.

Half a lap and she turned belly-up. The early afternoon sun baked her face. Maddie followed the dancing red and orange squiggles inside her lids. A man called out her name, not once—she counted them—but two, three, and four times. She should answer; he sounded upset. It felt so dreamy, floating like this…a little this way, then that…to the rhythm of the Latin rosary and the draining life in dying eyes. She lost count of her name; he still called it. She was running, and had almost reached Tim's waiting outstretched arms when hands touched her shoulders.

She dropped to a standing position. An elderly woman, with her red-smudged smile and supertight turquoise swim cap that pushed her brows over her eyes, pointed to a man, dressed in a hotel vest, precariously balanced in a kneeling position at the pool's edge. Maddie herself was teetering on a dangerously fine line. As she swam to the side, she was reassured that her survival instinct could still be trusted.

"I'm so sorry," Maddie told him. "I think I'm having problems with my hearing."

"I am glad to see you are doing well." The relief in the young employee's face was obvious. He had probably been given the responsibility of checking on her periodically, and there she was, passed out in the water. He held open a terry cloth robe for her, and she returned to her room. She decided to forgo anything physical and read mostly. Claudia and Marcus had not been notified about the event. She wasn't inclined to talk about it anymore.

By the end of a week, Maddie felt recovered, more or less. She also concluded there'd be a change of plan; she no longer wanted to stay in Rome. After the Vatican, she was hitting the road. Wouldn't it be grand if she found renewed faith there? Realistically, she worried there'd be bigger questions.

On the morning of her departure, Maddie got help from the desk in order to call Angelina. The girl was overjoyed at the sound of her voice. Angelina reported that their neighbors were helping them in so many ways. Her father was thankful to have his children, but her grandmother stayed in her room. She didn't eat…didn't talk to the priest. Maddie asked Angelina if she was eating and taking care of herself. Yes, replied the girl. She knew she needed to stay strong to take care of her brother and another younger sister. She wanted her mother to feel proud of the good job she was doing when she looked down on her. That's right, said Maddie, with utmost conviction; life after death was the one thing she was completely certain of, even if she no longer defined it as she once could. Before saying good-bye, Maddie told Angelina that her family was in her prayers, what few she offered these days.

The hotel taxi deposited her on the busy freeway ramp. The young driver got the biggest kick out of what the American was doing—he couldn't wait to tell his grandmother about her.

Maddie sat on the backpack with her thumb out, as if it were nothing. She already regretted not staying in Rome longer; however, as she waited to see who on earth was going to pick her up next, the fun that was inherent to the anticipation lifted her spirits, and she knew she was making the right move. Car after car passed. This wasn't the best time. People looked in a hurry. She did detect the smiles when they caught a glimpse of her before merging into the steady flow of traffic.

She could see his eyes; he had pushed his sunglasses up on his head expressly so she could. The fresh scent of his cologne wafted past the window when he lowered it to ask her destination—Maddie hadn't bothered with a sign today. West, she told him, to the sea. He cleared the seat beside him of a briefcase and some papers.

Fortunately, the gentleman was fluent in English. His name was Umberto, and he had just come from an interview and said he needed to make a quick stop at another company. That was OK with her. He'd been a casualty of downsizing. In his fifties, he was too young to retire, but too old and overqualified to be considered for most other jobs. He'd go to another country, if it meant a paycheck, but men his age were encountering the same prejudice everywhere. Maddie sympathized; there certainly was enough unhappiness to go around these days.

She sat in his parked shiny, red car and waited. It was a beautiful, modern section of the city, incorporating immense sheets of glass in the surrounding architecture. The sight of the cheerful masses that strolled along the wide boulevard, lined with thick palm trees, refuted a gloomy economy. It was an animated picture of energetic, fashion-conscious men and women; many of whom were joined at the elbow, laughing and carrying on. Maybe it was all a cover. Umberto looked equally presentable. She wondered how long he had been unemployed.

As he got comfortable behind the wheel, the Italian wanted to know which spot had been her favorite during her visit. Maddie told him that because she had gotten sick, she had had to miss most of the area, other than the Vatican. Umberto did a double take—how could she leave without having seen anything? If the traveler was headed nowhere in particular, and had no time constraints, why didn't she simply stay longer? Maddie looked directly at him and answered that she was at the wrong place, at the wrong time, last week. He understood and expressed his sorrow over the ill-fated casualties. She fought thinking about that idea: the possibility of death being their fate that day, but not hers.

Where was he headed, Maddie asked, wondering when she would have to transfer cars. To the sea, like her—but not before showing her Rome. Umberto was tired after months of job hunting and was going to give himself this day. Their meeting on this occasion was kismet, he told her. He had never in his life picked up a hitchhiker and honestly couldn't believe it when he pulled over for her. Maddie loved these moments. She was too pleased; but, she insisted, he had to let her pay for the gas.

They walked around ruins and stunning gardens, and ate at a couple of different outdoor cafés. Neither discussed much about their families or work. Umberto loved the movie Maddie had seen at the hotel. That served as a springboard for conversations about other films. She enjoyed his stories about Russia and the excitement that he had felt when its borders opened. His company in Rome had sent him to live in Moscow while they were building a branch office. He mentioned in passing that he had worked in advertising. Maddie believed he must have been outstanding in his field. Umberto was quick-witted and knowledgeable. Although he wasn't handsome, there was a rare genuineness in his speech and manner that drew people in. And it was being wasted now. At least Maddie was benefiting.

It was late in the evening, and they headed north through a string of coastal villages. Umberto pulled into an old farmhouse in Orbetello. A cousin's friend owned it, and there was always an open invitation to him...and guests.

Maddie excused herself after the late snack of cheese and a single glass of wine. The family who lived there was involved in a heated discussion about a local political scandal. Her newest friend gladly left them to see her to her room. He wished to say good-bye now, since he'd be leaving at five in the morning to get back to Rome, in time for yet another interview. The day had been exceptional.

After encircling Maddie in his arms, for a most enjoyable embrace, Umberto kissed both her cheeks and left. For once she wasn't too tired to change into a nightshirt. The sheets were stiff from drying outdoors. She should go back to the practice of hanging hers up; it was a special feeling from childhood, especially for her toes, which couldn't stop scratching against them. Her grandkids wouldn't know what she was talking about.

The window was wide open. Maddie convinced herself that she occasionally caught the scent of the nearby sea, but mostly the smell was of the backyard barn animals. The breeze caused the long edge of the crocheted curtains to repeatedly roll inward, tubelike, and then go flat again as the air sucked them slightly beyond the unscreened frame. This was no quiet place; the pigs never stopped snorting or the chickens their clucking. Maddie's dreams welcomed their timely intrusion. She hoped the strong odors and noises would keep her rooted in the present and ward off the recent sad images.

As she was pouring a morning cup of coffee, Maddie was told she should meet an aunt of theirs, who had already gone to bed by the time she arrived. The woman had been touring by bike and was going to sail back to one of her homes in France. The American could go along—she could tell people she hitched a ride on a boat; that was different. Maddie liked the idea, but didn't want to put the stranger on the spot; after all, what could the aunt say? Maddie sat outside to ponder the request, then decided that her presence on the boat would definitely be an imposition, and she left to collect her gear. She thought she should be able to cover a fair distance today by hitting the road this early. Heading out a side door, she heard...

"Mrs. Gulliver...Maddie Gulliver."

Caught in the act. Turning, Maddie beheld the happy face of a woman considerably taller than she.

"Ah, ah, ah...were you stealing away?"

Maddie smiled sheepishly. "If you must know...I thought I'd spare you." She hesitated...maybe this wasn't the woman. "You are the *zia*, right?" The aunt nodded, amused.

"Spare me what? Having company on my boat? Don't be silly."

Maddie didn't know what to say.

"Leave your bags. We'll go in an hour."

"Fine," Maddie said. "But go where?"

"Civitavecchia…the boat is there."

Maddie agreed to accompany their Aunt Sibylla to the bank. It was an opportunity to see the town. She followed the woman into the yard then stopped in her tracks behind one of the barns. Sibylla (whom Maddie suspected was older than she) had to be kidding. The woman pulled the cover off her "bike," a big, intimidating, glossy black Ducati racing machine. As if it were no big deal, Maddie was told to hop on the back, which she laughingly did, and away they flew.

CHAPTER 20

What bliss! Sailing the Mediterranean Sea. The heat and humidity were only slightly less oppressive than on land, but there was the psychological lift that came from being surrounded by elemental forces...and pure blue.

It stood to reason that all the reading material on the boat dealt with motorcycle racing. The Schedoni family was synonymous with the sport. Two of Sibylla's sons and three grandsons were consistently entered in events. Their interest was derived from the seventy-two-year-old titan, not the other way around. Sibylla had been riding since childhood. Her father had helped to maintain the military's fleet of motorcycles under Mussolini. Her husband, a racer, had ironically died in a fall from a regular street bicycle ten years ago—he had had a stroke.

The flamboyant *signora* liked her solitude—but not a quiet kind. Sibylla exhibited an exasperating restlessness. Her speech resembled her movements, fast and unfocused; the second sentence never followed the subject of the first. Adding to her idiosyncratic tendencies was the slender cigar that habitually bounced between her bright coral-painted, dry lips (even while she spoke). The madwoman was chopping parsley when she absentmindedly balanced the foul cigar on the edge of the sink. It ruined Maddie's appetite.

Sibylla darted over to a dusty lamp that happened to have caught her eye and started to clean the thing. Halfway into that, and while still filling the air with her empty rhetoric, she ran above deck to check things over, then ran back down to the chopping block. She picked up the detestable brown stalk of tobacco (which hadn't had time to burn out), then began to slice mushrooms before having finished with the parsley. That was interrupted when she didn't like the music. Sibylla skipped to the next CD, then the next. She didn't know what she was in the mood for...she would know it when she heard it. The woman would no doubt go on like this until tomorrow's docking. Maddie could feel herself becoming edgy. Hopefully the sailor wasn't an insomniac. An entire night of this behavior would send her overboard—Maddie, that was.

Although Maddie would kill at this point over the suggestion, Sibylla's hyperactivity was good for her. The Italian's fussiness agitated her to no end and therefore didn't allow for a moment's reflection. The memory of the Rome train station would remain shelved as long as she was in Sibylla's company. Maddie had this picture in her head of maliciously taking the Good Samaritan (who so willingly agreed to bring her along) by her ostentatiously bejeweled neck, furiously shake her wild white mop even wilder, then scream in her face...*Slow the fuck down!*

It was torture being at the mercy of someone else's schedule. When Maddie leaped onto the landing in Monaco the following afternoon, she breathed a huge sigh of relief. Now where?

"Maddie! I'm coming," the hoarse, overused, oversmoked voice called to her from below. Sibylla forced her duffel bag through the small passageway as she climbed up the steps.

Maddie honestly couldn't take one more second. What to do...what to do? She looked to the unfamiliar shore, then back out toward the equally strange yacht-heavy harbor, and drew a blank. When she found herself gazing straight down into the water, she believed she had discovered the only potential alternative.

Sibylla heaved one of Maddie's smaller bags over her other shoulder as a counterbalance and still managed to walk with a jaunty step. Her shipmate glumly dragged her pack and trailed far behind. Oh, God. What to do!

A pack of more than twenty skimpily clad, drink carting, and overzealous friends came running like maniacs to greet Sibylla. Right then, Lady Luck intervened. Sibylla let go of her bags as soon as she was engulfed by the mob, leaving parts of them exposed between all the jumping, excited feet. Maddie moved fast. Spying the strap on the ground, she yanked firmly and reeled hers out of the whirlpool. No one noticed when she tore out of there in the opposite direction. In two shakes, she found a clump of trees to hide behind. She sat on her reliable Patagonia "bench," wheezing from the workout. She peeked between the bushes.

"They're gone."

Maddie shrieked, bolted to her feet, and turned to face the soft-spoken person directly behind her. Her reaction startled the woman, who also screamed. Together they burst out laughing.

Adrienne Sunday had witnessed the entire scene with great amusement. She had noted this woman's anxious demeanor as soon as Maddie stepped off Sibylla's boat. Adrienne had just pulled up alongside them in her dinghy and had walked past her.

"Being blotto is a prerequisite for putting up with the Grande Dame. And since that's pretty much the general condition of the folks here, she has lots of friends. May I?"

Maddie nodded, and Adrienne took her shoulder bag.

"Come...I'm in the hotel. Am I wrong to assume you need a place to go?"

Adrienne's good nature rubbed off on Maddie, and soon she was on the rebound, especially when the top floor in the elevator was selected. The suite overlooked the marina. Maddie was told to make herself comfortable on the balcony while the coffee brewed.

"I'm sure I could never guess what business you're in," said Maddie. This degree of wealth exceeded her realm of comprehension—although back where she was from, the rest of the city generally thought that about anyone in Mount Sterling. Her eyes grew big when a dessert tray was placed in front of her.

"Cork," said Adrienne.

Maddie tried not to snicker. She directed her arm from one side of the room to the other in a long, sweeping motion. "All this...from cork? We are talking plugs, right?"

"That's correct," said Adrienne, grinning.

This new acquaintance was Maddie's age. Adrienne had studied painting in Provence during a summer break from Amherst College, way back when. That was where she had met her current husband. The two wouldn't marry until decades later, though...long after the deaths of her two husbands and the death of his first wife. Adrienne once ran an art gallery in Boston and had moderate success selling her work. Besides the usual midlife funk, she found herself having to deal with the depression that was inevitable after a couple of dead spouses. At fifty-two, Adrienne returned to France with the hope of regaining her lost purpose. She paused to take a bite. "And who should arrive, too, in search of some meaning after his loss?"

The coincidence prompted an, "Unbelievable!"

Adrienne and her new suitor kept in contact for a year, then married. His family included her in their time-honored business. Besides the endless numbers of bottles that required her product, Adrienne informed Maddie of all its other uses—for example, her company also manufactured flotation devices for the fishing industry.

"And what is your opinion regarding the synthetic corks used for wine?" Maddie truly wondered. "I read that they are supposed to be as good, if not better, than cork."

Adrienne smiled. "We certainly aren't encouraging the practice."

Changing the subject, Maddie asked if she had any children.

"Yes. A boy from my first marriage," said Adrienne, "and two daughters with my second husband. Now I'm a stepmother to seven children. I can't begin to keep track of the number of grandkids. It boggles my mind."

Maddie gave her the lowdown on her own family, which included the mounting resentment she had begun to unknowingly harbor that led to this journey. Adrienne played devil's advocate a few times. It was helpful, unlike when Ed took on the role; when he did it, his antagonism showed through loud and clear.

"No one is really to blame, Maddie…you and your husband were too immature to have taken on all that responsibility at your young ages…or to make the kinds of decisions that were required. I think you did an admirable job, considering. Who knows, had you been older and wiser, the outcome could still be the same. That's life."

Adrienne opened a bottle of white wine. It was uplifting to be able to discuss these topics and not feel under attack. Maddie wondered if the atmosphere would remain congenial if she brought up the subject of religion. She'd give it a shot.

Adrienne felt for Ed. "Your husband had no way of knowing what he was in for when he agreed to let you raise the children as Catholics. For that reason alone, I would never have married my current husband back when we first met in France. He's a Catholic. I certainly loved him at the time, but I understood the no-win nature of the beast." She smiled. "Poor choice of words."

"Why are things different now?" asked Maddie.

"Because…there are no babies to consider. I don't have to grapple with that issue and have it come between us. I'm also sure that the major reason his family was so welcoming to me, and willing to overlook my shortcoming"—she smiled slyly—"was because I'm not a divorcee…better that my husbands died than that."

Adrienne's comment made Maddie think about how her mother saved face after granting her father a divorce. Mrs. Morrisey told people that her husband had been injured during the war back in England. He was in a hospital and would require special medical care for the rest of his life. There was no reason for Maddie's mother to confess the lie because she had talked herself into believing the story. Ed, alone, knew the truth.

Maddie admitted to Adrienne that she hated floundering like this. Her religion had given her a lifetime's worth of comfort; she had no desire to part ways with it. This straying from its core teachings was unsettling to her. She alluded to an affair.

"There is something obviously missing in it, for that to have occurred," proposed Adrienne. An implausible notion to Maddie—the Church was perfect, the individual was not. "Do you feel as if you're going to hell, Maddie...not think...but *feel* that's where you are headed?"

Maddie looked into her own soul, and recalled when she wondered about that back in Paris. "No," she answered. After thinking about it some more, she said, "And that's not right...by all accounts, that's where I should be going...because I don't feel repentant."

Adrienne shook her head, grateful to have never been saddled with this guilt trip. "You want to believe there is a hell?"

"You don't?"

"No, I don't. Does Ed?"

"I doubt it." Maddie never dwelled on it; instead she prayed for him, that he would come to his senses and see the light one day. "Where do you think sinners go? You don't think they're punished?"

"It's beyond my comprehension, and anyone else's," said Adrienne. "If something isn't fact—meaning witnessed firsthand—it's conjecture. And don't give me the argument about accepting things on faith...we'll be talking in circles all night." She clinked Maddie's glass and downed her last drop. "I don't need the prospect of there being a God to encourage me to lead a good life. The satisfaction derived from acting generously and living truthfully is its own reward. That, for me, is a state of grace. I bet if your husband tried to put it in words, he'd probably say the same thing. As much as I can't fathom your winged angels and demons, you can't picture the abstract realm of my imagination. There's no problem with that until one person coerces another into accepting his line of thinking, and it's not natural to the other's way of understanding." She gave Maddie's hand a friendly rub, then cleared the table. When she returned, Adrienne told her guest that she was expecting too much too fast. "The questions you are posing are all new to you, Maddie. They take time to sort out."

"What if I continue to deviate from what I once believed was the gospel...and I reach a point of no return?" That really scared Maddie at the moment.

Adrienne consoled her. "With that many years of honest living under your belt, you're fundamentally sound. Stop worrying. Now tell me about your travels."

Maddie gave her an overview of each of the towns. While she talked, she watched the changeful expression in the woman's shrewd brown eyes. Her lashes were either coated in layers of the blackest mascara or fake. Her eyebrows were dark, but her smartly styled, chin-length hair was the color of the cream. The story abruptly stopped with the mention of Rome. Maddie's breathing grew rapid. She was unprepared for this.

It took a while for Adrienne to get the gist of what happened. Maddie's grief had taken its time to build, somewhat like Angelina's, and now it attacked her with a vengeance, culminating with this enfeebling crying. Unlike other occasions, when such deep-seated emotions were extracted from her, Maddie didn't—she couldn't—slip away into sleep...or a pool of water.

This chance meeting proved fortuitous. Maddie offered no resistance when it came to Adrienne's self-determined guardianship. She had met a woman who took the Golden Rule to heart.

The headwind whipped their faces as they skimmed the surface of the sea in the small motorboat. The fast speed made her pleasantly mindless. Maddie had no idea where she would end up, nor did she care. It was too noisy to talk. When they weren't staring across the world, they'd look at each other, and Adrienne would smile. Maddie could only picture herself returning one. There was no controlling the sag in her cheeks and the droop of her mouth.

So it began—the island hopping. Maddie found herself sitting on a new terrace each afternoon, sipping varieties of wine while the compassionate host (a virtual stranger) met with friends, allowing her time to just be. Adrienne did this simply because she thought it would do Maddie good.

On the fifth day, the women boarded an offshore yacht, one of those intimidating behemoths. The personal service was impeccable; the decor, out of this world—which was exactly how Maddie felt. The extravagance overwhelmed her. She much preferred the ambience of the small islands and their vineyards. The far-off shoreline was always within view, and she followed as the French coast seamlessly transitioned into the Spanish one. They would be dropping anchor near Barcelona's port.

Although Adrienne was relieved to see the forlorn traveler involved with her surroundings again, she couldn't resign herself to leaving Maddie by the side of the road to wait for someone to take her out of town. "Maddie," she implored, having circled back to her, "Barcelona isn't to be missed. Please reconsider." Maddie didn't feel up for a big city. She did take Adrienne's number, in case she got in a pickle. She was warned that finding a room would be a problem in Spain—this was vacation time. The woman had contacts everywhere to help Maddie out.

Maddie found herself in Tarragona for the day, in an amphitheater by the water. Three Spanish students had made room for her in their overstuffed little car. She took them up on their offer of spending the night at a friend's house, a few more hours down the road. Tomorrow, in Valencia, she would need to find another ride.

Valencia, the orange producing capital, was never overrun with visitors like other villages, so Maddie took the opportunity to rent a room. The previous night she had slept on a crowded floor in the middle of nine other bodies. She surveyed the dingy neighborhood while she waited for a bus. She was excited to be going to a Gothic cathedral, where she would see the goblet said to be the one used by Jesus at the Last Supper.

The cell phone kept losing signal. Maddie located a cybercafe, where she sat for two hours reading her messages and e-mailing everyone, including Joel. Claudia got on her case for not having contacted Marcus yet, let alone her. There was so much to tell them both; it made her head swim. Wasn't she doing a superb job of hurting people this summer? Maddie wrote the same thing back to each of them: *Sorry...so sorry...there is no excuse.* She studied the faces of other customers busily typing in the shop. *Took a tailspin for a bit...hope the dark episode is behind me. Thoughts of you give me strength. Love, Maddie.* Don't be alarmed, she told Ed, if he didn't hear from her for a couple of weeks. Things were going well, not to worry, it was just that communications were tricky in those regions...which wasn't true. She wanted to get lost, and feel beholden to no one.

Another night. Maddie slept on the beach with other students who had picked her up. The sand and hard ground were unpleasant. The next day, the wind whipped her in the face for hours as she sat in the backseat of a convertible driven by a young French couple. They knew of a lovely, refurbished hostel all the way down the coast in Gibraltar, where they were going to make a side trip before turning inland. It was a tourists' haven now, and Maddie thought about writing off the experience. But she didn't want to deal with catching a new ride. The monkeys were a joy, even if they didn't kiss hands or tip their hats. The hostel was a delightful experience with people from everywhere. As it turned out, she loved it.

CHAPTER 21

The balcony, three floors up, directly overlooked a canal, busy with fishermen. Distant ocean liners remained fixed along the horizon, camouflaged by haze and patchy clouds. As she lay sunning herself, Maddie thought about how she might have had to resort to sleeping on a beach again. Stranded beside bumper-to-bumper impatient motorists, and with no prospect of securing a ride, she had availed herself of Adrienne, who was back in France. Maddie had to call her from a pay phone, where she then waited for the taxi that would be sent to pick her up. Adrienne suggested she come up there to regroup, in Cadiz. Since ten thirty that morning (four hours ago), Maddie hadn't budged from her chair.

When she finally felt too hot, she went inside and stood in the center of the small, square room. Maddie had specified no five-star palaces, and gotten her wish. She turned in a slow circle. The space, with its bare white stucco walls, was adequate. Two huge white linen loveseats were crammed between a chipped white wooden dresser and several matching end tables. A squat, cabinet refrigerator with a microwave on top qualified the corner as the kitchen. The wall-to-wall, navy blue carpet must represent the sea. A digital clock forced her to finally consider the date: 16 *Agosto*.

She unconsciously lowered herself onto the couch and studied the number as if it held some cryptic significance. Claudia's birthday was next week. She would love to celebrate it with her and Marcus. Maddie was missing their friendship. "The middle of August…Good Lord," she mumbled, disbelievingly.

Knowing Ed, he had everything packed for Alaska. Maddie tried picturing him fishing with Tom. *Good for them*, she thought. Remembering her conversation with Carol, she wondered if Rima had really gone to Berlin; her granddaughter might be there now. Thinking about her family was no different than conjuring up grade-school classmates; their names, remembered with fondness, belonged to history. They bore no current relevance, not even Rima's. It was inconceivable, but true nevertheless.

"Why was I saved?" There, Maddie finally said it: the question that was the source of her malaise, underlying every waking and sleeping moment since that day. It required answering. She'd give the matter her full attention…tomorrow. It was enough that she finally acknowledged it. Although the day was far from over, and her empty stomach growled, Maddie went to bed.

She woke at nine and decided it wasn't too late for a swim. The outdoor pool was colorfully lit. Boisterous youngsters splashed a lot, so she went and sat in a dim, remote area, alone with her thoughts. She looked like a sulking child. One thing was certain: she required a sympathetic ear. When she divulged the news of the explosion to Adrienne, she hadn't had ample time to delve into herself. She had just begun to examine the nature of how the event had impacted her.

Maddie considered her choices. Too bad the substance of her phone conversations with Gary over the last years had dwindled to paltry small talk. The mother and son had actually enjoyed the best philosophical discussions when he was growing up. They never agreed, but he always gave her food for thought—as did Carol. The only philosophical argument that had ever seriously come between the two of them had been that confounding Communion, which was no small contention. For the most part, their chats never deteriorated into the ugly yelling matches she learned to avoid with Janet.

The grandmother didn't bother to bring up Rima's name. The two were cut from the same cloth, but the girl was simply too young.

Maddie would be curious to talk to Irene about Patagonia, and whether the woman was at peace with her decision to go there. There was someone who had definitely been tested over the years. She wondered if Irene had gone to Alcoholics Anonymous to overcome her drinking, and asked for God's help in her struggle. Did the reformed alcoholic owe her determination to him? Maybe Irene could render the needed counsel. She wondered what the woman was doing that very second, and tried to envision how her days played out in that oh-so-far-away place.

Although she valued the insight of several of her friends back home, especially the ones from church, their words were rote after the many decades; Maddie could anticipate how each would advise her. She treasured them, but she yearned to be enlightened.

Perhaps Ed held the key. There was a novel thought. Since taking his life by the reins, maybe he had precious pearls of wisdom to impart. She seriously entertained that idea while she changed out of her bathing suit into a T-shirt and underpants. The air was muggy, but the open window let in a cool breeze. The ceiling fans helped to keep it comfortable inside.

Maddie turned on the lamp next to the bed. Her fingertips tapped the phone as she counted back the time zones. He'd likely be eating dinner.

No one picked up; the answering machine wasn't turned on. He was never good about remembering that. Too bad ol' Big Red couldn't figure out how to grab the receiver. She was so happy that the dog's surgery had had a positive outcome. The vet had explained that the procedure was no miracle; it could really only improve the ability to distinguish between light and dark—and then only sometimes. Apparently, it was enough to restore the dog's confidence. She was curious to see the results for herself.

The troweled swirls in the plastered walls drew her interest, and she became lost in the designs. It passed the time. There was the layer of obvious cloud patterns. Looking closer, Maddie saw that a horse's nostril, along with a bobbed mane, stuck out vividly. Tedium with the process must have set in for the poor worker by the time he reached a lower right corner; a carelessly executed blob resembled a huge bouquet of ragged peonies. Above it, two swans glided side by side. The longer she immersed herself in the pastime, however, the darker the images became, until Maddie saw nothing but bodiless arms and heads, and smoke spirals…out of which eyes emerged and held her in their grip. She recognized them and trembled from a sudden chill.

The phone shook in her hands. This time, she got through. The voices in the background made her feel as if she were interrupting something. Maybe the kids were over. That dreadful, sinking feeling continued, and she hung up before saying a word.

Angelina and her darling little brother came to mind. Maddie imagined how different her own children's lives would have been if she had died when they were younger…and Ed had dictated the rules. He would have been forced into becoming more emotionally involved in their lives. She couldn't imagine that. And her children would have grown up without ever setting foot in a church. She couldn't imagine that, either. It would have made Carol a happy camper; maybe she would have smiled more when she was little. Maddie also contemplated what would have happened to their family structure if Tim had lived, and another of his sisters or brothers hadn't. And who might those miscarried babies have become? *"If" should be outlawed*, Maddie thought.

She took to staring out the window at the night. The bedroom wall was avoided. Her motives behind her charity work came into question. They were decidedly self-serving—a means of meeting fascinating people and of garnering a degree of clout that caused others to seek her out for favors. No doubt, the end result of her efforts benefited an enormous number of people. Maddie was ashamed to admit, though, that it was just a good cover.

The driving force behind Claudia's deeds, on the other hand, was genuine. It couldn't be denied that the actress's status generated the means whereby she obtained financial support, but then she would go and get lost in Africa, where there was no one to pat her on the back…and, if that weren't enough, she risked untold dangers. Claudia also personally tracked how the contributions were spent—every penny—and helped construct hospitals and school buildings with her own hands. Her concern for the welfare of others came strictly from the heart. "She's a truly virtuous soul," said Maddie, sitting there alone. As Claudia so emphatically pointed out to her in Bern, maybe Maddie was supposed to meet her…but for a different reason than the one her new friend had proposed, that of convincing her to see her father.

Maddie wondered whether the decision to go on this trip had truly been hers to make; perhaps it was really mandated, a test from above that she miserably failed. After a life's worth of devotion, why couldn't she hold up to the end? She had yielded to lust and betrayed her wedding vows. It was convenient to rationalize that the Church had proven unreliable; otherwise she would never have resorted to this promiscuous behavior. She scolded herself, because she knew better. In her worst times, she maintained that Christ never left anyone in the lurch. He could always be relied upon to be there.

And only he alone could judge. How dare she have looked down her nose at the squalid man in the Rome train station? Maddie assumed he was a homeless beggar and had regarded him as a lesser individual; the sin of that mistake was flagrantly pointed out to her now on the hotel wall. His eyes had appeared to her…and beheld her as they had for those brief seconds in the taxi—with kindness. It was a fact that God communicated in visions.

"I'm sorry; I'm so very sorry." The penitent apology was repeated until she wore herself out.

It wasn't even the weekend, and throngs of sightseers, mostly German, swarmed the streets. Maddie dove in. It was difficult for her to get into the spirit of the place. A teenager, standing outside a hair salon and smoking fiendishly, stomped out his cigarette when she passed and walked a few steps alongside her. In a disarmingly ingenuous manner, he asked if the *senora*, already very lovely, would like to treat herself to a new look today. His face was boyishly sweet. She expected to hear more of his spiel, but that was it. He smiled and simply waited for her to go inside with him—which she did.

Maddie lacked confidence in the hairdresser, who didn't look old enough to shave, and was apprehensive about the way she'd turn out. He told her he was from a village in the Pyrenees Mountains, and his family had come there every summer since he was born. His first passion was windsurfing; the second, thank goodness, was styling hair.

He liked showing off his extensive English vocabulary, which was impressive, although the wrong choice of word often made Maddie chuckle. He blabbed about everything under the sun. She enjoyed watching him in the mirror. Surprisingly, once he began to cut, he moved with deft precision. She didn't have to be talked into the color job. The outcome was impressive. The boy arranged her hair in a sexy loose upsweep.

Feeling peppier, Maddie decided a new outfit would be fun to buy. She spied a bold brown-on-white polka-dotted sundress on display in an out-of-the-way alley. Its flamenco-inspired design enhanced the figure, and more important, the skirt flounces looked fun to prance around in. Maddie was elated when she zipped up the back and found it a perfect fit. Her other clothes were tossed in the bag.

She beamed over having dug herself out of the dumps. Her mood was infectious. Everybody was returning her hellos, especially on the dock. Normally men who constantly flirted annoyed her. In parts of the world where ogling was a way of life, the indiscriminate behavior of lumping all women together was a real turnoff. So why did she play into the low-minded passes of these coarse fishermen today?

Her age should have been enough of a factor to inhibit the provocative wiles she openly demonstrated at each seller's stand. She was having a ball, making the most of the "come-on" eye contact, kicking those flounces, and leaning forward just the right amount to enhance the fullness of her breasts. The vendors, who cooked fish in the open, enthusiastically shoved samples in front of her to taste. A combination of squid and tuna was going to be tonight's dinner. She planned on enjoying it by herself back in her room, although she was acquiring plenty of invitations for company this evening.

No sooner had the door shut behind her when the self-condemnation resumed…and persisted. Maddie sat on the balcony, twirling tentacles around her fork. The teeny, toasted eyes were a macabre sight. She studied them. They were actually less threatening than the beautiful pair she had witnessed in her bedroom. She felt lonely and confused…and didn't recognize the floozy who had just been strutting her stuff today. Worse, she couldn't think of where she wanted to be…or with whom.

The television stayed on through the night and the next day. Adrienne called to ask how she was doing. Maddie lied. Her insides were still, the desires quelled. That frightened her. What if this was the decreed punishment for her misguided sexual thrill seeking? Her regained sensuality had proven itself vital, making a world of difference in her approach to each new day. The emptiness that plagued her now would inevitably kill her. That was no exaggeration. She sat crumpled in the corner of the couch, staring at the screen as if the Spanish would suddenly magically make sense to her. She went to turn down the speed of the ceiling fan.

There was a knock. The housekeeping staff always announced themselves first. Insistent, multiple beats rapped in succession, shaking the door. Her pulse quickened. She'd been sitting in a T-shirt and underwear and went to throw on a skirt.

"Yes?" she asked, with her ear up to the door. The peephole had been broken.

Whoever it was, they switched to a quieter tapping action, right in the spot where she stood listening. It seemed as if someone was playing with her…and it was disturbing.

"Madelaine?" The identifiable pronunciation stopped her heart.

What followed was a blur: the swiftly opened door, the tenacious embrace, the madly urgent scramble to the bed. The prospect of hell certainly didn't deter Maddie from accessing her supposedly lost libido. Marcus was to blame. He moved in all the right ways. How could she resist?

She smiled shyly. They had worn themselves out before even saying hello. She held on to his waist when he tried to roll away, keeping him inside her. He arranged the pillow on one of her shoulders in order to sleep there. She was impatient for him to want her again.

"Claudia told me about Rome. She e-mailed your granddaughter when we didn't hear from you in weeks. Rima's name was in her computer. Your cell phone hasn't been working."

Maddie didn't want to remember that last phone conversation with Rima, when she'd been given the silent treatment. She stroked Marcus's hair, his cheek, his chin. He was really here. *Stop talking*, she thought. She closed her eyes and waited; couldn't he tell? His arms slid around her, and she endured the momentary crushing weight of him while he expressed how grateful he was for her safety. The words of concern didn't end, but continued to sail into her ear until she silenced him with a kiss...and the waiting game ended.

Freshly showered, they sat on the balcony and enjoyed their morning coffee.

"How did you find me?" she wondered.

"Delectable."

It took a second...then she rolled her eyes at him. "C'mon."

"What do you mean? You called me."

Her face went blank.

Marcus could see that something didn't jibe. "I had a few neighbors over for Claudia's birthday. We celebrated early, because she was flying to Austria to be with her family. Someone called during the evening, but didn't speak. I checked the number and called it back. The name of the hotel meant nothing to me, and I almost hung up...when it occurred to me to ask if you were here."

That wasn't possible, thought Maddie. She could not have confused Germany with the States when she made the call. The numbers were completely different. She knew she had been operating in somewhat of a fog these last days, but was she really that out of it? Maddie tried to picture the hotel phone on the table, and tried to remember dialing. She didn't mention the mistake to Marcus. She was certain she had called Ed.

They decided to spend a leisurely day at the beach, regardless of all the people. Marcus's company comforted her. She wanted to tell him about what happened to her in her room the other day, but didn't want it to come off sounding like something from the *Twilight Zone*.

Just as they suspected, there weren't any open spots on the sand to throw down their towels. One excited family, recognizing the actor, quickly collected all their kids' toys and made a place beside them. *What a perk*, thought Maddie. Whenever Marcus sat up and looked around, tourists waved and called out their favorite roles of his. They respected his privacy, to the extent that they didn't ask for autographs.

As much as she loved to swim, Maddie didn't like the ocean. She really enjoyed her laps, and that was it. Marcus ran into the water several times to cool off, getting cornered by his fans on his way back to her. He engaged them by throwing a few Frisbees and chatting, and was good-natured when they suddenly produced cameras. She couldn't begin to imagine what that kind of adoration must be like, or how she would handle it. As she looked at the sky, annoyed by every hard lump of sand that protruded into her back, and feeling sleepy from her skin's rising temperature; she contemplated Angelina's mother's lost life. How many mothers and fathers were missing from this happy vacation picture right now?

Neither had gotten badly burned. Maddie's thighs bore the brunt of the sun, being the least exposed every day. Marcus's healthy tan (from sailing) proved he was still procrastinating, although he swore he was off to a good start with his book. He proudly admitted to being halfway done. She was duly impressed.

The balcony, thankfully, was more spacious than the room, but it was in clear view of countless other ones that overlooked the sea. In a tight but cozy fit, Maddie sat between Marcus's legs on the long deck chair. Her loose, cotton shirt made it easy for his hands to remain hidden while they explored her. She reached behind her, parting the towel tucked around his waist, then shimmied back until he pressed against her tailbone. They were oblivious to the horizon as it swallowed the last speck of light. The wine bottle was empty. Maddie forced herself to go inside and fetch another. While she was at it, she went to use the bathroom, turning on the lamp by the bed so she could see.

"Maddie? What the hell are you doing?" Marcus had come in when she hadn't returned to him. There was no anger to his tone; it showed worry.

He didn't startle her. The palms of her hands, level with her head, lay upon the wall. She turned and leaned back, and waited to see if Marcus could tell that he was being watched from over her shoulder. He grew impatient for an explanation.

"I am alive because I was constipated. How absurd is that?"

Marcus stood there, stumped. The festive music and ongoing merrymaking from other rooftops poured in through the window. He wondered if he should close it, but he didn't want to take his eyes off her for a second. After all, that was why he came—to be there for her. He guessed she didn't say anything on the phone because she had a last-minute change of heart, and didn't want to impose on him. He was glad to be the one she would turn to. The grisly ordeal had yet to be brought up.

It was hard to determine whether she was going to start into this now. Maintaining his watch, Marcus stepped to the closet and pulled on his pants. He sat at the foot of the bed, in front of her. His heart ached. She appeared sad, comfortless.

"The most beautiful girl sat across from me…with her whole life ahead of her." Maddie described her to a T, and the others…including the vagrant who was sprawled across the chairs. "One second, I was doubled over with cramps…the next second, when I looked up from the floor…" She shook her head slowly, not knowing how to describe the horror, the chaos. "Their faces still had a look of surprise." Marcus had to strain to hear her soft-spoken account. "The man beside me…had been thrown to the floor. Out of everyone who was in that enclosed waiting room, we alone lived."

There were long pauses. She managed a feeble smile when she told him about the exasperating Sibylla Schedoni. Who in Europe wasn't familiar with the antics of that kooky matriarch? He couldn't repress a short laugh when he envisioned Maddie marooned on the boat with Sibylla. Then he learned about Adrienne, and of all the rides offered to Maddie along Spain's coast.

That brought her to Cadiz. Only now did she look into Marcus's face for reassurance—before she concluded. He was looking at her so lovingly—maybe it would be OK. She needed him to see the conviction in her heart.

"When I recited the Latin to the dying mother, I remembered every word, after all this time, and without a mistake. It felt like I was part of a miracle, put there to help this woman find peace at such a despairing moment."

"It would have been a miracle, all right…if she had gotten up and walked away." His smirk put her on the defensive. She felt crestfallen.

"So sorry, Maddie. Really." Marcus sounded sincere, but he would require a muzzle if she continued with this nonsense.

There was no stopping now. "The fellow who was beside me, who ended up getting us out…he appears to me in this room, in the wall."

Marcus looked intently to her left and right. Then he faced the floor. This was more than he bargained for. He said nothing.

"I mean, just think about it, Marcus. I reacted to this man as if he weren't fit to exist. Me," she emphasized, "who's sidestepped my morals since arriving here. And then he comes to our rescue. The building was coming down around us. Fires were breaking out. The children and I would *not* have escaped if we continued sitting there any longer. His manner and expression were so…so…saintly." Marcus didn't budge. "Christ meant for him to be there."

Now her heart pounded. It sounded farfetched to her too—but it was what she firmly believed at this point. "I need to concentrate on becoming humble of spirit. He's obviously the reason I was protec—"

The fist flew past her line of sight so fast it had to have grazed her. The hearing went out of her left ear after the pugilistic punch to the wall, no doubt directed at the phantom eyes. She got dizzy from fright. Marcus ranted in German, hammering his opinion of all this malarkey next to the sides of her head. She felt faint.

And the cause for such ire: the evil-riddled dogma of the Church, her church, with its unmitigated hypocrisy and contradictions. That someone so dear to him should be infected in this manner was distressing to Marcus. The subject had never come up; Maddie had no way of knowing.

Marcus leaned forward and supported her rigid body against the wall; his gory mitts cupped her face. At once he got tearful. A crippled whisper pleaded for her forgiveness. She kept her eyes shut tight and prayed that he go.

His lips moved against hers when he next spoke. "So you're going to change your sinful ways because of a drifter…a bum." She heard his teeth snap together. "Consider his life, Madelaine." His dulcet and deliberate cadence had a somnolent effect. "There's nothing unusual about a homeless person sleeping at the station in the afternoon. Any other day, it might be the park, or under a bridge. He just happened to be next to you right then. And he was, without question, high on heroin…giving him that otherworldly look you imagine as holy. Who knows what holy looks like, huh?" She despised Marcus's mocking tone. "I'm sure he doesn't even remember what took place. The excitement shook him sober for a short time. That's all." Marcus stroked her hair. "As for your personal predicament…I'm sure others in the place were holding onto their stomachs as well. That's normal when you travel. Then something totally unforeseen simply happened, for no damn reason. Under different conditions, those leaning over might have been the ones killed. These coincidences don't seem extraordinary to me." His hands felt sticky. "But…if you *must* find something supernatural about all this, why not believe in the prayers of a heathen like me? Maybe mine have been the ones that saved you. Would that reaffirm your faith?"

Air bombarded her face and chest the second he moved away. She gulped it like a long glass of water after a day in desert heat. Her knees took her slowly to the ground. She dared to open her eyes. There were splatters of red. Using her shirt like a washcloth, Maddie lifted the hem and wiped her face and neck, afraid of touching her ears. When she built up the nerve, she haltingly moved her fingers over them. They were fine; she was intact…physically, at least. She looked up at the splotches on the wall and realized all the blood had come from Marcus. His fists had to be broken. No matter. Sleepyheaded, her crouched form involuntarily tipped to the side and lay inert on the blue-piled sea.

The job required a full hour and lots of elbow grease, but the wall got scoured to her satisfaction; there wouldn't be any questions from the hotel staff. Once the detergent foamed, it had become bright pink. The carpet was easier; the red was better hidden. Cleaning felt good, therapeutic.

Marcus didn't return that next day, or the next. At some point, he'd have to collect his shoulder bag; he would also want the straw-colored suit that had been carefully hung up. She never got a full view of him in it. It was expensive…silk, and smelled of his skin. Maddie stood caged in the closet—trapped by her emotions, like after Tim's death. She had never wanted to leave her son's closet; never wanted to leave the scent of him, the touch of his clothes, the stack of old piano books and Green Lantern comics, an outgrown baseball glove, and most of all, his boxes of marbles. There was no more significant place, after someone went. Who could guess the untold numbers that have become enshrined?

It was Friday night. The streets were alive. Maddie observed the gamut of behaviors from her upper floor. Hungry couples couldn't be bothered with consummating their appetites in the privacy of shadows. They stood in doorways, some lay on boat decks; one woman looked to be making the rounds on the laps of a spirited group of soldiers who were seated outside the restaurant, catty-corner to the hotel. Maddie wondered what it would feel like to be as shameless. It had to be liberating.

She uncorked the wine meant for the other night. The confession overshadowed the noise and was replayed a hundred times: the infidel had prayed for her.

While pouring a third glass, she glanced between the decorative bars of the wrought-iron hand rail and observed a nearby terrace. She didn't care if she was caught being a voyeur; after all, the three interlocked men, braided together like a pretzel, were doing it right out in the open.

It made no difference being tipsy; if Maddie had been dead drunk, her hallucinations still wouldn't resurrect the image. Marcus's fury had ultimately expunged it. She turned off the lamp. Overwhelming sadness sucked the wakefulness out of her.

The zip of the blind snapping up woke her. The sun struck her face.

"Rise and shine! A beautiful day awaits."

Here and there, she spotted bits and pieces of Marcus. Damned if he thought she was going to pretend like nothing happened! Maddie sat up in bed and blinked repeatedly to recover her sight. How had he gotten in?

"Come on." He started pulling the covers back. "No dillydallyi—"

"Cut it out!" She grabbed his upper arms and forcefully pushed him away. She was rubbing her eyes and could finally make him out, when the mattress jerked from his weight. There he sat, with head hung low. He looked guilt ridden. Good act; it didn't fly with her, though.

Marcus sheepishly asked, "Do you hate me?"

Maybe...now that he gave her a word to work with. He turned toward the window. "I hate me."

Oh, brother! His hands were bandaged. "Did you go to a hospital?"

He glanced at them. "Just bruised."

Hardly, she thought. "What makes you think you can simply waltz in here and expect me to go traipsing merrily off with you?"

Marcus couldn't assume a serious face, not in his present mood. He was operating in high gear. At least he had learned to lasso his tongue before a wiseass remark jumped out. He had no comeback. The wall drew his attention.

Speaking in monotone, between clenched teeth, Maddie berated him. "*You should've cleaned that fucking mess. You were responsible for it!*" She didn't hesitate using the obscenity.

He turned and greeted her icy stare with his own steely one. Mimicking her disparaging attitude, he shot back, "It would never have been necessary...if you hadn't said such a fucking...stupid...thing."

Neither backed down during this stand off. Maddie claimed a little religion would likely have gone a long way when he was growing up. Marcus countered with the argument that her life didn't sound so admirable because of it. Each felt justified regarding his and her respective stance on the matter.

It ended in a draw. Maddie coolly left to go shower while Marcus made coffee. He accepted that she'd be peeved at him for a long time, hopefully not indefinitely. She didn't dry herself off very well and simply spun her wet ponytail around a few times, then secured it with a clip.

The freshly ground brew (from the beans he so thoughtfully brought with him) tasted too good. It was a much-appreciated treat—that went unsaid. The two sat uncomfortably close at the little kitchen table, in silence. When had the place ever been this quiet? Maybe it was a religious holiday. Maddie crossed her legs, making sure that the robe covered her thighs. She observed Marcus's left leg; it bobbed up and down excitedly as he watched out the window, as if he had to pee. He knew he was getting scrutinized. His impatience grew beyond his control, and he started to squirm in his chair. Meantime, Maddie slowly, and loudly, sipped the coffee...as if it could possibly be as hot as it was fifteen minutes ago. The scene reminded her of the French movie she had watched while sitting in the bathtub in Rome. In it, the elderly couple had resorted to flicking paper wads at each other. Maddie refused a giggle. When Marcus finally looked at her, she held the cup in front of her mouth to hide her changing disposition. Her light eyes stood out against her tanned skin. He studied them.

"Dear Madelaine, would you please accompany me today?"

How sweetly he asked...so heartfelt. He was still a jerk. She kept him guessing for a bit.

"You're lucky you're so pretty without makeup."

He was too much.

"If you choose to come with me...you'll only need your bathing suit."

"I've had my fill of the beach."

"That isn't what I had in mind." No explanation followed.

When she placed her cup down beside his fingers, she saw how very swollen the tips were. The blackened cuticles and knuckles stuck out from the bandages like a bagged handful of fat, burned-out cigars. Marcus self-consciously withdrew them, leaned back, and rested his arms on his lap below the table. The bouncing leg must have worn itself out. Maddie was tiring of this banter. "I poked my head in all the local bars, thinking I would come across you."

Marcus shook his head and clucked his tongue, disappointed at her perception of him. "Believe it or not, I reflect on my actions." He let go a huge sigh. "My first response to something so upsetting...isn't to go and get soused. I'd like to think that I'm more introspective at this stage of life." As he stood, he added, self-mockingly, "It's not like I'm still only...fifty, you know?"

Although he didn't crack a smile, she found humor in his admission. Without skipping a beat, he insisted on knowing if she was going to come with him; he was going to leave.

They kept at arm's length from each other, literally and figuratively; anyone would have guessed they were strangers. Maddie was secretly thinking that she had to be a complete nincompoop for agreeing to go anywhere with someone who could behave as monstrously as he had. She was pleasantly surprised when he turned to the left and headed toward the end of a dock.

The wind was perfect. The Gullivers owned a similar catamaran, which they sailed on the Great Lakes. Their children always worked the ropes, but today, Maddie would have to be Marcus's hands. It wasn't a problem, but she knew her arthritis would flare up later.

Soon the seawall was out of view, and their excursion really got under way. The brisk speed created fun splashes. Looking at a map, Marcus mentioned they were nearing an area famous for its coves...and nude sunbathing, he added with a roguish grin.

Extra help was required to steer them clear of the rocks. Marcus gripped an oar, enduring the brief jabs of pain. Fortunately the current helped them along, and in no time they floated onto a serene turquoise pool. The temperature and humidity changed dramatically. Fluorescent lichens encrusted the mineral-yellowed surfaces, forming dazzling green ornamental patterns. The boat continued to glide down a far-reaching tunnel—an organic art deco grand hall of sorts, graced with smooth walls that arched high above them. Awestruck, the sailors strained their necks like first-time tourists taking in the great cathedrals.

"It's exquisite...absolutely breathtaking."

"Mm," agreed Marcus.

They drifted to a stop and sat idling on the smooth, mirroring surface. A dusty shaft of copper light cut through the upper atmosphere of the dome, linking them to the outside world. It was downright mystical.

Hardly a ripple moved through the water when Marcus gingerly stepped his way over to sit beside Maddie. The heat from his body took away the chill. Although they were disarmed of their furor for the most part, Marcus still had to answer to Madelaine Gulliver's time-honed accusatory stare, practiced on two generations of children—one that possessed the lethal power (in this mythical setting) of turning him into a block of stone. He knew to watch his words.

Now seemed like a good time. He reached for a canvas rucksack and checked the bottom to make sure it hadn't gotten waterlogged. His clumsy attempt at unbuckling the flap provoked Maddie into helping. Holding it open, Marcus invited her to see what was inside. Out came a book. Puzzled, she silently read the title. *Tales of Fishes*. By Zane Grey.

Marcus's breathing picked up. His chest moved hard against her arm. She flipped through the pages, mindful of the large type...and the comment she had once made about it to Tim.

"I thought we could share it," said Marcus.

The sounds of dripping water hitting stones and the echoes of squawking birds, way up high, stole her attention. In a reverent manner, the mother closed the cover and rested her hand on this treasure: the subject of her son's final dreams. Life, at the moment, was surreal and cause for meditation. Marcus tenderly kissed Maddie's neck. She accepted it. He kissed her shoulder.

Demurely, he asked, "Will you read to me, Madelaine?"

The touch of his tongue in her ear as it pronounced the *l*'s was startlingly electrifying. She agreed with a nod.

Marcus threw their towels over the life vests as a makeshift pillow and lay down beside her. Maddie turned to the first page, uncertain of what to expect.

"To capture the fish is not all of the fishing." She sounded out the foreign names and places. If she hadn't recognized the photograph on the front, the lyrical quality of the beginning paragraphs would have been enough to make her doubt that this was really the same book that Ed had given their son. When she paused after certain lines, Marcus nudged her, prompting her to continue.

As she read, she made herself more comfortable, positioning her long legs and skirt across Marcus's thighs. Her left hand secured the pages on her lap; she rested her right hand alongside the buttoned fly of his khaki shorts. Glancing up, Maddie saw that Marcus's arms fell in that vulnerable posture she so loved. The left one hung over his forehead. The other was stretched out to his side, but curled around so that his hands touched. He casually flicked at a nail, at the crusted blood. Her fingers crept between the open gaps in the material to touch his skin while she moved on to the following sentence.

Page eighty-five...the last one for a while. The astute Mr. Grey, in a clear and unaffected manner, conveyed the infinite scope of the oceans and the nobleness of a certain character of angler who fished them. The author's observations showed that he was governed by such integrity himself. This was a particularly beautiful, descriptive passage, the spirit of which lent itself to the couple's languishing mood. By the time Maddie reached the chapter's conclusion (dealing appropriately enough with a heaving sea), Marcus was looking at her with considerable need.

The Patagonia was much lighter. Extra shoes and sleepwear and toiletries had long since been discarded. Maddie felt emotionally ready to leave. These past days had been relaxing and healing. Marcus was going along in the taxi to the bus station. There'd be a couple of hours for her to daydream before arriving at Seville's airport, where she was catching a plane to England.

Until today, neither had known for sure if they would ever make love again. They had returned from their previous afternoon's sailing (where they had discovered a haven in that wondrous natural pavilion) without having engaged in true intercourse. That night, Marcus was relieved to have won his half of Maddie's bed, and that was exactly where he stayed. Maddie assumed that he had found another room in the area since fleeing from her place. If she had given the matter a second's thought, she'd have realized how problematic finding another room would be during the busy high season, although a pricier resort would certainly have put the actor up. With his hands wrapped, and no clothes to speak of, Marcus had asked a fisherman to sleep on his boat. Following several pleasant days of going to movies, eating out, wandering through shops, and friendly conversation, Maddie still chose to keep to her designated side at bedtime…and Marcus disappointedly resigned himself to his. However, the next morning—this morning—proved lucky. As they simultaneously rolled over in their sleep, the erection found a welcoming place to nest.

Her bags were loaded in the bottom compartment of the big touring bus. They stood off to the side in a doorway so Marcus wouldn't be recognized.

Before a final hug, he humorously noted, "I see that Claudia's persuasive personality finally got to you." The reference pertained to Maddie's last stop in London. She had decided to meet with her father after all.

"No, Marcus, it's not because of her."

"No?"

Marcus looked strikingly handsome in his silk suit. The cornflower blue tie brought out the color of his eyes. What a glorious lasting picture she would have of him. Maddie took his hands in hers. The bandages were off, and the blistered skin had been given a good scrub. She raised them to his tie. "Good match." He frowned and at the same time offered a modest smile.

"It's something your wife had said…about you resuming your role as a father." He looked at her with interest. "Marta was right…one is obligated to being a parent until the end. It isn't a title that can be renounced…not that I think my father ever tried to do that. He asked me to visit him when I was around thirteen. I remember wanting to go, but I felt an allegiance to my mother and didn't want to hurt her. It was as if he still chose me to be part of his life, but not her. My mother had never wanted to divorce him. She talked me into believing I would be in the way…just like your son always felt around you. My dad had a new wife, they were starting a new family…my mother said he didn't need a reminder of the past. I can understand where she was coming from, but still…that was pretty cruel. Fortunately, Ed's parents couldn't have been any kinder to me, especially his dad."

Marcus was happy for her and kissed her forehead. "I hope for both your sakes it's a positive reunion…I really do."

Their embrace was affectionate, not clingy; it was one reserved for those who were neither friend nor lover…but something different, indefinable, and in some regards more rewarding—the product of lifelong experiences.

"Before I go, will you please tell me why you pronounce my name like you do?"

They were feeling rushed. The baggage compartment of the bus had just been closed.

"It was my twin sister's name," said Marcus. "She died from pneumonia before we made it back to Germany. We were very young." Maddie knew he meant from South America. They had never discussed the hearsay, and she didn't ask if he was going to include that part of his background in his book.

The reality of her departure was starting to get the better of him; the sadness in his eyes created a lump in her throat. He added, "My mother never stopped talking about her…silly little things she used to say and do. I'm told we were inseparable. I have so few memories. I know we had fun together."

It was nice that he would share that.

Marcus ran with her; she was the last to hop on board. As she went to take her seat, she was jostled by excited passengers as they clambered to the left row of windows and started waving furiously and blowing kisses to the gentleman outside.

CHAPTER 22

The flight went by fast. Maddie thought about Ed the entire time. Marcus had given her an altogether different perspective of her husband. Any man, he said, who would give a boy such a book to read was unquestionably a full-fledged romantic. Marcus likened Ed's recliner to a magic carpet that transported the disillusioned husband and father around the globe to all its exotic fishing holes. While he slept, his son could accompany him in dreams. And what an admirable type of individual Ed wanted Tim to emulate, thought Marcus, referring to the anglers in Grey's book.

According to the author, a meaningful life was rewarded the observant man of passionate purpose, one sensitive to the balance of nature. Its lessons, if taken to heart, promised to make his soul as free as a generous sky across a bountiful sea. Maddie had scoffed at Marcus's over-the-top idealized portrayal of the man she beheld every day, zoned out for the better part of it. Now she wondered if Ed's world possibly entertained such satisfying fantasy.

Maddie's spirit withered when she thought about the unshared sorrows she and Ed had endured. Even though it was what they both had wanted, she realized they married too young…and had babies too soon. There was never an allotted hour for learning what each was all about. People were more pragmatic back then too; no one questioned much. At some point down the road, they should have addressed the increasing and festering discord. Then it was too late; she no longer cared to care…nor did Ed. She easily saw now why that happened—mainly because they were exhausted.

As Maddie walked to the baggage area, she was beginning to have reservations over meeting this stranger. She hadn't called her father beforehand. No harm done if she chickened out. Maybe she should just go spy on him. No, her emotions would certainly get the better of her. She could see herself flying into the old gent's arms…and giving him a heart attack.

The cab drove by many of the familiar sights seen on numerous television programs and in the movies. It was five thirty when she entered the family run inn situated in the outskirts of London.

While wandering the picturesque area in search of food, Maddie drove herself cuckoo trying to decide whether to call the man that night. She thoroughly hated that she was behaving like an insecure little girl.

She dialed the number. The phone was ringing. A tingling sensation rose in her chest and worked its way up to her jaw. She hung up and held fast to the nightstand, fearing she might keel over. How ridiculous! Working herself into a tizzy over this. A weight lifted off her shoulders when she finally decided to delay contacting her father until tomorrow morning. The late-night British telly was funny. It felt great to laugh out loud. She woke to the morning news and the soft glow of the lamp; its light still shone brightly because the outside world was dreary.

After her shower, Maddie sat on the bed and hugged a pillow to pacify her nerves. She believed she was ready and picked up the receiver. Again the lightheadedness started up.

In only twenty minutes, she had walked to the address. There wasn't as much as a bucket to sit on in the austere, narrow lane. So quiet, too, considering how close it was to the busy main street. Maddie stood on the bumpy cobblestone driveway, underneath an arch that probably housed an upper-floor bedroom. The homes were renovated stables, connected by these bridges. The units circled a courtyard. Unlike the cheerless exterior, the cloistered garden, with its decorative animal statues, floral trellises, and fountain, was charming and inviting.

The split-second noise of a latch, followed by a man stepping out, disrupted Maddie's thoughts. There was no time to hide. He offered a friendly "Mornin'." Her chest vibrated from the pounding blows of her heartbeats like an anvil being struck. She hugged herself and remained speechless. He must have thought her rude. He continued past her, tipping his cap. This second "good day" gesture still didn't elicit a response from her. There was no excuse; this must really insult him. When he disappeared behind the corner, she closed her eyes and drew the air deep into her lungs.

A voice rang out, "Excuse me, Madame…but are you lost? I know most of the faces around here."

The elderly gentleman had backtracked to the corner. He was around fifteen feet from her, so she couldn't see his features clearly. Also, the brim of his hat shaded his brow.

"Thanks, but I think I've found the right number."

"Oh? And what number might that be?"

Had there been robberies? Did she appear suspicious? The ripped square of hotel stationery was secured in her hand. The man noticed when she happened to scrunch it tighter in her fingers. Placing the handle of his cane on his forearm, he walked to her, then gently reached for her hand. "Let's see, dear." He straightened out the wadded paper and read the name and address. Without glancing up, he said, "Yes, you've indeed found it."

He folded it over as if to give it back…but he didn't. Maddie took a moment during the agonizing pause to examine him. He was maybe an inch taller than she, broad in the shoulders, trim…there was no belly pushing forward from under his tan, linen sport jacket. His wire-rimmed spectacles, cast downward, fit on a very straight nose. A shock of feathery snow-white sideburns twisted out from under the traditional Ascot cap. His hands were smooth, with no big, twisted veins or knuckles, but the skin appeared thin, like a moth's wing. Nothing could be detected by his expression when he looked up at her. She silently begged that he continue on his merry way and just let her be.

"You know, I may have an old mind…" He spoke solemnly. "…and old eyes, yet I still trust them to recognize my Madelaine."

The rewarding gleam of acknowledgment in his kind eyes allowed her, at that precise second, to believe she was the center of the universe. Madelaine Morrisey huddled inside her dad's arms, closed her eyes and let the tears fall. She listened as some passing clicking footsteps neared them and then drifted out of range.

After spending only an hour in his home, the daughter was astonished (and relieved) to see that the ninety-two-year-old man was still very active—and his mind sharp. In no way did he resemble the picture she had fought from taking hold of her imagination: that of a senile, wizen-faced, doddering old-timer. During the lulls in the small talk, the two simply stared…then they laughed. It was all too nonsensical.

They went for a stroll, arm in arm, around a pond at Hampstead Heath, the large area north of the city that included several parks. Her father belonged to a group of citizens who helped care for its flowerbeds. They had admitted defeat against this summer's heat. The wooded area with its meadows reminded her of home. He showed her Parliament Hill. It felt grand to be taking in this expansive view of London with the eyes of a child. She was fortunate to have found the man alive.

The cane served only as an aid for balance. Mr. Morrisey's snapping wrist motion paced it to his brisk step. On their way to a nearby restaurant, they took time to sit and watch boys and men alike sail their model boats on a shallow pond. Children ran with kites.

Maddie loved learning about him. The neighborhood chemist had operated his own apothecary shop. The terms evoked another period of history, ascribing a sense of wizardry to the profession—much more colorful than today's pharmacist. And, in fact, throughout most of his career, he had been responsible for mashing the ingredients needed to concoct various medicinal remedies. He proudly displayed his mortar and pestle in a corner curio. At age seventy-two, he let one of his employees take over. Maddie wanted to see the building, but, alas, erected in its place was a shopping complex with cinemas and retail stores. Such was the way of the world.

So how had he filled these retired years? Hopefully, Maddie thought, not by traveling the world…without ever stopping to visit her. Her father confessed to being a homebody and enjoyed nothing better than the grandkids' soccer matches and their musical recitals. He and his second wife vacationed in Scotland and Wales, but that was the extent of their excursions. She died five years ago, which was when he moved from their bigger house to his present home. Maddie couldn't bring herself to ask him if he ever dwelled on his first child. It sounded as if he had a wonderful relationship with his son, his daughter, and the five grandchildren. She tried to overlook the brief attack of jealousy.

Mr. Morrisey gladly rested his vocal cords and insisted that it was his Madelaine's turn to apprise him of her life. While they enjoyed their tea and sandwiches, Maddie attempted a brief summary, omitting the emotions that had ruled the events along the timeline, and which also seemed miraculously superfluous now.

When all was said, her father laid a hand on hers, then asked, "Is Ed a good man?"

The question was unexpected. She didn't need time to answer. "Yes…he's a very good man."

Her dad gently squeezed her fingers, reassured by the reply. *That's rightly what should matter most to a father,* she concluded.

Maddie would challenge anyone to find adequate words to describe her circumstances tonight. She lay in the guestroom, paying attention to every detail: the delicately drawn maroon and beige floral wallpaper, the pink-etched antique water pitcher and basin (which the family had probably used long ago), and three photos of several generations that rested on an antique dresser, purchased as new once. She felt all of her sixty-five years. It wasn't registering that the majority of them didn't include this important person. Her mood interchangeably went from joy to sadness. There were instances of true brokenheartedness; she desperately desired to reclaim the years and alter their course. Sleep was out of the question.

At one in the morning, the neighborhood was still. The temperature had to be below seventy. After months of intense heat, it felt chilly. Maddie quickly changed into a snuggly velour running outfit, then wrapped herself in the terry cloth robe her dad had given her. "Brrr…"

Warm milk and honey might do the trick. A conversation outside the door prevented her from turning the handle. She didn't want to interrupt his company. *Awfully late to be entertaining*, she thought. It was difficult to understand the mumbling. Her ear remained glued to the wall. Following several minutes of this covert activity, she came to realize that there was only a single voice; her dad was talking to himself.

Maddie peeked out of her cracked door. Shadows danced in crazy patterns across the wall at the end of the hallway by the stairs. Every floorboard creaked as she tiptoed the short distance to the master bedroom. She didn't wish to scare the old man. The door stood wide open, and she lightly tapped on it. The room was big, with a gorgeous four-poster bed. Her father sat in a chair off to the side of a small square cut-out fireplace that looked rather like an afterthought. No mantel. He saw her.

"Madelaine, dear…come in."

Oh, thank heavens…he was lucid. Maddie sat on the corner of his footstool, facing him. His world-weary eyes lacked color. Perhaps the tousled hair also came from restless tossing and turning. "My brain is befuddled," she told him.

He laughed. "Well, let's befuddle it some more. Why don't you grab yourself a glass of sherry from over on the desk."

When he realized there was no place for her to comfortably sit, he suggested that they go down to the sofa in the living room and start a small fire; so what if it was summer? He had found it impossible to sleep, too.

They honored her mother with a toast. In no time, flames spit and crackled. Her father stated that he seldom used this bigger fireplace—too much work. He reminisced a little about the war. It was never his intention to break up their family. But as the months went by…then a year…he fell in love with someone else. The room grew warmer, and Maddie took off the robe. Her father got up to go to the bathroom. She smiled to herself, imagining Claudia's reaction to all this.

He resumed his seat close beside her. His silky robe smelled of bergamot...Earl Grey tea, she decided.

"It's the bewitching hour, Madelaine, dear..."

"...when fantastic tales come to life, rhapsodized by an eloquent Moon on the illusory stage of Night." She giggled over the remembered line. She loved to hear her dad say her name, her full name...always followed by "dear." For some reason, her name had gotten shortened after moving to the States. "Regrettably," she sighed, "we have no tale."

Frederic Morrisey wagged an index finger, which landed on the tip of her nose and whispered secretively, "Ah, I would be remiss if I brought up the subject and then had nothing to show."

Maddie eyed him with curiosity; more so when she noticed that something lay hidden behind his left side. His hand glided to his lap, revealing *At the Back of the North Wind*. She immediately choked up.

"Promise me you won't cry," he said, "...or I shall. And that will get us nowhere."

"Mm-hmm," she sniffed, searching for a degree of control. Maddie curled up and held his arm. Since their copy had been in her possession when she moved to the U.S. (and unfortunately lost shortly afterward during another move), she asked, "Did you buy it for your children?"

"Amazingly, I found it during the war...lying on the floor of a library that had just been bombed. Not too far from us here. It lay there, only a bit singed, surrounded by volumes of other scattered, busted-up books. I couldn't believe my good fortune. It's as if I were meant to stumble across it...to serve as my lucky charm. Who knows, eh? A comrade of mine felt the same when he came across *Winnie-the-Pooh*, his own childhood favorite, which he stuffed in his jacket. Later, when I tried reading it to Kennith and Penelope, they showed no interest. Just as well; after all, it was our story, right?" He calmed her chin with his hand, then kissed her cheek.

"Right," she gasped, still trying to collect herself.

Once the cover opened, the magic unfolded, and it became possible for the North Wind, in the guise of a benevolent, flying lady, to sneak in through the holes of the loft, then back out, carrying the boy Diamond (and his dearest friend Madelaine) across the sky in a cloud of her black, flowing hair. And just has he had done back then, the reader embellished the plot with his own scenes. After flying over a prince's magnificent palace in Katmandu, they headed to view a family of singing dingoes in remotest Australia. The young father read to his six-year-old until they both fell asleep on each other's shoulders.

The embers had long died out. Her awkward position woke Maddie. She felt stiff. Fearing the same for her father, she gently shook him, and together they moseyed up to their beds for a little more shut-eye.

Over breakfast, she was informed that her dad's son and his family looked forward to meeting her. Penelope was on vacation, but she called to express her regrets, hoping there'd be another opportunity someday for the half sisters to become acquainted. Maddie hadn't taken into account this unforeseen predicament, though it only made sense that she should have. Getting introduced to these blood relatives was of no consequence to her. She didn't want to face the lucky ducks who had had this man all to themselves for their entire lives. He was hers now, during this all-too-short visit. Funny that one was never too old to revert back to childish tendencies.

Things rarely proceeded as expected. Maddie was old enough to know better than to walk into a new situation with any certain mindset. The Sunday afternoon dinner was delightful. Her half brother Kennith adored her, and repeatedly demonstrated it with hugs. He had married late in his life. His wife had also been older. At forty, she gave birth to the first of three children.

The family had exhausted their brains while trying to come up with something very special to give to their newfound relative.

The audience of adults listened to the preteens' much-rehearsed rendition of the lullaby *Too Ra Loo Ra Loo Ral*; a song which the first Mrs. Morrisey sang to her baby girl almost every evening; they were the first lyrics Maddie ever learned. When they finished, the two boys and girl eagerly kissed their "Auntie" on the cheek, being touched themselves by the resulting impact of their efforts.

Leaving was going to be tough, but the experience inspired Maddie to take a fresh look at her own convoluted relationships. She had too readily accepted the estrangements as being lasting. There was much to be gained by getting beyond the impasses. She wasn't naive about the challenging task; it was, after all, a two-way street. The long plane ride back appealed to her. There'd be lots of time to reflect. Her mood, in relation to her domestic front, was so opposite from when she had embarked on this trip. Now there was hope.

Although the remaining three days were spent doing mundane things, Maddie relished them: shopping at the local market, renting movies, afternoon tea, and so on. She liked accompanying her dad to the barber shop and hearing the men's idle talk. And he thoroughly loved showing her off. She wondered, as the unruly ends accumulated on the floor, if her hair was that incredibly white.

The rain began in the middle of Maddie's final night. The mood was low-key in the kitchen, where the father and daughter stayed up late, sipping a ritual sherry while they discussed a copy of the family tree that he presented to her. Mr. Morrisey expounded on the various lineages. His immediate descendant studiously jotted down the details. It would be a crying shame if these interesting anecdotes were lost to time. Maddie was pleased to know that she hailed from strong and long-lived stock, at least on one side. An industrious Penelope had visited Ireland to research Maddie's maternal history, along with some supposed illegitimate offspring. Many of her relatives had sailed to either America or Australia.

"Well, well, darling Madelaine. Is it likely I shall ever meet more grandchildren…or great-grandchildren?"

Rima would be tickled for sure. "I'm definitely going to pursue the subject."

Time was tugging at their heartstrings.

"Are you really doing fine with money? You'd tell me the truth?"

"Yes, Dad. We're extremely well-off, as they say."

He pursed his lips and nodded. "Good…good."

They wrapped their hands together in a knot and stared at them in the center of the table.

"Is there any way I can help you?" asked the newly self-ordained devoted daughter.

His wide smile measured his wealth. "I am set for the rest of my life." He patted the top of her hand. Once more, she occupied the entirety of his heart.

Kennith drove her to the airport. He felt no shame in hanging onto her at the curb. She had to pry his arms from around her waist.

"Please visit again, Madelaine. I cherish having a big sister."

What a precious thing to say. She hadn't given it serious thought…having a little brother. And she did feel sisterly toward him, now that he mentioned it. How would a meeting with Penelope have turned out?

Maddie dodged the flustered travelers who crisscrossed her path. She ambled along, contented. *Cherish*—who used that, except at weddings? It sounded natural coming from him; the sweet sentiment from a considerate brother provided a word to carry her home.

CHAPTER 23

As it turned out, the hours in transit consisted of nothing more than borderline sleep. Maddie got off the plane feeling as if she had waged war—an instance when too much sleep encourages more of it. Yawn after yawn after yawn...the waiting was insufferable. Maybe she had gone to the wrong baggage carousel. Her jaw was beginning to hurt. She was too lazy to concentrate on conquering the involuntary reflex, so the ache continued.

She fumbled inside her purse for her glasses. The emotional week had taken its toll on her eyes, and she hadn't been able to wear her contacts. The laborious hum of the machinery that sent the luggage circling around and around was about to do her in. "Finally!" Her bag was in sight.

"Maddie Gulliver!" A hand squeezed her elbow. "Oh...my...God! Maddie! It *is* you!"

If only she could claim a case of mistaken identity, but it was a neighbor from the next street...who insisted on giving her a ride home.

Maddie slowly sobered up once she started to talk a little. Mrs. Waverly was thanked, the car door was shut, and then lo and behold, she stood before her house. It felt as if a year had been jammed into the last three months. Keeping true to form, Maddie had let no one in on her return date.

It seemed fitting to enter the front door—like company—instead of her usual route through the kitchen from the garage. Even after touring the downstairs, she continued to sense this wasn't her turf.

It was two in the afternoon, and there was no sign of Ed. His car wasn't gone. Maddie rounded the kitchen corner and met Red head-on. His butt comically rested on the bottom step while his front legs held his chest and shoulders up at attention. His rigid posture remained motionless. How could he not recognize her? Did she look as different to him as he did to her? His blimplike middle was deflated.

"Red, baby? How ya doin'?"

The ears twitched. Maddie got down on her knees and extended her arms. He stepped cautiously, then stopped short of her. His failing old nose was busy trying to identify the essential perfume of this particular body. Then the whining began, and the tail spinning. He couldn't twirl around her...or lick her...or climb all over her fast enough.

It was definitely strange to have ol' Red trailing her up and down the steps. He hadn't been able to accomplish the feat in years. The place was remarkably clean and well-ordered. Most shocking was the basement. Gone were decades of stored tools and paints, forgotten carpets and old furniture. The missing workbench left a gaping hole in the far corner.

She went up to sit in Tim's room. At last it was reduced to only things. There was no remnant of him here anymore.

"Maddie?" Ed called to her from the kitchen. He had to have spotted her bag in the family room.

She listened to his footfalls as he combed the floor in search of her.

"Mad—"

Their eyes met as he retreated from the end of the hall. Neither could think of anything appropriate to say. He was going to tell her that he would have picked her up. Both took quick note of the other's general appearance. They met halfway and placed their arms around each other. It was cordial. They could be cousins. Maddie was aware of experiencing a long-forgotten sensation: Ed's hip bones. The dialogue jumped right into ineffectual small talk as they walked back to the kitchen, where she watched him put away a few groceries.

"Where'd you go? I saw the car was still here."

"Every couple of days I walk to Seton."

He said it like it was no big deal. At an almost-running pace, the store was forty minutes from their street. Maddie used to go when the kids were younger, and the grandkids. They had given up asking Dad (Grandpa) to join them. The exercise had certainly produced an astonishing change. Ed's belt was visible again, and his neck. He walked with an altogether uncharacteristic spring to his step. He looked happy.

Ed spent the next couple of days following his new routine: yard work and four walks. Matt required his assistance fixing a screen door. Maddie spied inside the family room several times, but never caught him in his chair. She phoned the kids (including Janet, who didn't answer) and grandkids, and invited them over on the weekend. She e-mailed her friends from the summer, unpacked, soaked in the tub, and best of all, lounged in her own bed (in her own room). However, unlike other mornings following a vacation—when she would stare up at the ceiling from her bed, recalling images from it—she could only picture Ed staring up at his, and wonder if he was thinking about her. She could go in and see.

Maddie was scouring the house and garage for a misplaced watch when the condition of it really struck her. The next time she saw Ed, she said to him with a questioning tone, "The place looks like it's ready to sell?"

Ed shrugged his shoulders and glanced around the uninhabited front living room. "There's too much to keep up with. Do you still want to take care of everything?"

He had actually gone ahead with his own plans. Maddie really didn't think her suspicion was going to be substantiated when she innocently asked. Her brain went blank for a second. Then she thought about the amount of time that had gone into choosing the fabrics, paintings, wall colors, and furniture; items which constituted their home. Glumly she answered, "Not really."

It was a revealing and sad moment—for both of them. Ed sat down on the piano stool. Maddie pulled out the chair from a beautiful, but never used, secretary at the other end of the room. There was more to ask, obviously.

Red wandered in and lay by her feet, licking her slippers.

Ed broke the silence. "Are you up for a stroll in Schiller Park?"

She was in a daze. "Let me get my shoes on."

Silly woman, waiting by the car; of course he would walk there these days. The couple covered the mile quickly, then slowed down to enjoy the winding paths. Colorful late-season wildflowers lined them. The giant trees were lush—must have been a summer of heavy rains. It was hard to believe that in a month, their limbs would blow naked.

Their sleeves sometimes touched. Odd that a man and a woman, married as long as they had, would be completely aware of it. At the halfway point, Ed sat on the end of a bench, allowing ample space for Maddie. She spared them the discomfort of being that close, instead choosing to stand by a tree. This was a gorgeous area. Would she be leaving it?

Ed watched Maddie as she took in the hillside. "You look like a flower child."

Maddie's spontaneous, contracted laugh was more a hiccup. She peered back over her shoulder at Ed, recalling her appearance in the "before" picture. Now, a single loose braid hung down her back. The salt-and-pepper roots were not yet the stark white of her father's color. Except for mascara, makeup was a bother. Her healthy color was leftover from Spain. An open-weave, light-blue crocheted smock hung over a sheer knee-length petticoat. And the shoes she had changed into for the walk—cheap, plastic flip-flops—unheard-of! "What can I say? It feels comfortable."

"Maddie, it wasn't intended to be a cut."

"Oh, no?"

"Not at all. I think you look...ravishing."

She thought she might laugh again, only there was nothing teasing about the way in which Ed was eyeing her. She picked at the bark of the maple. *Ravishing?*

"Do you intend to go back?" he asked.

He would wonder, after the way she took off. "No."

Maddie tried envisioning Ed with Lorraine and got nowhere. Maybe because her own infidelities hadn't left her feeling that she necessarily wanted a divorce, she presumed his didn't necessarily either. Lorraine was like Marcus, Maddie thought. They were able to successfully dissociate their emotions from the sex act and simply satisfy their bodies' needs. To an extent, because of Robert, Maddie now also had an idea of what that was like. Her attraction to the student had been strictly a physical one. Maddie thought about Lorraine's husband, Neil. He must have truly understood that his wife loved him; that Lorraine's insatiable desire was merely that. One could only guess how her actions might have affected their children, if they had had any. This would be an opportune time to raise the subject of Lorraine to Ed. When she didn't...and he didn't bring it up...Maddie wondered if things were going to be no different in their lives than before she left.

They walked home, this time with their arms brushing together constantly. And again, they were aware of it the entire way back.

The couple puttered around the yard. Maddie weeded the ferns. When Sarah came out to swing her children, she went over to say hi. During their chat, Maddie noticed Ed in an exchange with Lorraine outside her garage.

Maddie fixed sandwiches for their dinner and she and Ed ate on the back patio.

"So when were you thinking about putting the house on the market?" she asked, presenting it as if the decision could really be his solely to make...because that, incredibly, was his attitude.

Ed finished crunching his chips. "It isn't right to move before Red dies. It's just not fair to him. He'll never get used to a new place. Doc says he possibly has a couple years left…at the most. His liver's not so good."

When had she ever discussed the dog's health with him? This was funny. Then it wasn't. They chewed and watched the neighbors' comings and goings.

He continued matter-of-factly, "It doesn't make sense to give the house to the kids…or even divide the profit from the sale between 'em. They've gotten more than enough already." After a swig of iced tea, he pounded the glass down on the table as if to appease the hostility he still harbored over his wife's past indulgences. "I've given it a lot of thought, and I think Ivee should have it."

Ivee. *Ivee?* She said nothing, but continued to observe Ed as though he were some fascinating experiment. *What next*, she wondered. "Have you spoken to her about it?" Maddie had no problem with Ed's idea. Ivee's contribution to their household had been enormous, and never underestimated. It far exceeded a simple maid's role.

"I wanted to see if it was OK with you first." *Thanks for that*, she thought. "Maybe her daughter's family would want to live here with her, seeing as how Ivee's our age and alone. You know, the one that's a teacher. I'm sure she could find work in this district or in Seton. Times are different now. There are lots of African Americans in the school." He spoke with conviction. Since when had he broken the habit of saying "coloreds"?

His wife, confounded, sat listening. Ed couldn't be faulted for not considering all angles. Maddie wasn't going to bring up where he expected her to go after all this got settled. Normally, when her brain was in overload like this, the swim club beckoned to her. No more.

Cleaning up the kitchen made her feel as if she were truly home. The golden evening light drew her to the window. She was caught up in the clouds when Ed came in.

"I hate it when the days start getting shorter." Maddie agreed with him every year.

The familiarity of his voice was comforting. She smiled at him and looked back outside. In an offhanded manner, she credited him for doing an outstanding job of clearing out the basement.

"Tom helped a lot. I don't know that I could have trashed as much as I did without him constantly asking if I really needed it."

She crossed her arms and leaned against the frame. She wasn't going to miss this sunset. "How well did he do in Alaska?" she asked.

"It was slow going at first…then he really took to it. Did you see the salmon in the freezer?"

She was genuinely glad to hear the trip was a success. The sun was almost gone.

"What did you like best about your trip, Maddie?"

She looked at Ed, pleased that he would bring it up. He appeared interested. "That's a toughie." A massive cumulus cloud, dusted in pink, hung over a neighbor's roof. She found the answer in it. "I came this close to three Van Goghs." And she placed her hand on the window pane. When she turned, she was brought back to reality. All of her cookbooks were on the table, ready to be gone through and, for the most part, tossed or given away. Ed's housecleaning inspired her to do the same. Better to start now than wait to the last minute. With a sigh, Maddie lamented, "I look around…there's so much stuff. It's overwhelming. I don't know where to begin."

Ed's heart was in his throat. "You could start by making love to your husband." He didn't like how he phrased that…since it was he who wanted her. He braced himself on the end of the countertop and observed the wheels turning in her head—for the longest time. He wished to take back the words and ask differently…better yet, on another day.

Maddie went over and placed his hands on her waist. At six feet, Ed didn't seem to have shrunk in height over the years. That, or they were going at the same rate. He still looked down on her, if only slightly. They were uncertain as to how to proceed. Ed began to suffer from the kind of insecurity imposed by a blind date. Maddie felt for him; his lower neck was scalded red. She traced the perfectly trimmed hair from around his ear to the back of his neck. As much as she liked the German actor's mane, Ed's hair suited him. She had been taken with Ed's neat appearance the first day she ever laid eyes on him.

"What would make you happy, Ed?"

He had never been asked. And, in his present condition, he couldn't think. It gave Maddie time to study him, along with her body's response to this situation. Ed looked around, unsure of how graphic she expected him to be, if in fact he had interpreted her correctly. Maddie followed his eyes to the dim family room, to his chair…before he quickly turned his attention to the kitchen window. It was dark now. She asked him again, in a hushed voice, in his ear…to tell her.

He rehearsed the words one time in his mind. Out spilled his deepest desire. Neither could remember when they had last kissed like this, after which they embraced, enjoying a feeling of acceptance. Then Maddie led him to the other room.

This was too good to be true. Ed sank into his old recliner.

Maddie wanted to see and turned on the lamp behind the couch. Jokingly, she asked, "Out of sight, out of mind?"

"What do you mean?"

Using her chin, Maddie motioned toward the table. "The pictures."

After experiencing a fitful moment, Ed got up, and this time he led her by the hand down the hallway. The bed would be more comfortable, he said—Lorraine was never invited to it. His wife didn't give the matter a second thought as she went about her lascivious business.

The Gullivers tested their rekindled passions on a daily basis. And they were transformed because of it. Their family and friends witnessed a new level of mutual respect between them. That wasn't to say that either of them put the past to rest. Although they had made a pact to discuss and resolve issues pertaining to each of their children, and they solidified plans over the kind of life they wanted to pursue together in the future…they still ducked mentioning their indiscretions. Maddie watched Ed with curiosity whenever Lorraine came outside her house or pulled up to it in her car. She and Ed gave a casual wave, as did Maddie when she saw her. It was laughable.

Once word got out that the popular Mrs. Gulliver was back, the phone started ringing off the hook. Groups that wanted her help for their fund-raisers were relentless. Before she would offer her services again, though, Maddie decided to get her own house in order.

She was surprised by the new face at Mass. Her friends complained that it wasn't right for a man who had been married, and who had children, to become a priest. His vow of celibacy, especially at his age, didn't require the same discipline, and therefore degree of faith, expected of younger men. This was an instance when, listening to their reasoning, Maddie displayed the crazed look she sometimes received from her nonreligious friends. The debate over who was deserving of priesthood mattered little to her today. She could think of no one better to tell her troubles to, and went to see the priest that same week—because of his life's experiences.

The idea of unloading the house and hitting the road was exciting—that was the plan. Ed's goal was to fish in places he'd only read about—with the local disadvantaged youth. Maddie swore he was pulling her leg. He believed they would benefit from the meditative aspect inherent to the sport. Ed was forever leaving Maddie tongue-tied of late. Marcus had been right about him…he was a romantic. She wasn't sure what she would find to do in these places, but figured there must be something comparable. Maddie told Ed that they had to set aside time to visit family. This was workable, they concluded.

After crafting a well-worded letter for the benefit of their children, explaining their intentions, they turned on the radio, then snuggled up on the loveseat in front of the bay window to watch the squirrels and birds. Many of the leaves had changed colors.

Maddie didn't wish to put off getting them sent, and left to stick all the copies in the mailbox. When she didn't return, Ed got up to go to the front door. Glancing through the curtains, he panicked when he saw Maddie and Lorraine together at the end of the drive.

"Shit." How could he possibly think they would never talk? Not that Lorraine would say anything. Even if Maddie assumed something went on between them…who would have told her? After all, the next door neighbors had not cavorted out in the open. This couldn't be happening now, not when he and Maddie were on exceptionally good terms. He feared their plans were in jeopardy. The women stood firmly planted. Ed's chest was in a knot. He watched. Neither was expressive. Maddie stood with her hands in the pockets of her skirt, whereas Lorraine kept her arms folded. The suspense was too much. There were binoculars in the secretary. He was shaking badly. The instrument divided the sheers while his body stayed positioned behind the drapes. There! Something. He slid his glasses up and looked again. A blurry thingamajig went back and forth. "Oh, jeez."

Looking back over his shoulder, an indignant Red stared at him through the lens, then he barked toward the house, as if he knew what Ed was up to. Common sense told the spy it wasn't possible, but then…he wasn't behaving too rationally. The ladies started up the driveway.

Ed hurried out of the room and made it back to his seat just as Maddie was coming in. His heart galloped at a marathon rate. She sank down beside him and picked up where she left off…surveying the backyard and enjoying the waltz that currently played. She wore a cheerful expression. He didn't get it.

Surprisingly, none of their children tried to talk them out of their plans. Maddie knew they must have immediately called each other to discuss what was going on.

This was an introspective period. While she sorted and packed and tossed things out, Maddie thought about how much she had admired Ed's take-charge attitude when they first met. Once that authority diminished, he seemed emasculated. There was nothing appealing about a man then, especially if he was moody as well. Now she was finally given a reason for it.

While Maddie finished organizing files in the den, she looked back on one of her recent walks in the park with Ed. He had held her tightly against him as they sat on the bench, and he explained about Korea. She wasn't above blaming herself to an extent—for never having made the connection to his behavior. It wasn't normal to expect that these young men, boys really, after surviving the perilous conditions of war, should simply pick up their lives where they left off when they returned back home. She saw Verdun's rows of white crosses while he spoke. Then she thought about the soldiers currently stationed overseas, and the sustained suffering they and their families were yet to face. Ed poignantly noted that if only there'd been no more wars, especially Vietnam, those images from Korea wouldn't have constantly gotten rehashed. His spirit might have been allowed a measure of healing, and their future assured of more happiness.

Maddie found him dazzling that afternoon, even when next he laid it on the line about her spending practices with regard to the kids. His ardent gaze had almost seared holes in her head. Her answer to him was lame: She did it because they could, money-wise. It was all she could offer. Ed's look of dismay had conjured up a picture of the chef at the culinary class after her unimaginative response to his cooking challenge. She thought and thought to come up with a more satisfactory answer. There was only one according to Ed, who told her to ponder why she needed to show off to such a degree. There was no venom behind his remark.

On occasional evenings, during sunsets over wine, they talked about Tim. It hurt considerably. Ed saw magic in Maddie's recital of a few of Zane Grey's passages, and looked upon her like a vision.

Tim had also been the subject of Maddie's words with Lorraine at the mailbox. They hadn't even mentioned Ed. Maddie told her that she regretted having shut herself off from these particular neighbors after her son's death. It wasn't personal; she unfortunately behaved that way to even her family. The next-door couple must have grieved as if he'd been their own. Lorraine was deeply moved by the belated admission. The pain of the tragedy was permanently laid to rest. The love they shared for the boy radiated in their faces when they continued to relate a few of his antics.

At some point every day, Maddie thought about her dad; how could she not? As she gathered the bed sheets to do wash, she wondered: What if, like him, she got another twenty-five years tagged on to her life? That was a major chunk of time! Although it seemed like an eternity to children, they made it through all of their schooling within that period. Parents watched their babies grow into adulthood. People switched careers—some often. It was rewarding to think about sharing the bonus time with a partner. That made her all the happier over her reconciliation with Ed. For the most part, they were healthy, which was reason enough for a daily prayer of thanks.

Prayer…what about that? Maddie sat on the bed and watched out the window as Sarah's children headed down the road with a train of bikes and wagons, tied together with jump ropes. Their monster German Shepherd was the caboose. Ed came in and started laughing over the sight of the parade. He looked so good.

"You thinking about back when?" he asked, acknowledging her wistful expression.

"No…other things."

"Oh?"

He plopped down on the heap of bedding beside her and held her hands.

She studied his long fingers. "Wouldn't you be tickled to find out that I've come to question heaven and hell…and what constitutes sin…and a host of other things that used to drive you nuts?"

Ed didn't weigh in; he kissed her shoulder. He understood the magnitude of her problem. In as grave of a voice as Maddie had ever heard, he confided, "I've given this matter a lot of consideration while you were gone, and I decided that I want to convert."

Maddie pulled away and glowered. "No…way."

"I thought you'd be pleased," he said, sounding hurt.

"No fucking way!"

That had never—ever—come out of her. She caught the twitch at the corner of Ed's mouth, then he was unable to hold back his snickering. He loved that he really had her going. Off came the flip-flops. Maddie promised him that he was surely going to hell for this one. He insisted she thank him for helping her believe again in the hereafter. The fun-spirited wrestling led to kissing, and then they settled down. Maddie lay in Ed's arms. The fall air…the children's voices outside—it was peaceful. And the time was finally right. "Did you fall in love with anyone over there?" Ed wasn't bold enough to ask her point-blank if she had had sex.

Maddie formulated her answer carefully. "Not the smitten kind you may be thinking of." Referring to Claudia and Marcus, she said, "I met a couple of people whose company I really love. I'd like to remain in touch with them.

They're important to me." She paused, then added, "I do feel I have to atone for what I've done." That's as far she would go, before seeing what he had to say.

Ed kissed the top of her head. "I took up with our infamous neighbor...and I would really, really appreciate you not holding it against me." She chuckled and inched closer to him. They lay like that for a period, in silence. Then she giggled a little again.

"I wish I could have witnessed the attack."

"Don't, Maddie." Ed was glad she was taking the news this well, but he didn't want to continue making light of what happened. "It felt great after such a long time...just knowing the parts were still reliable, you know? Then, when I realized what you and I had been missing, I got furious. Jesus, Maddie...how did it come to this? You believe me when I swear that I've never done this before in our marriage, don't you?" She looked up at him and nodded. "I put a stop to it when you wrote," said Ed.

After considering the matter a little, Maddie voiced a concern, "It scares me to think that that we might throw this in each other's faces someday...when we're good and upset over something or other. You hear about that happening."

"I won't," promised Ed, with certainty.

"I won't either."

"I hate that you can picture the face of the person."

"It'll pass," she mumbled.

Ed ran his fingers lovingly along her arm. "I'd like to meet my father-in-law. He sounds like a wonderful man." Maddie kissed his hand. Then they drifted to sleep for an hour.

Claudia e-mailed Maddie a reminder about Lake Como. It was going to be tremendous fun, but Maddie felt it unwise to go. Her presence was required at home; Red's kidneys were failing. Following the event, Marcus called Maddie on her cell phone to tell her what a terrific "date" he had had with the charming and handsome cardiologist from Ohio she had set him up with for the charity fundraiser. There were lapses in their conversation. This was the first time they had heard each other's voices since the bus station in Spain. Marcus knew Maddie would be going through a lot in the coming months and didn't want to interfere. They had communicated with short e-mail messages—general updates, nothing more. Right now, it was excruciating how much they missed seeing each other. They eased into more discussion, until it finally felt natural. The worst hurdle, the initial contact, was over. It was smooth sailing from here on out with regard to the bond they had cultivated.

In reviewing her summer, Maddie concluded that she had just as much to learn at this stage of life as ever. The challenge now was to correct things that had been allowed to continue unchecked—a conclusion reached by Ed too. Maddie wished it weren't so, but she realized that people were forced into examining what was essential only when they were cornered. Hopefully solutions surfaced before one ended up in real dire straits, as happened to a few of those she had met during her stays on the road...and could have happened more than once to her in her own life. Maddie prayed that Amy wasn't headed for such a sink-or-swim scenario.

Amy kept their heads shaking in exasperation. During a recent meal with her parents, she said that she "got" what they were trying to impress upon her...but couldn't they help her out this one last time? She had asked the same question the previous month. The excuse this month was that she hadn't anticipated the heating bill going up for her apartment when it turned colder outside. She was short on cash at the moment. Her father asked where her paycheck went; she had a good job with an insurance company. When Amy shrugged her shoulders, Ed asked why she was tanned this late in the year. Did she have cable TV? Why did she need cable? The daughter looked pleadingly to her mother. Maddie asked how much it cost to have hair streaked, and what the going rate was for manicures, after complimenting Amy on her nails.

"OK, OK," said the daughter, in defeat. When they finished eating, Ed asked Amy if she was willing to sit down with him and create a reasonable budget. She definitely was, and they had fun squabbling through it. Amy's last holdout was her daily fix of lattes. Her dad compromised and ordered that she wean herself from seven to two per week. This was nothing to joke about to her. On her way out, he grabbed his wallet and handed her a few bills, asking if that was enough to tide her over. She was extremely grateful. This touching give-and-take raised a smile on Maddie's face.

The Gullivers were making headway talking to their sons. The reason Matt gave for not seeing his dad after his mom went away was that he couldn't believe what she had done, and didn't know what the heck to say to his dad. Gary surprised them. He sounded sincere when he said he looked forward to his parents' upcoming visit. He liked the idea of a threesome. Going home for the holidays, facing a houseful of in-laws and kids was more than he could take...which was why he always left immediately. He loved his quiet and solitude, but at the same time, he wanted to see his parents. Gary told his dad that he was sorry for how mean he'd been to him in the past. Ed brought up his own regrets. There were good spots for fishing around Vegas, said his son, and he hoped his dad would want to go with him.

Janet and her family remained distant. Ed told Maddie to just give it some time. If only a truce could be reached with her daughter before they left. The mother had written a one-page synopsis of her trip, which she mailed to Janet, revealing that the course she had undertaken in Europe was based on her daughter's journey. Maddie explained that she had located the envelope in the attic that contained everything she had saved. Maddie looked forward to the day they could discuss the different places. She told Janet that this discovery had come at an opportune time in her own life, when she was beginning to reassess her priorities. There was no reply to the peacemaking gesture. Janet obviously had other considerations in her life now.

Carol offered to make her home the future gathering place for holidays. No matter where they were, her parents promised to make a point of returning.

The Gullivers weren't so impractical as to sell off all their belongings. The children got first dibs on things, then their closest friends. The rest was placed in storage in the event that she and Ed wanted to set up house one day again. It seemed realistic to think that they would.

On the day of their departure, a lovely spring morning, Ed and Maddie woke to find their van decorated as if they were honeymooners (they had traded in both cars). Grandpa thought it was a surprise from Matt's girls, but Maddie recognized Lorraine's handiwork. No one else braided crepe paper or formed such elaborate roses. Lorraine was beside herself with joy when she learned that Ivee was going to be her new neighbor. The two could reminisce about the street. Best of all, Lorraine would have Ivee's grandson and granddaughter to entertain in her house. She even contemplated getting another dog to help break the ice with the grade-schoolers so they would want to come over.

The passing motorists tooted their horns as the couple went cruising toward the freeway with the colorful flying streamers blowing in the wind.

"Quick, Maddie...which way?" Ed slowed to a crawl a block before the entrance ramps.

"Ahhh...I don't know. The second one. West."

"West it is."

He reached over and gave her thigh a firm squeeze. Grinning ear to ear, the Gullivers couldn't believe this impromptu, catch-as-catch-can life. If it didn't work out, this supercharged morning alone would have made the venture at least worth attempting. With the sun rising to their backs, Maddie envisioned a day when they'd be driving along, and roll right into Patagonia, to the land of the end of the world. Ed reported that the trout fishing there was unparalleled. Which benevolent fate granted these two individuals their current lot? Every person Maddie and Ed were to encounter, from here on out, would reap the overflow of their abundant gratitude.

978-0-595-35099-5
0-595-35099-2

Printed in the United States
41042LVS00004B/251